THE VENTRILOQUIST

TERRY GARDINER

Published in Australia by Sid Harta Books & Print Pty Ltd,
ABN: 34632585293
23 Stirling Crescent, Glen Waverley, Victoria 3150 Australia
Telephone: +61 3 9560 9920, Facsimile: +61 3 9545 1742
E-mail: author@sidharta.com.au

First published in Australia 2023
This edition published 2024
Copyright © Terry Gardiner 2023
Cover design, typesetting: WorkingType (www.workingtype.com.au)

Gardiner, Terry
The Ventriloquist
ISBN: 978-1-922958-37-2
pp390

To Anne
You deserved better

Acknowledgements

My thanks to my editor, Dr Gail Wilson and to John Aylmer who helped with the details of the application to the RAAF.

Table of Contents

Chapter 1
SEX IN A PANDEMIC

This is a scenario most people would condemn, but here it is. Paul Arnold, a successful scientist and businessman, and pricey prostitute Rachel Doyle meet for sex in the middle of a pandemic. This is Australia, a liberal democracy, where the coronavirus was controlled better than in most other countries. There was an unusually good response from the public. Most had been willing to give up some fundamental human rights for the greater good to prevent illness and death caused by a virus, especially in the elderly.

When authorities initially published a list of activities to be banned during the pandemic, most Australians responded, not without suffering the inevitable loss of employment and curtailment of many normal activities.

The Federal Government responded appropriately to support businesses and employees who were denied funds because of the need to stop people from mixing and spreading the virus. Since this pandemic was caused by a different organism than past pathogens, medical authorities had to learn about the virus as the pandemic unfolded, but the basic responses were well-known. There have been many pandemics in human history, and lessons have been well learned. Part way into the pandemic, scientists had established that the most probable way the virus was transmitted was by aerosol from speaking, coughing, and sneezing.

The techniques used to limit the spread of the virus were first to reduce how an infected individual could spread the virus to others. That meant mandating that, with few exceptions, people were confined to their homes and later wore masks. There was hope that a vaccine could be developed, reducing the need for people to distance themselves from others.

On the lists of activities banned by various state governments, the banning of brothels was usually found near or at the bottom of these lists or in the states where brothels were illegal, not on the lists at all.

Brothels and prostitution are endemic. They are found in most cultures. Some are visible or do not seek to be invisible. Others are hidden but known to most.

* * *

What about Paul and Rachel?

Despite the rules about moving and mixing, Paul and Rachel reasoned that this need did not apply to them. Paul is seventy, does not suffer from erectile dysfunction, and has a normal libido for his age. His second wife, MacKenzie, died a year ago. His first wife, Louise, was disinclined to have sex after having two sons, so Paul occasionally used prostitutes to satisfy his needs. It was a different story with MacKenzie, who was quite demanding of sex. Paul was fine with that. MacKenzie, however, was not mentally stable, and there were periods when she denied him.

Rachel is twenty-three and loves sex. She is a sole trader who does not work in a brothel setting. She has needed frequent sexual experiences since her early teens. Her mother, Elaine, recognised this need – she felt the same. She had bought a dildo for herself and bought one for Rachel when she realised that Rachel was masturbating with her fingers. Because of this need and Rachel's good looks, they had discussed the possibility of a career for her as a prostitute.

Rachel was only sixteen when the decision was made. So, until she was of legal age, Rachel worked in a bookshop owned by her aunt's friend, Barnaby, in Derry, Northern Ireland. It was only a serious threat of disfigurement that drove her out. She fled to Brisbane, Australia.

At age twenty, Rachel was offered a significant sum of money as seed capital by an acquaintance. It was a loan at high interest, but it got her started and she paid it back in two years as agreed.

Paul's involvement in the embryo transplant industry meant that he at times met with wealthy investors. Dick Harmon, one of the investors he met with, passed on to him a copy of *Executive Desk*, a limited-release magazine for wealthy businessmen, published quarterly. It gave in-depth reporting on financial movement in the economy, but it also included a service section, including contact with high-class prostitutes.

Paul found several promising listings, but he chose Rachel because she claimed to have a "talking fanny", her Burning Bush.

The whole experience of obtaining an appointment with Rachel was unusual, to say the least. He was asked several questions about himself, which he felt had little to do with arranging sex with a prostitute. He had dealt with prostitutes before. That had been years ago, and he had not needed such services when he was married to MacKenzie. And Rachel was way more expensive than he was used to, but she offered something special that no other prostitutes had done.

He found the experience better than he could have wished for. But it also had a consequence he could not have imagined.

So, contrary to clear advice about spreading the disease, they met, breathed on each other for an hour, and then parted company. The work of epidemiologists who advise the government in times of epidemic or pandemic is statistical in nature. The advice they give to the government is an assessment of the risk threatened by, in this case, a variety of coronavirus.

Paul and Rachel assessed the risk as small enough for them to ignore it. Fortunately for the rest of the citizenry, they did not spread the virus.

Chapter 2
FRANK

S uppose you found out that you had a brother that you had never met. What would you do?

Let's further suppose that your father had changed his name while you were still in the womb. And finally, what if this brother was not interested in being found?

Frank MacGregor was born in Brookdale, Victoria and discovered that he had a brother whom he had never met. Frank was an inquisitive person and made it an ambition to find this sibling.

Frank was born in April 1963. It turned out to be an easy birth and his young mother, Madeline, was relieved. Her husband, Harvey, was relieved that he had escaped the Paradise Club, he hoped, forever. His libido was high, he was only forty, and when the period of Madeline's pregnancy denied him the sex that he craved, as in his first marriage, he found it elsewhere.

Frank was just seven when his father died. In his state of grief, the process of his father's will being challenged by his unknown older brother occurred without his knowledge, except that he did overhear the name Paul, in conversations between his mother and another man, her solicitor.

As Frank grew older, he became fascinated by his dead father's desk, which for some reason, was always locked. When he asked his mother about it, she told him that there were important things in the desk, and she needed to keep it locked in case someone stole them. He knew that his mother kept keys in a kitchen drawer, so when she was out of the house, he decided to look there for the key to the desk. He took all the keys he could from the drawer in the kitchen and tested each on the desk lock. None worked.

To hide his investigations from his mother, he replaced the keys in the kitchen just as he had found them. *Where could the key be?* He was stumped. He could not think of another place it might be. He suspended his investigation for now.

Frank was watching a movie where a man was looking for a key and found one taped to the bottom of a drawer in a woman's bedroom. At the next opportunity, when his mother was out, he went to her bedroom and searched under each drawer. He found nothing but as he was replacing the last drawer, he noticed a small envelope in the drawer on which the words 'desk key' had been written. He carefully noted how the envelope had been placed in the drawer so he could replace it just as he had found it.

He took the envelope and key to the desk and opened

it. He was unsure how long his mother would be out, so he re-locked the desk, kept the key and returned the envelope to his mother's drawer. He would investigate further when he knew how long his mother would be out of the house. It seemed ages before a new opportunity arose, but when it did, he opened the desk and began looking through the contents. There was not much that he found that was of any interest until he found a birth certificate for Paul Arnold, but Paul's father was listed as Harvey Arnold. It didn't make sense but then, in the same folder, he found the birth certificate for Harvey MacGregor with an annotation indicating that Harvey MacGregor had formally been named Harvey Arnold.

Now it made sense – he had a half-brother called Paul Arnold.

At this stage, Frank was only fourteen and there was little he could do to follow up his new-found knowledge, so he decided to pursue it when he left school.

Frank questioned his mother about Paul, but she was disinclined to talk about it, saying it was nothing to do with her or Frank.

Frank could not leave school soon enough. He hated it. The only subject that he did like was manual arts, where he learned some basic woodwork and metalwork skills, but more importantly, a common-sense approach to solving problems.

He decided also that he could not wait to leave the rural backwater of Brookdale soon enough either. There was little work locally for a school leaver, especially one like Frank who at fifteen had barely passed most of his subjects. His salvation came soon after he left school in the form of a military recruitment team that had come to Brookdale. As soon as he had laid eyes on the photographs of the F111 fighter jets, he was hooked. He wanted to join the air force. This ambition remained just that, for as a school leaver at age fifteen, he would have to wait until he was seventeen to apply to join the RAAF.

By chance, he managed to gain local farm employment as a hand harvester at Elders weeding and picking vegetables and fruit. This was difficult and dirty work, but he relished the outdoors. Because of his enthusiasm, he was also offered the chance to drive tractors. He soon became skilled operator and given the opportunity, he learned how to repair them.

As soon as he turned seventeen though, Frank bought a train ticket to Melbourne to find the RAAF recruiting office and applied to join.

His poor school record seemed not an impediment as the recruiting staff were impressed by the reference from Elders, his experience with mechanics and his obvious enthusiasm. He signed up and was given a ticket to fly from Melbourne to Adelaide for basic training in two days. He was rapt.

Frank arrived at RAAF Edinburgh just north of Adelaide and was immediately swept up into the process of becoming an aircraftman. Medical staff examined him and his fellow recruits, suffered several injections, and were shown their living quarters. Here it was demonstrated to them how to make a bed in an acceptable manner. Uniforms were issued and haircuts were performed, short enough to avoid lice.

Frank was taught how to shine his boots to the acceptable mirror-like level to avoid penalty and quickly learned that no matter how silly or outrageously ridiculous an order from an officer may seem to be, it must be obeyed. Intuitively, he understood that this was a process of ensuring that aircraftmen, soldiers and sailors alike, obey orders even if they did not understand or agree with them. Those recruits who did not understand or agree with this process could pull out or be dismissed in the first three months.

To add to the exhilaration that he felt in leaving Brookdale, he had escaped his mother's cooking which was rudimentary and unpredictable. The food at Edinburgh was great and there was plenty of it.

Frank endured the long runs and the camping out that was part of the course and enjoyed learning to shoot a rifle. He found that he was rather good at it.

At the end of basic training, he felt fit and ready to go. He was assigned to No. 292 Squadron, sensor operator training, where he was to learn about ISR (Intelligence Surveillance Reconnaissance) systems involving P-8A Poseidon, E-7A Wedgetail and AP-3C Orion aircraft.

There, he also learned of the planned use of drone aircraft, which flew at remarkably high altitudes for surveillance in the future. Frank was intrigued by unmanned aircraft, and when small remote-controlled models became available, he bought one.

Frank remained in sensor systems for the five years that he would remain in the RAAF. He parted on good terms with his military masters and entered the commercial field of electronics. At this break in his career, he thought, now twenty-two, he might look for his half-brother.

He had revisited the desk several times since first opening it and had had a copy made of the key. His mother did not seem to realise that he was investigating and did not to his knowledge open the desk herself.

Documents that had earlier made no sense to him now did, and he figured out where Harvey had lived and worked in Sydney in the suburb of Greystanes. In among the documents was a number with an address that he guessed was the family home.

Frank looked at the travel options: train/bus, 1400 km, one day and nine hours; plane, 1400 km, one-and-a-half hours. He could afford to fly, so he did.

He stayed in a motel close to the airport overnight and made his way to Greystanes the next day. The address he found in his investigations was 59 Elgar Street, so he tried there first. When he knocked on the door, it took about two minutes before he was confronted by a rather large middle-aged woman wearing a hijab who spoke no English. She seemed put out by being disturbed at whatever she was doing, and her hand movements indicated clearly that Frank should 'piss off', or so he thought. She shut the door in his face. Frank took off his hat and scratched his head. It did not help. He turned around in a circle. This did not help either. He closed his eyes. This did help. The image of a post office appeared in his mind, and he asked a passer-by for directions.

Once at the post office he spoke to Ashley Faith and

explained his problem as well as the incident in Elgar Street.

'Oh,' said Ashley, 'Mrs Arafat did not mean for you to piss off. She speaks no English but if you had gone there out of school hours, young Eli could have translated for you. She is only eight years of age, but she is the only one in the family who can speak English. In any case, you still would have ended up here. I know Paul continued living there until his mother sold up and went to live with her sister on the Gold Coast. The sister had lost, or misplaced, her husband as well, so they put their money together and bought a unit up there.

'It's hard to know where Paul might have gone but your best bet is to go to the electoral office. It's just around the corner. You'll be able to look up and see where all the Paul Arnolds in Australia live. I think Paul may still work for the CSIRO, so he probably lives in the Greater Sydney area. Good luck! Next, please.'

Stephen Burke at the electoral office was helpful and suggested that he begin searching the rolls in Sydney. The address for the only Paul Arnold was in Drummoyne. Stephen was helpful and gave Frank directions to the Drummoyne address.

The house was an unremarkable house in an unremarkable street. He knocked on the door: no response.

'He won't be home before six', a voice from next door offered. 'He works in Rozelle. So, he'll be a while.'

Mrs Royds was a small, grey-haired woman who lived next door. 'Are you a friend of his?' she asked.

'Not exactly,' said Frank. 'I'll go get a coffee and come back later.'

'Do you want to tell me your name in case he gets here before you get back?'

'No thanks,' said Frank as he turned to go back to a McDonald's he had passed on his way to Paul's house.

He returned at about 6.10 pm and knocked again. No answer. He was just turning to leave when a man came up the path, asking, 'Can I help you?'

'Well, I hope you can.'

Frank's gaze shifted from Paul to Mrs Royds, who was listening to the conversation. He looked back at Paul, who was now looking over to Mrs Royds.

'Maybe we could talk inside?' said Frank.

'Maybe we should,' said Paul, adding 'Good night, Mrs Royds.'

Paul opened the door, walked into a small entry, and turned to look up at Frank, who was considerably taller, and said again 'How can I help you?'

'I think we may be brothers, or rather half-brothers,' said Frank. 'Who are you?' said Paul, clearly surprised.

'Well, first,' said Frank, 'are you Paul Arnold?'

'Well, yes, but who the hell are you?' said Paul, clearly annoyed now. 'Frank MacGregor,' said Frank.

'And what makes you think we are brothers?' snapped Paul.

'Harvey Arnold was your father and my father as well,' said Frank. 'But you said your name was ... what? I've forgotten now,' said Paul.

'Frank MacGregor,' said Frank.

They were still standing in the small entryway and Paul's

neck was sore from looking up at Frank. 'Come into the living room and sit down, so I can sort this out,' said Paul.

They sat. Paul's neck felt better, but he was still angry. It had not been a good day at work and now this.

Paul pushed back his hair, frowned, and drew a breath. It did not help. He breathed out again. 'Let me get this straight, you think we are half-brothers because we have the same father, but if we have the same father, we should have the same surname. So, how come we don't?' said Paul. 'Harvey changed his name to MacGregor before I was born,' said Frank.

'So, do you have some photo ID to prove who you are?' Frank showed Paul his Victorian Driver's Licence. 'Okay', said Paul, 'we'd better talk'.

And they did, into the night.

Frank had brought with him some photos and memorabilia he had taken from Harvey's desk to show Paul evidence that they were truly brothers, and it did not take long, however, for both to be convinced that Harvey had been their father.

Importantly, as they talked, each decided they liked the other.

At about 10.30 pm, after exchanging contact details, Frank called a taxi to return to his accommodation.

Frank felt relieved that he had found his brother and that it seemed that each would like to include the other in his life.

Paul was surprised that this had happened and wondered why he had not sought contact with Frank when he did know that Harvey had a child from his second marriage.

He supposed that he just didn't care, until now. He was genuinely impressed by this young man who had taken the trouble to find him.

Frank returned to Adelaide, satisfied that he had found Paul and that it seemed they would, from now on, be part of each other's lives.

He began a new job with Telstra in the technical team, investigating and creating systems to support the new mobile phone network. He learned more about coding and designing the Code Division Multiple Access tower systems.

By the early 1990s, there was a strong demand for computer programmers, and Frank moved seamlessly into this field.

Paul and Frank had remarkably different pathways through the education system. Paul had been a stellar performer at the secondary level, achieving the highest possible ranking in his state with first-class honours in physics and chemistry with As in each of his other four subjects. He won a Commonwealth scholarship and so studied at Sydney University free of charge. Paul studied science, majoring in both physics and chemistry. In his final year, after gaining distinctions and high distinctions in his studies, he won the University Medal for Physics.

He faced making a difficult decision at this stage – to remain at university and follow the path of lecturing and research, or to follow a research-only pathway in an industrial setting. But he was approached by a recruiting team for the CSIRO to join their physics department in developing photovoltaic cell design. He chose to join the

CSIRO to pursue solar technology, but after two years he found a passion for an entirely different field in embryology.

Chapter 3
AEMON

Elaine was getting pissed off. The fellow she wanted to dance with simply wasn't asking her.

Why didn't she ask him? Oh no, that was not the way it is done. The man is supposed to be the one doing the asking. He needs to take the risk of being rejected. No way was she going to ask a man to dance and take the risk of him saying 'No thanks' or worse. She would just have to wait.

He wore a plain black T-shirt, jeans, a black biker jacket and good boots and looked pretty damn good.

In the progressive barn dance, he had shown a certain aptitude for dancing, and she could imagine being in his arms for a complete set of songs. But he wasn't coming over to ask her. *What could be wrong with him?*

She looked beautiful tonight, even if she did say so herself. She wore her best blue dress, a blue figure-hugging piece with noticeable decolletage, matching blue high-heel shoes, and just a touch of make-up and barely discernible mascara. *What was not to like?*

The music for the next dance, a waltz, was just beginning. He got up and walked her way. She looked away, not wanting to make eye contact for too long, only to find Barry Castle standing in front of her with his hand out and asking, 'How about it, Elaine?'

She hissed, 'Piss off, Barry, not now.' She was hoping the black T-shirt was still coming her way. He wasn't.

He veered off to the left and asked Margaret O'Brien to dance. She thought, *That's it, I'm going home. I have had enough.*

She walked over to where Barry was standing and apologised. She said she had not meant to be rude, but she had a headache and wanted to go home.

Where was her sister, Jesse?

Looking for Jesse, she felt a hand on her shoulder. She turned around and found herself looking at the black T-shirt!

He introduced himself, but Elaine, not wanting to appear too eager, said, 'It is nice to meet you. I'm Elaine, but I am going home right now. Maybe I'll see you at the next dance.'

Many of the young men Elaine met were pleasant enough, but most were unemployed and had few prospects of getting a job.

Elaine had done her research. She already knew about Aemon. She was a fixture on the Derry 'grapevine'.

Aemon was different – he was employed, had reasonable looks, and could dance quite well. Elaine was sexually attracted to several of the young men around her, including

Aemon. But she had to wait another week for another chance to encounter Aemon again. However, even then it did not go to plan.

She and Jesse arrived to find many couples dancing, but a quick 'recce' of the crowd disappointed her. Aemon was nowhere to be seen. She had a few dances but sat several out, becoming more frustrated as the night wore on. She had decided to go home early again when she spotted Aemon entering the dance hall. She remained seated but pretended to be speaking to Angela who was seated beside her.

Aemon stopped in front of Elaine, who paused just a little before looking up at him. 'Hi', he said. 'Would you like to dance?'

'Yes,' she said, taking the hand he offered, 'Have we met before?' 'Yes,' said Aemon, 'I'm Aemon and we met last week.'

Elaine was tempted to work this line of no interest a bit further but decided to be more gracious and listen to him, wanting to know why he had kept her waiting! She did listen, and it turned out that he had been delayed by work, and that, she thought to herself, was forgivable.

They danced and then danced some more.

When Aemon held her very close, she could feel the arousal in his body. She welcomed it, embraced it even. He could not know with certainty that it was welcome, but she had made no attempt to separate from his erection.

Near the end of the evening, they went outside to talk. The crowd and the music inside made conversation difficult.

He asked her to have dinner with him. Elaine accepted but declined to have him pick her up from home. She was not ready to have him know where she lived, so she arranged to meet him at *Sandino's* on Water Street near the Foyle Embankment. Sandino was an infamous Nicaraguan rebel venerated by the Irish Republican Army (IRA) as a hero.

The dinner went well. Aemon talked about himself. Elaine encouraged this, but he also asked about her and appeared interested in her life.

They both had a couple of drinks, but she noticed that he quit as soon as she did. It was good to know that perhaps he did not drink to excess.

Elaine noticed that many of the other patrons at *Sandino's* seemed to know Aemon and she correctly guessed that this was perhaps Aemon's favourite watering hole.

He offered to walk Elaine home, but she declined, saying that the bus stopped nearby, and she would see herself home. She still did not want him to know where she lived, at least not yet. Before they parted, Aemon gave her a chaste kiss on the cheek and asked if she would like to go to the cinema the following Saturday. Elaine gave an enthusiastic 'Yes' and arranged to meet him there on the night.

They saw *Who Framed Roger Rabbit?* They were still laughing and recalling scenes as they left the cinema.

Again, Elaine opted for the bus for the trip home alone.

They had two more dates before Elaine permitted Aemon to take her home and give her a more passionate kiss before saying good night.

After a few more weekly dates, Aemon was invited in to meet Elaine's mother, Adele, and her older sister, Jesse. Elaine's father, Leon, had died years before in a motorcycle accident. All three women worked: Adele as a cleaner, Elaine at a local Derry newsagency and Jesse as an accountant.

Adele warmed immediately to Aemon, but Jesse never felt comfortable with him.

Aemon worked for Patrick O'Sullivan, master plumber, and most of his work involved using a mini excavator to dig trenches and, occasionally, graves. He had regular work and was trusted and well-regarded by his boss.

Having sex presented Elaine and Aemon with several difficulties, not the least of which was being Catholic. Aemon did not own a car, and finding a private and safe place was very difficult. Both lived in small houses. Elaine shared a bedroom with her sister, and Aemon was boarding with his cousin, so sex was generally out of the question at either home.

Elaine had a very strong sex drive but was too Catholic to yield to the advances of any of the young men she knew. It was not so much that extramarital sex was sinful – you could be forgiven that in the confessional. It was fear of pregnancy.

She realised in her teens that she would have to satisfy her own needs by herself, so she purchased a dildo. She guessed that Aemon had made his own arrangements to satisfy his needs and believed it did not involve another woman.

So, it was understandable that both wanted a commitment to marry and a short period of engagement.

When Aemon approached Adele and asked her approval to propose to Elaine, she was delighted, gave him an enthusiastic hug, and said 'Yes'. Jesse was unhappy and told Elaine and her mother that Aemon was a loser and would surely make her sister miserable. When questioned, Jesse could not say precisely why she disapproved of Aemon. She was vague and claimed that it was just a feeling.

'Probably a feeling of jealousy,' taunted Elaine.

Whereas Elaine was 'a real looker', Jesse was just plain.

They announced their engagement to friends, family and the parish priest at a small gathering at *Sandino's*.

It was unclear to them both what licence it gave them to indulge in sexual activity while engaged, so Elaine decided that they should remain chaste until they married. Aemon tried on several occasions to test her, but her resolve on the matter was too strong for him.

They decided on a wedding date in January. They would make their vows at their local parish church and have a small reception at Elaine's home.

On 25 January 1989, Elaine and Aemon celebrated their wedding. They rented a small Toyota and set off for a three-day honeymoon in Ballycastle.

The long-awaited sex was extraordinary. They could not get enough of one another and so saw few of the local attractions.

Buying a house for themselves was not possible at this stage, so Aemon moved into Elaine's house while they saved for a deposit for a home of their own. This meant a substantial change in the Ryan household. Adele agreed to take Elaine's bed in the sisters' room. Aemon and Elaine moved into Adele's room. This rather tense arrangement lasted six months.

Jesse was not happy about living under the same roof as

Aemon and used her accountancy expertise to help them save for a deposit to get Aemon out of her domain as quickly as possible.

They decided that they did not want to become pregnant until they managed to get a home of their own. Elaine was not so Catholic, however, as to ignore the benefits of the contraceptive Pill and secured a script from her doctor.

Eventually, they found an affordable cottage in Bready just outside Derry. There was a regular bus service into Derry where they both worked. They moved into the cottage in October and soon after Elaine stopped the Pill. However, it was not until April of the following year that she became pregnant with Rachel.

Elaine's pregnancy was fraught. She experienced nausea during the first six months, and she suffered from gestational hypertension, which had to be controlled with medication despite her reservations about taking medication during pregnancy. This made it difficult for her to keep working at the newsagency, but she persevered because they needed the money to pay the mortgage.

Rachel was born at Waterside Hospital on 16 December 1990 after a harrowing thirty-four-hour labour.

Elaine and Aemon had decided that if they had a boy, he would be named Liam and a girl would be named Rachel. Aemon had agreed with Elaine that it did not matter whether it was a boy or a girl. It would be welcomed and loved. They hoped that their child would be healthy, the universal hope of all parents. However, Aemon secretly hoped that Elaine would produce a Liam rather than a Rachel. He was apparently ignorant of the fact that the sex of his progeny would be down to him.

On his second visit to see his wife and daughter, Aemon was confronted by a tearful Elaine, who told him that she was not ever going to do that pregnancy and childbirth again. 'Not ever!'

Aemon was taken aback by the outburst but reasoned that Elaine would soon forget the dreadful time she had had in having Rachel and everything would be back to normal. Elaine did not forget, and everything did not go back to normal. She began insisting that Aemon use a condom each time they had sex and soon arranged for them to visit their doctor, Elam Forbes. Aemon hardly knew Forbes, for he had no health issues himself, but they had met during Elaine's pregnancy.

At their appointment, Elaine told Forbes that she would never do it again! No way! Forbes listened to Elaine and suggested that she was probably suffering from postpartum depression and suggested the following:

She should sleep when Rachel slept, even if it meant that some household chores were left incomplete. He turned his attention to Aemon and said he might do more about the house while Elaine recovered.

She should discuss her feelings with Aemon and other family members and talk to other mothers. There was an active mothers' group in her vicinity. He gave her contact details. And importantly, make no major decisions any time soon.

'I'm sure that will help,' he commented, bringing the

appointment to an end.

After following Forbes' advice for three months with no noticeable effect, they went back to him, insisting that she be free of the real fear she had of becoming pregnant again, ever! Although he said nothing about the issue of having more children, Aemon had been a bit put out about taking up housework which was clearly Elaine's job. He mused that no more children meant the traditional divide between the sexes remained unchanged. Elaine would do childcare, cooking and cleaning until Rachel went to school, and he would be the breadwinner.

They needed Forbes' advice to prevent any further pregnancies. Rachel was asleep in Elaine's arms but stirred a little as they sat down for their appointment. Elaine stroked Rachel's brow, and she settled immediately.

'Let's begin with the obvious solutions,' said Forbes. 'You could go on using condoms, which are about ninety-eight per cent effective, but in real situations, let's call it eight-five per cent. They can fail, so you will have about a fifteen per cent chance of becoming pregnant with them.'

'Not good enough,' said Elaine. 'What else?'

Aemon was pleased about this; he didn't like wearing them anyway. 'There is the withdrawal method.'

'What does that mean? Not having sex?' said Aemon.

'No, not withdrawal in that sense. It means that when you feel that you are about to ejaculate, you pull out, withdrawing your penis so that semen does not enter Elaine's vagina. It can be effective, but you have to be disciplined,' said Forbes.

Elaine looked unimpressed. 'What else?'

'Well,' said Forbes, 'you could go back on the Pill.'

'How effective is that?' said Aemon.

'Studies have shown it to be 99.7 per cent effective, but in practical terms, about ninety-one per cent is a good indicator. So about nine or ten per cent of women could become pregnant even while using the Pill. 'That sounds...' said Aemon, but Forbes cut him off.

'Other issues can also affect its efficacy,' said Forbes. 'Efficacy?' said Aemon.

'Whether it works or not!' snapped Elaine. 'What other issues?'

'Number one, sometimes women forget to take it. If you miss a day, it may not work.'

'Two. If you vomit, the pill may come back up or not be properly absorbed.

'Three. You need to take it at about the same time each day, within about three hours. Otherwise, it may not work.

'Four. You need to have your new pack ready when the last one is finished.'

'Five. Some medications such as phenobarbital, an epilepsy drug, can interfere with its efficacy. And there's also St John's Wort. That can be a problem too.'

'Too many problems,' said Elaine, 'and some women I know got really fat!'

'That can happen too,' said Forbes.

'What else? I've heard about IUDs. What about them?'

'Personally, the results from the studies I've read show that there are too many things that can go wrong with them. Or Aemon could have a vasectomy.'

'You mean "the snip",' said Aemon. 'Does it hurt?'

'Not much, I've had one myself,' said Forbes. 'And it is about ninety-nine per cent effective and that's about the best available method. And it does not affect your libido or your erection.'

'Libido?' said Aemon.

'Your sex drive, your willingness to have sex,' continued Forbes.

'Oh, are you sure about that?' said Aemon.

'Yes,' said Elaine 'are you really sure?' She did not want Aemon going soft on her. 'Yes,' said Forbes, 'I know it's correct!'

Elaine and Aemon decided to discuss what they had learned from Forbes and made another appointment to see him in a week.

Rachel was a bonny girl and showed all the signs of being healthy.

After two days in the hospital, Elaine and Aemon took Rachel home. Rachel turned out to be an easy baby. She suckled readily, which Elaine enjoyed, and began sleeping through the night after only a few weeks.

Her development was normal. Elaine took Rachel for regular check-ups. She was walking just before her first birthday, and her language skills were developing normally.

During the time between appointments, Elaine and Aemon asked for advice from their friends and acquaintances about vasectomies. Ellis, one of Aemon's workmates, had had a vasectomy back in 1983, and he said it was the best decision he and his wife Ellen had ever made. However, their situation was quite different. They already had three children, so it was more of an economic decision and not one based on fear of pregnancy and childbirth. However, Ellis was able to assure Aemon that the vasectomy had not affected their sex life.

He did add one further piece of advice. 'If you and Elaine part in the future either through Elaine's death or separation, you may not be able to have more children. Yes, it was possible to reverse a vasectomy, but its success could not be guaranteed.'

No one in Elaine's social circle had any intelligence on vasectomies. Many had not even heard of the procedure.

So, based on Ellis's information and Forbes' own experience, they asked Forbes to arrange for Aemon to have a vasectomy on the NHS. The waiting period turned out to be fifteen months, so they decided to use condoms until he could have the snip.

Chapter 4
YOUNG AEMON

Aemon Doyle's first memory of a Protestant march was the day he and his father joined other Catholic protesters to hurl abuse at the marchers on the last day in October in Belfast.

This march was to celebrate Reformation Day, a day set aside to recognise the protest by Martin Luther against the Catholic church hierarchy.

This challenge was launched when the printing press made it possible for ideas to spread via the literate community quickly and eventually led to Protestantism. Aemon's father, Alex, regularly attended these events to express his anger for the Protestant marchers as they wended their way close to Catholic areas. He hoisted young Aemon onto his shoulders so the six-year-old could see the enemy and hear the comments yelled at the marchers.

'You're a lot of Prody bastards,' he yelled. If Aemon had not been with him, it would have been 'You're a lot of fucking Prody bastards.' But he did, on occasions, moderate his language in front of his son and some women.

It was a form of initiation for Aemon, but in fact, his initiation had begun as soon as he acquired language and heard all around him, the bitterness of adults about the rights they felt were denied them. For over three hundred years, the tension between Catholics and Protestants waxed and waned. Protests, bloody and bloodless, shamefully conveyed the message of hate from one generation to the next.

Aemon's education was incestuous. Biased, unreliable notions about the history of the Irish struggle for independence were taught along with good Catholic principles of caring for others and living a life within the parameters of law and order. These notions were handed on from generation to generation with the same result as incest in families – twisted ideas in place of twisted people.

Belfast was a segregated city. Most of the Catholic population lived in the west and north, and the Protestants lived in the east. As if by divine intervention, the sun always rose first on the Protestants.

Since 1969, peace walls began to be erected to prevent violent exchanges between Catholics and Protestants. In August 1969, Conway Street was ablaze due to a fire-bombing initiated by a paramilitary Ulster group.

A decision was made to erect fences to keep Catholics and Protestants separated. Initially made of barbed wire, the peace walls were upgraded to thick cement and steel up to eight metres high and stretching thirty-four kilometres in length.

Aemon attended a Catholic school. Not one Protestant family in Belfast wanted, or dared, to send their children where they might be indoctrinated into the Catholic culture and faith. Similarly, no Catholic school enrolled a Protestant child.

And so it was that Aemon and his fellow Catholic youth continued the tradition of hating anyone they identified as Protestant.

Aemon's mother was keen to have her only son have as many advantages as she could provide for him, so she arranged for him to have ballroom dancing lessons with Maureen O'Hara (not the actress), the daughter of her best friend.

They went with their mothers to a dance studio where Aemon took lessons from Freddie and Maureen took lessons from Gracie. Freddie and Gracie were professional ballroom dancers and won their fair share of competitions. After about a half hour, Aemon and Maureen were paired up to practise what they had learned. This worked quite well, although Maureen was a lazy bitch who leaned heavily on Aemon's arm when she tired. Despite this, they were awarded Highly Commended awards when they danced for both bronze and silver medallions.

During a school lunchtime break, a short time after their silver medallion awards, Aemon foolishly revealed to his best friend Tony Hegerty that he was taking dancing lessons and now had two medals. He had brought these prized medals to school to show his friend. When they went into class after lunch, Tony's arm shot up. Brother Francis, well-known for his sadistic nature, said irritably, 'What is it, Hegerty?'

'Sir, Sir, Aemon is taking dancing lessons, Sir! He has won some medals.'

'Oh, has he?' said Brother Francis as the class erupted into laughter.

'Well, why doesn't he come up to the front here and do a little dance for us!' he said. More uproar filled the classroom.

'Sir, Sir,' Aemon tried to say but was drowned out by the chanting of 'Dance, dance, dance' by the class. Brother Francis raised a hand that clutched a short thick leather strap, a sure sign that he wanted silence. The class cowed at this well-known tool of punishment and silence reigned.

'Now,' said Brother Francis, 'why don't you come up here, Doyle, and show us how you dance?' 'But, Sir, I am learning ballroom dancing, and I dance with a partner,' blurted Aemon.

'Oh, does that mean you won't show us?' said Brother Francis. 'It doesn't mean I won't, Sir, it means I can't, Sir,' said Aemon. 'Oh, what a pity,' said Brother Francis.

Some sniggering was now coming from the class.

'Would I be right in thinking that your partner is a GIRL?' Brother Francis placed great emphasis on GIRL.

Uproar again and the leather was raised again. 'Yes, Sir,' said Aemon.

'And who would this GIRL be, Aemon?' said Brother Francis louder than was necessary for the class was quiet again.

Aemon now totally embarrassed whispered 'Maureen O'Hara, Sir.'

'Come again, Doyle. I can't hear you!' Brother Francis

said even louder. 'Maureen O'Hara,' said Aemon barely able to speak now.

'MAUREEN O'HARA, THE FAMOUS ACTRESS?' announced Brother Francis and the class erupted again.

Brother Francis raised his weapon again.

As the class quietened again, Aemon said, 'No, Sir, Maureen O'Hara from Falls Park.' More uproar and the weapon was raised again.

'Well, someday soon, you and Maureen O'Hara will have to show us how you can dance.'

Aemon did not reveal this humiliation to his parents. He kept it inside. Soon afterwards, he asked his mother if he could finish the dancing lessons. He had already achieved two medallions, and that was enough for him, and although he did not tell his mother, he was a bit sick of Maureen. He wanted to concentrate on playing football which was far more acceptable to the malicious Brother Francis and his classmates.

He had learned a vital lesson about confiding in friends: make sure they can be trusted before revealing anything important.

The other important lesson was that those people with power, like Brother Francis, could humiliate others, and it was necessary to avoid situations wherever this could occur.

He also realised that violence achieved results. Brother Francis's use of physical punishment worked. Although clearly outnumbered by his students, he wielded power by dint of violence or threat of violence, and he had the backing of the school, the Christian Brothers, the community, the

Church and the parents. Students conformed or were punished, and they absorbed this idea that the threat of violence or even the threat of death by the powerful will win out.

In Northern Ireland, power resided in the British Government and its powerful military. To resist this power meant the threat of violence, incarceration or even death. Resistance to the British Government meant that the law was being broken and punishment followed.

In this uneven conflict, the use of violence to protest against laws that discriminated against some was met by greater violence by the more powerful, lawful forces.

If required, the government could establish rules to make opposition a crime.

Even peaceful protest could be legislated as illegal, so participants could be arrested and deemed terrorists.

A head-to-head conflict would never be successful, although many youthful fighters thought it would. Casualties occurred on both sides, and righteous militants became terrorists for breaking the law.

This resistance by Nationalists was visible to the young. Still, the more subtle political manoeuvring was known to only a few, and young firebrands like Aemon had to be tempered by older activists. Aemon's hatred of the British and Ulster extremists turned to a lifelong crusade to kill as many of these people as he could, if not with gunfire, then with bombs, kidnapping and probing at weak points in the British defence.

On 16 June 1971, Aemon's older sister, Sophie, was caught

up in a gunfight between IRA fighters and British troops. She was having her hair cut at the Shear Class salon when British troops ran past the firing back behind them. They were being pursued by a contingent of IRA fighters. They took refuge behind parked vehicles and returned fire. All those in the salon flattened themselves against the floor as hundreds of rounds were exchanged. Shots blew out the front window showering the salon in glass. Everyone in the salon was terrified.

An armoured vehicle arrived with fresh troops, and the soldiers began to move back towards the IRA fighters, now with the armoured vehicle for cover. A stray bullet entered the salon and ricocheted off a chair. It had sufficient momentum to pierce the base of Sophie's skull as she lay prostrate on the floor and destroyed her brain stem. It was a fatal injury.

It took three hours for the news to reach the Doyle residence. Sophie's body had been removed to the morgue at Forster Green Hospital, and it was here that Alex Doyle came to identify his much-loved daughter. Aemon and his mother were hysterical and stayed at the house with neighbours while Alex wept over Sophie's inanimate body.

Nearly a thousand people attended Sophie's funeral. Several were IRA fighters wearing balaclavas. Father O'Brien conducted the service and condemned the violence on both sides, but it was clear that most mourners blamed Sophie's death on the British. As Sophie's coffin was lowered into the grave, four masked IRA fighters produced rifles and fired shots into the air.

Sophie's mother and Aemon wept hot and bitter tears. Alex stood stoic.

Soon after the funeral, Aemon sought out IRA members in his community and asked for information about joining. He was referred to a recruiting officer, Paul McQuade, in Percy Street. McQuade could see immediately that Aemon was underage despite Aemon claiming he was eighteen years old. He also recognised that arming Aemon would mean that the boy would be a danger to himself and, more importantly, to other members of the organisation. He advised Aemon to take up a trade. The IRA, he said, was not just about fighters. The fighters needed logistical support, and there were many more working behind the scenes than there were fighters. He added, however, that support workers sometimes took up arms as well.

Armed with the hope of fighting and killing Sophie's murderers, Aemon continued at school and left at sixteen. Unemployment in Belfast was at thirteen per cent overall and significantly higher for the young. However, an opportunity came for him to participate in a government-funded course to learn how to use large industrial equipment. One of the men teaching the course took a liking to Aemon, and when a position came up at Farrans Construction, where his teacher worked, Aemon got the job.

Aemon was a good worker. He was punctual, obeyed instructions and learned quickly. After four years of working with Farrans, where he learned many useful skills and secured a licence to use backhoes and forklifts, he applied for and secured a position with Patrick O'Sullivan, master plumber, in Derry.

Chapter 5
BARNABY

When Elaine Doyle received her diagnosis that the lump in her left breast was malignant, her doctor suggested that further tests should be done to check other organs for the presence of tumours. Elaine was proud of her breasts and now they were killing her. She looked at her naked body in her mirror. Her body was still attractive, albeit with a change in skin colour. Her belly was almost flat, and her hips nicely rounded. She had not looked after her body as well as she should have and now her dark organs were conspiring to end her life. She knew that she attracted looks of lust from men and sometimes the lust was reciprocated but remained just lust, unexpressed for all but Aemon. He was a generous and thoughtful lover who brought her to orgasm often with cunnilingus before coming himself.

Of course, the passion of those early years had waned, but the sex remained spontaneous, if not regular. He failed only when he had been drinking, but this was not often, and it was forgivable.

Further scans revealed an extensive presence of cancer in her liver, lungs and pancreas. Her doctor sadly informed Elaine and Aemon that there was nothing that could be done in the way of treatment, but she would be provided with support and pain relief.

When Elaine asked, the doctor said that death was imminent, and she had about six weeks to live. At this Aemon gritted his teeth and tried to suppress a sob but it erupted despite his effort to swallow it. He cried and bit on his fingers as he tried to comfort a stunned Elaine.

Of course, the news was devastating for the thirty-eight-year-old but also for Aemon, Rachel and Jesse. Elaine's mother, Adele, had died of liver cancer three years previous, and it should have made both Elaine and Jesse cautious about being tested for breast and uterine cancer, but it hadn't. It now came into sharp focus for Jesse and for Rachel, who was badly affected by her mother's condition.

When her parents told her of the situation, her pale skin was further drained, and she became even paler.

Despite her own grief Elaine felt obliged to comfort those who would be left after she died. But this was beyond her now as the internal enemy sucked up her energy.

What began as self-pity evolved into monstrous anger at the Creator – *how could this be justified?*

What sort of god would rob her and her family?

Elaine decided that she would stay at home until such time that it was not possible to control her pain, and she would spend her final days in a hospice.

Who would guide Rachel through the latter stages of adolescence? Elaine had given a firm basis for Rachel's entry into adulthood and protected her from Aemon, but now secret plans needed to be made to separate Rachel from him.

Jesse and Rachel met on occasions when Elaine had enough strength to participate. The plan involved Rachel leaving their home and moving in with Jesse. Elaine asked Rachel if she wanted to continue with her plan to make her fortune using her body and if not, how could Elaine help her? Was Rachel still hoping to pursue this course?

'My body tells me that this is what I need, and I know that there will be difficulties, but I think they can be overcome, Mum, but I was counting on you to help me. But now you are going, and I am so sad. Sad, but not defeated,' cried Rachel.

Rachel reaffirmed the plans, but she needed assurance that her aunt could guide her through the early stages until she could carry on the business alone. They had all agreed that Rachel did not pursue the plan until she was eighteen and that she needed to continue her education or find a job until then. Rachel did not like school and the prospect of continuing she found unappealing.

So, she needed to leave school and move in with Jesse to escape Aemon. She had just turned sixteen when her mother died, and Jesse arranged for Rachel to move in with her while Elaine entered the hospice. Elaine also revealed that she had saved over six thousand pounds from her salary as a teacher's aide, which she had done since Rachel began school. She transferred the money to Jesse, who would look after it until Rachel needed it.

Aemon was ropeable that Rachel had left school and had moved in with her aunt but after a long chat with Elaine at the hospice he had to accept it, like it or not. Elaine showed Aemon a diary that she had kept from the first time he had entered Rachel's room uninvited when she was just thirteen, and every other time she had to usher him out since then. She told him that Jesse would have possession of the diary which contained this damaging evidence of his attempts to groom Rachel for sex and would be handed over to police if he interfered with their plans. She did not tell him of their plans for Rachel to be a prostitute, only that she would get a job and live with Jesse until she could look after herself.

Elaine's funeral was a tense affair with a large attendance noticeably divided into two groups. Just like a wedding, the groups assembled on opposite sides of the aisle.

And afterwards, there were, in fact, two wakes – one side gathering at the Ryan family home with Jesse and the other at *Sandino's* with Aemon.

Jesse looked for positions for Rachel in Derry and suggested she apply for one with her friend Barnaby McVeigh, who owned who Barnaby's Boutique Bookshop in Derry.

She set up a meeting with Barnaby, who was impressed with Rachel and said he could offer her a three-month trial. Rachel liked Barnaby immediately, he was so eccentric, and so she began on the following Monday.

Barnaby was a larger-than-life figure. He was an overweight, oddly dressed, jolly man whom she noticed slapped his knees when excited or when he was laughing. Barnaby wore faded brown corduroy trousers and shirts of many colours that often clashed with his trousers, and he owned a large selection of oversized polka dot bow ties. In the cooler months, he added a faded houndstooth jacket with obligatory leather patches on the elbows.

At first, the tasks that Rachel was given were cleaning and ensuring that after customers left, the books they may have disturbed were put in their correct place. Gradually, she was given more skilful tasks, including using EFTPOS and the cash register.

When business was slow, Barnaby checked to see how Rachel was coping. He had been at school with Elaine, although not in the same year. He would hold her when she needed to be held, give her chores that would take her out of the shop when he felt she needed a break, or just say how sorry felt but added, 'If this had never happened, I would probably never have met you.'

Barnaby had become a sort of icon of the Derry CBD. He was a very lively presence at the front of his shop, which featured a vast array of books that he imaginatively presented to passers-by. He waved and passed the time of day with anyone who came near.

He requested Rachel to wear a black outfit. He realised that Rachel's looks could benefit his business, but it should not detract from his extravagant presence.

So, Rachel came dressed daily in black jeans, a shirt and joggers.

It made little difference to male passers-by. She did not fail to impress.

Barnaby noticed this but realised that the business was attracting more males who sometimes bought books. He was outgunned in the looks department but was sanguine enough to accept it. Initially, Rachel was shown how the shop was organised and how he expected her to maintain the highly ordered display of books. Not all the books were new. Barnaby also collected old or antique books that he sometimes bought at auction. These books were precious to him, and he rarely sold them. Sometimes collectors of these books came in to inspect and buy. Still, generally, people wanted the latest editions or best sellers or favourite authors or the large offering of non-fiction books.

Rachel had not read much when young, apart from the required reading at school. She was a very social person not given to reading at home when she could be on her bike with friends on rides along the river Foyle and for picnics and the pure enjoyment of physical activity and fun. And at night, of course, there was television.

Because she had now left school and some of her friends had continued with their education, she began to lose contact with some of them. But she was still an active member of the group of young people with whom she had grown up. Some of the boys in the group sought to pair with her and she did separate and coupled with some of them. If the occasion arose where privacy was such that they could have sex, they did, and it felt great! She remembered her mother's advice and always carried condoms in her bag. She was also aware of her mother's advice about sex when she was so young. Elaine did not endorse spontaneous sex for Rachel at this young age and did urge her to be cautious.

There was a great deal for her to cope with, not the least of which was the grieving she felt for her mother. They had been very close as Rachel shared the experiences of her social life. The death of a parent is always going to be a life-changing event but particularly for someone young. There was also the issue of Aemon, who made it very clear, despite his anguish of losing Elaine, that he felt that Rachel was deserting him at a time when he was grieving. He was infuriated about Rachel living with Jesse, whom he loathed, and that she had left school without his permission.

He had hoped that his only child would be better educated than he and Elaine had been, and now Jesse was charting her future without input from him. He was further enraged that the job that Jesse had arranged for Rachel was dusting old books at that faggot's bookshop.

Did Jesse not understand that she had put his daughter in moral danger?

Aemon came to Jesse's house on several occasions to argue with her and to try to convince Rachel that she should move back with him and go back to school. After several doorstop arguments, Jesse took out a restraining order on Aemon, which compelled him not to come within 50 yards of her house. She agreed to permit Rachel to meet him at local public venues if she was present. Rachel felt sorry for her Dad but understood that she could no longer be with him unsupervised.

He would not give up, though. He went to the bookshop to try to convince Rachel to come home with him.

His presence and his demands to see Rachel annoyed Barnaby to the extent that he, too, threatened a restraining order.

This exacerbated the situation, and Aemon sought help from his IRA colleagues, Aisling Byrne and Jimmy O'Connor. He suggested that they might torch the bookshop in revenge. Both Byrne and O'Connor were well-known homophobes, and he imagined that they would support him with this. To his surprise, they threatened him.

'If you do this and the act is seen to be linked to us, someone will find you lying in a ditch with a bullet in the back of your head,' warned Byrne. 'The coppers here are not fools, Aemon, and we do not want any unnecessary attention from them.'

Rachel enjoyed the atmosphere of the bookshop. It wasn't overly busy, but she had to learn enough about books and the arrangement in the shop so that in the future Barnaby could confidently leave her in charge and he could attend an auction to value a privately owned library for insurance purposes.

In conversation, Barnaby noticed that Rachel had read very little and he gradually suggested that when it was quiet in the shop, she do some reading.

'How will I choose a book, Barnaby? There are so many here.'

He was ready for this and had an extensive list of titles to get her started, knowing that he could suggest more challenging adult books later. He suggested that she choose from *To Kill A Mockingbird* by Harper Lee and *The Giver* by Lois Lowry, which were often recommended reading in schools. She had not read either book at school. She chose *The Giver* because she thought *To Kill A Mockingbird* was a weird title for a book.

Rachel enjoyed the Lowry book, and as she read at work, she became so interested in the fate of young Jonas that she took it home to finish. It was the beginning of a love affair with books which became a lifelong passion.

Outside Barnaby's Boutique Bookshop was a sandwich board on which Barnaby advertised some of his stock. It changed every day, but there was a special space for 'Barnaby Is Presently Reading' and beneath that, he would insert the title he was currently reading. Barnaby was a very fast reader and this, too, changed almost daily. This often-meant sales! When people questioned him about his choices, they often decided to buy them.

As the months rolled by, Rachel and Barnaby became good friends even though some of her friends cautioned her about working with a queer. When this was first pointed out to her, she feigned understanding of the caution but did not understand what a queer was. It did not take long to find out. You can find anything in books or on the internet.

Her research led her to understand homosexuality, but she found it disgusting that men would do this with one another. As for female homosexuals, it was bewildering. She sought some advice from Jesse, a good friend of Barnaby. Jesse shared her opinion about the sexual activities of gay men and women but stressed that this did not mean they should not be respected as people. Sex, she emphasised, is a private thing, and the expression of love for another human being should not be condemned.

Armed with this new intelligence, Rachel sought not to strive to convert her friends to this way of respecting other people but merely remained uninterested in further discussing the matter. Barnaby was always on the lookout to improve his business. After all, it would provide him with funds for a comfortable retirement. The business needed to develop and be refreshed constantly.

He was an active user of social media, which he found very useful in locating new stock and ideas. He also embraced selling accessories for book reading, ebooks and audiobooks.

One day he had a 'light bulb' moment. His large collection of bow ties had been fashioned by a former lover and friend, Marshall James. He guessed there may have been material left over, and he asked Marshall if this were so.

'That's years ago!' replied Marshall, 'but I'll have a look and get back to you.'

About a day later, Marshall rang back to confirm there was plenty of material for each of the ties. 'Have you worn them out already?'

'No,' said Barnaby, 'here's what I want you to do for me.'

A couple of weeks later, Barnaby received in the post a cardboard box that he took back to his office. When he had examined the contents, he called to Rachel to put out the 'Closed but will be back soon' sign on the door and come to the office.

When she came into the office, she noted that he had cleared his desk and on it he had placed the parcel.

She noticed how excited he appeared and said, 'What's going on?'

He said nothing but raised the open box above the desk. Out tumbled several 'scrunchies' which she soon realised were of the same material as his bow ties.

'Oh, Barnaby!' she said as she embraced the smiling Barnaby. 'Now, each day we will match!'

She thought, *What a wonderful man I have been so lucky to meet.*

Barnaby's faith in leaving her in charge was tested in a dry run where he went out with a friend for coffee, leaving Rachel in charge. Unbeknownst to her, he was just around the corner for an hour and a half, giving her his most reassuring smile and his mobile number.

She had been very nervous about this responsibility and was greatly relieved when he reappeared at the front of the shop. She had sold four books, all by herself!

Barnaby had a strong sense of history and anniversaries, and as the anniversary of Rachel's first day with him approached, she noticed him in a state of intense secretive activity.

On the big day, they began as they usually did with setting up the walkway display and updating the sandwich board. At about 10 o'clock, a courier arrived with a bunch of beautiful flowers and attached to it was a card indicating that this was a momentous day and that the flowers were from Barnaby to Rachel. She accepted them with emotional tears in her eyes, noticing that he was teary too.

'Take them into the office and put them in water, Rachel.'

He looked up and down the street and went to join Rachel.

A couple of minutes later, they heard the bell on the front door, and Jesse's voice called, 'Can I get some service here?'

'I'll go, you finish with the flowers,' said Barnaby.

When Rachel was finished with the flowers, she went out into the shop and Jesse was talking animatedly with Barnaby. As she reached the front door, Jesse greeted her and indicated a second sandwich board, blank now, except for the lower right corner which read 'Rachel is presently reading'.

Tears all around again – tears of joy.

As Rachel wrote on her sandwich board, an older, quite handsome man passed her as he entered the shop – Kirby Mitchell.

Chapter 6
RACHEL VENTRILOQUIST

In the weeks after meeting Kirby, Rachel hatched a plan to get to know him better.

She needed to know how he might respond to an approach to discuss ventriloquism. The difficulty was that she did not want to reveal any plan to use this skill because it had not yet become clear. Barnaby was not privy to this information. Jesse and Rachel believed that he would not approve of prostitution as a suitable career for Rachel or anyone and may have plans to have Rachel take over Barnaby's Book Boutique when he retired.

She began by having brief conversations with Kirby each time he came to Barnaby's. She encouraged him to talk about himself, beginning with his life at school with Barnaby. After that, he easily spoke about how he had learned this skill and his various gigs in theatres and clubs worldwide. Kirby had performed in many countries, the USA and Canada included. He had toured Australia and

New Zealand and learned French and German versions of his routines.

Kirby now lived in Derry and often came by Barnaby's to talk with him, and they often went off to *Sandino's* for coffee and more chats about the 'not-so-good' old days. They could laugh at it now, but they were both scarred by their pasts; laughter masked deep feelings of rage against the people who had harmed them, including their teachers and the Jack Sweeney mob. Their lives as sons of single mothers meant poverty, privation, and exclusion.

At one of their meetings, Kirby asked Barnaby if he thought Rachel would stay with him. 'Look, I'd like to think so,' he said, 'but she's only seventeen and has a long life ahead of her, I'm sure. I think it grand if she could eventually take over from me when I retire.'

'When do you think that will be?'

'I'm not ready yet. Every day it is still a thrill when I wake each morning and realise that I'm still alive and my precious books await me at the shop. There is also the issue of Rachel's age. If I did retire in a few years, it's unlikely she would have the funds behind her to buy.'

When she had an opportunity to speak to him on his visits to Barnaby's, Rachel gradually steered the conversations to ventriloquism and how it was done. Kirby was chuffed that Rachel asked if she could try some words spoken without moving her lips. They both laughed at her early efforts, but she remained confident that Kirby did not realise that he was giving her lessons. She did not press him, and when he had shown one technique, she would go home, practise it and not ask for any more for short time. After a short interval, she would approach him again, show off a bit, and he would applaud her. But she would leave it there and practised until he came to visit Barnaby again. This exercise was to become a lifelong habit; she practised every night.

Somehow, she reasoned, this skill may become part of her presentation to men, but she wasn't quite sure how.

Rachel had a strong sense of commitment to establishing herself in her chosen career; she had an attractive young body and gregarious nature, and she enjoyed having sex. She had heard some women discussing sex in a manner which, to her, sounded as though these women regarded sex as something that happened to them, not something they did for their enjoyment. It seemed strange to her because she found it so enjoyable. Could it be that after years of marriage, sex was no longer enjoyable for them? If they were no longer enjoying it, she could imagine that they would convey this directly or indirectly to their male partners who, perhaps, rather than talk about the issue, would seek sexual satisfaction from women like her and be prepared to pay for it.

Gradually Rachel picked up enough for Kirby to realise that she could probably perform if she had a routine and dummy to use. It surprised him that she had learned so much from their conversations. One day he asked her if she planned to use her skill on stage.

'Do you plan to do what I have done? Because if that is your plan, you and I should have a long conversation about the consequences of such a career choice. I have had a fulfilling life in this profession. It has allowed me to travel worldwide, but it mitigated my chances of forming close intimate relationships. Now I have retired and returned to Derry where, fortunately, I have friends like Barnaby to count on to share in my old age. Many of the performers with whom I've travelled – singers, musicians and dancers – have, like me, been unable to maintain intimate relationships, or if they have, find them crumbling away under the pressure of continual travel commitments.'

Rachel was touched that Kirby thought her sufficiently skilled to make a career out of ventriloquism.

She said 'Oh, I am so happy to think that you believe that I could be a professional ventriloquist and travel the world as you have, but the thought of being on stage petrifies me; I just couldn't do it. But thank you so much for thinking that I could.'

'In a way, I'm grateful that you have no plans to use your talent as a stage ventriloquist but sad that your talent may not be used at all,' sighed Kirby.

'Oh, don't be too disappointed, I have already intrigued my friends at parties with my skill. It's a lot of fun to see them looking at a sock on my hand speaking to them. No, life on the stage is not for me, I would be too scared,' giggled Rachel nervously.

She wondered what Kirby and Barnaby would think if they knew she planned to be a prostitute.

Rachel's use of ventriloquism at parties reminded Kirby of some lean times he had when ventriloquists were finding it difficult to get bookings. Interests of the public changed over time and sometimes they were simply not interested in ventriloquism. Then an outstanding ventriloquist would make it onto a major TV show and immediately bookings would pick up again. However, in those lean times, Kirby had to put aside his notion of good taste and do a 'bucks' night.

The venue was usually a club, and the audience would be a group of boisterous young men. His act was to accompany a stripper hired for the occasion. When the girl had stripped, she would move about the now more boisterous young men, and it was Kirby's job to stay close to her as she approached each man. As she faced each one, Kirby and his dummy, Harold, would make suggestive comments about their genitals. Some got comments about the size of their penises and testicles, some about lack of use, and some about high frequency of use. The groom, of course, got the most suggestive comment, usually about him using his 'equipment' on the stripper before using it on the bride. Kirby was not proud of these jobs but sometimes it was necessary to pay the bills.

Rachel would sometimes perform when Kirby came by at Barnaby's. It was great fun and Barnaby loved to see them 'play' their skill. Rachel never stopped learning from Kirby. There was always something in the way he managed words for her to learn. Rachel had no trouble mastering the easy letters of the alphabet that could be sounded without moving lips, but how could B, F, M, P, V, W and Y be pronounced without moving lips? Kirby taught Rachel that for these letters, you had to cheat and use other letters in their place. For instance, N can replace M, and if done quickly in the context of a sentence, the audience would not realise that you have fooled them.

As a child and young adolescent, Rachel had a problem with bladder control. She was a bedwetter but overcame it with protective parental care. Elaine never reprimanded Rachel for bedwetting but supported her with gentle reminders about the toilet before bed and a supply of incontinence pants as a backup until Rachel could sleep through the night with confidence.

Rachel later had problems with urinating in times of stress or excitement. If she heard something particularly funny, she might wet her pants. Some teachers, unaware of her problem, roughly chastised her, again resulting in the extra embarrassment of pants wetting. This presented a somewhat more difficult problem when she was at school or out with friends. Extra underpants and padding were a help but treated only the consequences, not the problem. Elaine took a reluctant Rachel to her local GP, who said that in her experience with pregnant patients, Kegal pelvic muscle exercises often led to better bladder control. Rachel was grateful that the doctor did not require her to show her pelvic muscles and that the advice and diagrams in the brochures she received on strengthening these muscles were easy to follow.

Rachel recognised the need for a solution to this problem if she was going to have a normal social life away from the security of home. She practised daily – first thing in the morning and before bed at night. However, she did not stop when she gained control over her bladder. As she practised, she noticed an increase in pleasure when she masturbated. This intrigued her enough to explore the idea that these newly strengthened pelvic muscles could be consciously controlled to move the lips of her vagina. Exactly what use she could make of this new-found ability was not clear, but she put that aside for now and continued to practise. Rachel practised daily even though it would be years before her talking fanny became part of her profession as a prostitute.

Her business was launched soon after her eighteenth birthday and she noticed that several clients commented on her green eyes and red hair. One even commented that she had a Burning Bush. It turned out to be a 'light bulb' moment – a Burning Bush that could speak to clients! Now she realised the potential of including her talking fanny in her work as a prostitute. What other prostitute would be able to include this talent to give pleasure to her clients? But for now, she would have to think of a way to pull it off.

It would take some time for her to have the courage to try it out on a customer. First, she needed to practise in front of a mirror. A customer needed to concentrate on her fanny. Men did not need to be encouraged to look but they did need to see her vaginal lips ostensibly forming the words she was making. To maintain their attention the Burning Bush would need to make some naughty, bawdy comments. The best source of the appropriate words was from the clients themselves. Some were very vocal during sex using words to convey to her what they were feeling and hoping that she felt it too.

Before Rachel had an opportunity to introduce this talent

to her customers, she encountered Arthur Millar.

The frenzied activity after his intervention into her life meant that these plans had to be thrust aside as she fled Derry to Australia.

Once she had distanced herself from Millar, she would have to reshape her plan to fit her new environment. Her contacts in Australia were Fergus and Dawn whom she had never met.

In fact, she was now safe, but friendless.

Fergus was from Derry but his wife, Dawn, was an Australian.

Both seemed friendly and took her to the accommodation she had chosen, the Backpacker Central backpacker hostel in the middle of Brisbane. She soon discovered that the couple lived in Sandgate, several kilometres away near Moreton Bay, not that close by. Rachel was resilient and set about getting a job and making friends at the Backpacker Central.

This was only ever going to be an interim measure. She had a lot of work ahead of her to re-launch her career. She was now a nineteen-year-old and had used up substantial funds to escape Millar. Rachel did feel the excitement of sex, but it was not necessary for her each time she had sex.

It was a bonus for Rachel if a man brought her to climax and many were genuinely pleased that they had achieved it, but most were premature ejaculators. For these, she faked it if she thought they earned it.

She also realised that the Burning Bush was a rather untidy affair. She thought about ways to make it more enticing.

It was becoming fashionable for women to have their pubic hair groomed and shaped. Some even had it shaved off. Some surveys about sexual preferences showed that over sixty per cent of men preferred the naked vagina appearance. She went to a hairdresser who offered such a service and instructed her to shape her Burning Bush so that the vagina was not covered. The hair immediately around the vagina was cut short and then tapered away to each side.

'Looks like the parting of the Red Sea!' commented the hairdresser.

Rachel saw how easy it would be to trim her pubic hair and immediately bought a trimmer for herself.

Chapter 7
KIRBY MITCHELL

Kirby Mitchell walked past Rachel as she was working on her sandwich board and entered the shop. She noted that Kirby was an older man, around the same age as Barnaby. She heard Barnaby greet Kirby enthusiastically and then take him into the office at the back of the shop. As Rachel attended to business, she could hear snatches of their conversation as well as roaring laughter. This went on for over an hour at which point Barnaby came out and asked Rachel if she could make the pair a cup of coffee.

She agreed.

Once she entered the office with coffee, she was able to confirm that the handsome Kirby was indeed about Barnaby's age and that they were very good friends.

'This,' Barnaby said to Kirby, 'is my wonderful new assistant, Rachel.' Kirby rose from his chair and proffered his hand. Rachel felt a firm warm handshake from Kirby who said, 'Lovely to meet you.'

'Forgive my ignorance. I am so excited to see Kirby again that I have not introduced you, Kirby,' enthused Barnaby.

'Rachel, this is my very good friend, Kirby Mitchell. We have been friends since our first day at school. We have not seen each other for years and now he is back to live in Derry! It is just wonderful to have him back in my life. You see Kirby and I had to look after each other all the way through school.'

'I think,' said Kirby, 'that it was you, Barnaby, who did most of the looking after.'

They laughed again. Barnaby slapped his knee as he habitually did when overly excited.

'You see, I was not the scholar that Barnaby was. He helped me so much to understand at least a little of the stuff that the teachers were trying to teach me. Instead of going outside during recess and lunch breaks, Barnaby used to help me in the library to try to make sense of English and Maths. And importantly we did not have to go outside where the bullies hung out.' 'Do you remember Jack Sweeney and his mob?' said Barnaby.

'Now, let's not bore poor Rachel with our unhappy school day memories,' said Kirby. 'I'm sure we can find some things in our past that are a little more interesting than that.'

Just then the bell on the shop door began to tingle.

'I had better get out there and see to business. It was a pleasure to meet you, Mr Mitchell.'

'And it was my great pleasure to meet you, Rachel, but please call me Kirby.'

As Rachel left, Kirby turned to Barnaby.

"What a lovely young lady you have there Barnaby, and so polite as well. I wager she attracts many young men into your shop."

'Yes,' said Barnaby, 'and some of them even buy books. But many are after a date.'

'Do many of them succeed?' said Kirby.

'Some do, Rachel is keen on boys but there seems to be no one special,' replied Barnaby.

'I'm sure that someday there will be,' said Kirby.

'I think we still have a lot to talk about, Kirby. Why don't we meet for lunch on Friday? *Sandino's* is good, What do you say?' suggested Barnaby. 'I say yes, about twelve-thirty?' said Kirby, and they agreed.

Over the next few weeks, Rachel encouraged Barnaby to reveal more details about his good friend.

She found that Kirby and Barnaby had been born within a month of each other in 1942 and had been raised by single mothers.

Barnaby's father had died of TB when Barnaby was just three years old. Kirby's father was an American Army officer sent to Derry to help set up the secret Base One Europe, later called the Royal Naval Base HMS *Ferret*. Oscar Carmody had met Ella Mitchell at a local dance, and they had fallen in love. He needed permission to marry an Irish girl and approached the officer-in-charge, Major John Maxwell, with his plan to marry Ella. After enduring two weeks of military red tape, permission was granted. They planned to marry as soon as Oscar had returned to Ireland from Ohio, where his parents and family lived. He felt that he needed to tell his family in person about his plan to marry Ella and took leave to fly back to America Ella and Oscar were so excited to have their plans set in place that they celebrated their delight in the most intimate way possible. Oscar never returned to Ella. His plane was shot down by German fighters over the Atlantic on the way to the United States, and all on board perished.

Oscar had unwittingly left a part of himself to Ella – a part that was in time to become her much-loved son, Kirby.

Unlike his friend, Barnaby was almost a scholar. He did well at school and went on to complete high school, whereas Kirby left school as soon as he was legally able to do so at fourteen.

Kirby managed to secure, with Ella's help, an apprenticeship to Albert Schultz, the set designer at the Waterside Theatre in Derry. Schultz was an eccentric creative person, temperamental, and sometimes difficult to work with. Over five years of working with Schultz, Kirby learned his craft well, but more importantly, he fell in love with performing. He secured several minor parts in Waterside productions but was enthralled by ventriloquists who sometimes performed there. He was fascinated by Ray Alan and his dummy Lord Charles, and Peter Brough with his dummy Archie Andrews. Kirby decided that this was his calling and set about learning to be a ventriloquist.

This information about Kirby's life as a ventriloquist pricked Rachel's interest, although she could not envision herself as a stage performer. 'It is going to matter to me in the future, I just know it,' she mused.

Barnaby also revealed that after leaving school in 1958, he was able to find a position as an assistant to Edith Jones at her bookshop Derry Book Land. Edith was forty-eight years old and was looking to spend more time travelling the world before she became too old to do so. Her husband, James, had left her well provided for when he died during the War.

Edith was impressed by Barnaby from day one. He was well-dressed, punctual and outgoing. He impressed the customers with his light-hearted manner and genuine love of books. As time went by, Edith was also impressed by the continuing improvement in his knowledge of books of all types.

By 1978, Barnaby was the 'face' of Derry Book Land, and since 1972 Edith was rarely seen at her shop. She spent more time travelling and left Barnaby to conduct business for her.

Near the end of the financial year 1978, Edith offered Barnaby the opportunity of buying Derry Book Land. Barnaby had been hoping Edith would make this suggestion and felt ready to run the shop himself. The only thing standing in his way was finance. He banked at HSBC, as did his mother, Ella, and Edith. The manager could not quite handle the amount required and suggested to Barnaby that he speak to his mother and Edith about co-financing the loan. After extensive discussion, Ella agreed to put in eight hundred pounds which still left him six hundred pounds short. Then Edith made the remarkable offer of financing the six hundred pounds herself on condition that Barnaby pays her one hundred pounds per year for the rest of her life. All three met with the bank manager, who thought it a novel way of solving the problem but gave it his blessing.

The deal was done, and Barnaby became the proud owner of Derry Book Land.

Barnaby's homosexuality plagued his life from primary school onward. Other children seemed to sense a difference in him, and he was taunted for it. He was fortunate that most of his teachers recognised the difference for what it was, tolerated it but did not encourage it. Jack Sweeney and his mob were particularly difficult to deal with. They took every opportunity to harass him. Kirby was his only real ally at school.

To understand his homosexuality, Barnaby read extensively, including *Death in Venice* by Thomas Mann (1912), *The City and the Pillar* by Gore Vidal (1948), and *Maurice* by EM Foster (1914).

He also read about Alan Turing, one of the country's war heroes who had been disgraced after being found to be having homosexual relationships in the privacy of his own home. Turing's punishment was chemical castration, but he committed suicide in 1954 at age forty-one.

In 1982, after intensive campaigning, *The Homosexual Offences (Northern Ireland) Order* decriminalising homosexuality passed through the Parliament of Northern Ireland. Barnaby welcomed it but it had little effect on his life.

After a year of ownership, Barnaby decided to give the business a new name to make it more in keeping with his style of running a bookshop. He called it Barnaby's Book Boutique. It was a classy name and he loved it!

When ventriloquist Alan Kline came to Derry to perform

with his offsider Arnie at the Waterside Theatre, Kirby asked him to reveal the secrets of ventriloquism for a fee of twenty pounds and show him how to perform. Kline agreed. The money would be welcome when bookings were becoming harder to get. The basics were quite simple, Kline told him, and it just took practice, just as it would be to juggle or perform card tricks. The difference between juggling, card tricks and ventriloquism was the banter between the ventriloquist and his 'stooge', the dummy. That was where the real art lay.

So, it was up to Kirby now to practise the voice techniques that Kline had shown him, organise a dummy and develop an entertaining banter to use on stage.

With the techniques he had learned from Schulz, Kirby was confident that he could create his own, and he did. He called his dummy Harold after Harold Macmillan, the former witty and unflappable British Prime Minister also known as 'Supermac'. He studied archival film footage of Macmillan and worked up an act based on him.

Macmillan had held various Cabinet positions in the then-ruling Conservative government. He had been a captain in the Army during WW1 and entered Parliament during the Great Depression. He held several positions during WW2, much of it outside England. He took the position of Minister of State for Air in Churchill's post-war government, only to lose his seat when Labour won a crushing victory to oust Churchill's Conservatives. The Conservatives won back power in 1951, and by 1957 he became Prime Minister when the then Prime Minister, Anthony Eden, resigned over the Suez crisis. He had to work hard to re-establish good relations with the USA which had soured during the crisis.

There were turbulent times during his prime ministership, including the bolstering of Britain's nuclear capability and the Profumo Affair.

So, Harold, his dummy, initially talked with Kirby in a gentle and inoffensive way, but it soon became dated and new material had to be prepared. This was exhausting, and Kirby realised that focusing on Macmillan had to change into banter about the type of person Macmillan represented, the upper class.

Kirby's audience was generally not well off and was happy to laugh when a rich fellow was made fun of in a farcical way.

It would take many auditions to convince potential managers to take him on as a client, but he eventually succeeded with John Snow, who was also at the start of his career as an entrepreneur.

The career that Kirby had chosen had unforeseen circumstances, not the least of which was a life of constant travel. While this was initially seductive, after a few years, it became arduous.

Kirby formed few strong relationships with either sex. He remained a bachelor for life. His only constant personal connection was with John Snow, who supported Kirby when ventriloquism waxed and waned in popularity.

And so, it was in Barnaby's Book Boutique that the life of ventriloquist Kirby Mitchell intersected with future prostitute Rachel.

Rachel was seventeen now and was being pressed by several boys and men to have a steady relationship, meaning that they alone could date her. She resisted this and began to experiment with sex.

She remembered well the advice that Elaine had given her and took precautions to avoid pregnancy and HIV, which had been a scourge for years.

She loved sex and enjoyed it with several young men but was careful to avoid a repeat performance with any of them. It was once only for each one. This was okay up to a point, but there was some perception in Derry that she 'was anyone's'. This was unfair because she rejected more suitors than she accepted.

About this time, the idea of Rachel selling her body for money was again discussed with Jesse. They reviewed the original plan and implemented it soon after Rachel's eighteenth birthday. Her 'work ware' had been purchased, and Jesse had organised for a website to be set up. They decided that they would use several revealing pictures of Rachel but none of her naked, and in the pictures that showed her face, she would wear a mask that covered the top of her face, excluding her eyes and nose. In one of the pictures, Rachel would be shown posing as Marilyn Monroe in that iconic 'wind under the dress' picture.

Jesse had already agreed to terms for short-term room occupancy with three hotels in Strabane, Limavady and Newbuilding. She also developed a contingency plan for mishaps that might occur with Rachel's clients. Until Rachel felt comfortable with having sex with strangers, Jesse proposed to vet men wishing to use Rachel's service before they went to her hotel room. Wesley Franklin, an Anglican curate from Belfast, was their first customer.

Chapter 8
WESLEY FRANKLIN

When Wesley entered room 202, he was greeted at the door by a beautiful young woman. This was the most beautiful woman Wesley had ever seen! Rachel motioned for him to come in. Wesley was very nervous. A lot was riding on this occasion, and he wanted it to go well. Wesley had easily passed Jesse's scrutiny in reception.

He had to come to sit with Jesse as directed by the receptionist. She confirmed with him the service cost and that what he would be doing had nothing to do with love. It was about sex and pleasure only. Demeanour suggested to Jesse that this man was probably doing this for the first time and was perhaps a virgin.

Wesley was from Belfast and was the third son of a wealthy brewer. His father, Hercule Franklin, was the owner of Yarmouth Brewery in Belfast, established in 1890. The brewery specialised in Angel Ale and Portland Pilsner.

Wesley was not required to join the brewery like his older brothers. Hercule realised that at an early age that Wesley was a little bit feminine. He was not revolted by this but realised that the boy would have to find his way in life, different from that of himself and his other two sons. Hercule had had dealings with gay businessmen and at social events and found most of them charming. He had no problem dealing with what they might do in their private lives as long as it remained private.

So, when Wesley graduated from high school with good grades, Hercule rewarded him with an opportunity to travel around Europe for two months. Wesley was delighted and took up the opportunity with enthusiasm.

During the two months, Wesley found the greatest pleasure of travelling in Europe was admiring the wonderful architecture. He felt inspired by it and decided that he should be an architect. When he returned home, he told his father of his plan to study architecture. His father was pleased that his son had a plan for the future, and that he would support him.

He enrolled at Queen's University in Architecture BSc Honours and began the following semester. It did not take long for Wesley to realise that he did not have the natural ability to complete such a formally disciplined course. He quit the course with the regret that he would never be an architect.

His father was disappointed that architecture had not worked out for Wesley and suggested that Wesley take some time to think more about his future and that he may like to spend some time with his uncle, Michael, who was an Anglican priest in Derry. Wesley agreed and set off to visit his uncle.

Wesley had stayed with his uncle's family many times during school vacations. He enjoyed being in Derry. Michael had long been aware that Wesley may be gay and sympathised with him. He knew the road ahead could be difficult, given community attitudes towards homosexuality. He was an experienced man and was aware that some saw the priesthood as a solution to this problem.

Without addressing the issue directly, he did not ask Wesley if he was gay. He suggested that Wesley might find the study of philosophy and theology interesting and as rewarding as he had.

Wesley had much thinking to do. He did not understand his feelings about sex but thought that a course in philosophy might be the way to go. He enrolled at Queen's again, this time at the Belfast campus.

He found philosophy much to his liking, and it helped to focus his mind on his problem with sex. He continued through the philosophy course, extended through the theology course, and took up the position of curate at the Christian Fellowship church in Belfast.

Wesley was introverted and shy, and the idea of approaching a girl for sex was just too daunting. But in some 'locker room' talk he heard other students mention the benefits of having sex with a prostitute. He decided that this was an ideal way to test himself. He looked at websites where sex was offered for a price and was particularly interested in Rachel's site. The idea of having sex with a prostitute in Belfast presented him with a problem: someone might recognise him. Rachel was ideal; he could meet her in Strabane. Rachel charged much more than the others he had looked at, but he decided on Rachel because she was probably the best and he could afford it.

Wesley went to extraordinary lengths to avoid being found out about his contact with Rachel. He first calculated the amount of cash he would need to pay Rachel and the other expenses, such as accommodation and meals. There would be no electronic record of this adventure. He would not use a credit card for anything. He began weeks before his meeting with Rachel to withdraw small amounts of cash from his two accounts. He also regularly deleted the browsing history on his laptop.

Little did Wesley know this was Rachel's first time, not for sex, but for sex for money.

After greeting Wesley at the door, she took his hand and led him to the sofa. They sat close together, and he felt a pressing need to touch more than Rachel's hand.

His penis was hardening. She looked directly into Wesley's eyes. He had warm, soft brown eyes. Her eyes were green. Wesley had never seen such green eyes. His eyes drifted from her eyes to her breasts which were only partly covered by her dress.

She placed a hand under his chin, lifted it and looked again straight into his eyes and said, 'Would you like to see more of me?' Wesley nodded. Her hand drifted down to his penis. She lightly gripped it and added, 'I think you are pleased to see me already.'

She guided him gently to the bedroom where he was treated to sex by a woman rather than his hand and his imagination.

Masturbation was Wesley's only way of relieving his libido, but even after this glorious sex with Rachel, he could recall that sometimes when masturbating he had visions of naked young men – it was not always naked women.

He felt a bit better, but only a bit.

Wesley paid the one hundred pounds for her time and left the room exhilarated but still concerned.

Chapter 9
RACHEL BURNING BUSH

It had been more than a year since MacKenzie had died, and Paul was staying at Frank's apartment in Noosa. The conversation had turned to women, and Frank asked Paul what he was doing about it now that MacKenzie was gone. Paul had been married once but had been in a relationship with MacKenzie for more than twenty years.

Frank never had. He was one of those people "who did not buy books but used the library". 'I am not eager to get into another relationship just now, but I miss having sex.'

'So have you tried any "working girls"?'

'You wouldn't think there can still be many working now that this virus has turned up? But I have, and not so long ago.' 'Well, where do *you* find them, Frank?'

'I don't need them. There are plenty of women out there who like doing it with the right guy for free.'   'What about online dating sites?'

'Well, they seem aimed at starting up a relationship, and I am too set in my ways to do the relationship thing again. I think that I could not bear living with someone again. I just want occasional sex. I'd like sex with someone young and attractive, but I would not like to live with any of the young women I see around. I am not seeking a trophy wife. A good-looking prostitute is all I need.'

'Well, it's hard to know where to find them, and before you suggest it, I don't mean those you find on the streets up at the "Cross" so I decided to look in *Executive Desk*.'

'Couldn't you just pull yourself off like any other bloke without an available woman? You know, there is a lot of porn on the internet.'

'Piss off, Frank.'

'Did you find anything?'

'Well, I found Rachel. I decided she was the one and I went to her. It was THE event of my life.' 'Was she better than MacKenzie?'

'Oh, yes. This was pure poetry. But it was a staged event, not something that could be a regular thing.'

'How did you find her?'

'Well, I was given a copy of *Executive Desk* by a friend, and I found her contact details in the services section.'

'What is *Executive Desk*?'

'It's a magazine with an exclusive readership – only men wealthy enough to be on the AFR Rich List get a copy.

'What about rich women?'

'No, this is for guys only. It has many articles about business opportunities and biographies of rich guys.'

'So how did you get a copy? You're not rich enough to be on the *Australian Financial Review*'s (AFR) Rich List.'

'From a rich friend.'

'There is a services section at the back. Mainly pest exterminators, couriers and creative accountants.' 'What about plumbers, electricians and so on?'

'No, there weren't any of those at all.' 'I wonder why not?'

'Well, my friend explained that these are sections you don't find in regular magazines. For instance, "pest exterminators" is code for "hit men". If you want someone eliminated or killed, you can find people to do it in that section. If you need the body disposed of, you'll find those guys in the courier section. They dispose at sea – fast boats, deep water and cement shoes. And in case you're wondering, the creative accountants make sure that the money paid for these services can't be traced back to you.'

'So, was there a section in the services area for prostitutes?'

'Well, that term wasn't used. There was a section for "phallic therapists", and I could tell from the advertisements that that's what it was for.'

'Were there many to choose from?'

'Yes, several, but I chose Rachel because she sounded special.' 'What was so special? Did she have big tits?'

'Not especially, but she had a "Burning Bush" that speaks.' 'How could that help?'

'Frank, it was her fanny that could speak! Don't you think that's special? How many women do you know who have talking fannies? And her fanny is a "Burning Bush".'

'Why "Burning Bush"?'

'Look here at her website. What colour hair does she have?' Paul said, showing Frank Rachel's website on his laptop. 'Well, red.'

'Don't you get it? Red fanny – Burning Bush!'

'Yeah, pull the other leg, Paul!'

'It's true. I saw and heard it for myself.' 'What else did she offer you?'

'The best fuck ever!'

'Well, they would all say that. So how did you contact her?'

'The process began on WhatsApp and was quite long and believe me, quite extraordinary.' 'So how did it go?'

'There was a mobile number on her website to ring on WhatsApp between 9 pm and midnight, and I went into a session with Rachel. It began with her asking my name. I said it was Ralph.' 'Why?'

'I got nervous and thought that I should not give my real name.'

'She said, "I'm sure it's not. Nobody calls themselves Ralph these days, but not to worry. I'll soon know your real name. What do you want?"'

'I said, 'What do you offer? And at what cost?'

'"Well, you get to talk to my fanny, and she will listen and talk to you, and you will get the best fuck ever."' 'They all say that!' said Frank.

'What, talk to their fanny?' 'No, the best fuck bit.'

'"Look, I don't have time for this crap. Do you want to go on or not?"'

'I lied and told her I hadn't done this before.

'She continued, "Cost depends on your choice, but you

won't get much change from a thousand dollars." 'You're kidding!'

'"Look, I don't have time to haggle. If you got to this point, you must be well-heeled, all the men who come to me via *Executive Desk* are rich or very rich. If you don't want to spend the money, quit the session now."'

'What did you say to that?' said Frank.

'Well, you know I must have gone on, Frank, I told you I had spoken to her fanny.' 'Go on; what happened next?' said Frank.

'She asked me how old I was. I said forty-two-years-old.' 'You're nearly seventy. Why did you lie?' said Frank.

'I thought she may not go on with it if she knew I am so old.' 'Paul, you do not look like a forty-two-year-old,' said Frank.

'I had to tell her I was sixty-one years.'

'"Height and weight? Don't lie; you may lose your deposit." "What deposit?" I asked. "You have not mentioned a deposit."

'"We're getting to that soon. Height and weight?" she asked.'

'"One hundred and seventy-five centimetres and seventy kilograms," I told her.'

'"Religion?"

'"What difference could that make?" "Religion?"

'"Catholic." "Poor bugger!"

'"Are you married?" "Not anymore."

'"Figures. Catholics are not good at it. If we do meet, you will have to have a coronavirus test. Do you agree with that? If you don't, we can go no further with this."

'"I agree, but how come you have such a test that I have not heard of?"

'"I have friends that are pharmaceutically connected. If you look to the bottom left-hand side of the home page on my website, you'll see my account details. Transfer two hundred dollars into the account."

'"How do I know that you will just take the money and I will have paid two hundred dollars for this session?"

'"You'll have to trust me on that. If I did that, *Executive Desk* would not be happy with me. They know exactly how I operate. When the funds' transfer is complete, we can go onto the next stage and another deposit, or this conversation is over, and you won't be able to contact me again."

'"How much is this next deposit?" "Two hundred dollars."

'"Give me a few moments while I transfer the money." "You've got five minutes, or we finish here."'

'So did you transfer the funds?' said Frank.

'Are you a real idiot, Frank? I told you already I went on with it. Just listen and stop asking stupid questions.

'She came back onto the session and said "Paul, funds had been received". I asked how she knew my name was Paul.'

'"I have ways and means of finding information about lying clients. Your name is Paul Arnold. I use 'Verification IX' to check on people, who do you use? We are now at stage two. Are you ready to go on?"

'"Yes, I suppose so."'

'Did she sound sexy?' said Frank.

'Did I not tell you to stop asking stupid questions?'

'"Now I need a few personal details to finalise the deal. Do you have sensitive skin?" she asked. "Why is that an issue?"

'"It can be with some of the options you may choose."

'"Like what?"

'"Well, you may choose to be roughed up a bit or a lot. Some clients like it, you know, being spanked, or tied up." "Hmm, how would that work?"

'"Well, you can be tied up and I could punch you, a little or a lot. I wear boxing gloves. I don't like bruised hands. Body punches don't leave much bruising but if I punch you in the face you may end up bruised and bleeding. I could turn you over my lap and slap your bottom, some men like to be tied up during sex, you know, 'bondage'. It's up to you."

'"I may pass on the 'roughing up'." "What's your cock like?"

'"This is getting a bit personal!"'

'Boy, Paul, it *is* getting personal! What did you say?' said Frank 'Well, she gave me three options. Small, medium or large. I chose medium.'

'"Why do need to know about my cock?" "You will see it when we meet. I like to be prepared and have the best 'rubber' for you."

'"But condoms are not made of rubber."

'"I'll just make a note that you're a bit of a smart-arse, Paul. And remember: If it's not on, it's not on!"'

'Boy, she's right about that, Paul,' said Frank adding, 'although I don't think the virus comes through semen.' 'Shut up!'

'"I take it that you have been circumcised?" "I'm Catholic."

'"Yes, a smart-arse Catholic. What a combination! Not all Catholics are circumcised. Are you a premature ejaculator?"

'"Would it matter if I was?"

'"There are ways of minimising that and you may enjoy it more. So, are you?" "I don't think so."

'"How can you not know?" "Pass."

'"For security, I have Steve, my security guard, never more than ten seconds away. If you get over-excited or refuse to pay the final amount, Steve will be there in a flash, and he can be rather forceful."

'"Does this Steve cost extra?" "No. He is part of the package." "Thank God for small mercies."

'"Paul, some advice, Steve does not tolerate smart-arses well. Be careful what you say when you're with him. We can now finalise the deal and you can pay the final non-refundable deposit of two hundred dollars. Same deal as before: pay the money in five minutes or you have just paid two hundred dollars for some risqué chat online."

'"Just a minute, what is the length of time of this service?" "An hour with me will cost two hundred dollars."

'So, what happened next?' said Frank.

'Rachel came back to talk about the final details.'

'"I see that you are calling from Sydney. And so am I currently. I have a vacancy at 10 pm here next Thursday. Does that suit?"

'"Yes."

'"You should book a suite not a room for the night at the Admiralty in Potts Point. You'll pay only two hundred and fifty dollars if you mention my name. The evening with me will cost two hundred dollars. If you want to reconsider being 'roughed up', it will be an extra one hundred dollars, but you can decide on the night. Bring two hundred dollars cash in mixed twenties, tens and fives, and an extra one hundred dollars if you want to be roughed up.

'"There's one last very important thing. This is a one-off. You can never get a repeat service," said Rachel. "Why is that?"

'"I don't need repeat business. I have as much as I can handle already. I intend to retire young and rich. See you on Thursday."'

'And with that, she hung up,' said Paul.

'So, Paul, you've done four hundred dollars on deposits, two hundred dollars for Rachel, and two hundred and fifty dollars for the room. That's eight hundred and fifty dollars! Are you going for "roughing up"? I would! Just imagine a real stunner giving you some good old-fashioned biffo!' said Frank.

'Frank, you're acting as though I am about to go. I have been already and did not opt for biffo,' said Paul, exasperated. 'So, was it all worthwhile?' asked Frank.

'You bet it was. I'd pay two thousand dollars for another go.' 'So, are you going to tell me the gory details?'

'Only if you keep your stupid remarks to yourself.' 'What's the Admiralty like?'

'As you can imagine from the name, it is upmarket with a nautical theme. There are a few expensive-looking model ships in glass cases in the foyer and navy-blue detailing throughout. The room service breakfast was excellent, but it was disappointing not to have Rachel to share it with me.'

'Did she leave after the sex?'

'Yes, she arrived at 10 pm with Steve, who reappeared at 11 pm to take her away.' 'So, tell me what it was like when she and Steve arrived.'

'Just before 10 pm, there was a call from Reception informing me that I had two visitors coming up to my suite. At 10 pm, there was a knock at the door, and I opened it to see a guy dressed in black. The woman behind him wore a trench coat, mask, head scarf and dark glasses. I could not see what she looked like.'

'But you'd already seen her on the website and WhatsApp.' 'Frank, how did I say she was dressed? They both wore masks. She said, "Hi, I'm Rachel, and this is Steve."

'Steve pushed past me without making eye contact and began searching the suite. "What is that about?" I said.

'"It's just about security. Don't be alarmed," said Rachel.

'When Steve had finished his search, he said, "All clear". Rachel then entered. She sat on the sofa, still in her trench coat, head scarf and dark glasses, and said: "Could you go into the bedroom with Steve so he can complete the final security check?"

'"What's this all about?" I began to protest, but Steve barked: "Just do what the lady says!" This guy was not to be messed with, so I moved into the bedroom.

'"Take off your clothes and put that gown on." He motioned to the white gown on the bed.

'As I removed each item, he searched it, neatly folded each and put it onto an occasional chair. When he was finished, he produced a specimen jar and told me to spit into it. He took out a small device from his jacket pocket, a dropper bottle that contained a blue fluid. He added some drops of the fluid to the specimen jar and shook it. He looked at his watch for what seemed to be about a minute and said, "You're ready to go". He left the room without further comment and said to Rachel: "All clear".

'"Thanks, Steve," said Rachel as he left the suite.

'"Well, here we are. What do you think?" Rachel had removed her mask, coat, scarf and glasses to reveal herself. "I think you look fabulous!"

'She had long, red, wavy hair, wore a beautiful knee-length sky-blue dress with a plunging neckline with a gold mesh belt, and a pair of matching pumps with multicoloured sequins.'

'Pumps?' said Frank.

'They are flat shoes, no heels. She is quite tall. But let me finish. She has lovely green eyes set wide apart and milky skin, a lovely oval face and a high forehead covered in small freckles. She has a small jaw that is tapered to her chin with just a hint of a dimple. Around her neck was a fine gold chain with an emerald surrounded by small bright red stones. And best of all she was Irish! Such a lovely voice!' enthused Paul.

'When has being Irish ever been an asset?' 'The voice! What a voice!'

'What about Steve? Was he a monster?'

'No, he's of average build but he looked very mean. No, not mean, dangerous.' 'So, you invited them in. How long before the action started?'

'Rachel had a small bag that she put on the sideboard.

She then took both of my hands, and we swung around in the living room. She then took her hands away and swung around quickly in a circle. And what did I see? Her dress lifted to waist level to reveal beautiful slim thighs and very brief black knickers just like that ionic pic of Marilyn Monroe with a suspender belt holding up her stockings!' enthused Paul again.

'Paul, calm down. What is a suspender belt?'

'Frank, you are possibly too young to remember suspender belts but before those horrible very unsexy tights girls wear now, they used to wear very alluring suspender belts to hold up their stockings. If a girl gave you a flash of her suspenders, you knew you were on! The suspender belt had four or five clasps holding the stocking tops to the belt and if you were lucky you could undo them with your teeth.'

While Frank went off to 'powder his nose', Paul reflected on the process that he had gone through to meet Rachel and, in the telling, realised that the seemingly unnecessary questions Rachel asked were simply to help her assess the risk she would be taking with potential clients.

For Rachel, of course, it made sense that even with Steve close by she could be vulnerable to dangerous clients. Seeing and hearing how they responded to being mildly provoked on WhatsApp allowed her to gauge the level of risk she was taking as a sole operator.

The experience with Arthur Millar was forever imprinted on her mind.

With Paul, she detected no malicious intent – just a need for good sex with a beautiful young woman.

Chapter 10
RACHEL

As soon as Frank returned, Paul went on.

'Rachel smiled seductively and said, "Why don't you just relax so we can get on with this?"

'I swallowed. This was really happening!

'"Get a drink for yourself and a tonic water, no gin for me, then join me in the bedroom."

'"Don't you drink, Rachel?" "Sometimes, but never on the job." "Oh, why is that?"

'"This is a serious business that I run, and it requires my full attention. Alcohol or any other drug would diminish my performance.

'"You do understand that this is a performance. It has nothing to do with love. But it is something I do for enjoyment too. I love sex, but I don't have to accept all applicants. If I don't like the man on WhatsApp I just don't go ahead. This a potentially dangerous business, which is why I have Steve. You are paying a lot of money for something you could get for free from someone else. I think that you expect to be very impressed, and I believe that you will be."

"'If I may, I'm interested to know how you came to be doing this."

"'If you want to spend some or all your time talking about me, you're welcome. Most clients are happier talking about themselves. In fact, the service I offer has, to a large extent, been shaped by numerous doctors, lawyers, policemen, accountants, politicians, priests and others who have unwittingly given me ideas to make my services develop to the point that you see today – sort of like evolution. Even you may make me think about honing my skills further."

"'Even me?"

"'Well, you have come across as a bit of an arsehole so far but even arseholes can be useful."

"'Why an arsehole?"

"'You have proven to be a bloody know-all and a tight arse. Nearly all my clients are wealthy and consider the money they spend on me is well spent. On the other hand, you may have recently become wealthy and don't yet know how to *be* wealthy. You are, after all, a graduate of Sydney University with a degree in science. Graduating in science doesn't guarantee wealth but I have never serviced an honours graduate before. Maybe they do better making money."

"'How do you know that I am a scientist?"

"Verification IX tells all!"

"'I did graduate as a physicist, but I soon moved on to other things." "Other more lucrative things?"

"'You could say that. But let's get back to you. How did

you become a..." "professional?"

'"Well, yes."

'"That's quite a long story. Remember, you have one hour. There can be no extensions and no repeat service. So why don't we get on with the task at hand and talk later if time allows."

'"Task at hand? You consider this a task?"

'"Paul, this is my profession and, as with most other professions, it is to perform professional tasks. You know, like a doctor taking blood pressure. Are we going to talk or are you going to fuck me?"

'"Well, since you put it that way, okay." "Let me take that gown off so we can begin." I was shaking all over.

'"Don't be afraid, I'm not going to punch you. You did not want to be roughed up.

'"Why don't you slip behind me and unzip my dress?"

'Paul, this is the bit I've been waiting to hear about!' 'Steady on, Frank.'

'She let the dress slip down to the floor.' 'What was she wearing underneath?'

'Not much. She remained facing away from me but guided my hands to her breasts.' 'I'm busting to hear what happened next, Paul.'

'She took my hands again and guided them to cup her breasts. She took in a breath; she was enjoying it!'

'Paul, this is agony, go on!'

'She swung around and pushed me gently onto the bed and I sat down looking straight at her.'

'Paul, I'm getting a hard-on just listening to this.'

'Well don't go discharging in your pants, people may guess what you've been up to.'

Paul had a hard-on too.

'"Well," she said, "it looks as though you are pleased to see me, and I'm pleased to see what you have for me."

'She walked away from the bed, turning slowly as she went. This meant that I could enjoy her from all sides. What a sight!

'She sat down on a chair, slowly unclipped her stockings from the suspender belt, removed them and slowly walked back towards me.

'She gently pushed me onto my back with my dick pointing towards the ceiling.

'She stood beside the bed and invited me to remove the suspender belt.

'As I did so she wriggled her hips a little so that my hand brushed across her fanny. She gave a little moan.

'When the belt was off, she leaned down towards me and indicated with her finger the clip on the front of her bra. I didn't need to be told what to do and I was soon looking at two luscious white breasts sprinkled with a few tiny freckles.'

'So that just left the frilly black knickers. Paul, you were so close!'

'Rachel put her thumbs in the sides of her knickers and slowly eased them down, revealing her fanny which she referred to as her Burning Bush. And as she did, the lips of her fanny said, "Hi there, Paul, we meet at last".

'Now her fanny was not just a thicket of bright red hair, it was carefully groomed so that the hairs surrounding her vagina were cut short, then less so for the hair further out. It was a professional cut, a truly sculptured Burning Bush.'

'What! Paul, this can't be true!' 'I kid you not!'

'"Welcome to the gates of Heaven, Mr Adequate Paul," the fanny said.

'What was truly remarkable was that fanny had no Irish accent.'

'Paul, are you sure this really happened? Maybe she spiked your drink. What was your drink by the way?'

'Does it matter, Frank? It isn't an important part of the story.'

'Then Rachel spoke: "Point your weapon this way while I slip on his raincoat."

'"Yes," said fanny, "If it's not on, it's not on!" 'It was Rachel's turn. "I think I shall stay on top and be in control. Are you okay with that?"

'"Paul, I'm picking up a vibe that you are about to unload. Slow down and look at my face. Try to forget tits and fanny for a bit. Look at my face and run your hands through my hair. Think of me as your first love. Remember how careful you were not to spoil that first time with her."

'Try as I might, Sally Burton's face would not appear. I could not conjure it up while looking at this beautiful creature.'

'So, what happened then?'

'Well, I fucked her.'

'Details, Paul.'

'Frank, you know what a fuck is like.'

'Details! Details!'

'Just listen, Frank.'

'Rachel said, "I remember that in our chat you were a bit vague about premature ejaculation."

'And at that point, Rachel rolled off me and sat astride my thighs and lifted fanny off me.

'"Hey!" said the Burning Bush, "I haven't finished!"

'"Don't be so greedy!" said Rachel gently fondling my balls. A voice from below said, "I want to swallow you."

'With that, Rachel lowered herself onto me, silencing fanny. "You know she shouldn't speak with her mouth full," laughed Rachel.

'Bliss! Followed by more bliss. Suddenly Rachel lifted off me again, saying, "You're about to pop your cork. I bet none of your lovers has ever come. Have they? Or maybe they just pretended? You have a hair trigger down there.

'"Never mind that, come back here," said Burning Bush.

'Rachel fingered the base of my penis to keep me on the boil for a couple of minutes, then lowered herself back onto me.

'"You nearly set a record for the fastest fuck I've ever had," said Rachel. She continued the treatment, stretching seconds into minutes until as she lowered herself for the fourth time. I experienced THE orgasm of my life!'

'So, what did you do afterwards?'

'We lay side-by-side on the bed. She had her back to me, and I had my arm over her. We were silent for a while then I said, "Do you ever do this with a naked fanny?"

'"Certainly not," said Burning Bush. "I wouldn't be a Burning Bush then. And besides, the girls who do that look prepubescent. Some guys, I guess, like fucking little girls."

'"Well now, what about it, Paul? Are you up to it again?" whispered Rachel. "Yeah, Paul what about it?" said fanny.

'I wanted so much to do it again. I knew that there would never be another opportunity. I looked down at my flaccid penis willing it to show some interest. The spent condom was still on,' sighed Paul.

'Rachel said, "Let's get rid of this first," and removed the condom. "Let's see if we can stir up some enthusiasm down here."

'She rolled me over onto my back again and began to massage my penis, at the same time lowering her breasts onto my face. It was in vain. Try as I might, I could not get it up again.

'She rolled off me and looked at the time. "Okay, it's time to pack up and go," she said. And with that, she slipped off the bed, gathered her things and dressed quickly. In no time, she was as she was on arrival, cloaked in secrecy.

'I paid the two hundred dollars as agreed and thanked Rachel.

'I added, "I know you said no repeat service, but maybe you could make an exception?"

'"I'll take that as a compliment, Paul, but no repeats."

"Could we at least have dinner?"

'"Paul, we shall never meet again."

'At 11 pm, Steve knocked and entered the suite. He made eye contact with me and held it longer than necessary. He seemed hostile. Rachel said, "I'm fine to go, Steve."

'Steve gave me a withering look, said nothing, and

escorted Rachel out of the suite.

'I never saw Rachel again, but I always look out for her whenever I'm out and about,' said Paul ruefully.

'There's not much chance of running into her in Sydney, mate!'

'But, Paul, do you think other chicks are born with talking fannies. I've never come across one myself.'

'Frank, no woman has ever been born with a talking fanny. Rachel is a ventriloquist!'

After Paul's appointment with Rachel, Steve drove her back to her apartment. On the way, Rachel ventured: 'You seemed a bit stern tonight, Steve. Is something wrong?'

'Not really,' he lied. 'Some of your clients are real dickheads, and that guy was one.' 'I thought that initially, but he turned out to be polite and thankful.'

'I have a day job tomorrow with an overseas client at 10am. Will you be able to be there, or will you send one of your associates?'

'Same hotel?' 'Same hotel.' 'I'll be there.'

Something was bothering Steve, and it wasn't something he wanted to talk about with Rachel. This Paul guy had upset him in a way none of Rachel's other clients ever had. He thought most of them were jerks and losers, even though they were usually 'loaded'. He wondered how he could deal with this feeling. This was a situation he never dreamed he would face, ever.

By the time he got home, a plan had formed in his mind, but he was not yet sure if he would implement it. He would sleep on it and decide in the morning.

Unfortunately, sleep eluded him that night, and to be able to sleep again, he needed to resolve this unlikely situation. But he gave himself one more day to think about it, and after Rachel's next client, he decided to act.

Chapter 11
STEVE

It was 7.30 am and Paul was leaving home to go to his office in Rozelle when his phone rang. He continued walking towards Victoria Road to catch his bus. He took the call. It was from an unknown number, and he wondered who would be calling so early.

'Hi, Paul speaking,' he said

'Paul, we need to meet. Be at the MOMA Coffee Shop at 11.30 today.' 'Who is this? What do you want?' said Paul.

'I know where you live in Drummoyne, and I know where your office is. Just be there, or I may come calling after dark.'

The line went dead. The caller had hung up.

This was a frightening situation. Paul sat at the bus stop. His bus went through. Whom could this be? He rang Frank. The call went through to voicemail.

He caught the next bus. He tried Frank again. Still voicemail. He had a seat. There were few passengers at this hour.

'Who could the caller be?'

He played the call again in his head. It was a man who sounded polite, to begin with, but became very threatening when Paul protested. It made no sense.

He was still trying to work out who it could be when he reached his stop in Rozelle. He walked to his office. As he entered the office, he put down his phone. Suddenly it had all the appeal of an Eastern brown snake.

He decided to check his emails. Maybe that would help with the dread he felt. There were no new emails.

He picked up the phone again, rang Frank, and got voicemail. Should he ring ooo?

What would he say? What could the police do for him?

He decided to continue working on his report on frozen embryos. He opened the file.

It was only 8.45 am and he could not concentrate on the report. He rang Frank again. This time Frank answered.

He told Frank what had happened. Frank listened and asked Paul to repeat what he had said. 'Look, Paul, I am in Noosa now. I can't come with you. You'll have to do this yourself. Just go to meet him. It was a man, wasn't it? It's a public place with plenty of people around and if he does try anything, ring ooo for help. Let me know what happens'.

The bus to Circular Quay and MOMA took about twenty-five minutes, so he took the bus leaving Rozelle at 10.45 am. As he travelled in, he wondered how he would find this person.

He then supposed that the man would know him and seek him out at MOMA.

Maybe this was an attempt at blackmail, someone who

recognised him at the hotel with Rachel. He arrived at 11.15 am and took a seat in the cafe at the front looking out towards Sydney Harbour. A voice from behind him, 'Come back and sit here.'

Paul looked around and saw a man in sunglasses beckoning him. He got up and walked back to the man's table.

He was happy that there were dozens of people in the cafe. He sat opposite the man who had now removed the sunglasses. Paul was astonished. It was Steve, Rachel's bodyguard.

'I recognised you the other night but saw that you didn't recognise me.' said Steve 'My name is Steve Arnold.'

'So!' said Paul, then the 'penny dropped.' 'Steve Arnold. My son, Steve Arnold!?'

'We haven't seen each other since you were a teenager. You are still not familiar. I still see Rachel's bodyguard.'

'A few years ago, I was involved in a jet ski accident and had serious facial injuries. My face had to be reconstructed, but my friends say that I'm still recognisable.'

Paul looked hard; yes, the face of his younger son was still there. 'Well, I am surprised that you contacted me,' said Paul.

'I am still surprised myself. It took me a couple of days to decide to go ahead with arranging a meeting with you.'

'You and I are the only ones left in our family.' 'Has your mother died?'

'So have Grandpa, Grandma, and Benny.' 'What! Benny is dead! How could that be?'

'He was killed when his motorbike hit a tree.' 'Why didn't you tell me?'

'Well, we did not think that you deserved to know. You were no longer part of our lives.' 'Shit, when was that?' '1986.'

Paul was stunned. He hadn't often thought about his family but somehow assumed they were still living.

'When did Louise die?' '2001. She had liver cancer.' 'So did her mother.'

'Mum never got over Benny's death. Grandpa died in 1983. She took over the farm when Grandpa died then Eric inherited it but sold it after Grandma died. Neither Benny nor I were interested in farming. And Eric wanted cash to help him with his family. She became involved in the Japanese Garden and Culture Centre in Cowra. Grandpa was a driving force in establishing the Centre and urged Mum to be involved as well.'

'I'm flabbergasted, our whole family gone!'

'Well, it hasn't been *your* family for a long time. You abandoned us a long time ago. Maybe you should have thought about us more often.'

Paul resisted the urge to tell Steve why he had 'abandoned' his family. Over the years of marriage to MacKenzie and being in therapy with Stone, he had come to understand that the problem was not just Louise, he had a part as well.

'Yes, I was a bit of an outlier in the family even when we were together. But I had hoped that you would all be okay. Did Louise ever remarry?'

'No, a few guys were interested, but she seemed content being single and helping Grandpa with the farm and the Japanese Gardens project.'

'Where are they all buried?'

'Both Benny and Mum are buried with Grandma in the Cowra cemetery, but Grandpa gained permission to be buried with the soldiers who lost their lives in the Breakout.'

Paul now needed to know more about what happened to his family. But he asked Steve how he came to be working for Rachel.

'That came about because of my accident. My good mate and business partner, Dan Overton, had bought a new jet ski and was keen to show me what it was like. I wasn't so keen, they reminded me a bit of motorbikes, and I did not want to end up like Benny. But Dan convinced me to ride with him on Moreton Bay. He had a very powerful machine, and even with the two of us, it flew! He was making a turn when something hit him in the face, breaking his prescription sunglasses, and the machine veered out of control. At that time, Rachel's friend, Fergus, was launching a jet ski for Rachel to have her first ride. Our ski hit their ski, side on, at high speed. Our ski was projected into the air, about two metres, I am told, and we landed about twenty metres up the beach. On landing, Dan luckily landed on his feet, and he sort of "ran", then tumbled in the sand to a stop.

'My landing was less well-executed. My face hit part of the ski, and I landed face-first into hard sand. Since my stopping was quite abrupt, the damage was quite significant. My neck was broken, and I was unconscious.

'Dan recovered quickly and ran back to help me. A few onlookers were also ready to help. Dan checked for breathing and pulse, they were both all right. But when Dan began to straighten my neck someone in the crowd shouted, "Don't move his neck!" "Who said that?" Dan asked.

'The man kneeling beside him said, "The redhead over there", pointing to Rachel.

'Dan looked at Rachel. He guessed that she could not be a doctor, she was too young, but she may have been a nurse.

'"It is best left to the paramedics when they get here. You may cause further injury if you move him. If he is breathing and has a pulse then he will be okay until the ambulance arrives," said Rachel Ten minutes later, the ambulance arrived with two paramedics. They did not move me right away either. They asked witnesses for some details of the accident but most of their questions were directed towards Dan who had some minor facial injuries. They asked him if my present position had changed. Had anyone moved me? Dan looked over towards Rachel and indicating with his hand, he said "The redhead over there was very clear that he should not be moved until you got here." "Well, she was right; more damage can be done by 'helpful' witnesses moving victims with serious neck injuries," said the paramedic as his partner applied a brace to my head and neck.

'Dan went over to Rachel and thanked her on my behalf. "How did you know not to move him? Are you a nurse?" "No, I just read a lot," Rachel told him.

'When the paramedic went to assist his partner to load me into the ambulance, Dan went over to Rachel to thank her again.

'"When Steve recovers, I'm sure that he would want to thank you in person. Here is our business card. I'm Dan and he is Steve. If you could call me in a few days, I can let you know how he is doing. Maybe you can call him when he is allowed to take calls. Please call, we owe you," said Dan as he handed Rachel their card.

'She did call a few days later but I was still unconscious. Dan asked if he could note her number so that he or I could call when I recovered. She agreed but it was weeks before I was able to call back. To make sure that I did not move my head, I was placed into an induced coma for six weeks. When it was safe for me to be taken out of the coma, I found that I remembered nothing about the accident but had been very fortunate that my spinal cord was not broken. It had sustained serious bruising and swelling. So, it was more than six weeks after the accident that Dan told me about it. When he did tell me about it, he emphasised the fact that a pretty redhead had possibly saved me from becoming a paraplegic. When I suggested that I call her, I asked "What is her name?"

'"Oh," he said, "I forgot to ask. I'm sure she'll tell you when she answers her phone."

'I did call her and asked if she would come to see me in the hospital so I could personally thank her. I met Rachel at the Royal Brisbane Hospital. She still had our business card and she asked me about the business. That's how it came about that I am her minder; I make sure that clients like you treat her well.'

'What exactly is the business that you and ... what's your partner's name again?" Paul asked. 'His name is Dan Overton and our business is Arnold and Overton Security.'

'Look,' said Steve, 'I think I've said enough. If you want to know more, you can go to our website. He got up to go.' Paul grabbed Steve's arm, whose hand was still on the table.

'Just a minute, we haven't finished,' said Paul, still holding Steve's arm.

Steve looked at his arm being held but did not pull away. Instead, he slowly raised his eyes to look directly into Paul's eyes.

He said, 'Let go or you may find *yourself* in a neck brace.'

'Benny never recovered from you bailing out of the family. He thought he had to look after Mum as a sort of substitute husband. Do you remember when we said goodbye to you that you gave each of us something special?' said Steve.

'No, I don't recall what it was,' said Paul.

Steve pulled his arm away. 'You touch me again and I'll break your neck.' 'Hold on, what did I give you?' said Paul.

Steve stood, glaring at Paul, saying nothing. Then, 'I should have known when I first saw you at the hotel. You're an arsehole and this was a very bad idea.'

'You can't leave it just like that, I'm your father and deserve respect.'

'Respect? You walked out on us. You destroyed Benny's life and left Mum without support. You should have been ashamed of yourself.'

'Will you stop lobbing these past tense, perfect conditional verbs on me and listen!' 'What?'

'Just a minute, your mother made life miserable for me. It was unrelenting.' 'What do you mean, unrelenting?'

'After she had you, she declared that there was to be no

more sex in our relationship. She just didn't like it. Are you married, Steve? Would you put up with that? What would you do?'

The pair now had the full attention of the other diners.

'Look, I was only twenty-eight years old when you were born, so that meant sixteen years of unrequested celibacy for me. All that time sleeping together in the same bed with a woman with a very enticing body that moved away when I touched it, or said, "Please don't touch me, Paul, you know I hate being touched."

The crowd in the coffee shop were fully engaged in the drama unfolding before them. Paul and Steve were engaged in full eye contact. Neither said a word. Then.

'What did I give you?'

'You gave me a fine gold chain with a Saint Christopher medal. Maybe you should have given *that* to Benny. Patron saint for travellers. Maybe it would have helped him to avoid the grave. And Benny, you gave him your wedding ring. You may as well have sent him a letter telling him to take over as the husband you failed to be.'

Steve turned and headed towards the exit.

A man seated at a nearby table began to clap. His wife slapped down his hands, saying 'It's not a play, Robert!'

Paul slumped in his seat.

He left MOMA and took a taxi straight home.

He called Frank and told him what had happened.

'Shit, mate, that's a bit of a surprise. Are you going to see him again?' asked Frank.

'Not any time soon. I might end up with a broken neck. He clearly blames me for destroying his brother's life.'

'I get it.'

'Giving Benny my wedding ring sent him a clear but malevolent message. Benny was a bully, and I was always protecting Steve from his sarcasm. I did not like him.'

'Maybe you should check out Steve's website and try to find out about Benny's death. Try the back issues of the local Cowra newspaper,' said Frank.

Chapter 12
THE DREAM

'Steve'. He looked up. 'Over here.'

He looked to his left. It was Rachel. 'Come over here.'

She was kneeling on a blanket on the grass.

She wore a large floppy hat, a sky-blue bikini bottom, and a wet, white T-shirt that clung to her body. 'I'm coming.'

She smiled.

It was a smile that said, 'Come and join me.' He felt the beginnings of an erection. 'Come on, Steve. I want you.'

Want? He hoped he was getting the message right. The message for which he had longed.

Her shoulders, upper arms, flat belly and even her navel and breasts clung to that T-shirt. Her nipples were erect.

He pulled off his shirt and paused to shake off his board shorts 'Mm,' she said.

She held out her arms towards him.

He was possibly five metres away from her now.

He noticed movement to his left and looked that way. As he did so, Rachel looked to her right.

They both saw a dark figure moving towards Rachel. She screamed.

'Steve, help me.'

Steve started to run towards her.

It felt as if he was running in chest-deep water.

Before she could stand up the dark figure of a man flicked off her hat and pushed her down. 'Rachel!' yelled Steve.

He was still metres away.

The man said, 'You should have paid!' 'Millar!'

He produced a bottle and removed the lid. 'Steve! Help me.'

'You should have paid.' He began to pour.

She raised her right hand.

The liquid fell striking her hand. Her hand began to melt. A loud scream. 'Rachel.'

Steve seemed no closer. Millar continued to pour. Rachel continued to scream.

Steve continued to run on the spot. Rachel's arm melted. Millar kept pouring.

He directed the liquid onto her head. Her lovely red hair melted. Then her face.

She no longer screamed. Steve was no closer.

'Steve, wake up!' Dan's voice. 'Do you often go to sleep in the office?' 'We have two interviews to do.'

When Dan returned from New Zealand, Steve filled him in on the proposal to work for Rachel. Dan had no problem with working for a prostitute. They deserved to be able to conduct their business without fear for their safety like anyone else.

'Given what she has done for us, I'm inclined to give her a service at cost. If not for her, you would not be in this business with me. Let's work out the cost to us if one of our staff does the job and if it's you or me, we should do it for free, let's say for a year and renegotiate for a more permanent arrangement after that. What do you think?'

'I agree. Let's propose that and see how she feels.'

The dream had shaken Steve, but he told neither Dan nor Rachel about it. It was his problem and he wondered why it affected him so much. He felt that it was emblematic; something he had to act on. Steve wanted Rachel but she had made it clear from the beginning that she was not interested in a relationship with him or any other man. This did not, however, mean that he could hope that she may someday change her mind.

Steve met again with Rachel to finalise the deal. She was happy with the arrangement that they settled on – a one-year contract with the option to extend after one year.

Their offer to Rachel did not show their pro bono work. They wanted to do something for her but did not want to make it too obvious.

Rachel had also attended some sessions with Chris Lattimer, who was the scriptwriter chosen by Matthew to improve her bantering skills for Burning Bush.

Chris was delighted with his brief to work on clearly outrageous dialogue that a ventriloquist-prostitute was going to deliver from her vagina.

They had two sessions and both laughed throughout their time together.

When they completed the work, Chris gave Rachel printed copies of the script they had created together, saying it was the most interesting brief he had ever had.

'Good luck, darling. I think you're onto a winner there,' he said as he escorted Rachel to his office door.

Before having photos taken, Rachel needed to purchase suitable clothes for her work and the website. It was good fun, but it would have been so much better to do it with a friend. She tried taking Matthew and Tuesday, but only once. Matthew liked everything, he didn't discriminate, and Tuesday quickly became bored.

Toni Blakely at Flash Bulb Photography took her work very seriously and excelled in it. She had taken some wonderful shots of Matthew on his jet ski, used in promoting the new Krogan skis from South Korea.

Rachel had decided to conceal the upper part of her face for the photo shoot and had purchased several masks that covered her eyebrows and part of her nose. The holes for her eyes were large enough to display her sparkling green eyes to the fullest. It added a bit of mystique to the image, but it meant her undisguised image was not made available to clients until they contacted her on WhatsApp.

Rachel had forty images taken by Toni Blakely to be used on the website which was now completed except for the photos. She arranged another meeting with Annie Oakley, and they discussed their use. She decided that they could be cycled through with six images on at any one time.

Annie showed Rachel how to access the site and change the range of photos as she wished. Most of the apparatus of the business was now complete. On the website was a mobile phone number with which potential clients could engage her service.

Unlike the plan in Derry, where Jesse vetted the clients, Rachel would do this herself using WhatsApp. To keep herself safe, she engaged the clients in apparently silly questions about themselves. It involved questions about their bodies and even questions about religion and whether they had been circumcised. Of course, she did not need these details, but it allowed her to gauge the prospect of violence. If they could not tolerate mild sarcasm and irony, then she would probably reject the application.

This initial contact through her website was in two stages. After the first series of questions, she offered the option of ending there or going to the next stage, which required them to deposit two hundred dollars into the account listed on the website. After another shorter series of questions, another deposit of two hundred dollars was required.

The deal would then be finalised by the client selecting a hotel from the list on the website and booking a suite, not a room, at the mutually agreed date and time. They would pay two hundred dollars in cash on the night of her service. It was important that her website attract men with money to spend, and plenty of it.

Annie Oakley suggested carefully chosen keywords that would be captured by Google and direct men with plenty of money and not 'tyre kickers' as she most eloquently put it. So, she included 'sensual female available', 'superior', 'premium', 'exotic', 'once in a lifetime', 'self-made man' and 'hey, big spender', which she thought, with the obvious class of Rachel's images, would attract men who could afford it.

She also suggested the statement, 'If you must ask, "How much?" at the beginning, you probably can't afford it'.

Annie said, 'We will need to fine-tune this as we go. Guys who would look but not buy will waste your time.'

Her plan was nearing completion, and Rachel was ready to launch it but thought she would need to be free of Amelia and have a place of her own. She found that she could afford a furnished studio apartment in the CBD for about the same money she was paying Amelia.

Frankly, she was over Amelia, her ultra-tidiness and her constant criticism, and the bonking arrangement was no longer just a funny issue to include in her conversations with others.

At this point, she contacted Jesse to discuss this issue and report on how much of her loan from Matthew she had spent. Her computer skills had improved, and she felt confident enough to prepare a simple financial statement, which included copies of all the receipts she had learned to photograph on her phone and email to herself, then forward to Jesse.

Jesse was pleased with Rachel's ability to be conscious of her spending and believed that soon she would not be a necessary part of Rachel's finances.

At this point, Rachel was still working at the bookshop and had been befriended by a regular customer, Janet

Freeman. Janet was a voracious reader who realised that Rachel was a fascinating person to talk to, and they began to meet, sometimes at lunch and after work. Janet, like Rachel, had no tertiary education but read widely and was doing an online course called Career Planning For Success. She worked as a secretary in a legal firm in the CBD. Like Rachel, she was ambitious and planned to have her own business. She was delighted to hear about Rachel's plans and admired her ability to use her body to make money.

Like many young people, she was beginning to question the efficacy of marriage. At twenty-six years old, she was happy to live alone but took up the chances for intimate relationships, enjoyed them, and moved on. She did not plan to have children.

So, Rachel joined Janet in an informal discussion group that met on a Friday night to talk about themselves and their opinions about life. All these young people were concerned about the actions of politicians, most of whom they distrusted.

Rachel enjoyed the vigour of the discussion and was comfortable with her contribution. At her first meeting, she was introduced to the group by Janet and predictably, she was asked what she did for a living. Her unembellished answer was greeted initially with silence, but it was short, and the conversation continued without further debate about her chosen career.

Rachel was comfortable in her body but realised that besides keeping her femininity attended to daily, with her pelvic floor exercises and ventriloquism, she also needed to stay fit.

She had noted Amelia's choice of tennis, but she was not a fan of competitive exercise, and now that she had moved to her apartment in the CBD, she found Flash Fitness, a twenty-four-hour gym, just a few metres away and joined up.

Her parting with Amelia was not acrimonious.

Amelia was in her new job as manager of a medical centre and earning much more money, and she was ready to move on and upgrade her accommodation. They gave the required two weeks' notice to Dariush and Marinella and moved out on the same day.

Rachel's social circle had expanded considerably, and at the discussion group and the gym, she encountered several men who wanted to date her. She decided that none would succeed. She did not want to have sexual relationships with men in these two groups and politely declined each offer.

Finally, everything was in place, and Rachel patiently waited for a response. However, she did not have to wait long.

Craig Belling was a fifty-five-year-old barrister from Sydney who had come to Brisbane to speak at a conference about domestic violence. Craig's wife, Ellen, was lovely but showed signs of age. Craig still felt twenty-five, and his libido was that of a twenty-five-year-old. Ellen's was about that of a seventy-year-old. So, he often took opportunities to satisfy himself with top-class prostitutes. While browsing for possible services in Brisbane, he came across Rachel's website.

He rang the advertised number on WhatsApp and was

confronted by a beautiful redhead. 'This will be interesting,' he thought to himself.

Rachel asked for details about himself that were very amusing for securing a sexual encounter. He correctly deduced that this was part of an act and answered with humour.

He chose Hotel Lyon from her list, and they met at 8 pm the next day.

He felt alarmed when he opened his door and found a young man dressed in black and a woman who stood behind the fellow. His thoughts immediately went to the prospect of being mugged. The woman spoke up quickly, perhaps sensing his fear and assured him that Steve, the man in black, was there to protect her. Steve moved past Craig into the suite, but Rachel remained outside. 'It's clear here!'

Rachel entered and sat on the lounge.

'Could you please go into the bedroom with Steve?' Nonplussed but cooperative, he stepped into the bedroom.

After a few minutes, Craig came out in a white gown, followed by Steve. 'All fine.' said Steve, who left immediately.

Rachel had divested herself of her outer garments and sat on the lounge.

'Your pictures do not do you justice; you look beautiful. But what was that all about?' he said, pointing to the bedroom.

'Long story, but it's really about my safety. Now let me attend to you.'

They both lay panting on the bed. It had been robust, sensational sex.

She had come infrequently but welcomed when it happened.

'That was, without a doubt, the best sex I have ever had!' said Craig 'How did you come up with this? I have never experienced anything like it.'

'Trade secret.'

In the time he had left, Craig asked Rachel about her past. She gave him an abridged version.

Then it was all over. He paid the two hundred dollars, Steve came, and suddenly she was gone, leaving Craig with mixed feelings about the uniqueness of the experience.

Chapter 13
HAYSEEDS

Steve, of course, had his uncle Eric, his aunt Molly and his cousins Fossie and Ted, as well as Paul, but he had little contact with them.

He was urbanised. He loved city-dwelling and, really, this lot were definitely 'hayseeds.' Steve had been born in Sydney, as had Benny. When they returned to Cowra soon after Louise and Paul separated, both initially were happy to be back at their grandparents' farm. It was fun for a while. Their farm experience was a vacation activity – two or three weeks, then back home to the more familiar environment of big city Sydney. Soon, both tired of the smallness of Cowra.

When they arrived in Cowra, Benny was halfway through Year 10 and Steve halfway through Year 8. It was not long before Benny had his first fight, the first of many. Most of his classmates and teachers disliked him. Benny was a bully, and the person he most enjoyed bullying was Steve.

He would pursue teasing until Steve reacted, then claimed superciliously, 'I think I touched a nerve there.'

Paul spent much of his time at home separating the boys and punishing Benny's bullying, but it was ineffective. Benny continued harassing Steve and Steve was always whingeing about it.

During a family gathering to celebrate Molly's birthday, Nick overheard his grandson Benny telling Steve their Aunt Molly was a hayseed. Her whole family were hayseeds.

Nick took Louise aside and warned: 'If you can't control Benny, then I may have to do it for you.'

'Dad, I'm doing my best, but he doesn't take my correcting him seriously. He is too big and too confident.'

'Louise, you have already made serious mistakes in your life like failing university, failing marriage and now this. You can tell him this from me – he won't ride my bike if he can't be civil.'

The only way out of this was to leave the party and try to talk some sense to Benny on their way home.

'Benny, Grandpa heard what you said about Molly and her family.'

'What?'

'You said that they were hayseeds.'

'Well, Mum, they are! Have you heard what Molly said about Cowra Show? All that bullshit about country music?'

'Benny, please stop. They are family.' 'Yes, they're family hayseeds.'

He ruffled Steve's hair saying 'It's catching too. Soon, Steve here will become a hayseed as well.' 'Benny, please stop!'

Louise was tempted to challenge him to call her a hayseed but thought better of it. Instead, she mentioned Nick's threat about the motorbike.

Benny did not comment on this, but he stopped bullying Steve for a while.

Nick was a lousy bastard. When Louise and the boys returned to Cowra, he offered no sympathy. 'You had a good marriage, Paul is a nice bloke, earning good money, and you walk away. You can stay with us for a while, but you'll need to find a place of your own soon. You must have done well out of the divorce. I can employ you here. I know you'll be useful, but I couldn't pay you much of a wage. You don't make much on a farm these days. We've been in a drought here for years.'

At school, Benny did very well, well enough to begin an Arts degree majoring in English and History to become a teacher. He found accommodation with a friend of his mother in Glebe a walk to the University of Sydney.

Benny began well at his studies, but as time passed, he attended fewer and fewer lectures, played more and more snooker, and drank more and more ale at local pubs.

He soon found himself out of depth with the subject matter and became depressed and homesick. He went home. He could not face upcoming assessment tasks.

Benny enjoyed niggling his mates. Most of them did not like him and were quite happy that university had been too much for him.

On his return, with his mother's help, he managed to get a traineeship at a local stock and station agency.

On the other hand, Steve was an average student with no desire to go to university. Instead, when he finished Year 12, he applied for a position with the Commonwealth Bank and began work in the Cowra branch. He took the earliest opportunity to transfer to the city. After five months in Cowra, he set off to the Castle Hill branch in Sydney's north-west. He did not stay long there and soon moved first to Bronte, then Armidale, where he met Kate. She was just so sweet, and he began to think about her as a possible partner in life. They dated for nearly a year, but as Kate was moving towards marriage, Steve was moving away from that goal. He had been invited to meet her parents, and he and Kate had driven together to the Gold Coast, where Kate's older sister and her family lived. He found all of Kate's family dull, much like the hayseeds of Cowra.

As a result of this visit, he decided two things: He did not want to marry Kate or anyone at this stage of life, and he wanted to go back to city living.

Steve was a coward. He could not tell Kate that he had no desire to marry her, so he applied for a transfer to Brisbane. When it was approved, he packed up and left Armidale and moved to the Chermside branch. He left Kate a letter apologising for this lack of decorum. He found accommodation in Fortitude Valley and was quietly absorbed into the community.

Steve played squash, and in doing so, he met his best friend and future business partner, Dan Overton. Both were highly competitive, and over drinks after a game one night, Dan challenged Steve for them to compete in a different sport. They were drunk, and without thinking it through, Dan challenged Steve to beat him in a contest to reach a black belt in karate. Neither had any experience in martial arts, but Steve boozily agreed. They agreed to sign up with Ajax Karate in Chermside.

After an intense eighteen months, they progressed through the various competency levels. Their teacher recognised the struggle as each tried to outperform the other.

He wisely chose to award both with their black belts on the same night.

Meanwhile, Benny was making a good living out of the hayseeds around him. He learned that his opinion of these people was best kept to himself and that some of the hayseeds were quite smart.

To enhance his city persona, he decided to buy a motorbike.

He wanted a bike that would enhance his public profile but found that getting a licence was long and the power of the bike was limited until he gained a full licence. He and Steve were both allowed to ride Nick's Honda 150 when they visited the farm, and both were already competent riders. It was annoying to wait so long to get a full licence. He had to endure three months on L plates, then three years on P plates. He bought a used Honda 250 to see him through this training period. As soon as the training was over, he sold the Honda and bought a three-year-old Ducati Hypermotard with the full kit, a top-of-the-market helmet and a standard helmet for a pillion, full leathers and boots, and top-grade leather gloves.

He looked super cool, which was the general idea, and the red bike drew attention from the hayseeds. Girls and young women vied for his attention, hoping for a ride on this phallic machine. Benny selected a few of the prettier hayseeds and took a high-speed ride to Koorawatha, about twenty-seven kilometres away, just for coffee. Initially, it took nineteen minutes to travel this distance, and he aimed to get it down to fifteen minutes.

Impressive! Other men in town had bikes, usually older guys reliving their youth on a Harley. Many farmers had Ag bikes, and some loved comfort on two wheels and had Goldwings.

But Benny's Ducati outshone them all.

Steve had left Cowra in 1981, but he soon had three trips back to attend funerals.

First, Nick died of a heart attack in his shed while sharpening his chainsaw. He and Maggie had their day punctuated by meetings for morning tea, lunch, afternoon tea and dinner. Maggie began to worry when Nick did not come to the farmhouse at the usual time for morning tea and found him unconscious on the ground in the shed. Louise was out in the paddock somewhere and did not respond to Maggie's cries for help. Her panic meant she did nothing else to get help but stayed, imploring Nick to wake up. Eventually, it dawned that she should call the ambulance. The ambulance arrived ten minutes after her call, but for Nick, it was too late.

Nick was eighty-one and had not changed his will, so Eric inherited the farm, and Louise inherited a parcel of shares. Maggie was devastated by Nick's death and seemed to lack the energy to go on. She had relied on Nick for everything, and now she fell into a deep depression. She could not manage the simplest of tasks. Louise moved into the farmhouse to care for her, but one morning less than three months after Nick died, she simply did not wake up.

Louise had kept the farm going after Nick died, but now with her mother dead, the farm was released to Eric. He generously offered it to Louise to buy, but it was financially beyond her. Eric put it up for sale but paid Louise a generous amount to keep it going until it was sold.

Since Louise was not a potential buyer, it was recommended to Eric to sell it at auction. He was anxious to get the money to expand his freight and removalist business. There were several potential buyers in the district, but he was advised that this property could interest buyers anywhere in Australia. It was a great package. He took advice from his real estate agent to list the farm for sale in all national newspapers. It caught the eye of a broker in Sydney, Peter Farrell, who specialised in bringing this form of investment to the notice of people who were earning a lot of money and were looking for a way to minimise their tax. Farrell was recently contacted by Kim and Clarence Martin, lawyers making millions. He did some homework and produced a figure that would make this property a great tax dodge – better than the bottom-of-the-harbour scheme they had recently used to avoid tax.

Farrell knew that the Martins would not want to operate the farm themselves, and they instructed Farrell to find them a manager. He found that Louise was already managing the farm well. Before the auction, he approached her with a proposal: if his bid was the winning one, would she be willing to continue managing the farm with a surprisingly generous salary?

Farrell had plenty of cash at his disposal from the Martins and just kept upping the price at the auction until he won.

So, surprisingly Louise finally got to run the farm herself and felt that despite Paul she had eventually got her way.

So, Steve returned to Cowra for his grandparents' funerals. A bloody nuisance coming from Brisbane and twice in the same year. At his grandfather's wake, he was subjected to the rest of them – Eric, Molly, Fossie and Ted. He stuck with Benny, who seemed to have outgrown his bullying, but he found soon enough that Benny was just as obnoxious as ever after a few beers.

He vowed that hell would freeze over before he came back to Cowra again, but three months later, a tearful Louise contacted him about her mother's death.

Shit! He would go but excuse himself from the wake.

Hell had almost frozen over when three years later, Louise called to tell him that Benny was dead.

Benny had been to the dirt bike races in Woodstock which was 21 km north-east of Cowra. Jamie, his mate from the stock and station agency who lived in Woodstock, had invited him to the races. Benny had never seen dirt bikes and enjoyed the noise of screeching engines and the drama of the race when much of the time, the bikes were going sideways. It was dusty, dirty and exciting.

Jamie and Benny had three or four stubbies as they watched the races, and Benny decided to take the Scrubby Rush and Pine Mount roads back to Cowra after the races. Sometimes Cowra police set radar traps on the alternative route, the A41, and he did not wish to be caught again. He had been fined twice and had lost points for speeding on the A41. There were some great sweeping curves on Pine Mount, which suited the Ducati.

About three kilometres from the junction with the A41 was a tight turn to the right, followed by a sweeping left, and into a straight kilometre before the hard right onto the A41. He wound up the Ducati to nearly 160 km/h on the straight. About halfway along was a crest at which he first became aware of the two kangaroos. There were groves of trees on both sides of the road, and one of the roos jumped off quickly to the right. But the other remained fixed in the middle of the road, staring at the oncoming Ducati. Benny gambled that this roo would follow its mate and veered to the left to avoid a collision. The roo did go that way, but the front wheel of the Ducati was now on gravel, travelling at over 80 km/h. It began to buck and fishtail. Benny had lost control and, in seconds, lost his life as the Ducati plunged into a large gum tree. It was now about 11.30 pm, and the wreckage of the accident was not easily visible from the road.

When Benny did not turn up for work on Monday morning, Jamie rang Louise to see if he was all right. Louise told him that Benny had not come home on Saturday night, and she had assumed that he had stayed on in Woodstock with Jamie. When he told her that Benny had headed home late on Saturday, she became worried. She frantically rang everybody she knew that Benny might be visiting, but when no one had news of him, she became panicky. She rang Jamie again, who told her that Benny had left Woodstock at 11 pm on Saturday and had intended to take the Scrubby Rush road home.

A now desperate Louise rang Sergeant Barry Grimes and told him of her anguish about Benny. Grimes told her not to worry, that young people tend to go off without telling anyone, but he would take the police cruiser to the Woodstock road and check.

Grimes believed the worst police duty was notifying parents of a child who had been killed needlessly in a road accident, and he now faced it with Louise Arnold. He knew her parents had recently died, so this loss was monumental.

Steve was shaken severely by Benny's death. He had driven the twelve hours to Cowra for his grandparents' funerals but did not trust himself to drive that long in a state of grief, so he took the plane.

Louise, of course, was heartbroken by Benny's death and clung to Steve. She pressured him to stay with her longer than he wanted to stay in Cowra. Both of them had thought about letting Paul know that his son was dead, and Molly had offered to do this for them. They declined, saying that they could look after this, but they did not discuss it further, and it was never done.

Steve thought the hayseeds seemed to being doing well for themselves. Eric now had two trucks which he and Ted used to service Cowra and nearby townships. Molly worked at the local supermarket and had just taken up an assistant manager's position. Fossie had worked at the Cowra Tourism Association. He and Benny had secret jokes about Fossie, particularly about how she dressed. He could not recollect what she had worn at their grandparents' funerals. Still, here she was for Benny's funeral, wearing a dress with a pattern of large red-and-yellow hibiscus and army boots. Her shoulder-length hair was piled on top of her head and held in place by a black Nike baseball cap, with black insulation tape on each arm just above her elbows.

'Benny would have been delighted,' thought Steve.

It was interesting to note that, by now, Eric had moved out of Nick's shadow and rather than being part of Nick's patriarchy, had formed his own. Just as Nick dominated his wife and children, Eric now dominated his.

But did he really?

Molly noted that Paul had not attended his son's funeral and assumed that Louise had decided not to tell him. Her sister-in-law was a queer fish, and Paul Arnold was a prick! And as for their sons, they were cheeky smart-arses. She had never liked Paul. She found him impossible to talk to. She knew no one who had completed a university degree other than him and was not surprised when Benny went off to university as well, but she was delighted when he failed and returned to Cowra. Initially, he was subdued and withdrawn but he soon overcame the defeat and returned to his obnoxious old ways. He returned, bruised by his experience in Sydney, which was in sharp contrast to her and Eric, who had a wonderful time together, leaving Cowra and pleasing themselves.

While she and Eric were having a whale of a time for more than two years on the road, she realised that Eric was, unintentionally perhaps, setting up his patriarchy as their relationship matured. She was not concerned because she knew Eric was susceptible to her suggestions and took many of them on as his own. When they returned to Cowra, she had assumed the power behind his throne and steered him away from working with Nick, who was a cheapskate and would have paid Eric a pittance to work on the Dole farm. After a couple of false steps that she did not oppose, they eventually rented a home just outside town, which was what she wanted and pretended that Eric had handled the accommodation issue so well.

The townsfolk and farmers saw nothing inappropriate in Eric's leadership of his family. Patriarchy was a model that had served country folk well for centuries, so why mess around with it? Everyone knew their place and stayed in it, except for Fossie Dole.

Fossie was a free spirit and ignored all attempts by her parents and her teachers to manoeuvre her into her allocated role as a firstborn female in a country town. She was not out of control – far from it, she had her sense of control and firmly resisted measures to make her conform. She was not abrasive or rude, she just convinced people trying to change her to submit and give up trying.

Molly wondered if any man would be strong enough to pair with her and at times thought that Fossie's partner may turn out to be a woman, but up to this point in time, Fossie had not paired with anyone, and perhaps that's what her plan was. Do you have to have an intimate partner? Perhaps not.

The last Dole hayseed was Ted. It was not an abbreviated form of Edward. He was christened Ted which was maybe a mistake. Dole is a name crying out for more syllables in the Christian name. His school friends could not be defeated, though. Many Australian children have their names changed. It is a national sport. Both Benny and Steve had their names shortened by their friends, and Ted was to be no exception. It was a challenge, and it took a while to emerge as Cham. It was still a single-syllable name but stuck because of its inventive origin. It came about because of classroom discussion, which featured pictures of reptiles, and there was much interest in the chameleon. Some smart fart at the back of the class yelled, 'Chameleon. Ted is a chameleon; he blends into the background', which was true. Ted always tried to avoid attention, and so it fitted. But chameleon was a bit of a mouthful and is inevitably shortened to Cham. His family did not participate in this tomfoolery, and he remained Ted at home.

Molly and Eric had often discussed their future, and considering Eric's inheritance, the future looked bright. They were all working. The kids stayed home and paid board, and Eric's business flourished with gentle guidance from Molly. She recognised, however, that his plan for handing on when he died was quite firm. Ted would inherit the business and conform to the patriarchal model entrenched in the local community.

What about the house?

Molly had a whiff of women's rights and was edging Eric's thinking towards a fairer deal for Fossie, whom she noticed had been influenced by current expressions for women's equality in the press. Perhaps Fossie would get it.

Chapter 14
QUILTY

On a warm night in January 2020, Jack Quilty manoeuvred his telescope to observe the sky adjacent to Venus. He checked his notes. He had noted on his last observation that an object that he did not recognise was still there. He checked on the internet for reports of similar sightings but found none. This was beginning to become exciting! He had known of other amateur astronomers who had made discoveries before the professionals, but he never thought it would happen to him. He noted the somewhat fuzzy appearance of the object and took several more photos. He recorded the data that he knew the 'pros' would require for them to believe him and sent it to the Siding Springs Observatory.

Jack could hardly believe the controversy created by his discovery, a comet from deep space, from outside the solar system! He was chuffed when the press named it the Quilty Deep Space Comet, although there was some speculation that it was not a comet.

Jack remembered that the first known object of interstellar origin that had entered the solar system in 2018 had similar properties to comets. The object was called '1/2017 U1', later named 'Oumuamua'. Here was the second, and he had seen it first!

Jack had lived on the Harrison Pastoral Company's cattle station since 1975 after Cyclone Tracy obliterated Darwin.

Warnings from the Bureau of Meteorology about the imminent approach of Tracy were largely ignored by the good citizens of Darwin, who had seen cyclones come close before and failed to take the precautions advised by the weather forecasters. Consequently, when it struck with wind speeds exceeding two hundred kilometres per hour, Jack's mother, a Larrakia woman, was in a drunken stupor outside a local pub and was killed instantly when part of the pub roof fell on her. His father, a public servant in town planning, had just begun kidney dialysis. Although he survived the cyclone, he died a few days later in an Adelaide hospital of kidney failure.

Jack's science teacher, Fred Wilson, who had fostered Jack's interest in astronomy at school, understood that he would need help. He found Jack huddled in the bathroom of his home and took him to the allocated gathering site on Darwin's football ground. After speaking with some of Jack's extended family, he arranged to take Jack to Harrisons and set him up to train as a jackaroo. Jack never left the Territory. He enjoyed his work at Harrisons and bought ever more sophisticated telescopes.

As a result of Jack's discovery, Paul, who had a passion for star gazing, convinced Frank and his two teacher/farmer friends, Jason Irwin, and Jill Anderson, to join him at the Cathedral Reserve Camp in the Blue Mountains to admire the discovery and to tell them some exciting news.

Paul had met Jason and Jill when the three had become involved in an exciting project to import frozen Angora goat embryos from South Africa. Jason and Jill had made good money out of the project. Paul could not invest personally because the project involved technology he was developing as part of his work at the CSIRO. Several investors made big profits on the frozen embryo technology before government action on biosecurity concerns meant that new regulations rendered many business plans based on the technology unprofitable. Many investors lost money and the frozen embryo technology was no longer seen as a profit maker.

However, Paul believed in the technology and was determined to try it on a different venture. He left the CSIRO to concentrate on further developing the technology and set about devising a way to use the technology for people.

Jason brought with him the telescope from the high school where he worked as the science coordinator. Quilty was a bit of a letdown – it looked more like a fluffy ball than a comet. Jason remembered being similarly disappointed when his science teacher showed him Comet Halley in 1986.

After an evening meal the four friends sat around a fire talking about this and that, Paul said 'I have an announcement to make.'

'Not frozen walrus embryos?' quipped Frank. 'Can't you ever be serious, Frank?'

'Not often, especially after that ventriloquist story you told me.' 'What ventriloquist story was that?' asked Jill.

'Never mind Frank, Jill. You know how he is. Too vivid an imagination!' said Paul, giving Frank a withering look.

'But, Paul, it's such a happy story,' said Frank smiling first at Paul then at Jill. 'Shut it, Frank,' hissed Paul, 'or I'll shut it for you.'

'Oh, please don't, Paul. I would be so scared!' mocked Frank but he knew he had pushed this far enough and asked, 'So what is your announcement?'

Paul did a silent count to ten to relieve the irritation Frank had caused and said: 'I am writing a book!'

'About what?' asked an incredulous Jill. She added 'Paul, you can't even write a decent email. What makes you think could write a book?'

'Maybe it will be a textbook about embryology,' ventured Jason. 'It would still have to be written well.' insisted history teacher Jill. 'Well, it's not a textbook I'm writing, I'm writing about God.'

'Paul, you can't be serious. I'm surprised you even believe in God,' Frank exclaimed.

'Look, just listen a while and I will explain.'

'The latest theories we have about the origin of the Universe are all about the Big Bang,' Paul began.

'I thought you said the book was about God,' interjected Frank.

'For Christ sake, Frank, just listen. I'm getting to that,'

hissed Paul, angrily.

He mentally counted to ten again before continuing: 'I now believe that for the Big Bang theory, the "singularity" these physicists refer to, was in fact God. The singularity contained all that is God.'

'What about the problem of how the singularity, or God as you refer to it, was itself created?' said Jason.   'That is not a problem at all but let me come back to that point later,' said Paul 'Nearly all religions have a Creation story,' said Paul, 'but this is how I see it.'

He continued, 'God decided that It needed company. So, It decided to create some Beings like Itself to keep It company and adore It. Firstly, there were just two others, referred to as the Son and the Holy Spirit. This was not enough, so It created a whole legion of Beings called angels. This seemed to work out well for a while, but some of the angels started to believe that they were just as good as God and maybe a bit better. Some of them staged a coup, and this meant trouble in paradise. A war erupted, and with the help of some loyal angels, God quashed the rebellion. God demoted the rebellious angels to beings, but It was so angry at being challenged, It just EXPLODED. That was the Big Bang. So, the observable universe consists of remnants of God and various angels, which may eternally expand or collapse back to reform God. I think that the universe will collapse back, and God will reassemble Itself. It doesn't matter that God is now in a diaspora, It is still God and continues to be. It put the idea of having company aside as one its less successful ones.

'And also, the explosion or Big Bang if you like, means that the composition of matter in the universe is homogeneous. Further, remember that we are all made up of stuff that was originally in the stars. That stuff contains part good stuff from God and Its supporters and part bad stuff from the evil Lucifer and other bad angels. We all have about equal parts of good and bad. You know, Yin and Yang!'

'Paul, I have a problem with this idea of what created the singularity. Surely something had to come before,' said Jason.

'That's where you're wrong. There is no before – before, after and now are concepts of TIME and time is a human invention. It just helps us to make sense of change. There is no concern here for God. Mind you, this God is not perfect as the Christian God is thought to be. It does not know everything, and It does make mistakes.'

'The scientific evidence seems strong to me, Paul. I've read some of Stephen Hawking's stuff, and it seems pretty sound to me,' said Jill.

'I'll bet you don't understand the mathematics behind it. Hardly anyone does, except a few other eggheads like his mate, Roger Penrose. And the fact that they have to invent up to nine dimensions to account for it, is farcical. The whole idea beggars belief. What's wrong with the notion of gravity given to us by Newton? Those space/time diagrams of Hawking and Penrose leave me cold. Most of us can cope with three dimensions, but nine? Give me a break!'

'When are you going to begin your book? said Frank.

'Oh, I have started already, I have been thinking about this for ages,' said Paul

'Well good luck with that, Paul. But I think your notion is a bit out there,' said Jill.

'All new lofty ideas are considered out there when they were first proposed. Remember what happened when Galileo proposed that the Earth revolved around the Sun?' said Paul smugly.

'That may be so, but I don't think of you as a twenty-first-century Galileo,' said Jill.

The conversation continued into the night, and after they retired to their tent, Jason and Jill continued with the issues raised during the conversation.

They could not decide if Paul was serious about his book or whether he was delusional. He had, after all, been so affected by MacKenzie's death just a year before. His reaction to Frank's comment about a ventriloquist seemed so odd. Why was he so unwilling to talk about it? Could that be an indication of his state of mind? They had never heard him talk about religion except for his unhappy recollections about being raised Catholic.

The Paul they knew was intelligent and articulate. He was well-read and kept up with current affairs. They tried to recall if Paul had made any comment on the conviction of the now-disgraced Cardinal George Pell or his guilty verdict being overturned in the High Court, but neither could remember discussing the issue with him.

Just before they went to sleep, Jill said, 'I think we should keep a close eye on him, Jason. He may be depressed, and we know he is still grieving for MacKenzie. Let's invite him to stay with us at the farm for a week. I'm sure he would love to see how our alpacas are doing. Why don't you ask him tomorrow before we leave?'

'Yeah, I'll do that.'

Jason did ask Paul to come to the farm the next weekend. Paul said that he'd love to.

He arrived on the following Friday evening and presented Jill with flowers from his garden and Jason with two bottles of wine.

Jason prepared barbecued meat and Jill did the salad. They ate on the veranda and enjoyed the view across the paddocks to the hills beyond. The conversation was easy. They had been friends for years, but it was not quite the same without MacKenzie.

Jill said, 'It's been a year since MacKenzie died. How are you handling that?'

'You know it's difficult not having her around. I miss her, and there have been times when I cry for her. But in another sense, I feel released – released from the pressure she put on me to be something I'm not. And I don't have to deal with Stone.'

Jill and Paul knew about Stone. She had been MacKenzie's psychiatrist for more than forty years.

Chapter 15
BIRTH AND BEYOND

Paul went to his friends' house the following weekend after seeing Comet Quilty and talking about his writing. He showed Jill and Jason an example.

'You know that my writing has been in response to Stone's pressure on me about MacKenzie. Together, I thought they were manipulating me; to make me more accountable as her carer. It seemed that my life was being moulded to fit MacKenzie's needs. I needed to have something separate from being a carer. I found quite by surprise that I could think and write creatively, and the process seemed natural.

'I did not begin with any great plan. I just wrote about myself and from there new ideas seemed to flow naturally.

'This is a fragment of my writing that directly reflects my own experience. The earliest part of life is unknowable in the sense that the primitive brain cannot remember but it can feel.

'You may think that I can't write but look here.'

Paul produced a folder containing three A4 sheets.

'This is what I wrote about BIRTH. Here, you read it and tell me that I can't write. It's a first draft only but I reckon that you'll recognise that I can write insightful stuff. Go on read it.'

And he handed it to Jill who read the following:

*   *   *

BIRTH

Ever since I began as a single cell formed from the union of ovum and sperm, I AM. I am alive and I begin an odyssey called life, a continual battle against ENTROPY. I require energy to stay alive and more energy to grow.

I begin by accepting energy from whence I know not. Both ovum and sperm carry enough carbohydrate energy to sustain the dividing zygote, now referred to as a blastocyst that implants itself into the uterus where new blood vessels form to supply nutrients and oxygen.

I proceed to exist. Time passes.

What is time?

I am now AWARE. I know not how.

Beyond awareness comes FEELING. I know not what it is.

Something is changing! I have been in a state of just BEING and now something is changing. Before I was in a state of BEING, I was in a state of AM. This is difficult to explain because back then I had no words, no ideas, just feelings. It was *feeling* that changed me from AM to BEING.

The most important feeling was comfort. I felt comfortable most of the time and it was, well, pleasant. Now I am being not comfortable. I feel pressure. I feel I am being squeezed.

What is comfort like? A sense of wellbeing, a sense of not having to seek energy to combat entropy. Before, I had no need to *do* anything, I just had to BE. I could feel parts of myself, and I could feel things going on. Things that were happening to me.

I AM ALL AND EVERYTHING.

THERE IS NOTHING ELSE BUT ME.

There was a regular pulsing in me. At this stage, all feeling related to ME. I was everything! Much later I would learn that the pulsing inside me was my own heart beating. Back then, though, I had only feelings.

The squeezing continues, but in bursts, with quiet times in between. What is happening? When I was just BEING I sensed things, that I later learned some were sounds. The sounds I was hearing now were very strong. This was not comfortable. Now my head is being squeezed big time. Is this the end? Is my time up?

I wish that things could have just remained comfortable. Why this change?

I decide to embrace a new feeling – fairness, and this is not FAIR!

Push and stop, push and stop. On it goes. I feel my head is being squeezed out of shape. Is this the end?

No! Suddenly my head is squeezed out of my world of former comfort followed by my left shoulder. The rest of me quickly follows. I am out and I am not happy!

What is waiting outside?

What does OUTSIDE even mean?

Two fleshy scoops I later learn are hands, the hands of another being move me and I feel I am being prodded and poked. Something is shoved into my mouth. Stuff is poured into my eyes. I decide to express a new feeling: ANGER. How to do this? It seems to come naturally. I fill previously unused lungs with air and squeeze it out through a wide-open mouth. The indignity, a new feeling, of it all!

Sounds, that I would later learn were sounds of joy followed my anger.

'It's a boy,' a voice says. This made no sense then, but I came to learn later that this was significant. Now I was wrapped up, placed on some sort of device and someone announced, 'Seven pounds, three ounces.' From there I was placed gently on the body of the one I would later know as my mother who cooed and stroked my nose.

This was just not on! I squawked again but it had all been too much and I slipped into a deep sleep.

When you are born and for weeks afterwards you don't see very well, so I was more aware of sounds, smells and touch. The sound, smell and touch of my mother were the most important parts of my life in the outside world. While inside my mother, there had been no sense of hunger, but now it became especially important, and my mother looked after this well. The smell of the milk on her breast was all I needed to solve my new hunger problem.

Now it is not at all surprising that I don't remember any of this. Back then I acted on feelings until I gained the tools to form memories, language. But feelings are never replaced by memories and language that help guide us all through life.

'It's a boy!!' This was an important point, and it is worth noting here that being a boy in my first couple of years really meant little me. It seemed that everyone was a boy. My mother and father were much the same to my untutored eyes, but bigger, save hair length and clothes; until Robyn came along.

Just before my mother gave birth to my brother, her friend Joyce visited us at our house with her daughter, Robyn. She and I were about the same age, nearly three. While my mother and Joyce chatted in the lounge room, Robyn and I went to the laundry. Honestly, I do not know why we did it, but we decided to take off our clothes. Maybe we thought they needed to be washed.

We were both shocked! If I had had the words I have today, I think I would have said, 'What happened to you?' Part of her equipment seemed to be missing! There between her legs was a deep gash. My equipment was in its proper place between my legs. I stared at Robyn's lack of equipment in amazement. I noticed the Robyn also looked puzzled. I can only imagine what she may have been thinking. Maybe it was something like: 'I've been robbed!' or 'What has happened to mine?'

We did not have time to discuss the issue further in the limited language we had then because Robyn's mother suddenly appeared at the laundry door and squealed 'ROBYN', picked her up, gathered up her clothes and quickly left the scene. My mother appeared as well. She said nothing to me but hastily pulled on my pants from around my ankles. The incident was never spoken of or discussed again.

Soon after the 'incident in the laundry' my brother was born. I could see very early on that he was properly equipped, unlike poor Robyn.

I did not like him much.

Now I did not see much of my father in my years as a child. 'Where's Dad?' I would say and my mother would usually reply 'He is at work.' Dad worked five-and-a-half days each week. When he left for work I was often asleep, and when he came home, he would spend time with me. But the time was short, and I was tired and put to bed early. I had no chance to see his equipment and presumed that he was intact just like my brother and me. It would take a stroke he suffered at age sixty-eight when I had to assist him to urinate into a toilet bowl that I at last confirmed it. It was a difficult moment for both of us; me having to hold his penis to direct the urine into the bowl and for him the indignity to be in such need. I am weeping for us as I write this.

I never saw Mum's equipment but was reacquainted with her breasts when she was feeding my brother and my sister.

My parents were very reluctant to discuss anything to do with sex and my mother seemed very ill-informed about her own sexuality. By my late teens and my own burgeoning sexuality, I realised that my mother and father hated each other.

I learned about sex from secondary sources – 'knowing' friends and their sniggering comments about girls, and a book *Attaining Manhood* left out by my father for me to find when I was about fourteen. I still knew little about sex as a feeling. *Attaining Manhood* was basically about the biology of sex, not how to experience it. But I knew that wonderful feeling I got when unexpectedly I had an erection.

I discovered this in the bath and experienced the joy of stroking my penis but was at first shocked when a thin milky fluid emerged.

Oh dear, have I broken something?

No.

This stroking was to make future baths a real treat.

But I digress – back to my mother. When my sister was born eight years after me, my mother seemed pleased but puzzled and my father was ecstatic. However, she was hiding something: ignorance! Her ignorance was exposed only when I completed a course in zoology at university.

My mother had had a torrid time medically soon after her marriage. Several visits to hospital for several conditions, including an ovarian cyst which resulted in the removal of that ovary, and her first pregnancy that resulted in the death of her first foetus which was a boy. Now, for whatever reason, my mother believed that one of her ovaries produced boys and the other, girls so, to her, the surgeons had removed her girl-producing ovary and she was destined to produce male children only. When I was showing off telling her that the sex of children was determined by sperm not a woman's ovary, the mystery of my sister was finally explained.

*   *   *

When Jill had finished, she handed the sheets to Jason who began to read. They remained silent until Jason had finished reading.

'Well,' said Paul 'What do you think?'

Jill spoke first: 'I think you may be on to something here. There's a need for some editing, of course and opening paragraphs are a bit contrived, but I think you have taken on a very difficult task trying to give an account of the birthing process from the infant's point of view. My advice is to have a professional editor read it and get their opinion. I could ask at school to see if any of the teachers knows of one. May I take this to see what I can do?'

Jason said 'There is an issue with the title of course. The story is about more than birth. You'll need to change that.'

Paul was delighted that both gave guarded approval of his writing. He told Jason to keep that copy. He had the file on his word processor.

Writing would be a mechanism for him to clarify his views on abortion.

After his rapid uptake of biology, having shifted from physics, he formed the opinion that once fertilisation had occurred life had begun, and he rejected the idea that this life could be terminated by doctors whose major aim in their profession was to preserve life. For a woman to have the right to kill the embryo within her is tantamount to murder.

Some argued that in the early stages of development, the embryo/foetus was not a sentient being but were willing to concede that after a certain stage of development, it would not be proper to abort. This stage seemed arbitrary, and

Paul argued that a fertilised ovum was a life, and it could not be proper kill it.

Some argued that a single cell, a fertilised ovum, could not be counted because something living could not be so, as it would be incapable of awareness of its environment.

This was nonsense, of course, there were thousands of examples of single-cell organisms, amoeba and paramecium for instance, which showed awareness to light and other stimuli.

He wanted this message, the right of a human zygote to live, come through in his writing which would have a broader emphasis on awareness in the main character, based upon himself throughout his life and the consequences of a life without constant awareness. Paul realised that many of the big errors he had made in life, such as marrying Louise, were the result of spontaneity born out of lack of awareness and not taking time to assess his situation, which had led him to make rash decisions.

Much of the input about abortion came from religious groups. Although he could not believe in God, he had already the seed of an idea to consider the current cosmological view of physicists of the origin of the universe with a blend of religion with the idea that the Big Bang singularity was, in fact, God which had exploded because of a mighty battle with the forces of darkness.

He looked forward to creating a novel, *God and the Big Bang.*

Chapter 16
MACKENZIE

I t was 9.30 on Sunday morning, 1 September, when Frank's phone rang. 'Hi, how's it going, Paul?' said Frank.

'Oh, Frank, MacKenzie died this morning. Can you come over? I really need your help.'

'I'll be there in 15 minutes,' said Frank and hung up. He changed quickly into jeans and a T-shirt, grabbed his phone, wallet and keys, and headed for his car.

True to his word, Frank arrived at Paul's in 15 minutes. He knocked on the front door. Paul called out 'Come in Frank, it's open.'

Frank found Paul slumped on the sofa sobbing. He still held the phone in his hand. Frank gently took it from him and placed it back onto its stand.

Paul struggled to speak: 'Frank I. I. I... can't speak, I am shattered!'

Frank sat beside Paul and wrapped his brother in a comforting embrace. He pulled Paul's head over to his shoulder and stroked Paul's hair.

'Oh, mate. Oh, mate. You poor bugger! What happened? I thought she was getting better.'

Paul sobbed and sobbed. He could not speak.

There was a knock on the door. A voice called 'Paul, is everything okay?'

It was Paul's neighbour, Elliot. Frank called for him to come in.

'What's happened?' asked Elliot.

'MacKenzie died this morning.'

'Oh no. Paul, I am so sorry,' said Elliot who sat on the other side of Paul and took his hand and stroked it softly.

Later Paul recovered enough to tell Frank and Elliot the full story.

*   *   *

MacKenzie had been hospitalised to attend to a faulty valve in her aorta. The operation had been successful in that the valve had been correctly repaired but internal bleeding had made her condition parlous. She spent the next nine days in intensive care during which she made a little progress and recovery. However, she had been intubated and oxygen was supplied to help her compromised breathing.

Paul spent hours each day with MacKenzie at the hospital and reluctantly had been given permission to stay overnight on what was to be her last night. They spent an almost sleepless night but enjoyed many loving and intimate moments which made Paul incredibly happy.

Their relationship had been tempestuous, and each at one time or other had said: 'I want out of this.'

They both fell asleep sometime in the early morning, and when he awoke at about 6 am, Paul kissed her and said 'I'm going home to freshen up. I'll be back in an hour.'

Paul had been home only ten minutes when a doctor called to say that MacKenzie had died only minutes before.

Frank drove Paul to the hospital to see MacKenzie. Paul could not believe that the vibrant woman he knew was now silent, breathless, inanimate.

He lent down a kissed her cheek but then noticed that the tube into her nose was still in place. He called angrily, 'Nurse come in here!'

When she came in, he said, less angrily, 'Please remove that tube!'

The nurse apologised and quickly removed the tube.

Paul held MacKenzie and wept.

He tried to speak to the doctor who had called him earlier but was unable to, so Frank asked 'How did she die? We thought she was getting better.'

'MacKenzie was a high-risk patient, and the surgeon would have discussed this with her and her husband.'

Frank nodded and put his hand on Paul's shoulder. He pulled Paul towards him and placed Paul's head on his shoulder.

'Oh, mate. Oh, mate,' cried Frank as he too felt the loss of his good friend.

The doctor showed Paul and Frank to another room and told Frank that she would be back soon with a counsellor to help.

A nurse asked if they would like a tea or coffee and Frank ordered two coffees.

The doctor, Raylene Atkins, and counsellor, Eric Judd, came in and eventually succeeded in calming Paul to the point where he could converse with them. Dr Atkins explained to Paul that MacKenzie had died suddenly, probably from heart failure. She noted that MacKenzie's records showed that her heart was already in a perilous state before the operation. It was a risky operation but necessary due to the dire situation with the valve. She said that they had done all they could, but in the end the assault on her body by the operation was just too much for her heart.

Paul had MacKenzie cremated. She had not wanted a funeral or a coffin or to be buried. She had just wanted Paul to sprinkle her ashes on her precious garden.

And this he did.

MacKenzie and Paul had met at Oscar's, a well-known wine bar for more mature adults to find a new partner. Most were divorcees, with a few widowed people as well. Paul was sitting with Alice, who was a fifty-one-year-old widow. He had managed to extract her from her group of two girlfriends, and over a glass of wine, they were finding out about each other.

Soon afterwards, MacKenzie came in with her girlfriend Zoe, who was looking for a man but was timid about going to Oscar's. She had not wanted to go alone and persuaded

MacKenzie to go with her. MacKenzie had been divorced twice, or almost twice, and was not looking for another man living with. That night she was not looking for another man.

Men! She thought they were not worth the trouble of catching, bedding and living with. So, if she found someone suitable to catch and bed, she could leave out 'living with'.

Or so she thought.

She and Zoe looked around at the available males, evaluating each, when MacKenzie's gaze fell upon Paul. She was impressed but decided she would not pass on this intelligence to Zoe. Perhaps she would have him for herself. She excused herself from Zoe and moved to the table where Paul and Alice sat. She introduced herself and sat beside Paul. MacKenzie was very articulate, and when she found out he was with the CSIRO, she dominated the conversation with her extensive knowledge of science, for she, too, had studied science at university. But in typical MacKenzie form, she had not completed the course. She had been at, or near the top, in each of her subjects but was dismissive of her lecturers and tutors, whom she thought were incompetent 'bozos'. Partway through her second year, she quit pursuing a career in landscape gardening. She now owned a landscaping business in Sydney's north-west. Alice gradually realised she had no hope of winning Paul, excused herself, and went back a bit teary to her girlfriends.

MacKenzie looked back over to Zoe, winked, and waved, a signal that Zoe should make her own way home. She was going to this guy's home, and she would get home by herself.

There was a little light entertainment at Oscar's that

night, and MacKenzie organised Paul to sit beside her for the performances. The last act was a juggler whose stage name was Rusty Balls.

After Rusty Balls, MacKenzie whispered to Paul, 'Are you going to take me home now?'

'Okay,' said Paul, 'Where do you live?'

'No, I mean your home. I live a long way from here.'

MacKenzie was more handsome than beautiful, but she had a strong personality, and at forty years old, she was an attractive woman. She was born Isobel MacKenzie Lloyd but hated being called Isobel and, worse still, Issy, so at eleven years of age, she announced to her parents that she wished to be called MacKenzie. Her parents were surprised but knowing her to be incredibly determined, gave reluctant approval.

At Paul's home in Drummoyne, she relaxed in his loungeroom and while Paul organised drinks for them both, MacKenzie examined the wall hangings and other items. There were few and MacKenzie was unimpressed.

Paul brought in the drinks, and they sat close together on the lounge. MacKenzie put aside her drink and took Paul's away as well. She reached over him and drew him into an embrace. As they kissed, she slowly reached down to feel his erect penis.

She said, 'Adequate', kissed him even more passionately than before and finally said 'Where's the bedroom?'

Paul thought *'Adequate?' Louise had never commented on his penis and so this surprised him.*

Paul led her to his bedroom, and he had the best sex in his life. After the sex-drought of his marriage to Louise, he felt as high as a kite.

MacKenzie stayed the night with Paul and early in the morning, before he had a chance to prepare breakfast, he heard her summoning a taxi. He called out 'Won't you stay for breakfast? It's Saturday'

MacKenzie replied 'My music lessons start at 9 am and I'll be teaching all day.'

'I thought you had a landscaping job,' he called from bed.

'I do, but I teach music to kids on weekends.'

MacKenzie lived on acreage in Arcadia in Sydney's north and was in the process of divorcing her second husband. Before leaving, she said 'I want to see you again. Come to my place next Friday night so I can enjoy you all over again.'

After showering, MacKenzie took a taxi home and left Paul to wonder where this was all going. He had been separated from Louise for over a year and so had lost contact with his sons, Benny and Steve.

After MacKenzie left, Paul began to ponder on her comment about his penis. What had she meant by it? He had not made it a habit of examining the penises of other men. There was little opportunity to do so, anyway. So how could he know what sizes were out there?

'Adequate' – it seemed to imply borderline small. Maybe

this was why Louise found sex with him so abhorrent. Maybe he was not even touching the sides of her vagina. Why had she never said so? But he mused that MacKenzie seemed to be happy with his equipment and was asking for more.

When he and Louise had separated in 1989, Benjamin, age fourteen and Steven, age twelve, went with their mother when she returned to her hometown of Cowra. Louise did not contest his application to the court for a divorce, but she did claim sixty per cent of the value of their home in Drummoyne on advice from her solicitor because of her relinquishing any claim on Paul's superannuation. Paul agreed to pay for child support until each son had finished school. The divorce meant that Paul had to pay out on the house in Drummoyne to Louise and deal with the mortgage they had already had, without any contribution from Louise who had worked part-time at the local swimming pool. Although it was difficult, his bank accepted his application to refinance.

Paul really wanted a partner with whom he shared his interests and ambitions as well as being a willing partner in sex. Louise had shared none of his interests, had supported his ambitions, but found sex with him unappealing.

The following Friday night at MacKenzie's house, a lovely brick home on ten acres of bushland, they shared a meal by candlelight. Afterwards, they sat on the balcony and enjoyed the last of the cabernet shiraz that Paul had brought with him.

It was late. When there was a break in the conversation, Paul stood, said that he should be going, thanked her for a lovely meal and headed for the front door. MacKenzie walked with him but when he reached for the door handle, MacKenzie said, 'Wrong door', and indicated another door to the right. She opened it revealing her own bedroom and said, 'This is where you should be going.'

Paul did not go home on Saturday. He spent the time that MacKenzie was teaching, investigating the shops at nearby Galston, and brought back meat pies for lunch. After the music lessons, they went to a local Chinese restaurant for dinner. Nor did he go home on Sunday. He stayed. They talked, they had sex and continued this cycle until Monday morning. They both had work commitments – MacKenzie had her landscaping to manage, and Paul had his frozen embryo research to continue.

It was an amazing experience, and Paul was looking forward to the next Friday when they could do it all over again.

This arrangement continued for a couple of months until MacKenzie suggested that Paul move in with her so she could enjoy him every day. She suggested that he rent out the house in Drummoyne and the rent would help pay off the mortgage.

'Have you not heard of negative gearing, Paul?' said MacKenzie.

Of course, Paul had heard of it, but he had no idea how it worked. MacKenzie added 'How about I arrange to set it up for you?'

'Sure.' said Paul. MacKenzie knew about finance, and he appreciated her help.

Paul was now forty-five and thought that it was not too late to begin again. He had never been close to his sons. When he was at home, he could not bear the rubbish that Louise and the boys watched on TV and usually went back to his office to read or listen to classical music. On weekends he took the boys around as they played soccer or swam. When it was finished, he usually played tennis or squash, anything to avoid Louise who was beginning to hate him.

Louise had always wanted children and Paul sensed that she would submit herself to intercourse if there was a chance to conceive again. He made a case to her that they should limit themselves to two children. They had limited resources and could well support two children but would be less able if there were more children.

When Steven was just four months old, he told her that he wanted a vasectomy and had, in fact, made an appointment to have it done. This surprised Louise, but she reluctantly agreed. Paul had his snip the following Thursday.

Paul moved in with MacKenzie and commuted to work from a nearby railway station to the city and then a bus to Rozelle where he had his office and lab.

MacKenzie sold her landscaping business and bought a Harvey Norman franchise in the north-east of Sydney.

Paul thought, '*This is the life.*'

But like all thoughts of a rosy life ahead, his thought was badly flawed.

About six months after he moved in with MacKenzie, Paul proposed. MacKenzie was a little taken aback. She had done that twice already and it had failed. It should be noted that she did not say that SHE had failed, just that each marriage had failed.

Her first marriage to Graham was a disaster. He was abusive and on occasions hit her. He was also unfaithful – his last lover was his secretary. He continued his violent ways with MacKenzie and at one time knocked her out. MacKenzie could not understand his abusive ways and lapsed into deep depression. Her GP was anxious for her mental health and recommended a special clinic for people with what he called mental breakdowns. It was at this clinic that she met Dr Stone who would dominate the rest of her life.

Stone was a well-known psychiatrist in Sydney and with a reputation for her novel approach. She was one of the first to prescribe Prozac when it became available in Australia and actively campaigned for its inclusion on the PBS. She prescribed doses of Prozac which were well above the recommended dose drawing the ire of her colleagues.

When Stone was accused of inappropriate sexual behaviour with a troubled young woman, she was found guilty and struck off the register of medical practitioners. She told MacKenzie that it was a stitch-up, and she believed her. She never doubted that she was innocent. She stayed with her patient until she died.

Chapter 17
MARRIAGE AGAIN

When MacKenzie left the private clinic where Stone was a consultant, she returned home to Graham. She felt more empowered now after several sessions with Stone and took the out-of-character step of warning Graham that she would contact the police if he hurt her again and she would divorce him if he did not stop 'playing around'. Graham was apologetic and promised never to hurt her again. He said that he never really wanted to hurt her; it was just that sometimes she made him so angry that he lost control and hit her. Stone predicted that he would say this and advised her not to get into a discussion about blame because it never worked. They also discussed the cues that made Graham angry and violent. Stone recommended she avoid these, if possible, but she was not to sacrifice herself to his unacceptable ways.

Graham claimed that his infidelities were just about sex – they never really meant anything. Sometimes he was in a position where sex was offered. The time and place were suitable, maybe at a conference he was attending, and he took the opportunities available. It didn't mean he loved these women. Stone advised MacKenzie not to challenge his account but to firmly remind Graham that such behaviour would not be tolerated anymore, and she would divorce him if he did it again.

Graham apologised profusely and promised to mend his ways. And he did, for a while.

About two months later, MacKenzie and Graham were discussing their credit card statements and MacKenzie questioned three transactions for hotel bookings made by Graham. He became defensive about being questioned, then angry. He stood up and said that he was going out. MacKenzie followed him to the front door and asked if he had a whore waiting in a hotel room.

Graham swung around and backhanded her. MacKenzie fell and hit her head hard on the tiled floor. Graham swept on out through the front door without looking back, leaving an unconscious MacKenzie behind.

He drove off a minute later.

When he returned two hours later feeling better that he had worked out a way to justify the hotel bookings, he found the house empty. MacKenzie's car was in the garage, but he could not find her.

Alan Doughty, MacKenzie's next-door neighbour, was drying dishes when he heard the argument. He was used to hearing MacKenzie and Graham arguing, but it had not occurred for months. However, something was different this time. The yelling had been brief and was followed by silence. Then came the sound of Graham's Monaro backing rapidly out of the driveway.

Something did not feel right, so he went over to investigate. He found MacKenzie unconscious at the front door with blood coming from a wound to her right eye.

He immediately called ooo and asked for an ambulance and the police.

At the North Shore Hospital doctors found MacKenzie had sustained an orbital rim fracture on her right side and concussion caused by hitting her head on a hard surface.

Alan went to the hospital to give information about the incident to the medical staff and the police. MacKenzie remained unconscious while police took a statement from Alan and the medical staff. Once the statements were taken, police went to MacKenzie's house to speak to Graham. He had not yet returned, and they asked Alan if he knew the Monaro's number plate. He did and police issued an all-points bulletin for Graham's vehicle with an order to stop the vehicle and detain the driver on suspicion of assault occasioning grievous bodily harm.

Graham returned home before he could be stopped by police.

He searched the house for MacKenzie and noted that her car was still there. *Where could she possibly be?* He was searching the grounds when police arrived and put him under arrest.

At the police station Graham was questioned about injuries to his wife, who he now found was unconscious in hospital. He soon realised that he would require legal advice. He stopped answering questions and asked to call his lawyer.

Stone was called to attend MacKenzie at her request when she regained consciousness the next day. Stone immediately arranged for several photos of MacKenzie to be taken and requested copies of notes made by each attending physician and nurse. Once she had done this, she asked MacKenzie if she had made a statement to police. She was unclear on this but thought that the police had not returned to speak to her. Stone advised her to say nothing to police yet. She should claim that she could not remember the incident. Stone told her she would arrange a friend and lawyer Patrick Stevenson to speak to her first. As a result of this manoeuvring, Graham was not charged with any offence because MacKenzie claimed that she remembered nothing of the incident. She assumed that she had fainted because of the argument, had fallen and hit her eye socket on the table near the entrance, then she hit her head on the floor.

Stone advised MacKenzie that if Graham was imprisoned over this, he would come out seeking revenge or arranging from his prison cell to have her assaulted.

MacKenzie recovered from her fall, then immediately applied to the court for a divorce.

Stevenson sent his file for MacKenzie's divorce application to the court. It included the photos of her in hospital and statements from medical staff that attended her to Graham's lawyer with a suggestion that Graham does not contest MacKenzie's application for a no-fault divorce.

The court granted MacKenzie's application, and the judgement was finalised some months later.

At property settlement meetings, the same damning evidence was presented and MacKenzie's claim for sixty per cent of the estate was granted.

Their house, two investment properties and a share portfolio were liquidated and MacKenzie invested her share into the house at Arcadia. She had enough left over to set up a landscaping business. The north-west area of Sydney was booming, and she worked hard on this business. She did most of the work herself with the aid of some rented machines. But she was a bit greedy and found that she needed to take on some muscle to keep up with the demand.

She hired Phil, who got her pregnant. Worse still, he wanted to marry her!

It was not in MacKenzie's nature to have an abortion. They decided on a quick wedding with no guests and Phil moved in. Being pregnant was not conducive to the physical work of landscaping and in her fifth month she developed cramps and miscarried.

Phil was a good worker and good in bed, but he was a yobbo and not really husband material. She offered him a cash settlement to separate and divorce. Phil didn't mind, MacKenzie had some strange friends who were up themselves; a bit like MacKenzie herself. She was good at sex, but so were lots of women and his good looks made him very attractive to female yobbos.

MacKenzie was in this position when she came across Paul.

'Paul, marriage again?' said MacKenzie. 'You can't be serious. I've done that twice already and we both know how that worked out. And you have done it before, and we know how that worked out too. Let's just be satisfied with what we have – a loving relationship and a good life. Let's not mess it up with marriage!'

Paul was disappointed with her response, but he was not about to give up.

'I'd feel much better about our relationship if it was formalised by marriage,' said Paul

'Paul,' said MacKenzie, 'I know what's driving this and I am telling you that it is not a good idea. You Catholics are so tied up in knots about sin and guilt you just can't see that marriage is the cause of relationship breakdown. We are not going to produce any children to be protected by the legal nature of family so what's your problem?'

'My problem, Macca, is that I love you and I think that the promises made when marrying are important and need to be stated in public.'

'You mean that I should promise to love, honour, and obey you in public! You can't seriously believe that I am going to OBEY you? This relationship we have now is based on mutual respect, or that's what I thought it was. And are you going to claim conjugal rights if I'm not in the mood? And would I need to break off the relationships I have with my male friends because I'm married? Forget it, Paul, I'm not doing it!'

Paul was taken aback by the force of her response and decided that it would be appropriate to retreat now and approach her at a time when she was more amenable.

Amenable was not a word that came quickly to mind when describing MacKenzie. That is not to say that she was difficult to be with, but she did have certain core beliefs that could not be challenged. One of these was her idea that once in a relationship, a man should not be sexually attracted to other women or at least not show it. Paul was often called upon to defend the position that a man could be sexually attracted to other women, he just chose not to act on it.

This situation was highlighted in an incident soon after they met. MacKenzie arranged for her good friends and recent newlyweds Bill and Cathy to join her and Paul at an Italian restaurant for dinner. Paul knew little about either Bill or Cathy. He was seated beside Cathy at the table and began asking her questions about her life. This went on for some time and he felt the tip of MacKenzie's shoe striking his shin and foolishly failed to understand what it meant.

Then MacKenzie got up and indicated that she was off to 'powder her nose'. This should have alerted Cathy that she should accompany her, but Cathy failed to recognise or act on this signal. Consequently, when MacKenzie returned to the table, she sat and gave Paul a kick that could not be ignored. As he turned to ask her what it was for, she stood up, threw her napkin on the table, and shouted, 'How dare you!' as she ran out of the restaurant in tears. Paul made some vague arrangement with Bill about the payment then ran after MacKenzie whom he found sobbing at their car.

'You drive me home, pack your bags and get out of my life!' she shouted.

Most of the night, they argued back and forth. MacKenzie

was sobbing and shouting, and Paul was pleading the case that he was unaware that he had done anything wrong.

'I was just talking to Cathy. What's wrong with that?' he said. 'Her hair was on your shoulder!' MacKenzie shot back.

Fatigue more than force of argument meant that they eventually went to bed, after Paul coaxed MacKenzie back from the guest bedroom where she had retreated in distress.

Because of this incident, Bill and Cathy were never spoken to again.

Paul was blamed for MacKenzie's loss of her good friend, Cathy, and for the rest of their time together MacKenzie would regularly accuse Paul of being unfaithful by having Cathy's hair on his shoulder. MacKenzie continued to see Stone once per week. She no longer charged an excessive fee as a medical doctor and now practised as a counsellor.

She continued to exert a strong influence over MacKenzie for the rest of her life.

MacKenzie and Paul never married. Their relationship endured many potential schisms and, at the very end with MacKenzie in hospital, their last hours together were the best they had ever been. MacKenzie had been denied food by mouth and Paul spent their last night together giving her juice from small sponges. At times she was delusional and asked him to take sweets from a dispenser on the wall. The dispensers were for disinfectant foam and although she asked him for the sweets many times, he gently reminded her that there were no sweets there.

The loss of MacKenzie was both painful and a release.

His time with her had been a time of personal growth.

She made him appreciate the fact that he could not be a 'good guy'. It made no sense that this state could be sustained and like everyone else, he had a dark side. It had never occurred to Paul that he would have a dark side. He had been taught by his parents to consider others and his Catholic upbringing reinforced this. He was always nice.

In his first marriage, despite Louise's lack of intimacy with him, he felt that he had been a considerate husband. He never expressed his anger with her for this. He was always polite and never aggressive. MacKenzie would later point out to him that such behaviour cannot be sustained, and he was left with this unexpressed anger even after he and Louise had divorced. They had never discussed the feelings they had for each other.

However, his personal growth would always be limited by his remnant Catholicism.

Chapter 18
PAUL

Yes, Dad, I'll get the first flight available.' Louise put down the phone.

'Paul, can you come here?' He was in his study.

As he came into the living room, Louise said 'Oh, Paul, that was Dad. Mum has liver cancer.' She began to cry.

Paul walked over to her and took her into his arms.

'I'm so sorry, Lou. Maggie has always been such a healthy person. What are you going to do?' 'I'll fly down tomorrow. Will you be okay with the boys? I don't know how long I'll need to be there.'

'We'll be fine. Won't we, boys?'

'Are you going to visit Nan, Mum? Can I come too?' said Benny. 'And me too.' said Steve.

'No, not this time. Nan is sick. I'll be back as soon as I can.' 'Ooh, Mum.'

Louise did go the next day.

She called that night to say she was bringing her mother

and father back to Sydney for her mother to attend an appointment with an oncologist at Prince Alfred Hospital.

The boys were delighted that their grandparents were coming to visit, although they did prefer to go to Cowra to be with them on the farm.

Maggie's oncologist said that it was fortunate that the cancer had been detected early and for the present, at least, it could be treated with tumour ablation.

Louise's parents did not stay long. They were worried about their animals being looked after by friends.

Paul was grateful that Louise's mother and father were not staying. It meant that he had to give up his study, which doubled as the guestroom.

He had to put up with Louise's lack of intimacy because of the children, but he did not want to put up with her parents as well. He knew that being married meant having some sort of relationship with in-laws, and really, Maggie and Nick were okay, provided he did not have to be with them too often.

The big problems were Louise's brother, Eric, his appalling wife, Molly and their children, Fossie and Ted.

It was like dealing with bird shit on a Panama hat.

He would probably be safe from them this Christmas, which his mother, Silvia, was hosting this year and fortunately, Eric could not travel to Sydney as he was unable to get time off work.

Paul already had in mind a divorce from Louise as soon as the kids left school.

As a child, Paul's mother took him to Mass every Sunday.

Harvey, his father, never came with them. It seemed that he was needed at the Paradise Club nearly every day, for something. Paul wasn't troubled by Harvey's lack of attention, or thought he wasn't, and preferred to be with his mother. Silvia, too, seemed to be content with Harvey's lack of presence in her life. In fact, she suspected that he had a mistress or even mistresses. He had begun seeking sexual relief elsewhere during her pregnancy with Paul and, frankly, she was happy for other women to satisfy his needs. He had a substantial income so she and Paul were well catered for.

Paul attended a local primary school in Parramatta and then the selective James Ruse Agricultural High School and did remarkably well. The Catholic schools in the area were not up to the standard that Paul's intellect required. He matriculated and completed an Honours degree in Physics before taking a position at the CSIRO.

At CSIRO, he began in work as part of a group researching photovoltaic cell efficiency, but after two years in this field, his attention shifted to embryo transfer and implantation in sheep. This came about because of several discussions he had with his colleagues about abortion. He strongly opposed it and wanted something done about it. Someone had said, 'Then, why don't *you* do something about it?'

Paul was not a campaigning and protest type of person, but it occurred to him that there might be a scientific solution rather than a political one.

He requested a transfer to a group researching embryo collection, freezing and storage, and was given tacit approval with a proviso that he quickly learned a lot of biology.

This was a work that occupied Paul for nearly ten years.

During this time, he spent some time in country New South Wales, and notably in Cowra, where CSIRO was located, working with Nick Dole, whose South Suffolk sheep were part of his research. Paul was attracted to Louise, Dole's daughter, and she to him. It started with conversations over tea in the Dole kitchen and moved onto attending social gatherings together, then to dates. They eventually became sexually intimate, but the opportunities were limited.

Their courtship extended over three years because Paul's research was done primarily in Sydney, so they saw each other only on his visits to Cowra. Louise was Nick's much needed support in running the farm particularly with the scientific aspect of embryo harvesting and transplanting.

With the possibility of the relationship becoming more serious, Paul began to plan for the future. He was earning good money and living at home with his mother, Silvia, meant that his expenses were low. He invested in a house in Drummoyne, a three-bedroom brick veneer cottage, and rented it out while he lived with his mother in Greystanes.

Paul brought Louise to Sydney to meet his mother and his friends as they were thinking through the likelihood of marriage.

Marriage to Paul was an important step to take for Louise, knowing that her plans to take over her father's farm when he retired would be impossible, and she knew it would be difficult for her to fit into Paul's academic world in Sydney. If she moved to Sydney, Nick would perhaps need to employ someone to replace her; it was already becoming difficult to manage by himself.

There would be no sense in handing over to her brother, Eric, who was a disaster. By now, Paul was thirty and Louise was twenty-seven.

They spent a lot of time talking about plans to wed – on the phone, and when Paul was in Cowra and in Sydney.

Nature nearly made the decision for them when Louise revealed that she was pregnant. This was clearly not the plan!

Each had an opinion about how it could have happened. Unfortunately, it was not discussed, and they reacted to the situation, rather than consider any other options. Paul did not know Louise's opinion about abortion. They had never discussed it. Having their child aborted was an option Paul would certainly not support. And as each agreed later, perhaps the reasons for marriage were not strong enough to proceed. The decision to marry and live in Sydney would mean that Louise's plans for her future as a farmer were to be abandoned in favour of Paul continuing his career. And now with a baby in the mix, any hope of moving back to Cowra to be a part-time farmer and help Nick was quashed.

Paul's insistence that he pursue *his* career, which was after all, more important than Louise running a farm in Cowra set the scene for her to punish him by withdrawing conjugal rights. She never made it clear to Paul her frustration at abandoning her dream, and he never asked why she withdrew from intimate contact.

The arrangements for a wedding in Cowra were swiftly

made and reception held on the Dole property. Jason Orr, Paul's good friend from the CSIRO, was best man and Louise's cousin Pip was matron of honour. Paul declined the offer of having Eric and Molly included as groomsman and bridesmaid in the wedding party and Louise was pleased to have Paul blamed for any perceived slight.

Like countless other couples before them, they headed for the Gold Coast for a one-week honeymoon.

Fortunately, the lease on Paul's house in Drummoyne was expiring two months after the wedding, so in the meantime they lived with Silvia in Greystanes. This turned out to be a strained period for all concerned and each was relieved when Louise and Paul moved to Drummoyne.

Louise flew to Cowra when she could during her pregnancy to spend time with her parents. The pregnancy was uneventful, and she gave birth to Benjamin in the Westmead Private Hospital. Maggie came to Sydney for the birth. Nick was unavailable due to shearing of his beloved South Suffolks. He considered babies to be woman's work and doubted that he could be of any use in Sydney.

Paul had other ideas for this developing technology involving embryo harvesting, storage and implantation and believed that it could be developed for human use. He had strong feelings about abortion and although did not openly support the movement against abortion or the struggle for women's rights, he had quietly begun to study the complicated nature of embryonic development of humans.

He realised that experimenting with women using embryo implants was not an option to achieve his plan for saving unborn children at this stage, and looked for possible candidates, perhaps using other primates. It did not take long to realise that these would be too expensive and the gestation period too long.

Then he happened upon an article in the *Scientific American* about spiny mice, which unlike other rodents, had a menstrual cycle like that of humans and other primates. Other rodents and most placental mammals had an oestrus cycle.

Paul developed a plan to harvest the embryos that were unwanted by women, freeze and store them for later implantation into the wombs of women who wanted children but for whatever reason were unable to conceive. The main problem was that the embryos would be well advanced as the women would not know of the pregnancy for some time after fertilisation. This was not, of course, going to save all the embryos unwanted by their mothers from being murdered, but it could save some. It required techniques to overcome the rejection of a developing embryo by the surrogate immune system.

Paul first applied to the CSIRO for a research grant to pursue this idea, but it was rejected, he believed, on political grounds. Governments were wary of becoming further involved in the abortion issue than they already were, and government was the main source of CSIRO funding. He was aware of the Antiabortion League organisations in Australia and approached the NSW branch for an interview in which he planned to explain his proposed research. He prepared well for the interview with fund-raising committee.

He realised that he would have to sell them a comprehensive plan and reassure them that his research history with the CSIRO showed that he was a competent person to do such research.

His current work was not corporate, and science alone here was not enough. He needed funding from non-government sources.

The committee listened with interest to his idea of first establishing basic principles using spiny mice. Embryos would be taken from pregnant mice and implanted into surrogates. If successful, the technique might be developed for humans.

The committee members were familiar with the basics of human reproduction, but most were unaware of the detailed knowledge of embryology that Paul was bringing to them.

Many were cognisant of the techniques used in the process of IVF, some of which Paul claimed could be utilised in his proposed research.

The committee thanked him for his presentation and asked him to attend another meeting the following month.

Paul felt that the committee was favourably disposed to his proposal, and this was something that it could support him in.

In the second meeting, he was greeted with enthusiasm as committee members set about asking questions about his research and what he believed would be the cost. The Antiabortion League organisation already had several corporate sponsors which it thought would back this proposal and the committee believed that, given the nature of the work to be done, there could be several other corporates willing to come on board.

Paul was cautiously optimistic about the enthusiasm shown for his idea, as he understood some great ideas remained just that: great ideas, never to be implemented, including the Sarich Orbital Engine and Synrock, both Australian inventions.

To float his great idea, he would need support and he was asked to put to the committee a proposal which would fund his research for the next five years. Paul outlined for them the time and resources of some of the CSIRO research proposals had required and agreed with them that a five-year plan would be realistic.

This was a large undertaking, but the committee members said that if it saved even only some lives, it would be worthwhile. Some members of the committee suggested that government funding could be applied for, but this proposal was voted down – abortion was too divisive an issue for government intervention.

Paul's work with the CSIRO was nearing ten years and he was now considering resignation to take up a position with the Antiabortion League. He had sourced office space in one of the back streets of Rozelle only a short bus ride from his home in Drummoyne to continue his work.

He knew that he would need someone with IVF background and other staff to manage the project, but this was not his expertise and left it to the committee to employ a manager for the business.

He submitted a proposal to cover a salary for him over

the five-year period with possible extension of a further five years.

He ventured his salary should be one hundred and twenty-five thousand Australian dollars per year and would include the basic entitlements for an employee. His entire work history was as a full-time employee, and he was not inclined to operate as a contractor or consultant. This was a large sum for the committee to deal with.

The League employed an accounting firm, Michelson and Mead, to complete a cost analysis for ten years. It did not disclose to Paul the analysis for the project. It stipulated that they would own the intellectual property created during the project and would commit to five years only at this stage and that they could not pay him more than one hundred thousand Australian dollars per annum.

Paul was concerned about the intellectual property generated during the project becoming the property of the Antiabortion League and consulted his accountant, Ted Fisher. Fisher told him to check the situation with a lawyer before he signed any contracts with the League and that one hundred and twenty-five thousand Australian dollars was pie-in-the-sky stuff.

Paul's solicitor confirmed that his accountant was right. The company which paid his salary would own his research findings during his employment.

It was not exactly what he wanted, but he had to accept that compromise would always be an issue in negotiation.

It was a pity that this had not occurred to him in his agreement to marry Louise.

Chapter 19
LOUISE

Louise Dole was born in Cowra, NSW, in 1943. She was schooled in Cowra and, from a young age, looked forward to taking over the family farm. Perhaps she did not realise it at the time, traditionally farms were inherited by sons, not daughters, and Louise had an older brother, Eric. Eric's birth had been a difficult one in which the umbilical cord had been wrapped around his throat, compressed the blood vessels in the cord, and deprived his brain of oxygen for some minutes. Eric survived, but as a result, his brain suffered minor but significant damage.

Although Louise was born four years after Eric, her rapid development soon exceeded Eric's. This did not escape the notice of their parents. Eric was slow to walk, slow to talk and struggled at school.

Eric's father, Nick, was optimistic and hoped that one day Eric would be able to take over the farm, but as Eric progressed through adolescence, this optimism waned. Eric was able to carry out simple tasks when directed to do so, but he could not be relied upon to complete tasks involving a series of steps. Someone needed to be with him to guide him through these steps. Nick was patient, and he provided Eric with the supervision he required.

It became apparent that while Eric struggled with farm chores, Louise mastered them quickly and loved doing them.

Eric finished high school at the end of Year 9, and Nick offered him a job on the farm, which Eric declined, but he did agree to stay on until he secured his driver's licence. He dearly wanted to escape the confines of home and the smallness of Cowra. He wanted to travel, and although Nick and Maggie were reluctant for him to embark on travel by himself, they gave him their blessing and a Holden ute to pursue his dream. He planned to go to Queensland, where he had once heard that it was "beautiful one day, perfect the next".

Maggie cried as he drove out of the farm and Cowra. She and Nick had given him some money and made sure that he was able to access the funds in a bank account that had been set up for him. Eric promised to keep in touch by phone each Sunday night.

And he did.

He did not, however, disclose to his parents that he was not travelling alone. Eric's girlfriend Molly, who was eighteen years old, convinced him to take her with him. She packed a few things into a bag, left a note to her mother indicating she was leaving home and was picked up by Eric early one Friday morning on the corner of College Street and the Midwestern Highway. They headed north towards Queensland, with Eric behind the wheel and Molly with the Gregory's on her lap. They were as happy as two pigs in mud!

The two had a wonderful time. They picked fruit and did other farm work. They put up fences, painted sheds, mustered cattle and did roustabout work with sheep shearers. They slept in haysheds and shearers' sheds and sometimes in the back of the ute. They occasionally came back to Cowra but stayed only briefly. Work was easy to find, and they often had several options to choose from.

During the time of Eric's journey, Louise completed Year 9 and told her parents that she wished to leave school and take up work on their farm.

Nick and Maggie wisely advised that since she had good school grades that she should continue to Year 11, thereby extending her chances to seek non-farm work and perhaps go onto university.

Nick still held onto the chance that Eric would someday return to Cowra, settle down and with the experience of work behind him take over the farm.

The school counsellor agreed, and she advised that Louise continue to Year 11 and suggested that she might then seek tertiary qualifications, perhaps in agriculture.

Louise did not suspect Nick's secretly held hope for Eric to take over the farm, and since she quite liked school agreed to continue her studies.

Louise and Eric were small children on the night of 5 August 1944 when their father was urgently requested to man a Vickers machine gun at the prisoner of war camp just outside Cowra when it was rumoured that there was to be a breakout by Japanese soldiers.

Nick had been born in 1902 and when war broke out in 1914, he was only twelve. After trying unsuccessfully in 1916 to join the army, finally, in early 1918, he was accepted and trained to use machine guns including the Vickers.

Although trained, he never engaged with the enemy and was demobbed in 1919. He was fortunate to be spared the Spanish flu which killed more people worldwide than WW1 but succumbed to a strep infection leading to rheumatic fever in 1923. By 1939 when WW2 broke out, he was not medically fit to enlist, and farmers were encouraged to stay on the land.

Nick arrived at the prison camp compound and was ordered to one of the towers armed with the Vickers. His skill with the gun was instrumental in saving the lives of many of the prison guards and other Australian personnel.

But he was forever haunted by his killing of dozens of young Japanese soldiers, many of whom were unarmed. The other tower with a Vickers was over-run by the Japanese and the operators slain, but not before they disabled the gun by throwing away the bolt mechanism.

Louise completed high school with good enough grades to enter university, but by this time Eric and Molly had returned to Cowra, for Molly was expecting their first child. The nomadic lifestyle was not conducive to rearing a child and Molly wanted to be close to her mother during her pregnancy. Although the strained relationship with her mother prompted her escape from home in Cowra, it had somewhat normalised in her absence. Molly and Eric moved in with her mother, but it quickly became evident that this situation would not last.

They tried next to move in with Nick and Maggie, but this too was fraught.

Eventually, they sought and took a lease on a farm labourer's cottage where they were able to offset part of the rent with farm work.

With her family's support, Louise, who was not sixteen years old, decided to go to Hawkesbury Agricultural College to study agronomy. She managed to stay for two terms before homesickness overwhelmed her and she returned home.

This was a time when student welfare was not widely available, and students were expected to act as adults and just get on with it. Louise was an introverted soul and made friends, but slowly. Her decision to return home was welcomed by Maggie but Louise felt that she had failed.

Nick took a different approach. He did not support or condemn her decision but saw it as an opportunity to continue farming as his health declined. Rheumatic fever had damaged his heart and he secretly withheld it from his family.

Despite several offers for work on his father's property, Eric's need for independence was strong and he continued to find work elsewhere, and it was not just farming work. He was a careful driver; his father had taught him well, so he found work driving delivery trucks as well as tractors and forklifts.

With Eric's clear desire to work elsewhere and Louise's

to work on the farm, Nick reluctantly admitted defeat and accepted the fact that Louise would work with him now, but that hopefully Eric would take over eventually.

In his will at this stage, the farm would be passed onto Eric when he died with the proviso that Maggie could choose to live in the farmhouse as long for as long as she wanted. He was now presented with the dilemma of choosing between his children. If Louise took an essential role in running the farm, how could he not leave the farm in equal share to both?

Although it was not normally the case, Nick sought counsel from Maggie, and they jointly discussed what to do. They first ruled out Maggie taking over – she was a woman. Maggie suggested that both children inherit the farm. Men did farm work, and women helped by cooking, cleaning and having male children to take over the farm. Maggie had done well with this with the exception that Eric was born 'unwhole'. Maggie would have to live with this failure for the rest of her life.

But that was the past and now they needed to face the present.

They decided to address the problem with their solicitor, Wally Taylor. After Nick had explained their situation to him, Wally pointed out that many women had taken over farms while their husbands were away at war and in some cases still did, when their husbands were killed or seriously injured in battle.

'Times have changed, Nick. Many women have shown that they can manage farms as well as men. In my experience, some have done a better job of it than their men.'

This advice was not warmly received by Nick, but he grinned and shook Wally's hand.

'I wonder how many quid that lot of bullshit will cost me?' he thought as he left Wally's office. When he returned home, Maggie asked him 'How did the meeting go?'

'He wasn't much help really. Just let me think this through, Maggie.'

'Okay, love. You know best.'

Nick made no change to his will, and on his death the property he had fashioned on inheriting it from his own father would go to Eric. However, he did not leave Louise out completely. In good years when profits were high, he had invested in shares. These he would pass onto Louise. If he died first, Maggie was eligible for the age pension, she would remain for as long as she wished in their house and be financially supported by Eric and Louise.

For the next few years Eric continued to work in Cowra. He and Molly had a second child and Louise worked on the farm with Nick.

There was an unexpected consequence of Louise's time at Ag College. She had a brief romance with Craig Charles who went on to complete the course. He took up a position of agronomist with the NSW Department of Agriculture and was assigned work in the Central West and Orana region in which Cowra was located. When Craig's work took him to Cowra, he took the opportunity to call in on Louise. Louise proudly introduced him to her parents, and while Maggie was off preparing afternoon tea, Nick, Louise and Craig discussed farming. Craig gave them the benefit of his knowledge of new farming techniques. Nick had already noticed trends that Louise had learned at college and she and Nick had had good results with artificial insemination with their South Suffolk stock.

Craig had an interest in Spider Lamb syndrome which occurs in black-faced sheep such as South Suffolks. Craig was impressed by the progressive attitude that both had for their farm and mentioned that his friend, Paul Arnold, was working at the CSIRO on embryo transfer in sheep. Before going that day, he mentioned to Nick and Louise if they may be interested in supporting such research. They both expressed an interest and agreed to receive a call from Paul Arnold about being involved.

When Craig eventually caught up with Paul, he mentioned the Doles and their progressive approach to farming. Craig gave a very good impression of the South Suffolk property and suggested that it could supply Paul access to a well-run farm already using the best technology. It was also important to Paul since the South Suffolks would provide a more inclusive range of sheep breeds for his research.

Paul contacted the Doles initially by phone and spoke with Nick about his research with embryo transfer. He followed up the conversation and posted a written detailed model of his current research and asked Nick to comment on it. Although Craig had mentioned to Paul that Nick's daughter was seriously active in the farm operation and that she had completed part of the studies of agronomy, the feedback that Paul received, he thought, had come from Nick only, and if he had been told about Louise, he had forgotten.

Paul was impressed by Nick's response, written by Louise, to his research model and he sent Nick a proposal to include the South Suffolks in his research. Nick and Louise considered his proposal and decided that it would be advantageous to be included and they could garner valuable insight into the work of the CSIRO with sheep product development. This breed was a good commercial proposition because of its height, rapid growth to maturity, fine texture of the meat, and a good quality fleece. To protect Australia's position, along with New Zealand, as the largest exporters of lamb and mutton in the world, the CSIRO worked continuously to improve the standard of the Australian sheep industry.

When Paul managed to take the time to personally assess the Dole operation, he was pleasantly surprised to find that Louise was an equal partner to Nick in this enterprise and that he immediately fancied her.

Chapter 20
IRA

Aemon led a double life. To most people, he was a devoted family man, loyal husband to Elaine and loving father to Rachel. He enjoyed time with his mates as well and could often be found at *Sandino's* drinking with his friends. But he did not overdo it. He neither drank to excess, nor was he at *Sandino's* every night. He would have been described as a moderate drinker who was rarely drunk. It was at the times when IRA activities were in the news that he tended to drink too much.

This was indicative of Aemon's darker side.

Aemon was an active member of the IRA. He was not a fighter as such, but he had an important role in the logistical operations of the organisation. As a youth in Belfast, he had been drawn to the IRA as had many of his friends. However, when his older sister, Sophia, was killed by a stray bullet from a nearby gun battle with the British military, he was devastated and vowed to avenge her death. When he was fifteen years old, he volunteered to fight. The IRA officers who heard his request 'to kill every bastard Englishman he could get a hold of' decided that Aemon would be a risk to himself and, more importantly, to the organisation if he was armed. So, he was assured that although the organisation needed no more fighters at present, it did have need of logistics support, and so Aemon found his niche in the IRA.

Initially, Aemon joined the Belfast Brigade which had three battalions and 1200 members. One of these was the Derry battalion. Aemon joined Derry battalion when he moved from Belfast to take a job with O'Sullivan's there. There he boarded with his cousin Alan's family. His position at O'Sullivan's and his liberal access to machinery made him increasingly valuable to the logistics arm of the organisation. Aemon used O'Sullivan's excavator to bury newly smuggled arms, explosives, and other munitions in secret locations near Derry.

O'Sullivan chose not to be aware of this.

Doing this type of work meant that he had knowledge that only Aisling Byrne, battalion commander, and Jimmy O'Connor, his deputy, were privy to. Therefore, Byrne and O'Connor had to trust Aemon. Unbeknown to him, they had tested him on several occasions, and he had not let them down. So it was that Aemon with Byrne and O'Connor became part of a clique in the organisation which took the hard-line view that continual harassment of the British was the only way to achieve the ends of throwing them out of Northern Ireland and the final unification of the Irish nation.

Byrne was a member of Sinn Fein, the political wing of the IRA, and had become frustrated by the attitude of the party to abandon military action in favour of negotiation with the British and their allies in Northern Ireland.

After years of negotiation in the 1990s, a bargain was struck with the IRA, represented by Sinn Fein, and the British Government and all but the Democratic Unionist Party and some minor groups in Northern Ireland to begin peace negotiations. A final ceasefire was declared in July 1997.

The Good Friday Agreement was reached in 1999, but this was rejected by the Real IRA (RIRA) whose members now included Byrne, O'Connor, and Aemon.

Aemon did not discuss his political ideology with Elaine or her family. His attitude to news about the unrest in Ireland when he and Elaine were living with Adele and Jesse formed part of Jesse's disapproval of Aemon. She felt his anger and frustration and it was contrary to her own feeling that Ireland deserved peace rather the bitter war in Northern Ireland.

He spent less time with the RIRA during the period of negotiation. Because of his new role as a husband and father, he less often met with Byrne and O'Connor, but he kept abreast of the ongoing negotiations with the British. The fact that Sinn Fein continued talking to the British was anathema to him. He wanted to continue punishing them for killing Sophia.

By 2000, the RIRA had made many attempts to disrupt the life of Londoners including a bomb placed at Hammersmith Bridge which detonated but failed to cause substantial damage. Three bombs were placed around the Ealing Broadway station, all of which were located by police who neutralised each one.

A more ambitious attempt was made to bomb MI6 headquarters in Vauxhall using a rocket launched by a Russian RPG-22 launcher. The rocket caused only minor damage to the eighth floor of the building. Aemon had been involved in the acquisition of the explosives, the rocket and its launcher, and was pleased the British were still being harassed. But he needed to have more causalities to satisfy his hatred of them.

Rachel was thirteen years old when she began to menstruate and Aemon's feelings of love for his daughter evolved into lust and his dark side became noticeable to Elaine.

She watched as the looks of sensual desire, once reserved for her, were now being directed to Rachel. When Rachel came home one day from school early, looking distressed, Elaine took her aside and asked her 'What's wrong, sweetheart?'

Rachel cried and said between sobs that she had been bleeding between her legs. She had not told her teacher what was wrong, but she asked if she could go home as she was feeling very sick. She was sent to the front office where she received a leave pass to go home.

'You know what this means, don't you?' said Elaine.

Rachel replied grumpily 'Of course I know what it means, I've learned about it at school. It's the beginning of my periods.'

'But do you understand about periods?' said Elaine softly.

'Well, the uterus bleeds once a month and I have to put something on to absorb the blood.' 'I don't want to be picky about this, but do you know why it bleeds?'

'Not exactly.'

'If you didn't understand, why did you not ask?'

Rachel shouted, 'MUM! I was with my friends, and they already know all this stuff. I couldn't show that I didn't understand!'

Elaine took Rachel into her arms and said quietly in her ear 'It's time you did find out. I shall tell you all.'

'Let's do this step by step; you can tell me what you know, and I'll fill in the bits that you don't know or understand.'

'Mum, this could be very embarrassing.'

'Look, it's just you and I here. No sniggering girls, just us, and I am not embarrassed talking about sex. You tell me what you know, and I shall confirm it if it's true and correct it if it's not. How does that sound? said Elaine.

'It could still be very embarrassing,' grumbled Rachel.

'Let's begin where you are now. Your uterus is bleeding because it was getting ready to receive a fertilised egg and that didn't happen. It didn't happen because a fertilised egg means you have had sex with a boy or man. Are we okay so far?'

'Yes, it's okay,' mumbled Rachel, clearly not liking what was coming.

'Let's address the fertilisation bit; you do understand that your eggs are in an organ of yours called...'

'Yes Mum, I know that I have two ovaries and that's where the eggs come from,' interjected Rachel. 'Our teacher showed us diagrams of the female reproductive system as well as the male one. Lucy, the girl sitting in front was making an O with her finger and thumb and was poking another finger through it when the teacher had her back turned. She was giggling and thought she was so funny. Our teacher went through the various parts and showed us how the eggs were released from the ovaries and travelled down a tube – I've forgotten its name. She said that it was in the tube or the uterus that an egg might join with a sperm and cause fertilisation.'

'Well, that's a rather good start. Did she tell you how the sperm got there?'

'Helen put up her hand and asked that, but the whole class laughed loudly, and I could see our teacher Ms Moss was embarrassed. When the class calmed down, Ms Moss showed us the male diagram and told us where the sperm were made and how they got into the female part. Then Helen asked, "How does the sperm get into the vagina from the penis? It looks limp to me". Again, the class laughed so loudly that Ms Moss was unable to be heard.'

'Honey, did you laugh too?

'Of course, I did, I thought it so funny,' giggled Rachel.

'Your teacher had a tough time with you girls. I don't envy her having to do that job.'

She continued 'It's better done in private. Sex is a private thing and best done in the way we are doing it now. I think they do it in schools because some parents don't do it. There are many reasons for this, but I think the main one is that they are too embarrassed and leave it to the school to do.'

'Why didn't you tell me about it?'

'It was a matter of timing. Of course, I planned to tell you, but you have grown up faster than I thought. I apologise for not getting it right. Did Ms Moss show you how the penis changes so that it can enter the vagina?'

'She told us that it became erect but did not have a diagram of that. Helen asked, "Why don't you have a diagram. Don't they make them?" Just then the bell went for the end of the lesson.'

Elaine asked Rachel if she had more questions, but Rachel said, 'That's about all I want to hear now but there are other things I'd like to find out but I don't feel well enough to talk anymore. I think I'll go and lie down. Thanks for helping me with the tampons and the talk, Mum.'

Over the next the next few weeks, they had several conversations about sex. Elaine asked Rachel if she masturbated but Rachel did not know what that meant and said that it was not mentioned in sex education classes at school. When Elaine asked if she had ever put her finger in, Rachel, red with embarrassment had said no, but admitted soon after that she had.

Elaine told her that there was nothing to be embarrassed about and that most girls do it and found it very pleasurable. She told Rachel that she could do it anytime she liked in the privacy of her own bedroom.

Later, they dealt with choosing who to have sex with, the importance of refraining from sex until she was legally old enough to do so, and when she was old enough to make sure that her friend wore a condom. Elaine bought some condoms and showed Rachel how to fit it onto her own dildo. They laughed a lot doing this, and when Elaine offered to buy Rachel her own dildo, Rachel replied 'Yes, please.' Rachel grew into adolescence slowly, becoming at sixteen years old a real stunner.

She went out with many boys during adolescence but always in groups with other boys and girls. She liked many of them but there was no one special.

During adolescence, Elaine noticed Aemon's growing interest in Rachel. One night when Rachel was just fourteen years old, he entered her room after coming home drunk from *Sandino's*. He moved over towards the bed but as he reached out to touch Rachel, Elaine appeared at the door and said quietly 'I don't think you should do that. Why don't you come into bed with me?'

Aemon swung around, startled, and said 'She's my daughter, why can't I touch her?'

'It's no longer appropriate for you to be alone with Rachel. You must resist the feeling you have for her now and be only a father to her,' said Elaine. She led him back to their own bedroom. Aemon slumped onto the bed and fell asleep fully clothed.

The next day Elaine bought a wireless pager with a call button. She explained what had happened the night before and showed Rachel how to use the pager. If Aemon came into her room at night, she was to press the button to alert Elaine.

She told Rachel that fathers sometimes had sexual feelings for their daughters, but it was not allowed. In fact, it was a criminal offence if a father had sex with his daughter. She was sure that Aemon would not do it again. Aemon had apologised to both Elaine and Rachel, adding that he had been drunk and had mistaken Rachel's bedroom for his own.

This was not the only time that Aemon attempted to molest Rachel.

Later incursions into her room were all attempted when he was drunk. Each time he was thwarted. When Rachel was just sixteen years old, Elaine was diagnosed with breast cancer and died a few months later.

Chapter 21
ARTHUR MILLAR

As time went on and the number of clients grew, Rachel and Jesse neared a position where they were making more money than they were spending. They were finally making a profit!

Then came Arthur Millar.

Arthur Millar passed the vetting scheme with Jesse well enough. He was well-dressed and did not appear to be abnormal in any way. In fact, he was charming and quite good looking.

For the vetting, the potential client was asked to take a seat in the reception area of the accommodation he had chosen. Here Jesse would speak to and assess him. Anyone whom she considered 'weird' would be told that the appointment had been cancelled.

Millar went to his room and after a briefing with Jesse. Rachel followed.

The sex they had was pleasant enough and he requested

none of the fantasy options that some clients asked for. After the sex, Millar suddenly produced a small spray bottle and sprayed the contents into Rachel's face. 'What do you think you're doing?' Rachel said, annoyed by this.

'Imagine,' said Millar, 'if that had been concentrated sulphuric acid instead of water?'

As he said this, he produced a short sharp knife and pointing it at Rachel's naked breasts, said 'And imagine that while you are coping with acid on your face, I cut those pretty nipples off your lovely breasts? What sort of future do you think you would have in this trade?'

Rachel was both very annoyed and very frightened. She screamed at him to 'Get out!'

He flicked her fee onto the bed beside her and said, 'You'll hear from me soon about a plan that I have in mind for you.' 'Get out!' she screamed again.

At this point, Jesse entered the room and Millar departed.

Rachel was now sobbing, and Jesse took her into her arms saying, 'What's wrong?'

It took Rachel nearly an hour to regain her composure enough to tell Jesse what had happened. 'Oh my God!' said Jesse 'What can we do about this?'

Since neither could get much sleep that night, they spent the time together assessing what they could do. Rachel's work was illegal, so approaching the police was not an option.

'You will need a "minder",' said Jesse.

'But we don't know what this Millar, if that is his real name, wants,' said Rachel.

'Oh, I think that is clear enough. He is going to offer

you a package to protect you from himself. This is a protection racket.' Jesse's brain had shifted from empathy to accountancy mode as she weighed up the pros and cons of dealing with Millar and running the business.

She said to Rachel, 'Millar is a parasite and as such is committed to taking from the host but not killing it. Despite what we see in movies, these parasites need the hosts to prosper, not die. It ensures the parasite an ongoing income indefinitely. I suspect that Millar is a canny businessman and as such will be willing to negotiate the terms of his proposal. Let's hear what he proposes and decide based on that.'

Two days later, an email was received from Millar outlining his service contract details. The details made no reference to the type of service he was demanding, just the cost (two hundred English pounds) to be paid on the 27th of each month in a manner to be outlined later. He also mentioned how much he had enjoyed her services and that she could expect his friends to take advantage of her too.

This final reference unnerved Rachel anew and she wailed, 'I can't go on with this, Jesse, I have to quit!'

Jesse pondered the situation they were in and finally agreed that to go on was too dangerous. A fresh approach was needed to ensure Rachel's future.

Meanwhile, Rachel continued working with Barnaby.

It was 21 June 21 when Millar turned up at Barnaby's. He wandered in randomly picking up books and putting them down again, then he saw Rachel attending to a customer further back in the shop. As she turned to speak to her customer, she spotted Millar who waved. A feeling of terror arose in her gut, and she felt faint. She was composed enough to accompany her customer to the desk and complete the sale of two books.

As the customer left, she looked over again to Millar who motioned to her to come over to him. Rachel felt sick but she gathered her wits and went over to him.

'What are you doing here?' she hissed at him.

'Why, I am looking for a book,' said Millar 'A book about a young woman who pays her friend to look after her.' 'I'm not paying you anything!' she hissed again. 'Get out of here!'

Just then Barnaby came from the back of the shop and noticing the redness of Rachel's face, he asked 'Can I be of any help here? 'No,' said Rachel 'The gentleman is just leaving.' 'That's right. I am just leaving.'

He handed Rachel a slip of paper on which were written his banking details. 'Thank you for your help, miss, and you, sir,' said Millar smiling at both as he left.

He was just at the door when he turned to Rachel and said, 'Don't forget the 27th', and. 'Was that man harassing you, Rachel?'

'Yes Barnaby, he was. I think that you and I and Jesse need to talk.'

That night, Rachel and Jesse revealed their after dark activities. Barnaby was surprised at what they had engaged in. He thought it was a dangerous occupation and said so. However, that was by the bye now. It had already been done and the circumstances that they were in now needed to be addressed quickly. There was no point in discussing what should or should not have been done in the past. They needed to deal with the issue at hand: Millar!

Arthur Millar had not always been in the protection racket business. He had begun in a career of insurance salesman in Belfast and had moved from there onto insurance claims assessment. He noticed that the system of insurance claims lent itself to possible fraud. He decided that he could possibly make more money than his meagre salary at the insurance company by going into private consultancy. He took leave from his work to 'test the waters' to see if he could succeed in the new venture and if not, return to boring assessments.

He researched the areas near Derry and decided on Newbuildings, a large village 3 km south of Derry, as a possible target. He left his flat in Belfast and stayed in Derry for two days. He travelled to Newbuildings to check possible businesses that he could burn down. He decided on two – a hairdressing salon and a cafe. For these two premises he could gather intelligence and planned to first burn down the cafe and about three months later, the hairdresser. He returned to work in Belfast.

It was a wintry Sunday night when Millar approached the rear of the cafe. There was no CCTV here, and he avoided other cameras around the shop. He wore a dark overcoat and woollen cap. He had parked his hire car outside the town limits to avoid detection and walked to his target. When it was impossible to avoid CCTV, he put on his clown mask.

There was a large gas cylinder at the rear of the cafe, and he carefully collected combustible materials in the yard and placed them against the gas cylinder. He set it alight and swiftly left the area taking the same precautions that he had on his approach.

Millar had never done anything like this before and was not certain that it would cause any damage at all to the building. He was heartened however, when as he reached his car, a mighty boom came from behind him.

The gas bottle had exploded.

He lit a match and set the clown mask on fire before dropping it to the ground.

Millar drove back to Belfast, making sure that he did not speed or in any way attract the attention of police.

News of the explosion was covered by the national news services with speculation that it was an IRA job. But after days of waiting for the IRA to claim it for their own, police concluded that it was arson and were trying to locate any suspects that may have had a grudge on the cafe owner. Officers from the anti-terrorism squad had quickly dismissed the IRA theory due to the very amateurish attempt to blow up the building.

As it turned out, there were several suspects, all who had issues with Marcus Thomson, the cafe owner. Police interviewed six possible suspects including Thomson's wife, but each could account for their presence at other locations on the night. Police published poor CCTV images of the suspect with no result and the investigation stalled.

Some weeks after the cafe had been torched, Millar went back to Newbuildings and spoke to several businesspeople. He identified himself as a private detective and former military intelligence officer. He told them that he could find out who was responsible for the fire at the cafe and that he could ensure that the person could be persuaded not to torch their properties. He gave each an assurance that their property would be safe if they paid him a monthly fee of two hundred pounds. He gave each a week to consider his offer and gave each the number of a pay-as-you-go phone and encouraged them to call. He warned that if they did not contact him, the arsonist could strike within days.

After Millar had departed, the newsagent Clyde Palmer contacted police in Derry. He gave a statement and handed over Millar's card for forensic analysis. Examination of the card showed evidence of Palmer's fingerprints and DNA only. Millar had been careful to handle the cards only when wearing gloves.

Police arranged for each shop owner approached by Millar to come to Derry and help to create an artist's impression of the suspect's face. It was a good facsimile of Millar's face and brought many reported sightings but not of Millar. This news frightened Millar and he decided that his arson protection racket was just too dangerous and began to consider other less hazardous ways of making money.

Inspiration came to him while reading the *Belfast Chronicle*. At the back in the Services section were several advertisements for sex. He decided to try one out. The girl was very young; Millar guessed her to be barely eighteen or so. Could he offer her his protection for a reasonable amount?

He thought not. The girl charged too little, and the service was provided in her bedroom when her parents were absent from the house. No, he needed a target in the high range – a prostitute who operated in hotel rooms and provided great sex for big money. These women were sole traders without the protection provided by a brothel and as such could be vulnerable to his scheme.

He had read recently that the rate of acid attacks in the UK was among the highest in the world. This, he thought, was the way. All he had to do was threaten with acid. The woman would be with him alone in a hotel room and he could threaten her with an acid attack, not by him directly, but by any new client she may have. She would never know if her next client would splash acid in her face. Millar would offer her an assurance that it would not happen for a fee of, say two hundred pounds per month. Rachel was Millar's first victim.

Rachel was not alone in being targeted by Millar. He set about adding numerous possible protection clients to his list. The list was quite lengthy.

Millar had no intention of throwing acid in anyone's face. He calculated that while not all would submit to his threats of disfigurement, there would be enough to make this enterprise work.

Chapter 22
MILLAR'S FUTURE

Millar was unaware of the danger he was putting himself in with this new enterprise. He had little idea about how the criminal world operated. He had no criminal record himself, but he was aware that in his own work criminals were active. These individuals were trying to make money from fraudulent claims on their insurance policies. Most of these were not part of any criminal organisation, although Millar was aware of some multiple offenders who had developed systems to enhance their chances of succeeding in fraud.

So, just as he had blundered into the fire protection racket and failed, avoiding apprehension by authorities, he now blundered into a very dangerous game dominated by organised crime.

Rachel was only one of a dozen prostitutes that Millar threatened with disfigurement and in doing so exposed himself unwittingly to some very dangerous people.

After threatening 'Lolita' at a hotel room in the Angel's Dust Hotel just outside of Belfast, he was attacked by two large men wearing balaclavas A hood was placed over his head, and he was bundled into a van and driven to the Belfast Harbour shipping container area. Here in a small office, he was beaten severely by the two men. Consequently, he gave up his phone, his wallet, his address, his keys, his computer access code and his banking details. They placed the hood back over his head. He heard the van start up outside. The only sound he could hear now was water lapping up against the piers and the scuffing of the shoes as one of his captors moved about in the office.

'Please, I've given you all you wanted. Can't you just let me go? I don't know who you are or what you look like. I won't say anything to the police. Please just let me go.' The response was another heavy blow to his face, followed by 'Shaddup!'

About an hour later the van returned. The driver came into the office and Millar heard them talking.

He heard 'Did you get it all?' and 'Sure did, and I have his computer as well.' 'Great.'

After a few moments of silence, he felt hands undoing the buttons on his shirt, then a long very sharp blade was expertly driven between his fourth and fifth ribs into his left ventricle. He died within two minutes. He was bundled up into a large canvas bag together with some heavy chain and carried to a waiting boat.

It was already dark when the boat sped out of the harbour unnoticed. About three miles offshore the bag with Millar and the chains was thrown overboard.

He was never seen again.

First to notice Millar's absence was his supervisor at Phoenix Insurance, Don Davidson, who called Millar's phone after he had failed to turn up at work the day after his disappearance, a Wednesday. The call rang out and went to voicemail.

When the same happened on Friday, Millar's boss was not worried – he was pissed off. When Millar failed to turn up for work on Monday and his phone was still going to voicemail, Davidson stopped making caustic remarks to the voicemail and began to feel worried again. He decided to go to Millar's flat to see if he was okay. No one responded to his knock, so he tried the next-door neighbour's door. A Mrs Flynn answered the door and when asked said that she had not heard Millar in his flat since Wednesday night. She said that he had come home about 10 pm and after a few minutes went out again. She had not heard him come back. Davidson thought about breaking a window to gain entry but decided to call police instead.

The weekend had been difficult for the Belfast Police, and they were slow to respond to Davidson's request to come to the flat. When an officer did come, he told Davidson that he could do nothing. He was not going to damage private property based on the occupant not turning up for work for three days.

Davidson was now fuming again and when he returned to his office, he asked his secretary to find a contact number of a next of kin for Millar in his personnel file. The contact was Millar's mother.

He rang Eileen Millar and asked if she had heard from her son. She told him that Millar had failed to call her as he usually did on Sunday, and she was worried that he had not responded to her calls to him.

Davidson, armed with this new intelligence rang Belfast Police, Lisburn Road division, and was put through to Sergeant Margaret O'Reilly in Missing Persons. He told O'Reilly what he knew and gave her Eileen Millar's contact details. O'Reilly told both Davidson and Eileen that it was not unusual for people to be missing for a few days and told them to contact her again if Millar had not turned up by Wednesday.

Millar did not turn up on Wednesday, nor did he return his mother's calls, and a tearful Eileen Millar contacted O'Reilly again. She turned up at Millar's flat with a constable later that day and after some loud knocking and yelling, O'Reilly instructed the constable to force the door open.

They found a tidy flat without any signs of a struggle. They noted that a computer desk did not house a computer. The wardrobe contained a range of clothes and an empty suitcase. They made further notes about the appearance of the flat and took several photos.

O'Reilly informed Eileen and Davidson that Millar would now be deemed a missing person. Just before O'Reilly put down the phone, she asked Davidson how Millar got to work each day. Davidson said that Millar drove a Ford Fiesta. O'Reilly asked if Davidson had a number for it because there was no Fiesta at the flat.

Davidson did not know the number but thought that it may be on Millar's personnel file. He promised to check and ring back. Davidson rang back within minutes, gave O'Reilly the number, and added that the vehicle was red. They now had a missing person and a missing car.

O'Reilly visited Phoenix Insurance to question Davidson and others in the office about Millar. She learned that Millar was a prompt and reliable in his work and that had recently taken some days off but could offer no details about Millar's whereabouts during that time. She questioned the other people in the office but found that Millar had not revealed his plans for his days off with any of them.

She next questioned Millar's mother about her son's social and family life. There were no other living relatives, and he did not inform his mother about relationships he may be having or have had.

It was a puzzle. O'Reilly saw little she could go on with and so she attended to other cases of missing persons. A clue came her way a week later when the Police computer matched her Millar file with a complaint by the manager of the Angel's Dust Hotel that a red Ford Fiesta had been taking up a car parking space outside his premises for over a week and that he wanted it moved. The number matched Millar's car.

O'Reilly got back on the case. She questioned the manager and showed him a recent photo of Millar supplied by Eileen. The manager said that he could not recall the person in the photo booking a room at the hotel recently. He offered to show the photo to other staff who might remember him and report to O'Reilly if any of them recognised Millar.

She arranged for the Fiesta to be brought back to the station for examination by Forensics. The tests revealed some recent receipts for accommodation in Derry. She followed these up but gained nothing further that they did not know already but they had at least found Millar's car. She reviewed her notes and noticed that neither Millar's phone nor his wallet had been accounted for. She rang Davidson and told him the news. She was about to ring off when a thought came. 'How was Millar paid his salary?' she asked Davidson.

'All our staff salaries are paid directly into their nominated bank account,' he replied. 'Is it possible to send his banking details to me?' she said.

'I'd have to ask the legal department if I am allowed to do that. I'll get onto them now and get back to you.'

'It's important. If we have his banking details, we can see if he has a credit card as well. That would allow us to track his movements by the transactions made since his disappearance,' she emphasised.

'Legal tells me that we would have to get Mrs Millar's permission to do that. Can you manage that?'

'I'm onto it,' she said and hung up.

Mrs Millar was pleased to give her permission. She just wanted to find her son. Once O'Reilly had the credit card details, she could track his movements. Records showed that the last transaction was made on the night of Millar's disappearance and that the balance of the account was now zero. There had been no further transactions since the night of his disappearance. The transaction previous was interesting though. It was for seventy pounds paid to the Angel's Dust Hotel.

O'Reilly thought, '*This was awfully bad news. This fellow is dead. Someone has murdered him, milked his bank account, and probably disposed of the body.*'

But she wondered why an insurance processor would be disappeared and killed.

She was disinclined to tell Davidson and Mrs Millar of her opinion and reassured them that the investigation would go on. She would continue to search for Millar.

She was surprised when she received a call from Eric Simms, the night manager at the Angel's Dust Hotel. Simms told O'Reilly that he recognised Millar. He added that a reservation had been made for that night. The date matched that of Millar's disappearance.

'Did Millar book the room?' asked O'Reilly. 'No,' said Simms, 'but he did pay for it.'

Simms added, 'It may interest you to know that it was booked for short-term occupancy. This was common practice for rooms booked for prostitutes. That may be significant to your investigation.'

This was sounding like an organised crime prostitution racket.

She contacted the Belfast Tactical Response Group (TRG) and briefed them on the Millar case. The TRG took over the case from there, but promised O'Reilly that they would keep her 'up to speed' as the case progressed.

Meanwhile, frantic steps were being taken to organise Rachel's escape from Millar, but unbeknown to those involved, Millar was no longer a threat.

Chapter 23
ESCAPE TO AUSTRALIA

Edgar Rice Burroughs was not a writer. In his Derry shop he repaired gearboxes and differentials. He had two sons who worked in the shop, Fergus, and Alan. The business had been set up in 1951 by Edgar's father, Ainsley Burroughs, who had married Iris Dawe. Iris was a prolific reader of Edgar Rice Burroughs. She could not believe her luck, not only to marry Ainsley, but to have a son she could call Edgar Rice Burroughs.

Edgar married Emily Strachan in 1981 and Fergus was born in 1982, followed by Alan in 1983. After he had completed his apprenticeship in motor mechanics, Fergus applied to the Australian Government to migrate there.

He had been entranced with Australia since completing a project on the Great Barrier Reef in Year 6. His work was judged the best in class and when his award was made, he announced, 'I am going to live there one day!'

Several in his class openly doubted that he could fulfil

his wish, but Fergus was determined.

He was a great fan of Steve Irwin, the Crocodile Hunter, and was in Australia when his hero died from the barb of a stingray off Hamilton Island in September 2006.

His skill was in short supply in Australia, and he was readily accepted as an immigrant. Fergus promptly found work at a motor mechanic business in Hexham, near Newcastle, eventually buying it from his boss who was nearing retirement. It was close by the Hunter River where he found Dawn Drummond, his future wife, and a love of jet skiing.

After buying a basic model ski, he graduated to bigger more powerful skis and then entered jet ski racing.

Fergus won several important races, and his name became well known in the sport, so much so that he sold the gearbox and differential business and set up a jet ski sale and service business in Nobbys Beach in Newcastle. This was an inspired decision. Nobbys was *the* place to surf and enjoy jet skiing in Newcastle. The business for jet skis was growing fast. Not only were young people with disposable incomes buying jet skis, so were surf lifesaving clubs.

However, his dream was to one day move to Queensland. So, he decided to try his luck in the Brisbane market over the border in Brisbane. He leased a shop in Sandgate and sold the business at Nobbys.

It was courageous decision, because other jet ski businesses were already established in Brisbane, but he wanted to live in Queensland. He continued to compete in jet ski races and won many more races than he lost.

He was at home celebrating his latest victory when he received a phone call from Derry. It was his brother, Alan. Could Fergus help a girl in trouble?

'Have you got some girl pregnant?' said Fergus.

'Of course not, Jesse Ryan is our accountant and a friend. The girl is Jesse's niece, Rachel,' said Alan.

Fergus replied that he could not help if she were pregnant.

'No, she's not pregnant, but she needs help. She's flying to Brisbane, and we'd like you to meet her and help get her to her accommodation there,' said Alan.

The story about the threats to Rachel by Millar were revealed, with the exception that she was a prostitute, and a plea was made to him to look after her when she arrived in Australia.

Could he perhaps find her a job? Her experience working for Barnaby was outlined and her good looks were emphasised.

'Where is she going to stay?'

'A place called the Backpacker Central.'

'Okay send me her flight details.'

Fergus offered to meet Rachel, speak with her, and help if he could. He could not guarantee that he could find her a job, but he would try to help.

Fergus was a bit puzzled by the lack of police involvement on this issue but decided to leave that until he met Rachel.

There was a lot to be done to arrange Rachel's flight to Australia. Jesse and Barnaby handled her safety.

Jesse watched over her at home and accompanied her to work where Barnaby took over for the day. It was necessary to keep both Millar and Aemon away from her.

Millar was not seen but they assumed that he could take advantage of any lapse in security, so this was a tense time.

And Rachel had no passport.

This was a serious drawback given the urgency of the situation and it became more complicated when they realised that it would take up to six weeks to get the passport.

Jesse remembered that a friend had to get a passport quickly and found that it was possible to get one in a week. But since Rachel had been born after 1 January 1983, they would also have to produce a copy of her father's or mother's birth certificate as well as her own.

Aemon, of course, was not pleased to be asked to cooperate in this, but with the weight of evidence about his behaviour with Rachel so great, he caved in and handed over Rachel's and his birth certificates. With help from Jesse and Barnaby, Rachel scraped up enough money to pay for her passport and a one-way flight to Brisbane where Fergus promised to meet her.

Her flight was arduous. She had never spent so much time sitting and a small child some rows behind was distressed and cried much of the time, causing angst among her fellow passengers. Her flight on Virgin included stops at Heathrow, Dubai and Singapore and took a total of twenty-eight hours.

Fergus and his wife Dawn were there to meet her, Fergus in T-shirt, shorts and thongs, and Dawn in T-shirt, jeans and runners.

It was stiflingly hot. Rachel had never felt such heat. She was grateful that they had an air-conditioned car. The drive along the airport link road took about thirty minutes, with frequent stopping. It meant, though, that Rachel could take in one part of the large metropolis that was Brisbane. Most of the pedestrians were dressed similarly to Fergus and Dawn and many were barefooted.

She had booked in at the Backpacker Central Hostel for two weeks while she looked for work. Fergus and Dawn gave Rachel a contact phone number and waited with her during her booking in at the Backpacker Central. Once she was in her room and settled, they said goodbye, realising that she would need to rest after her long trip.

Barnaby had written Rachel an excellent reference for her work with him and her first foray into the Brisbane jobs market was to visit several bookshops in the city.

Brisbane was by far the biggest city Rachel had ever been in. Belfast, the biggest city in Northern Ireland had a population of about 250,000 people. Brisbane had more than two million people. Public transport was good, and she was able to visit several of the ten shops on her list.

She struck it lucky at Blake Books next to the Gnocchi Italian restaurant on Givan Terrace. The owner, Lola Smythe, loved Rachel's accent and was impressed with Barnaby's reference. She gave Rachel a month's trial beginning the next day.

She returned to Backpacker Central immediately and called Jesse to tell her the good news. In her haste to call, she forgot about time zone differences and Jesse had to answer the phone at 1 am. She did not complain. She was so delighted that Rachel was off to such a great start.

Lola Smythe had one other employee, Amelia Haworth, who had moved from Cairns to Brisbane to escape her violent husband. She was an attractive brunette with deep-set brown eyes. She had not revealed the violence of her past to Lola or Rachel nor her urgent need to establish herself by finding more satisfying and better paid work than as an assistant in a bookshop.

She had wanted to become an invisible entity of the city – to see but not be seen for protection against being located by her husband, Adrian.

She arranged a change of phone number with her service provider and offered the number to no one.

She blocked caller ID when making calls; of which there were few.

Amelia knew that Adrian would not be taking her break away well. She also he was clever enough to find her if she left clues for him.

They had friends because of their work. Adrian worked at an advertising agency and Amelia in medical administration. Because they had decided to be childless until they had established a home there were no friends because of childcare or school.

This decision meant that a break from Adrian was less painful for her. She left him to sort out the rental property that they had shared in Edge Hill and at three hundred and twenty dollars per week, he could afford it. She had no immediate plans to divorce Adrian. She had yet no new man in her life and at age twenty-eight, she was in no hurry. She did wonder what she had missed in their courting phase that left her open to physical abuse, and, of course, there was that financial control that should have alerted her.

She would not let that happen again.

Amelia was a competent tennis player and had enjoyed tennis competition in Cairns and found quite by accident that she was living close to the Roy Emerson tennis centre in nearby Milton. She bought a racquet and some suitable clothes and joined up for a mixed social on a Friday night.

Tennis is the best sport because men and women can compete in mixed doubles. One could do it with golf and lawn bowls, of course, but she had no interest in those sports. There were six courts at the complex and facilities for social mixing between and after games. There were several young men players and she soon found herself being asked for dates. She was choosy. While she did accept some men who did end up in her bed, she did not sleep with all of them. When the sex was over, they were sent home and she only ever had two dates with any one of men. After that, she reasoned that they believed they owned you and she was not ready to be owned. Before she dated any of the men, she took the time to watch them playing and otherwise interacting with the women, trying to gather clues for suppressed violence. Some she observed did show some signs. One married couple played on Friday nights. Amelia noticed that when they were playing against each other, the man made every effort to hit the ball directly at his wife.

In one game when they were playing against each other, the woman had a partner with a very weak serve. As he served his terribly slow second serve, her husband slammed it straight at her at the net. However, just as he did so, she squealed and ran off the court. Many of the spectators thought it was as funny.

Amelia made a mental note not to date men who played like that.

She had found accommodation within the city, but she was paying too much for the privilege. She had the cash she had extracted from her husband and had decided that he would not find her. She used no credit cards and paid for everything with cash even if it was becoming an easier way to pay using cards. The felt it had become more difficult and sometimes inconvenient to use cash.

However, the high-rent and low-wage situation was causing her to resort to use up her savings for living expenses. She had two ways to remedy the situation: get a better paid job and/or find someone to share the rent.

She was in this frame of mind when Rachel appeared at Blake Books. Rachel had replaced Sarah, an unfortunate looking girl who had left Brisbane to care for her ailing mother in Nambour, a situation she had only escaped two years before. Her father had since died, and reluctantly Sarah returned to Nambour to look after her mother.

Amelia and Sarah had not been close, certainly not close enough to invite her to share accommodation, but she did feel for Sarah as she tended her resignation to Lola to head north back to Nambour. Meanwhile, for Rachel, the heady days of life at Backpacker Central were beginning to wear thin and she began to concern herself with finding a more stable place to live.

She had had numerous offers for sex at the Backpacker Central but had declined them. She was especially regretful to turn down an achingly beautiful Iranian man whom she could have taken to her room and ripped off his clothes. No, the lack of personal privacy there made her turn down the offers. Another problem for Rachel was the frequent use of party drugs among the backpackers. She was not averse to smoking a joint or two, but cocaine, heroin and ecstasy were rife there, and that was a worry. There was little violence there because of drugs. The only incident she personally witnessed was when a young Scottish woman under the influence of ecstasy attacked her cousin with a butter knife. He had not suffered serious injury, but it took three men to disarm and hold her down until police and paramedics arrived.

Some of the Backpacker Central residents had moved on to shared accommodation situations, and Rachel began looking for similar situations. She found and applied for a property in Mount Gravatt. It was a four-bedroom house with two bathrooms. She would be sharing with three other young women at a rent she could just afford. She went to the house on the following Sunday.

It was with some anxiety that she faced an interview, not with the property owner, but with the three other young women who rented the house. Two of the women seemed pleased at the notion of having Rachel as a housemate but the third, a Brit called Felicity, was less than willing. Felicity left the meeting early claiming that she had another date, mumbling 'bloody Irish' and left it to Margie and Sue to make the decision.

'Don't worry about Felicity,' they said, 'she can be up herself sometimes.'

Margie and Sue agreed to have Rachel stay and she moved in on the following Saturday.

Rachel soon found that living with three women had its drawbacks. After some difficult issues with Felicity, she began looking again perhaps with male housemates.

It was about this time when Amelia suggested something that could suit them both.

Rachel and Amelia did not share a break together but there were times during the day when trade was slow that presented them with time for conversation.

Amelia asked Rachel how her accommodation was working out and when Rachel indicated that she was on the lookout for an alternative, she offered to share accommodation with her.

Chapter 24
AMELIA

Sunday came and Rachel made her way to Hayward Street, Paddington by bus and some small distance on foot. On her way, she passed Blake Books and realised that the apartment would not be far from work. She took this as a good sign. She had also purchased a posy of flowers for Amelia at Roma Street station.

She could see as she approached the apartment that it was an older building and showing its age. It needed painting, the front garden was a mess, and the fence was broken in several places. But the lawn had been mowed.

There were two front doors, and she chose to ring the buzzer on the left as instructed by Amelia. Amelia appeared at the door in seconds. She had seen Rachel approach from the upstairs window. She was delighted to receive the posy and showed Rachel upstairs from the small entrance to her apartment.

Rachel did not know what to expect but she was impressed

by the orderliness of the living room as they emerged from the stairs. Amelia offered coffee which she quickly prepared in the kitchen. It was served in

pleasantly fine china mugs. The apartment was furnished which pleased Rachel for she had no furniture of her own.

The furniture was old, dated and a bit worn. However, it had a clean, fresh look. Amelia had placed several throws over the leather lounge suite, mid-blue in colour, to cover worn sections. There were two armchairs over which she had placed burnt-orange throws to complement the blue of the sofa.

Amelia had chosen interesting pieces to enhance the lounge area. There was a small dining table with two

wooden chairs and a small wooden coffee table with a Laminex top. Both were topped with stylised fish ornaments. A colourful, new-looking, modern rug was placed under the coffee table. There was a large electric radiant heater under the window. A narrow wooden bookshelf rose to half ceiling height, with figurines reflecting a nautical look outnumbering the books.

After they had finished their drinks, Rachel was given a tour of the apartment. There were two bedrooms, both with double beds, a dated but functional kitchen, one bathroom with a shower-over-bath arrangement and a separate toilet. The shower curtain looked new, featuring fish, starfish, and shells – perhaps a replacement made by a fastidious Amelia.

There was no separate laundry and, in its place, a front-loader washing machine was set up in the kitchen.

As they walked around the apartment Rachel realised that Amelia appeared to be serious about 'order'.

She would learn soon enough that Amelia was obsessed about order. Rachel was assigned space in the

refrigerator and shelves in the kitchen cupboards and Amelia informed Rachel that it would be important that they agree on schedules for cooking, showering and laundry times.

All wet areas had linoleum floor covers and all other rooms were carpeted. The carpet was new but of a

cheap and uninspiring blue material which Rachel thought was more suitable for shop ware. When they had

completed the tour of the apartment, they returned to the living room to discuss the possibility of

Rachel joining Amelia.

The apartment was not a great place to live but its advantages – room of her own, reasonable rent, proximity to work, internet access and even sheets on her bed – seemed to outweigh the disadvantages of a shared bathroom, kitchen, toilet, and laundry, together with limited refrigerator space. It was more expensive. She could only just afford it, but it was as private as accommodation could be, given her present accommodation was with three other young women.

Amelia further explained that the owners of the apartment, Marinella and Dariush, lived in the apartment

downstairs. They were a young couple who had bought the property as an investment and a first step in owning their own home and bring up a family.

Marinella, who was of Greek descent, worked as a dentist's receptionist and Dariush, whose parents were Iranian immigrants, was a motor mechanic. Amelia was on good terms with them, and they were cooperative, helpful landlords. They offered a private rental agreement with no agent involved so they could offer it at a lower price.

On balance, Rachel thought that the apartment was reasonable and that for now she could tolerate living

with Amelia. Amelia explained that she had been so thankful to find this place when she moved from Cairns about a year before. She had been an office manager in a large medical practice there and moved to Brisbane because of her violent husband, Simon.

Simon had a good job in advertising that paid well and had regular hours. When they were first married, they had agreed that they would each contribute twenty percent of their salaries to a special account in Simon's name to save for a home of their own. After two years, Amelia asked for access to the account that Simon managed. The account was in his name only and Simon was reluctant to give her access and put her off with assurances that all was well. Amelia was beginning to wonder why she had allowed this to happen in the first place. She became anxious about his reluctance to give her access to the account and one Friday night demanded access.

His refusal led to an argument that escalated into a fight in which Amelia sustained a broken wrist and spent a night in hospital. The treating doctor was suspicious of the story that Simon told of Amelia's injury and questioned Amelia privately about it while she was being transported to X-ray. Her account did not match Simon's and she encouraged her to involve the police. She was reluctant to do this given

Simon's extreme remorse, but she warned him that she would involve police if he ever assaulted her again.

Simon was full of contrition and vowed never to injure her again.

Amelia talked to her friends about the issue, and they all agreed that she should have access to the account, but counselled Amelia not to broach the subject for a month or two. After three months her wrist was fine and Simon had been very attentive, so she decided to ask for access to the account again. Simon told her that she did not need to see the account; that all was well. However, this time, Amelia had calculated that the account should have about twenty-seven thousand dollars in it, and again pressed him for access. Simon challenged her lack of trust in him and turned the argument back onto her. She pressed ahead, demanding access. He pressed back challenging her lack of trust in him. The argument again escalated into a fight and ended when Simon punched Amelia in the face rending her unconscious and with a broken jaw.

He panicked when he could not revive her but did check to see if she was breathing and that she had a pulse. She was breathing and she did have a pulse, but still he could not get a response from her when he begged for her forgiveness.

Finally, he realised that Amelia needed an ambulance and rang ooo. When the paramedics arrived, Simon claimed that Amelia had fallen and hit her face on the corner of the heavy marble coffee table in the living room. The paramedics had seen scenes like this multiple times, and both realised that this was yet another example of domestic violence.

Simon followed the ambulance which took Amelia to the emergency department at the local hospital. He was with her, still unconscious, when she was assessed by a neurologist, who said that this was a serious case of concussion and she scheduled Amelia for a CT scan immediately.

The scan showed evidence of her brain bouncing around in her skull and was more consistent with a punch than the fall described by Simon. Amelia remained unconscious and could not verify Simon's account of the incident. A review of Amelia's admissions to hospital revealed the prior wrist injury and prompted the neurologist to notify police.

Surgeons operated on Amelia that night to repair her fractured jaw.

However, the neurologist was genuinely concerned that she had not regained consciousness prior to or after the operation. It suggested to her that there could be significant brain damage and that Amelia may need extensive treatment to restore possible loss of cognitive function.

Amelia did not regain consciousness until the next day and police would not come until she could speak with them. Simon remained with Amelia through the night and until she awoke. She recognised him but was

otherwise confused to find herself in hospital and could not speak.

Amelia's doctor notified police that she was able to be interviewed at about 10 am, but since she could not speak, they would have to be satisfied with written notes. The neurologist insisted that she be present during the interview.

They arrived at 12.15 pm to take her statement. Simon was

still with her pleading with her to substantiate his account of the incident, but by now she was lucid. She would not reveal her intentions about the police and left him worrying what she would tell them.

When the police did arrive, Amelia related that her recollection of the incident with written notes.

She claimed it was too difficult to speak also that she was still hazy about the incident. She confirmed that she should be able to respond to their questions with handwritten notes. She wrote asking if they would give her more time to clearly recall the incident.

As soon as the police had departed, she motioned Simon to come close. She wrote an instruction for him to call up the account details on his smart phone. He refused.

She wrote that unless he did, she would reveal what had really happened and have him charged with

assault. Again, he tried to bargain with her, claiming that she did not trust him.

She agreed with him. She did not trust him, but he could trust her to tell the truth to the police.

Finally, he produced his phone and brought up the statement of transactions over the last two years. The total was $12,679. She told him to transfer twelve thousand dollars into her personal account. Simon refused claiming that these funds were joint savings towards saving for a house. Amelia pointed out several withdrawals, some as much as four hundred dollars. Why would there be any withdrawals from this account at all? He pointed out that there were also extra deposits made by him over and above their salary deposits. Again, the question arose: why would this happen?

The discussion continued, but Simon could not explain the withdrawals, the deposits, or the fact that they did not have nearly twenty-seven thousand dollars.

Amelia wrote 'Okay, I shall tell the police that you punched me last night and I shall also press charges on you for assault. Remember that the last time I ended up in hospital was due to you. That will not look good when I tell them that you were responsible for that as well.'

Simon still refused but by the next day when the police were due to return to take Amelia's statement, he

was pleading with her to see reason and support his version of the incident. 'What good would it do them if he ended up in jail? How could they save for a home then?'

Amelia's nurse came to tell her that the police were on the way to her ward to take her statement. Hearing

this, Simon finally relented and transferred twelve thousand dollars to Amelia's account.

When the police came Amelia recalled that she had tripped on their rug and had fallen onto the coffee table. She was so sorry to have wasted the time of the police, but the fall had made her very confused for a while. But it was now clear that it was just an accident.

Both police attending were unhappy with her claim and after asking Simon to vacate the room they told

Amelia that she ought to tell the truth. It was evident to them and the medical staff that she had been punched by her husband and had sustained a serious injury. And experience told them that if women allowed husbands to get away with it, it would happen again, sometimes with fatal results.

As they were about to go, she wrote, 'I know you are right, but I am dealing with this myself.' When they left, Simon returned and was so grateful to hear that he was not to be charged and he promised never, never to hurt her again.

Amelia wrote, 'I know you are so sorry, and I believe you will never hurt me again.'

By now Amelia was exhausted and her jaw ached. She had two small plates screwed into her jaw to hold

the fracture in place and she now needed pain killers and rest. She was responding well to the treatment for her broken jaw and for the serious concussion she had sustained. The oral surgeon who had managed her operation was pleased that she was able to manage to eat very soft foods and that judged that she would be able to speak in a few days.

A speech pathologist visited each day to check on her progress. A neurologist assessed her

cognitive state with simple tests of memory and understanding to appraise her recovery from the concussion.

She confirmed that it was serious, and that Amelia would take some time to recover. She had been prescribed pain relief and antibiotics each day, and she had suffered no side effects.

Simon visited each day after work and Amelia gradually encouraged him to talk about the savings that had gone missing. He was reluctant at first, but eventually admitted that he regularly gambled online. He vowed that he would win back the money as he was becoming more experienced and was winning more often.

Amelia was alarmed at this and pleaded with him to stop gambling. Simon laughed at this suggestion asking, 'How else will I get the money back?'

At this point, Amelia decided that the only solution was to completely break away from him and start a

new life elsewhere.

Simon told Amelia that he and two friends planned to fly down to Bathurst for the Bathurst 500 motor race Friday night, but he would be back to see her immediately afterwards. He had done this the previous year so she knew that he would not be back until Tuesday. It was time to move! She booked a seat on the train, *Spirit of Queensland* for Brisbane on Saturday.

She asked Simon to bring in a few items from their unit into the hospital so that she could enjoy some time outside in the fresh air. He brought in a couple of dresses, some shoes, underclothes and jeans. She thanked him and with as a big smile as she could manage and told him she hoped he enjoyed his time at the '500'.

She did not say that she would not be there when he returned and that there would be no forwarding address left at the hospital. She was going to leave many personal items behind, but she reasoned that her safety was more important. However, it was with great sadness that she was leaving friends behind, people with whom she could no longer meet with in case her whereabouts were revealed to Simon.

She was feeling elated that her escape plans were working

out so well. All she had to do now was book a taxi to go to her bank on Thursday, advise them beforehand that she planned to withdraw twelve thousand dollars in cash at 11 am, come back to hospital and have another taxi booked to take her to the Cairns railway station in time for her to catch the 8.30 am train to Brisbane on Saturday,

She did not check out of the hospital.

On Friday she took a taxi home and packed for her escape.

She relaxed with the idea that she would just go to a hospital in Brisbane when she arrived. It would be just 'too easy'. There were other critical issues that she needed to resolve in Cairns.

Her job at the medical centre was precious and she hated letting them down but hoped that they would

understand when she told them of her decision to flee but did not say where. Many of her colleagues were

aware of Simon's toxic behaviour and some had advised her to leave him when he had broken her wrist.

She rang Vince, the owner of the practice, from the taxi on the way to the Cairns railway station and told him about her flight from Cairns and that she would not be returning. She did not say where she was headed. He understood her circumstances and said that he would arrange for all her entitlements to be put into her bank account. She told Vince that she would be changing her phone number so that Simon would be unable to contact her, and she asked him to tell her colleagues of her leaving the practice for personal reasons.

She slept most of the twenty-five hours to Brisbane and when she arrived took a taxi to the Royal Women's Hospital.

She explained her situation and was placed in a medical ward while staff called Cairns Hospital for

her medical records.

She spent three days in Brisbane Women's and used the time to search for accommodation. She found the

house in Paddington and arranged to see it on the following Saturday.

Amelia's story shook Rachel. In her family she was unaware that any such situation existed. She thought that issues such as domestic violence probably happened but were not discussed. She wondered about her parents' situation but could not recall any evidence of violence or financial coercion. Of course, there were Aemon's attempts to sexually abuse her, and she noted that this was a family secret. Had Elaine told anyone about it?

She ventured a guess that Elaine had told Jesse, but Elaine had told Rachel not to reveal it to anyone.

'So, what do you think?' asked Amelia.

'I think it would suit me just fine,' said Rachel. 'How about I move in next Sunday. It will be a relief to live with less female company, which meant a lot of noisy sex.'

Since both were sexually active, they agreed to purchase a good pair of wireless ear buds to be used when the other was entertaining a man.

Chapter 25
FERGUS AND DAWN

Fergus met Rachel at Sandgate station as arranged. He was driving an old model Toyota four-wheel drive with lots of promotional signage for the products and services of his business. He gave her a peck on the cheek, took her bag and placed it on the back seat. 'Good trip? How long did it take to get here?' he asked as he set off towards his home. 'Yes. It took about an hour,' said Rachel, already feeling more at home hearing his Irish accent.

The trip to the house lasted only ten minutes and the conversation was filled with news and remembrances of Ireland. Each intuitively knew that this was the only time they would have to discuss these issues.

He was keen to know why she had suddenly fled to Australia, and she was just as keen not to tell him just yet. He would have to prove to her that he could be trusted to hear the full story.

As they pulled into his driveway, Fergus said 'I guess

that's the end of Irish news until I drive you back to the station on Monday.'

It was the May Day long weekend in Queensland and the barbecue organised by Fergus for his friends was to be held on Sunday to celebrate. None of them had an interest in the history of May Day but were happy to have the opportunity of getting together with friends and in Queensland the climate was such that an outdoor gathering was easy to organise. The house was on Flinders Parade and had stunning views across Moreton Bay. It was an older home with four bedrooms. The master bedroom had an ensuite and the other three bedrooms were serviced by a large bathroom and separate toilet.

It was a traditional Queenslander layout with a double-entry stairway to the elevated broad timber veranda which extended around the four sides of the house. The walls and ceilings were of tongue-and-groove timber, painted a pleasant cream. At ground level the front section was covered by a wall of tall white timber pickets, spaced to allow the flow of air under the whole building. On the southern side there was access for two vehicles.

There was an extensive subtropical garden, with solar-panel lighting beginning to come on as daylight faded.

It was one of the biggest houses she had ever been in, for most of the homes she was familiar with in Derry were much smaller.

Rachel had bought a posy at Roma Street Station, and she handed it to Dawn at the front door.

'It's lovely to see you again!' said Dawn as she received the posy.

'It's great to come and see you and your lovely home. Look at that view. You can see right across Moreton Bay,' said Rachel.

The light was fading now, and Dawn said, 'Yes but you will see it better in the morning. Your bedroom is on the eastern side of the house, so you'll get the morning sun. Sunrise is about 6.15 am. Are you an early riser?'

'Yes, but not that early! I call seven o'clock early,' said Rachel, and they all laughed. Rachel thought *This is a good start. I feel welcome here.*

'Why don't you show Rachel to her room, Fergus, and I'll get us some wine. Do you drink wine, Rachel?'

'Oh, yes, and it doesn't matter what colour,' said Rachel.

'A woman after my own heart!' said Fergus, 'Make it red, love. And can we have some crisps as well?'

'You mean chips, Fergus. In Australia we call them chips.'

'Oh yes, I forget. Chips then.'

'Rachel, he does this every time!' said Dawn. 'Wait a minute. What do you call them, Rachel?'

'Do you mean those thin, salted potato slices? I call them crisps.'

'See, I told you so, love. There you have it. I think you are outnumbered on the potato crisp thing,' said Fergus. And they all laughed again.

Again, Rachel thought, *These are good people and are making me feel very much at ease.*

Rachel returned to the living room after she had unpacked her things. Her bedroom had a large bed with a doona with a pale pastel covering featuring Australian flora. There was a chest of drawers with fresh white daisies in a crystal glass vase on top. There was a large hanging space with sliding mirrored doors. Bedside tables on each side of the bed featured small, cutglass vases containing native violets. A large overhead fan was positioned above the bed. She noticed that all the interior doors featured stained glass in a simple pattern of red and yellow square or oblong pieces.

The whole house had dark polished timber floors. In her room was a colourful rug with a marine theme. The guest bathroom was connected to her bedroom via an internal door. She noticed that a similar door connected the next bedroom as well. It was a good look and she decided that Fergus and Dawn were both proud of their home and had added features which make her feel welcome.

She sat next to Dawn on a large sofa while Fergus poured the wine. He handed each their glasses and Dawn said, 'Well, here's to you, Rachel. It's good to have you visit us at last!' 'What would you be doing in Ireland on 1 May? Do they celebrate Labour Day there?' 'Oh, yes, they sure do. In Derry it's a very special occasion. From 29 April to 1 May there is a music festival in Macosquin at Mary Pat's Bar. A big marquee is set up there and there's all sorts of music played ...'

Rachel's eyes watered up as she felt the pain of being homesick.

Fergus noticed and he moved over to sit next to her, and tears came to his eyes as well. Dawn felt their pain and cried along with them.

'Will you look at us, all crying. But it's natural to feel sad about being away from home. We call Australia home now, but I know that both of you will always have a fondness for Ireland. And particularly Derry,' said Dawn.

She added, 'I haven't been there yet. Fergus has promised to take me there soon, but we would need to have someone to manage the business while we are away. And that's not possible yet.

'Fetch the tissues, Fergus, while I attend to dinner. And don't tell me it's supper. I call it dinner.' And she marched off to the kitchen.

'Yes, dear,' said Fergus.

Dawn brought a large lasagne to the table together with a tossed salad and garlic bread. Rachel wondered a bit why there was so much food for just three of them. She took a portion of each. Fergus took his portion next, and Rachel realised why Dawn had served up so much food. Fergus took an enormous serving of lasagne and garlic bread and no salad. Dawn did not seem to mind being left with just a small portion for herself.

The conversation over dinner was both exhilarating and tiring for Rachel. Much of it consisted of questions to her by Dawn and Fergus, and therefore she did most of the talking. Although the issue of her flight to Brisbane was hinted at, it was not put to her as a direct question. But she was constantly aware that it might be the next question.

After finishing the second bottle of wine, Dawn suggested that Rachel may like to retire. Fergus offered a glass of his best port, but she politely declined. She asked Dawn if she could help with cleaning up, but Dawn said, 'Oh no, that's Fergus's job and besides most of it we bung into the dishwasher. You should head off and get some rest. You'll need it for the BBQ. These mates of Fergus are a lively lot.'

As she headed off to her room, Rachel reflected on 'bung' and the 'lively lot'. Australians certainly had their own version of English.

Since her room was adjacent to the master bedroom, Rachel did not do her usual practising of the skills she had learnt from Kirby, but she still did her pelvic floor muscle exercises.

Sharing the house in Paddington with Amelia meant that she had to explain to Amelia 'the other person' in her room when Amelia asked about the other voice.

Rachel decided that the only way to explain the other person was to tell a partial truth. The absolute best lies are those that are nearly true.

She admitted that she was practising ventriloquism but was vague about telling Amelia why.

'It might be something I could do in the future, but not just yet. But I need to do regular practice to keep the skill.'

Amelia agreed with this. She was a strong advocate of self-improvement and doing the right thing.

So, although tired, Rachel performed her pelvic girdle exercises. The lips of her fanny visibly moved under her command. Her future customers will be astounded by the movement of these lips with the thrown words. These lips would say very naughty things and delight them. She also planned that it would be a one-off. There would be no point in doing it repeatedly for one client. She would limit her customers to a once ever service and there would be no repeats. However, she was not ready to re-launch her career. There were several steps to be taken before she would do that. One of those steps was to find a minder. She needed to feel safe from protection racketeers like Millar.

She woke with the sun and a raucous noise of birds, seemingly right outside her bedroom. She'd had a good night's sleep and could smell bacon. She loved bacon. She showered quickly, put on shorts and a T-shirt over her togs and followed her nose to bacon. She found it on a BBQ where Fergus was busy with tongs and fork shifting bacon around on a BBQ plate.

'Take a seat over there, early bird,' said Fergus as he prepared eggs for frying. 'How many eggs would you like with your bacon?'

'Oh, two, please.'

'There's coffee in the plunger and tea bags if you want a cuppa.'

'Where's Dawn?'

'She gets to sleep in on a Saturday. She deserves it.'

'That's so nice,' thought Rachel. *'They sound like a happy couple.'*

She noticed that the eggs on the plate all had unbroken yolks. 'How do you make sure the yolks don't break?' asked Rachel.

'Always break them at the bottom and open the shells from the bottom and Bob's your uncle.'

'Bob's my uncle?' replied Rachel 'What does that mean?'

'It means that everything will be fine.'

Rachel thought, '*How quaint. Another Aussie phrase to remember.*'

Just then a medium-size bird with a fearsome looking beak landed on the table. Rachel pulled away, not knowing how to react to this unexpected intrusion.

'Don't worry about him,' said Fergus, waving the bird away from the food.

'That's a kookaburra. You've probably heard him and his mob this morning. They may have woken you. They're a bloody noisy lot.'

'And over there on the grass, that looks like a magpie, but I have seen some smaller black and white birds as well,' said Rachel.

'They're probably butcher birds or peewees,' said Fergus. 'You're out of the city now and you'll see a lot more birds here. Have you noticed swarms of small, colourful birds, also making a lot of noise? They're lorikeets.

'Bung some bread into that toaster if you want. One for me too if you would.' Fergus brought over a platter with four eggs and a huge pile of bacon to the table.

Rachel took two eggs and two rashers of bacon and a slice of toast. Fergus took two eggs, a slice of toast and pausing with tongs over the huge pile of bacon still left, he said, 'Will you be wanting any more bacon?' 'No, thank you.'

With that Fergus scooped the rest of the bacon onto his plate. They ate in silence for a while, then Fergus asked, 'I'm intrigued by you coming to Australia with such haste.

Can you tell me why it had to be that way?'

Rachel knew that she would eventually have to face this question and she had prepared to give an answer that was a partial truth – a lie, but ninety per cent true.

'Fergus, you, and Dawn have been so kind and helpful to me. Keeping in touch by phone, and now this invitation to your beautiful home to meet your friends, it's just wonderful. You deserve to know what happened.

'I had a date with a man for dinner. I thought he was nice; you know, polite and thoughtful, and afterwards he took me to a hotel. I knew what this meant. It meant that we would have sex, and so we did, and the sex was good, I really enjoyed it. But afterwards, as I was relaxing, he produced a small bottle from somewhere and splashed a liquid onto my face. It surprised and annoyed me. I told him to piss off and what did he think he was doing. He laughed and said it was only water but then he said "What if it had been sulphuric acid? Anyone you date from now on may be a friend of mine and could use sulphuric acid on you but if you pay me one hundred pounds per month, I'll make sure it doesn't happen."

'I screamed at him to get out and he quickly did. I was so frightened. I got dressed and quickly went home to Jesse.'

'Fuck!' said Fergus, then quickly, 'Sorry about that. Jesus, no wonder you had to get out of there. Did you call the police?'

Rachel was also prepared for this.

'There was no point really. It would be his word against mine and in fact he was only guilty of throwing water on my face. But for me the threat of disfigurement was too awful. I would not know if he could carry out his threat if I did not pay him. I had to escape.'

Just then Hank appeared. He had come through the gate to the backyard, as everyone did. Hank was a mechanic at the jet ski business and a good friend of Fergus and Dawn. He was an important part of the success of the business.

'Hi, Hank. Have a seat. Would you like coffee? Oh, pardon, Hank, this is Rachel. Rachel this is Hank.'

'Nice to meet you,' said Rachel and extended her hand.

Hank took it, shook it and said, 'It's good to meet you at last. We've heard a lot about you already.'

'Thank you,' said Rachel.

The handshake and the concurrent eye contact took a little longer than it should have and Rachel instantly regretted it. She had given Hank an unintentional signal.

Surprisingly, Fergus noticed it too and immediately attempted to defuse it. 'How is Ross and the plans for the wedding?'

'Ross and her mother have everything in hand. They've even chosen my suit. All I must do is turn up.'

'And pay for the drinks. Let's make sure get your part right.'

Rachel sighed silently, *'Thank you, Fergus; I owe you one.'*

'So, what can I do for you?' said Fergus, pouring Hank a coffee.

'I need to adjust the impeller pitch on my machine. Do you have a trailing edge gauge that I could use?'

'This is shop talk, Rachel, would you excuse us while

Hank and I retire to the shed? Take a swim if you like. The water is not too cold.'

'Thanks, but I think I hear Dawn in the kitchen. I'll take these dishes in to be washed.'

'It was nice to meet you, Hank,' she said as she handed him the coffee Fergus had poured for him.

'I suppose I'll see you again tomorrow at the BBQ,' said Hank.

'Yes, and I look forward to meeting your fiancée, Ross, as well,' said Rachel feeling some relief after the mess she had made on meeting Hank.

She made a mental note to be careful when being introduced to Fergus's male friends.

Chapter 26
HARVEY

Email to Frank MacGregor

I'm moving out of Arcadia in two weeks' time to 243 Blake Street, Balmain, so when you come to visit me that's where you'll find me until the lease is up on Drummoyne in July. Paul

The email sounded odd to Frank. Why was Paul moving out of Arcadia? It didn't make sense. He called Paul that night. 'Why are you moving out of Arcadia?'

'It doesn't belong to me, and the new owner has it up for sale.' 'New owner? I didn't know that you had sold it.'

'It wasn't mine to sell.'

'Surely you inherited it after MacKenzie died. She had no other relatives or am I missing something?'

'No, there are no other relatives. She left it to Stone.'

'What! You must be kidding me. Left it to Stone, that charlatan!'

'I kid you not. She also left her all her jewellery and about $50,000 in a savings account. She did not leave her loot to Stone herself, but to her daughter.'

'Why to her?'

'MacKenzie was worried that her daughter, Emily, who is mentally handicapped, is going to be left uncared for when Stone dies. Since Stone was struck off for medical malpractice, she has been unable to accumulate wealth enough to have Emily looked after when she dies. Emily is unemployable.'

'Surely you are going to challenge that. I know you weren't married, but surely you were in a de facto relationship, and you have rights to inherit. What claim does she have?'

'Her main claim is in the wording of the will. She gets it all.'

'That may be, but I've heard of many challenges to wills lately and I'm sure you would have a good chance to have the will overturned.'

'You would be too young to remember this, Frank, but I challenged Harvey's will and lost very badly. I did not get one cent from that old bastard. I am not going to expose myself again to the judiciary. In Harvey's case, he left what he had to your mother and nothing to me, his son. And the judge thought I was a bit dodgy, thanks to your mother's barrister. I was made to look a fool and I'm not going through the whole court thing again.

'In addition, MacKenzie left a six-page handwritten letter, saying what a lousy partner and carer I had been in her later years of declining physical and mental health. She wrote her will and the letter, I suspect, soon after her operation to remove her gall bladder, when we had some serious disagreements over each other's behaviour.'

'I don't remember that.'

'Well, I do, only too well.'

'What happened?'

'Well, when I arrived to see her in ICU, she was out of bed sitting on a chair. I asked how she was.

'She did not reply to that and pointing over to her left said, "That nigger over there is my nurse". I looked and saw a coloured woman wearing a hijab.

'I said, "Shush, you shouldn't say that". MacKenzie said, "Well, she is".

'I thought it better to change the subject than argue. "I hope you'll be out of here soon".

'MacKenzie said, "Did you bring some extra codeine for me?"] I said, "You know they won't allow that".

'"I asked you to bring it". Her voice was rising now.

'"I told you that the hospital will not allow you to have extra medication".

'"Fuck you, what am I going to do for pain relief?" With that, she went over to her bed where her nurse had her Webster-pack containing her extensive array of medication. MacKenzie whisked the Webster-pack from the nurse's hands and began removing some tablets from it. The nurse grabbed the pack as well and so began a tug-of-war over the pack. I was both appalled and angry.

'I said, "I'm leaving. I'll come again tomorrow when you can behave yourself. Don't try to call me, I'm turning my phone off". And with that I flounced out of the ICU.

'That was back in 2016, and MacKenzie never forgot, and I was never forgiven. You experienced that for yourself on occasions when we did not get on at all that well.

'Besides, I think I may be on the verge of a breakthrough on the frozen embryo transfer for Egyptian spiny mice. I have been working on this for years and I think I nearly have it. At present, I have fifteen embryos, previously frozen, transferred into the wombs of surrogates. If I can achieve success in twelve of them, I shall have technology that I can direct to the Antiabortion League for the human trials and continue with the salary I am getting now, and Stone can piss off with MacKenzie's money.'

'That would mean that you let the bastard win,' Frank said. 'What about the NDIS? Would his daughter not qualify for that?'

'I don't know. As I said, MacKenzie set this up in 2016 and the NDIS was just beginning then. Look, maybe she will, maybe she won't. I don't care anymore.'

'So, do you think that the IVF people will be interested in this new technique of yours?'

'Well, not specifically them, but think about it, the abortion issue raises its head regularly and this could be a technology that would remove the need for abortions or at least some of them. Embryos could be harvested from the wombs of women who, for whatever reason, don't want to be pregnant, then frozen and made available to couples who cannot conceive.

'The League pays me an extremely attractive package now for the spiny mouse research and they have already expressed an interest in me being involved in the human trials that lay ahead. This will set me up for a comfortable retirement.

'If my technology works for Egyptian spiny mice, then there's no good reason that it won't work for humans.'

* * *

Harvey was born in Parramatta and attended the local state schools. He disliked school and those charged with educating him felt the same way about Harvey. He and his teachers were relieved when, at fourteen years of age, his parents agreed that enough was enough and it was time that the reluctant schoolboy got a job!

Harvey's parents looked for opportunities for employment locally but found nothing suitable. Then, Anthony Hordern & Sons began advertising for young men to be trained in retail where there were ample opportunities for promotion to management.

It did mean train travel each day to the Sydney CBD from Parramatta, but his parents thought that Harvey could manage that. He applied for an interview and was accepted for a meeting with Mr Clark, the recruiting officer at the main Sydney store. Harvey had never taken the train to the city by himself, so his mother accompanied him for the interview.

Mr Clark looked at Harvey's school results and frowned. But he looked through some teacher comments and found one of interest. Michael Taft, Harvey's manual arts teacher, had praised Harvey's work with woodwork, with special mention of Harvey's care with tools and their replacement when they had been finished with for the day.

Clark thought, *'This is a mind that values order'*. He knew that people with this trait generally made good employees. He wrote 'suitable applicant' on Harvey's file and thanked Harvey and his mother for coming.

'But he didn't ask me many questions, Mum,' said Harvey on the way home.

'No, that's a bit unusual, I'll grant you that, but he seemed to like the way you looked, and I noticed that he paid particular attention to your school report.'

'But my school reports are always lousy.'

Harvey was a good-looking young man and given the right guidance Clark thought that he was very suitable Anthony Hordern's salesman material. A few days later a letter from Hordern's arrived, offering Harvey a three-month trial at the Sydney store, beginning on the following Monday. The wage offered was the standard junior rate of one pound nineteen and six pence per week.

Harvey was rapt. He called to his mother 'Mum, I got the job! I'm going around to Freddie's to tell him the news!'

He flew out of the door with the letter clutched in his hand.

He tripped and fell at the front gate, grazing both of his hands on the gravel.

It didn't matter. He got to Freddie's with blood-soaked hands, but pride in his heart. 'Freddie, Freddie, I got a job!

I'll have nearly two pounds a week!'

Freddie was happy for his friend but pissed that he didn't have a job and had to remain at school.

Harvey began work the following Monday, wearing the trousers and jacket his mother had selected for him. He also wore two bandaids on the palms of both hands.

His mother advised him to be respectful of the adults he was working with, avoid showing the bandaids, and eat the lunch she had packed for him.

It was liberating to be going to work by himself on the train. He travelled to the city with hundreds of other workers. He was stoked!

When he arrived Anthony Hordern's, he went to the main desk at the front of the store. In his letter he was told to report to Charles Simpson. He asked the lady at the desk to speak to Mr Simpson. As he was waiting for Simpson, he looked around him. Even now, at the beginning of the working day, the store was full of life. Harvey was going to enjoy this.

Charles Simpson arrived. He was a spare man in a dark suit with a white handkerchief protruding from the breast pocket. He was an intimidating figure.

On request, Harvey produced a crumpled letter of offer. His mother had tried her best to straighten out the creases and remove the blood stains.

Simpson looked at the creased and blood-stained document with disdain on his face. This look was not altogether unfamiliar to Harvey. He had seen it regularly on his father's face and on the faces of his teachers.

The joy of seeing happy shoppers and helpful staff that had filled the sails of his spirits. Maybe working was going to be just like school!

'Come with me,' ordered Simpson.

As he turned to follow Simpson, a voice from behind the front desk said 'Welcome to Hordern's, love. You'll be okay.'

With his sails somewhat re-inflated, Harvey followed Simpson to Menswear on the ground floor. Here Simpson stopped. He handed the letter which he held between one finger and thumb to Mr Hunter, saying, 'Harvey Arnold, three-month trial. He's yours.'

Mr Hunter was an overweight man, perhaps in his fifties, dressed impeccably in a light grey suit, white shirt and a purple bow tie. He looked fondly at Harvey, winked, and said 'Don't worry about Charles. He is very unhappy now and is taking it out on everybody, not just you. We all hope he'll be feeling better soon.'

'Now look at you, a handsome young man and well-dressed. I see that your Christian name is Harvey. We're a bit posh here at Hordern's, so when we are on duty, you will call me Mr Hunter and I shall call you Arnold. That's a good start. Let's walk around Menswear and acquaint you with our kingdom here. You'll also meet your fellow Menswear staff.'

Harvey met each of the staff, all of whom wore suits. They seemed genuinely pleased to meet him, but the suits worried him. He had never owned a suit. His family could not afford it.

Alex Hunter was sensitive to the feelings of his customers and his staff, and he noted the look of unease on Harvey's face as he met the menswear staff.

When they had finished the tour of the Menswear kingdom, Hunter took Harvey to a small office to talk.

'Welcome to menswear, Harvey, I think you'll fit in well here, but I sense that you may be overawed by all the suits. If you continue with us, then one day you will own a suit. We like our staff to be dressed extremely well and eventually wear a suit. Hordern's offers staff a wonderful discount on suits, and you can pay it off. Don't worry about it now. Let's get you started as my personal assistant.'

This was the beginning of a happy period in Harvey's life. He enjoyed his work, and he eventually bought a suit.

But after six years he could see that the prospect of promotion was low and he felt ready for something different, so he began looking for something outside retail.

One Saturday he found just what he was looking for. In the *Sydney Morning Herald* classified section, a job for an assistant manager was advertised at a new club, The Paradise Club, near Parramatta in the nearby suburb of Fern Hill.

During World War Two, Lieutenant Colonel Richard Myers was stationed at the Leiei gold mine in Papua New Guinea, commanding a battalion of engineers to protect the mine from the invading Japanese. He did a remarkably good job, for the Japanese did not actually get close to the mine.

Myers kept his men busy with exercises to defend the mine. The mine continued to produce gold and a lot of it. Myers had four trusted officers, all engineers, to design moulds for pellets of gold that could fit into a pocket. He redeployed the staff of accountants and inventory personnel to other duties and replaced them with trusted officers. Four of these officers were charged with smuggling regular quantities of this pellet gold back to Sydney, where they were ordered to bury it in a secure place. Only Myers knew the locations of all four stashes of gold. Each officer was sworn to secrecy about the location of his stash.

Myers was a busy man. He had long wanted a business of his own and he had taken every opportunity to gain management skills in the Army. So, as he worked his way up the promotions ladder in infantry, logistics and catering, he gained the skills to run a medium-size business. Along the way, he had to punish soldiers who had acted illegally. In so doing, he learned the skills of acting illegally that the soldiers had devised to avoid detection, and how to avoid it. The war would end soon, and his plans to build the Paradise Club were well under way. He had secured the backing of Jack O'Neil, a local Fern Hill councillor, and had purchased fifty-three acres of land in Fern Hill.

He submitted plans for a luxury clubhouse with a compact nine-hole golf course designed by the noted golf course designer and Texan, Garfield Hackett II. Myers figured that members would care less about golf and would be more interested in the illegal gambling and prostitution that the club would secretly supply. A brief for plans for the building was given to architect Bob Agnew, a former schoolmate of Myers. It was to be essentially a building within a building, with two secret entrances to the inner building access not shown on plans submitted to council, but which would be added after final building approval.

Myers had commissioned four Sydney jewellers to gradually convert the stashes of gold into cash to pay for the construction of the club. The price of gold at the time was fixed at $US35 per ounce and Myers had managed to smuggle over five hundred pounds weight to Sydney, amounting to $US300 000, when the average wage in Australia at the time was five pounds per week. The club had just been officially opened by Councillor O'Neil when Harvey presented himself for an interview. He was impressed. The smell of fresh paint mixed with the seductive smell of new leather was everywhere. This spelt luxury, and the club was just that, luxurious.

His interview was with Captain Ralph Montague. Harvey did wonder why he was being interviewed by a captain and if it would be a ship's captain or an army captain.

Chapter 27
PARADISE CLUB

It turned out that Captain Montague was a soldier, not a sailor, who had not yet integrated back into society and imagined that he was still among soldiers. He tended to bark rather than to give orders and he made it very clear to young Harvey that he expected absolute loyalty to the club and, more importantly, to him personally. He read the reference written by Mr Hunter from Anthony Hordern's.

'I see you are nearly twenty years old. What do you expect to make of your life?'

Harvey had never been asked such a question and frankly had never thought about it. He had a 'weekend' mindset – how long was it until the next weekend? Or a variant – how many days to Friday? Intuitively, he did not reveal these feelings to Montague and for some unaccountable reason, although he had never thought about it, blurted out, 'To have a wife and bring up a family, sir.'

Montague smiled, apparently approving of such a goal. 'Do you have a fiancée or steady girlfriend, Arnold?'

Harvey had neither but was thinking that his first answer had set the tone for the interview and answered that he had a steady girlfriend which of course he didn't. Another smile from Montague told Harvey that he was 'in the groove' here. Montague pressed ahead with this theme. 'Do you expect to marry this girl?'

'Not until I am twenty-one, sir, and that I have her father's permission, sir.' Another smile.

Montague asked several more questions about Harvey's experience with Anthony Hordern's and seemed impressed with Mr Hunter's reference and soon brought the interview to a close.

'I have two other candidates to interview. I shall contact you by letter – it seems that you do not have the phone on at home – and let you know of my decision.'

On the way home Harvey assessed his chances. He was ecstatic that he had managed four 'sirs' during the interview and felt that he had impressed Montague.

'How did it go?' asked his mother when Harvey arrived home. 'I think I did rather well,' he replied.

'What is it like, the club, I mean?'

'I only got to see reception and the captain's office, But it did smell good.'

One week after his interview, Harvey received a letter from Montague indicating that he was being offered a three-month trial at the Paradise Club as assistant manager.

His mother was tickled pink with the news. His father

grunted something unintelligible. Harvey did not own a car nor did his father and he had not yet learned to drive, but there was a bus service to Fern Hill and the Paradise Club.

He arrived early for his first day at the club, which impressed the captain.

He began the day in Montague's office where there were three desks and office chairs. Montague invited him to sit in one of the leather chairs which faced his own impressively large desk of shiny dark timber. He told Harvey first about the club and then about the duties he would be performing. Montague stressed that he would be closely monitored over the three-month trial to determine if he was to be offered a permanent position. His job in the simplest terms was to do just what Montague told him to do. Harvey noticed the lack of clutter on Montague's desk. It had a phone, an ink blotter, a couple of sheets of paper, a family photo and an expensive looking fountain pen. Montague asked Harvey to turn and look at the other two desks. One had a typewriter, an in-tray, an out-tray, a comfortable office chair, a four-drawer filing cabinet and a small bunch of fresh flowers. Indicating this desk, Montague said, 'That is Mrs Gifford's desk. You will address her respectfully as Mrs Gifford and me as Captain Montague.'

Harvey stifled a laugh, thinking '*I wonder if I need to salute?*' Montague then indicated the third desk which had an office chair.

'We can decide what you will need on your desk when necessary, as you go. You'll meet Mrs Gifford later. She is out of the office at present collecting documents from the director's office. I shall take you around to meet the other staff. We'll begin at reception.'

Harvey met several staff members that day, not remembering their names but thankfully most of them wore name badges.

He was also introduced to Colonel Myers who did not wear a badge but was unforgettable with bright, but greying, red hair and moustache.

Myers' office was even more luxurious that the Captain's with a suite of leather chairs, Chesterfields, a dining table with setting for six, numerous lamps and what appeared to be a large map of some place in New Guinea.

The following Friday and Harvey had a date with Silvia, a new girl in his life, that he had met a local dance. She was a good-looking girl. All his girlfriends had been lookers. Harvey himself was a looker and he knew it. Nearly all the girls he had dated were lookers. He was rarely declined a dance or a date when he asked. His current girlfriend Prue had a friend called Helen who had recently said to him while dancing 'You are so up yourself, Harvey, you think you're the bloody ant's pants.' This was a bit of a shock. Most girls he danced with looked swooningly into his eyes, a deep blue, and he enjoyed this adoration. He remembered, though, when examining his face in the mirror for pimples one morning that his eyes were perhaps a little bit closer together than he liked.

He looked into Helen's less than swoony eyes and calmly replied 'You know, Helen, you're right. These eyes of mine are little bit close together. None of us is perfect.'

She huffed.

He made a mental note to not ask Helen to dance again.

*   *   *

Harvey's experience with sex was extensive. Even at barely fifteen years of age he had the attention of many young girls who worked at Hordern's or nearby businesses at lunch time and one particularly assertive nineteen-year-old who worked in Hordern's Lingerie department took him to a seldom-used storage area in the basement and educated him in the basics of sex.

He never forgot Tracy from Lingerie. But there were plenty of girls to choose from and he chose plenty.

When Harvey was at school there was no sex education and his parents, each perhaps thinking that the other would do it, told him nothing but Tracy certainly knew how to educate him. She had her own condoms and insisted that Harvey wore one each time and advised him never to have sex without one.

Tracy soon tired of being teacher and sought satisfaction from others. It did not matter. Harvey was no longer a virgin and was able to tell his mates about what they were missing. Few of them believed him or claimed that they will still virgins themselves but hoped that it was true and that there would be a 'Tracy from Lingerie' for them in their lives.

Harvey was twenty years old when a new girl, or rather, young woman entered his life. He had a well-paid job at the Paradise Club and had recently acquired a car, a Vauxhall, much to envy of his friends.

Silvia was a new girl in town and when she turned up at the local dance Harvey was one of the first men she danced with. She was pretty and attracted a lot of attention from the local men and boys. After a few weeks, Harvey asked her to the 'flicks' and she had enthusiastically agreed.

Since he had her to himself for a few hours he was able to find out more about her. Her father was a pharmacist who had recently bought a pharmacy in Parramatta. He owned four other pharmacies already and her mother worked in the Parramatta branch.

By this time, Harvey had found a few places to take willing young women for sex that were reasonably safe from interruption, and he now had a car as well. Silvia was as keen as he was to do it. They were so keen that Harvey forgot, and perhaps Silvia did not know about, condoms.

Harvey continued to date Silvia, but she was not the only one.

He had recently dated Prue again. Prue had been a bit resistant to his pressure for sex in the past, but perhaps she noticed that he was dating others including that new girl, Silvia, and was assertive enough to signal him that he just might get his way if they dated again.

And they did and he did.

It had now been a year since Harvey became assistant manager at the Paradise Club. He had been consistently observed by Montague as promised and he consistently satisfied the Captain.

He had met Mrs Gifford soon after the tour of the club when he and Montague returned to the Captain's office.

She was old enough to be his mother; most of the others he met were older than him but not as old as Mrs Gifford. Everybody had a badge, except, of course, Colonel Myers, and on the badge was the person's full name. His had Harvey Arnold but there were some exceptions to this, including Captain Montague who appeared not to have a Christian name, and Mrs Gifford, whose badge also had no first name.

Much of Harvey's work was to supervise other staff which was technically the Captain's job. Once he had learned what Montague wanted of him, he was increasingly given the supervision of most of the other staff. His task became monitoring the others but certainly not to direct staff himself. This was Montague's work and after doing the rounds of the club several times each day, Harvey was to prepare a written report for the Captain who would act if necessary. Montague did not receive Harvey's handwritten reports which had to be typed first using a format of his own liking. Harvey gave his handwritten notes to Mrs Gifford who formatted and typed them. This task was top priority and Mrs Gifford was instructed to drop any other task, type Harvey's notes, and then place them on the Captain's desk immediately.

This situation meant that Harvey was in the office at his desk much of the time making sure that his report was legible. In the beginning his reports were not legible, and Mrs Gifford often returned them to Harvey with instructions to convert it into correct English.

At first Harvey thought '*Strewth! This is just like school!*' But it wasn't, and Mrs Gifford patiently led Harvey through the grammar that he had failed to learn at school. Her patience and good will resulted in Harvey's reports being returned with fewer and fewer corrections. He learned from her the importance of accurate reports which should never be ambiguous. Now seeing the importance of language, he finally recognised that this was what his teachers had tried to do.

Montague also had duties aside from acting on Harvey's reports. He also monitored the handling and ordering food and wine for the restaurant and drinks available at the bar and the operation of the golf course. There more than forty workers on the staff.

Captain Montague was pleased to have Harvey gathering intelligence about the running of the club and seemed to come to his office less frequently.

This set up a situation for which he was not prepared.

Mrs Gifford and Harvey were often in the office without the Captain and so a relationship of trust in one another developed. This was a powerful bond that the Captain failed to recognise.

While the documentation of the club's work ended up on Mrs Gifford's desk, Colonel Myers had his own personal secretary who also produced documentation – about what? Where did Montague go when he was not in his office? Harvey, who moved around the club several times a day noting how other staff were working, hardly ever saw the Captain in the club. A check of the parking area revealed that Captain Montague's Humber was there, so he had not left the club. So where could he be?

One day, handwritten notes from Myers' office mistakenly turned up on Mrs Gifford's desk. She was amazed at what she read. It seemed to her that the financial documentation that she dutifully typed and filed was not the only financial record for the club. These unexpected documents showed substantial amounts of money Mrs Gifford knew nothing about.

What could be going on to generate so much money? And, since she knew that the books prepared by her for the accountant were for taxation purposes, it seemed this revenue collected by the club was not being declared to the tax office.

How could the club be making so much money and who ended up with all this cash? Mrs Gifford thought that this would have to have come from secret illegal activity. She was well aware that these activities could be prostitution or gambling. She did not move around the club much. She was confined by her work to her office, so she asked Harvey to be on the lookout for this illegal activity.

Harvey asked her what should he be looking for? She could only think of things she had seen in movies like roulette wheels and card games. She dared not think about what you would see in a brothel, but Harvey had an idea of what a prostitute would look like. As with many of his naive ideas about society, he was wrong. The scantily dressed women that he imagined were not what prostitutes looked like.

Did they have any particular look?

He began to look at the club in a different way. Instead of watching the staff, he began to watch the members. He noticed that although several members entered the club, he could not see them in the club. Where could they be?

He discussed this with Mrs Gifford, but she had no idea about it either.

Meanwhile Harvey continued his dating, but on a recent date with Silvia – they were using condoms now – Silvia mentioned that she had missed two periods in a row.

'We don't have to have sex if you're having your period. Just let me know and we can have a date a bit later,' said Harvey, not understanding what she was getting at. 'Harvey, it's not about having sex. It means I'm pregnant!'

'Don't be silly, how can you be pregnant? I always wear a condom.'

'Not on our first date about two months ago. Harvey, what are we going to do?'

Chapter 28
HARDLY HARVEY

Although Harvey had noticed that some patrons whom he had seen entering the club had disappeared soon after, he began to doubt what Mrs Gifford thought about the documents that had mistakenly landed on her desk.

Eventually the penny dropped, and Harvey realised that the two manned doors within the club that Montague had told him to ignore were probably entrance ways to a part of the club he had never seen. He asked Montague about these doors and why they were staffed. Montague told him that this was not a part of Harvey's supervisory role and that these men reported directly to Colonel Myers.

One day after giving the situation more thought, he suggested to Mrs Gifford that maybe the Colonel had another business and that the documents had nothing to do with the Paradise Club. Since they were unable to find evidence of gambling or prostitution it was just an assumption on their part.

Maybe it could be dangerous to be meddling in affairs over which they had no control.

But Harvey's attention to the inner workings of the Paradise Club now turned to Silvia. On their next date Harvey asked, 'How do you know you're pregnant?'

Tracy from Lingerie had not spent much time on this lesson in sex and really Harvey had little idea about periods and pregnancy.

'Harvey, I don't have time to explain it to you. Believe me, I am pregnant and my father is not going to be happy about it.'

Briefly the thought '*Well, let's not tell him*' did pass his mind, but fortunately it did not emerge as a suggestion.

'We need to get this over with, right away, Harvey.'

Another brief but more lingering thought '*Well let me know what he says*' did not come to his lips. 'We need to do it now,' said Silvia.

'Well, it's a bit late tonight, perhaps we could do it tomorrow,' ventured Harvey.

'Harvey, drive me home, right now. It won't get any easier if we put it off.'

Harvey was not sure if Adrian and Madge even liked him. Especially Adrian who had seemed distant when he met Harvey. His only recollection of Adrian's actual words was 'Make sure she's home by midnight!'

Harvey did not expect violence, but neither could he rule it out.

Looking back on the experience Harvey thought '*How am I going to enjoy life if I am going to be ordered about by this clearly enraged father and weeping possible future mother-in-law?*'

Of course, a situation such as facing potential parents-in-law was never going to be easy, but at least it did end. He was ordered out of the house, leaving Madge and Silvia in tears and if one could measure high blood pressure by the puce colour of Adrian's face, he was possibly on the verge of a heart attack, but Harvey was unsure whether he should be pleased or disappointed by not being ordered, never to come back, ever.

Two days passed before Harvey was contacted by Adrian at the Paradise Club telling him he was to come to Silvia's house that night. It seemed to be more of an order rather than an invitation and he weighed up his options.

'*Go and face the music, whatever that might mean. Or not go.*'

Harvey, at this stage had not shared news of his impending parenthood with his own parents, which it seemed he would be left to do without Silvia whom they had not met. In fact, Harvey had never brought any of his girlfriends to his house. Perhaps his subconscious warned him that such a step would lead the girl to imagine she was more important than she was.

Despite him telling Montague about his plans to marry and raise a family, it was never his plan. Harvey's interest in each of his girlfriends was for sex and now he had stumbled onto a different pathway. He reasoned that it was possible that the path may not lead to marriage and that Silvia's parents may choose, either to send her away to some distant location where disgraced young women were cared for, and the baby when born would be placed with a couple who could not conceive, or they would arrange an abortion for her.

When he visited Silvia's family that night, he was hoping that the news would be good – either of the above. It wasn't.

Adrian immediately took charge of the meeting and rather than offering any options, Harvey was told that he and Silvia would be married the following week but not in a church. When married he and Silvia would move temporarily into a flat while Adrian would organise a proper home for them and the baby.

Silvia seemed relieved that her father had taken responsibility for her future, but Harvey, seeing that other options were not even discussed, had mixed feelings, including being trapped and resentful. Silvia could recognise his unexpressed feelings perhaps better than her parents and her subconscious was gearing up for the trouble ahead.

They were married the following week.

Harvey had to quickly arrange leave from the club. Silvia worked for her father, so her leave was not an issue.

The wedding was on a Tuesday morning and the happy couple immediately took off for Nelson Bay, about three hours' drive away, where Silvia's family had a holiday home.

Silvia's parents and Harvey's mother were the only people to witness the marriage. When told of Harvey's unexpected plans to marry in just a few days, his parents both guessed what was happening.

Lois, Harvey's mother, was teary and wailed, 'We haven't

even met her yet.' Mick, his father grunted, 'Couldn't keep it in your bloody trousers, could you?'

When told of the wedding plans his contribution was, 'Well you won't see me there, I'm working and don't expect no present either.'

He did at least agree to meet the bride before the wedding and was cordial with Silvia until she was leaving with Harvey to be driven home. 'I pity you, lass you've got a real stinker there!'

Harvey had never thought about honeymoons; he reckoned that he was on a perpetual honeymoon with freely available sex and with a variety of partners. When they settled into the holiday home, Harvey was initially happy that sex was available all the time. However, reality quickly showed that Silvia did not want to be penetrated several times a day and he realised that he wasn't up to it as much as he imagined.

More reality. When sex was not the activity he thought it would be, he found that they did not really have much to talk about.

What had he done!

They tried walks, going to the flicks, eating out, as neither knew how to cook, hiring a boat and fishing, but neither had any experience. They also tried reading which was not one of Harvey's usual activities.

Both were relieved to return to Parramatta to familiar surroundings.

Adrian had rented a flat above a shop that sold children's toys in the CBD and both for now at least returned to some degree of normality. They both returned to their jobs and in the evenings and weekends found ways of avoiding each other. Silvia was becoming a reluctant partner in sex and Harvey was becoming weary of her excuses. As the months rolled on and Silvia began to show Harvey's preferred position, on top, became uncomfortable for them both. His angle of entry had to be altered and she complained of his weight on her and the baby.

To his credit, Harvey did not complain much and he simply reverted to type and sought satisfaction elsewhere with young women with good tits and flat bellies. He was handsome, still young and good at it. There were enough young women about who did not care that he was married, they just wanted what he had always wanted, sex without responsibility.

Adrian was not finished with Harvey, not by a long shot. Soon after returning from the honeymoon, he was summoned to Adrian's study for a chat about finances. Harvey was quizzed about his savings, which were modest, his salary and his prospects at the Paradise Club.

Adrian was rightly concerned about his daughter and the child she would produce in about six months. He would help them to have a proper house for a home and that his daughter and her child would be cared for under his supervision. He had begun to refer to Harvey as 'Hardly' and their relationship was barely cordial. Harvey avoided conflict and arguments by simply not participating. Some may have viewed this as a weakness or cowardly, but they would be wrong. He absorbed criticism and slights but never forgot nor forgave them. He would happily piss on his father's grave when the old bastard died, and he proposed to do the same on the remains of 'he who must be obeyed'.

He wasn't sure how or when Adrian and Silvia would have to pay for their treatment of him, but they would. He cooperated with Adrian and found to his surprise that 'he who must be obeyed' had a good grasp of budgeting and there were noticeable improvements in his finances. Adrian insisted that Silvia keep her current bank account and that Harvey would have no access to it. By the time baby Paul was born, Harvey and Silvia would have substantial savings, but not quite enough to put a deposit on to a home.

Adrian selected a two-bedroom cottage in nearby Greystanes, semi-rural at the time, telling Silvia and Harvey that it would be a worthwhile investment, but that he would own it.

He sought information about Harvey's prospects from Jack O'Neil whom he knew well. O'Neil reported back that Harvey's supervisor Captain Montague was very pleased with Harvey's work. He found him well- presented, punctual and loyal.

Adrian then set up a plan to supplement the shortfall they had in deposit on the house he had selected and underwrite the mortgage repayments. Silvia and Harvey would move straight into the fully furnished house – the furniture and appliances were his wedding gift to Silvia – as soon as the baby was born.

Meanwhile Harvey and Silvia continued working. Silvia ceased work at the pharmacy in the final month of her pregnancy.

It was an uneventful birth. Paul did not cause too much pain on Silvia as he exited her womb and at seven pounds thirteen ounces, he was average size for male births at that time. Harvey did not make it to Westmead Hospital for this event, he was busy at the club, but his son's birth meant more restrictions on his life and so Paul, too, was to be resented as much as Silvia and Adrian. Meanwhile, events at the Paradise Club unfolded in an unexpected way.

Captain Montague's work of supervision became erratic, and he sometimes failed to act on Harvey's intelligence concerning his fellow workers and so attention to tasks became slack, unexplained absenteeism and theft became commonplace; so much so that Harvey at times reluctantly had to remind Montague to act. It became apparent to Harvey and Mrs Gifford that Montague had a drinking problem. As many returned soldiers with memories packed with horrific images of the carnage of war, he self-medicated with alcohol.

Some days he simply did not come to work at all and this of course came to the attention of Colonel Myers. It saved Harvey and Mrs Gifford having to report their observations to Myers.

Myers, too, was spared the task of confronting Montague as one night he and his precious Humber ran off the road and hit with a tree. The Humber had no seat belts (cars at that time rarely did) and his body was found several yards from the car. He was pronounced dead at the scene with multiple fractures and broken neck.

Myers was genuinely fond of Montague. He was a

favourite and he was saddened by his passing. He arranged for Montague's funeral and assured his wife and child they would be looked after financially. Captain Montague was only fifty-five years old when he died.

The Captain and three other officers under Myers' wartime command formed the Paradise Club's board of directors but there were two other board members who were not on the executive and had no voting rights. One was Councillor Jack O'Neil and the other Sergeant Peter Martin of the Parramatta Police.

Myers was comfortable enough to take advice from the other board members but claimed the right to overrule them.

He was now placed in a situation where he would have to replace Montague. He and the other two

executive board members were too busy dealing with issues arising from the running of the gambling and prostitution to take over Montague's work as well.

Should he bring someone in from outside the club or promote someone?

None of the soldiers he had commanded had the organisational skills he required to run the business apart from the former officers who were already on the board. He called a meeting in his office to discuss the issue but did not include O'Neil or Martin. Their role was to watch his back and he paid each a healthy remuneration to ensure that this lucrative but illegal operation was not investigated by the council or police.

He called for Mrs Gifford to bring to his office all the files she had relevant to Montague's work and invited her to stay and over a cup of tea and discuss their contents. He asked how Montague created the files and she informed him that the raw data was gathered by Harvey, typed up and formatted by her and passed on to Montague for action. When pressed, she revealed what she and Harvey had done to support the Captain when his poor health was impinging on his work.

Myers asked more questions about the Captain's office routine which included her assessment of Mr Arnold. She gave Myers the impression that Harvey had done well after a slow start. He had, over the course of five years at the club, become well suited to continue the Captain's work until the Captain was replaced.

Myers thanked her and she returned to the office to tell Harvey what had happened. Next Myers called Harvey to his office to assess if he could replace Montague.

He had the documentation of the Montague's previous two years. He questioned Harvey about the tasks that Montague had set him. He noted the format Montague required of Harvey and Mrs Gifford to present to him and that it would require him to act on the intelligence collected to document the action he took in response.

It was immediately obvious to Myers that the Captain had failed to act in several cases, and this correlated with some stock losses and unexplained absences by club staff.

He asked Harvey why he had not reported it.

Harvey replied that he and Mrs Gifford had discussed this but were both fearful that it may result in them losing their own jobs.

Myers went back to his two fellow officers and discussed Montague's replacement. They were unable to think of anyone to do the job and finally agreed to advertise in local and national newspapers.

There were fifteen applicants for the position, including three women, whose names were immediately deleted, bringing the number to twelve.

Some of these were eliminated after their CVs were found to be unimpressive and they decided to interview five, one of whom was Harvey.

Mrs Gifford had helped Harvey to prepare his application for the position and she did a marvellous job. At the interview, Harvey performed well, comparable to the others but his main advantage was that of him being currently in the position.

He got the job!

Despite a temptation to pass on the good news to Silvia and her father, he kept it to himself. The position meant a substantial increase in salary but also a commitment to available to the club in emergencies, no matter what time. Silvia became used to Harvey's absences and his calls to let her know that he would be late home.

This was the situation that was presented to Paul as he grew up. His father's lack of presence in his life, he took to be normal until it became obvious to him that his father was not at all like his friends' fathers. Since Harvey did not seem to make any effort to bond with him, Paul forged bonds with his mother and her father.

Meanwhile Harvey created a new bank account into

which he funnelled the extra money from his new position. He viewed this slush fund as a down payment on the payback to Silvia, Adrian and his pest of a son. He was not sure yet how it would be used but he felt the deception itself was a good start.

Harvey was thirty-five and Paul fifteen when Harvey's father, during a particularly robust debate at a Parramatta cement works where he was union rep, had a massive stroke and died, intestate. Harvey could barely suppress his joy that the old bastard, who never left Harvey anything more than a noxious odour in the toilet, had inadvertently left him half of the old codger's estate.

Mick and Lois had a marriage typical for the times. It was a patriarchy – Mick earned the money and Lois did as she was told. Mick handled the money, gave Lois cash for groceries and other household items, paid the mortgage, electricity and gas, council rates and various insurances. Lois knew not what her husband did with his wages; she just knew that this was what was supposed to happen in a marriage and accepted it. Mick did not encourage Lois to associate with other women who may introduce her to other ideas.

He did not care for ideas which were not compatible with his own.

Mick took a newspaper each day but did not leave it at home where Lois might be infected by ideas of others.

When Mick died, Harvey was stoked. But when he heard that Mick had no will, he was silently jubilant.

He was aware of his mother's limitations and moved quickly to take advantage of them. She had been a loving, but rather colourless mother and he would help guide her through this loss. How could she manage without Mick? The answer? She had him! And he would be just as manipulative as his father.

He arranged a private funeral, just he and Lois attended. He did not want to pay any more than was necessary and he certainly not going to host a beery wake for Mick's fellow unionists. Next he approached a Parramatta solicitor to arrange for the settlement of Mick's estate. Harvey and his mother were the only living relatives and so the estate was divided 50 per cent each share.

He decided not to have the house sold and claim his half, leaving his mother to find other accommodation, but he failed to encourage his mother to make a will, knowing that if she too, died intestate, he would get the lot anyway. Harvey had hit a purple patch. First his undisclosed manager's salary and now this unexpected double bonus of exit Mick and hello Mick's house!

He did not inform Silvia of his father's death; she had no contact with Mick or Lois and did not need to know. Take that, Adrian!

Harvey took on all of Mick's responsibilities. Lois was eligible the widow's pension and he saw to it that this was used to pay her bills. He rarely had to supplement her income; her life was simple and sedentary.

He was aware that he would never get any money out of Greystanes house. Adrian had a firm grip on that and even if Adrian died, it would go to Silvia and certainly not to him.

Chapter 29
FLIGHT FROM PARADISE

Harvey was relieved that he had obtained the reference from Myers. He had never been invited to join the inner circle of the Paradise Club, but this did not trouble him until the almost simultaneous change in fortunes of O'Neil and Martin.

O'Neil surprisingly lost his seat on council to a celebrity Labor candidate in the recent council elections and Martin was under investigation over missing drugs, confiscated by him in a raid. Harvey by now had been working for the Paradise Club for almost 20 years and he heard on the grapevine that these circumstances may mean trouble for him. The Colonel gave him a reference.

Harvey was no intellectual, but he did have common sense. He knew by now what was going on in the exclusive part of the club. He also knew how some patrons of the club gained access to it, but he was still concerned about becoming involved in quite obvious law-breaking enterprises.

To gain entry, first, you had to be a member of the club or signed in by a member; and second, you asked the receptionist 'How is Colonel Myers?' Then a card would be issued to you and this you presented at one of the manned doors for entry to the casino.

Harvey resented paying for Paul's needs as much as he deplored paying for the mortgage on a house he would never own. He seemed forever having to pay out for something. This kid was going to pay back, big time!

But how?

He was confident enough that it would happen, and he was working on a plan for it.

He had stopped looking at Paul's report cards soon after the kid had topped his class in Year 4. It made him more and more determined to punish the little blighter.

How had he and Silvia produced such an egghead of a child?

In 1962, the oral contraceptive Pill was released onto the Australian market to married women, together with a luxury tax of 27.5 per cent. It represented a huge step forward for the feminist movement, which, while applauding its release, deplored the fact that it was not available to single women and that it was considered a luxury.

This was the '60s for Christ's sake!

Women had shown themselves quite capable of replacing men during the WW2, in everything from making munitions to taking management positions.

Coincidentally, in 1962 Mrs Gifford retired from the Paradise Club and Harvey, although he had found working with her immensely beneficial at the beginning of his career at the Paradise Club, now knew enough to no longer rely on her. All he needed now was someone who could type and take orders from him.

So, he decided to brighten up his office with Madeleine, competent typist and eminently beddable. She was pretty, curvy and not *too* bright. Mrs Gifford was dangerously bright. And he found when he first enticed Madeleine into bed that she was among many young single women who had found a way to obtain a script for the Pill.

Harvey wondered about this, but still used a condom with her. During their courtship, he began to realise that condoms, although they worked well with a notable exception – his irritating son – it would be so much better if he didn't have to use one.

So, he stopped.

Regrettably, Harvey did not research the Pill. But if he had, he might have found that it offered nearly one hundred per cent protection *only if it had been carefully managed*. Some women who failed to take it regularly were still prone to pregnancy. Madeleine acquired her script by having her mother obtain it for her and so missed the doctor's explanation of how it worked, and the importance regularly taking it at about the same time each day. She also did not read the leaflet attached to the drug when she bought it. It worked so well. She could have sex without risking pregnancy and, for her, the fact that she was not ovulating meant she had little or no period cramps or bleeding.

So, Madeleine became one of Harvey's mistresses. He

liked variety but only on his terms. He treated them all well if they were compliant.

But when Madeleine announced that she was pregnant, Harvey was stunned and exasperated.

'How could you possibly be pregnant? Are you not taking the Pill?' he questioned. 'I couldn't believe it myself but apparently it can happen if you miss taking it for a day or two,' she sobbed.

'Well, did you miss taking it?' said Harvey in a managerial voice.

Madeleine sobbed, 'I may have missed once or twice, but I didn't know it was so important.'

Harvey had special feelings for Madeleine, she was fun to be with, more so than other women, especially Silvia.

It was time for his plan to separate from Silvia to take shape and include this new circumstance.

He quickly surveyed the club managers' positions vacant in the papers and found that a recently established golf club in Victoria was looking for a manager who could get the club started and to hire new staff to run it. Harvey noticed that the club would prefer to employ a local, but when he looked at Brookdale where the club was being built, he reckoned that there would be few there to match his experience. The town had a population of about five thousand and was about 135 km from Melbourne.

He also needed to be difficult to find, and immediately applied to the Office of Registration of Births, Deaths and Marriages to change his name to MacGregor after his favourite tennis player, Ken MacGregor.

He also applied for mail redirection first to Brookdale Post Office, which he would later amend when he had found a place to rent or buy. This way made it more difficult to be traced by Adrian or Silvia.

He applied for the position and was called for an interview.

This meant that Harvey would have to fly for the very first time. His TAA flight from Mascot took him first to Melbourne. Greg Hunt, the club's president, was impressed by Harvey's application and offered to collect Harvey at the airport. By offering to bring him to Brookdale, he would have a chance to sum up him during the trip. Harvey did not fail to impress. He had made a good impression on most of those he worked for at the Paradise Club, including Colonel Myers whom Hunt had phoned to enquire about Harvey. By the time they arrived in Brookdale, Hunt had made up his mind that Harvey should get the job and felt that he could convince the other panel members as well.

There were six applicants chosen for interview in Brookdale and Harvey's experience impressed the panel and he was offered the position.

Back at the Paradise Club, having obtained the position, he sent his assistant Jamie out for inspection of staff, arranged coffee for himself and Madeleine, locked the office door and had a 'heart to heart' about their future. He could have questioned the legitimacy of her claim that he was the father of her incubating child, but he really believed her, and, in any case, he was about ready for flight. It was time to escape Adrian, Silvia and Paul.

He proposed two options for Madeleine: one that she

accompany him with their unborn child to Brookdale, or two, stay here in Sydney. If she opted to stay, he assured her that he would support their child, and she would keep her job at the club. He emphasised that she must decide within two weeks, for that was when he was to begin his new job in Brookdale.

This had taken Madeleine by surprise. *'Where is Brookdale?'* she thought.

'Will you marry me? I know you're married already, but I want our child to be legal.'

'I think you mean legitimate and yes, so do I,' replied Harvey.

The salary offered was less than he was getting in Sydney, but to buy a house in Brookdale would be a lot cheaper than in Sydney. And importantly he needed to escape possible prosecution in Sydney and fast.

Madeleine had come from Bathurst to Sydney to escape her uncle, turned stepfather. When she was just two years old her father, a radio operator on HMAS *Yarra*, died when it was sunk by Japanese cruisers in the Indian Ocean.

Initially caring for his sister-in-law, Madeleine's uncle then courted her mother and eventually married her in 1945. She never got on with her new father, a warden at Bathurst jail, and as soon as she was able escaped to Sydney to begin her adult life. She and her friend, Esme, shared a flat in Parramatta and did temp office work until Harvey hired her. Madeleine was not seriously bright, but she was witty and humorous to be with. She was also flexible enough to fit into Harvey's plan for a new life.

This was a bold but necessary step to take as it appeared that the Paradise Club was about to be investigated for hosting illegal gambling and prostitution. It was also highly likely that there would be an investigation by the Australian Tax Office. Although Harvey was not privy to discussions of the board or its decisions, he may be implicated in any police, council or Australian Tax Office investigation because he was the manager of the club.

Harvey had been very well paid by the club and there many perks of office such as cheap drinks, convention trips and a car allowance. This allowance covered maintenance costs of running his car, access to the club account for fuel, and registration and insurance costs.

However, given this largess, the club expected him to be available to the club 24/7. Although rare, there were occasions where he had to intervene in disputes between members or guests and staff, between members and members, and between the club and various unions. As a result, he had sustained a broken nose and incurred the wrath of members or their guests when he exercised the right to eject them if they disturbed the peace within the club. But it was all useful experience and would stand him in good stead in the future. He was not required, though, to exercise these powers over patrons of the gambling and prostitution element of the club. Myers had his own minders to cope with unruly guests in that division of the club.

The Brookdale Memorial Golf Club was planned to be built on one hundred and twenty acres of land in East Brookdale, adjacent to the Ellis Bay Wildlife Reserve.

The clubhouse, landscaping and golf links were nearing completion when Harvey was given the position of manager. It would be his job to oversee the final stages and employ the staff required to operate the club.

He found temporary rental accommodation that was furnished while he looked for a house to buy. Fortunately for him the rental market was soft and there was plenty to choose from.

Harvey reckoned that he had become rather astute at judging the motives of others and felt confident that Adrian would play into his hands relating to the issue of divorce.

Once he had absconded from Sydney to an unknown location, he predicted that Adrian would advise Silvia to seek a divorce and he would not oppose it. He would be quite happy to accept blame and since there was no chance of him attaining any advantage from the estate, he could begin again taking the accumulated funds of his undisclosed increase in salary with him. He would deal with the expected divorce proceeding by employing a Melbourne solicitor. He also decided to assume his new identity after the divorce settlement. Once he had the divorce he could go ahead and marry Madeleine.

Except for bedding various women and financing Paul's expenses, Harvey spent little on himself. He was unaware that he was conforming to his parents' practice of frugality and the Paradise Club had allowed him to save a large proportion of his salary.

At the time of his escape, Harvey had just turned forty and Madeleine was twenty-one. Their child, Frank, named for Ken McGregor's more famous doubles partner, Frank Sedgmen, was born in April 1963.

Authorities never found Harvey in his new life in Brookdale.

Did they ever try? Harvey did not know.

As time went by he thought little about it. The expected filing for divorce came and went with little effect on his life and he began to settle into an almost monogamous life. He no longer sought illicit relationships but would happily accept opportunities if they came his way.

He also bonded with Frank in a way he never had with Paul.

Unfortunately, the bonding was suddenly severed when Harvey experienced a massive heart attack when driving home one night from the Brookdale Memorial Golf Club.

He managed to keep enough control of his car to be able to pull off the road and come to a stop. He was unable to seek help on this section of road and died shortly after the car came to rest.

His body was found the next morning when a passing motorist recognised his vehicle with lights on, parked in a peculiar fashion on the side of the road.

Harvey was forty-seven years old, and Frank was seven when he died.

Madeleine was distraught, and Frank was bewildered by his death, but she believed that Silvia and her family should be notified.

She had her solicitor contact them through the Paradise Club, which was now a legitimate business, and Myers and his fellow directors were now serving jail sentences for a variety of crimes.

There were unforeseen circumstances when Harvey's first son, Paul, applied to court to amend Harvey's will to claim part of his father's considerable estate. Some two years earlier, Harvey moved his mother into a nursing home and leased her house for rent which he collected on her behalf.

Chris Lomax, who acted on Madeleine's behalf, assured her that this claim would not be accepted by the court and that she should not worry. Harvey's estate was sufficient to keep Madeleine, who was eligible for the widow's pension, and Frank. But worry, she did, until Paul's claim was rejected by the court, and she was awarded costs, which had to be borne by Paul.

Paul was chastened by this and later regretted his rashness.

Chapter 30
THE BBQ

Rachel stood in front of the full-length mirror. She was naked. What did she see?

Long, wavy, red hair past her shoulders. An oval face, slightly flattened at the chin. A high forehead lightly freckled.

Red eyebrows. Bright green eyes. Small, freckled nose. Bow-shaped sensuous lips.

High full breasts in the 'Goldilocks zone'. Narrow waist.

Rounded hips. Long, slim legs. And between them, her Burning Bush.

She lay down on the bed and pondered the potential of this body. *Can it really make me a living?*

Was there a future for the plan devised for her with her dying mother and Aunt Jesse? Millar and the subsequent flight to Australia had changed everything.

Should she just find a nice guy, marry and have kids? She closed her eyes.

Amelia had married a nice guy and what happened there?

She moved her vagina. *She had gained control of it to make it appear to speak. She was a competent ventriloquist.* **This part of her plan was in place already. What was left to be done?**

A lot!

And she did not have Jesse close by to help her. How could she set herself up as an outstanding prostitute in this totally new environment?

She did not know it then, but the answer to that question would come in just a few hours. She stretched out and reached for her dildo. It wasn't in her bag. *She must have left it back in Paddington! Shit!*

'*Oh well***' she thought '***I can always use my hand.***' And she did and felt a lot better for it.**

Suddenly her thoughts flicked back to her mirror image and her talks about sex she had had with her mother. She remembered Elaine telling her to be relaxed about her sexuality, that it was appropriate for her to enjoy her sex alone and had given her a dildo to enhance the effect.

She remembered Elaine filling the gaps in her knowledge about sex that she had picked up from her friends and from sex education at school. Most importantly, Elaine counselled her to dismiss the teachings of the Church about sex. It was to be enjoyed and not something to be ashamed of.

Then another thought; the animated video in a sex education class showed the sperm, hundreds of millions of them, ejaculated into the vagina, all madly swimming towards an ovum that was being coaxed along by the cilia in Fallopian tube down towards the uterus.

'Ejaculated,' one student had asked, 'what does that mean, miss?' Loud sniggering came from the back row of the class.

'It means that the sperm were projected into the vagina,' answered the teacher. Another question, again from the back row, 'What projects it, miss?'

'Well, as you saw in the video, it's the penis that has entered the vagina,' said the teacher.

Again, from the back row, 'I've seen my older brother's dick and it doesn't look like the one in the video. It's sort of floppy and hangs down.'

This observation is met with class-wide laughter.

After struggling to regain control of the class, the young teacher offered, 'Under some circumstances, the penis becomes hard and erect as you saw in the video.' A supplementary question followed, 'What circumstances are those, miss?'

'I think we will leave it there for now,' she said, after again struggling to regain control of the class. 'Please write down your homework for Wednesday.'

It occurred to Rachel that her teacher had not explained why all the sperm were frantically swimming towards the ovum, although she had said that many of the sperm died in the acidic environment of the uterus, and many had been destroyed by the immune system of the women.

So many of the sperm were destroyed on their quest to reach the ovum and then only one of the many left was accepted by the ovum. Once one sperm pierced the cell membrane of the ovum, a chemical change in the nature of the membrane made it impervious to the entry of any more sperm. At this point she shuddered at the thought of her parents having sex. Despite Elaine's liberal ideas, she could not visualise her mother's acceptance of Aemon's dick being planted into her or the fact that she enjoyed it!

This was a man that had tried unsuccessfully on several occasions to have sex with her, his daughter. No, it didn't bear thinking about.

But then the thought, despite her revulsion of Aemon, that the fateful union of sperm and ovum had resulted some twenty-one years later in the person she saw in the mirror, just minutes earlier.

She jumped up again, gazed in the mirror, lifted her boobs up a little, gave them a squeeze and shuddered.

That felt so good! Time to get ready.

She put on her swimsuit. It was one-piece which covered everything and hid nothing. Her curves were on display. She subdued the display a little with a loose white cotton shirt, jeans, socks and sneakers. She applied basic make-up, a little eye shadow and some powder to her cheeks. *She was ready to go!*

She decided on a strategy to meet these new people; she would be at the table for lunch before other guests arrived. This way she would meet them as they arrived and not be introduced to an already formed group.

She entered the kitchen to find Dawn just pouring herself coffee.

'Want one?' said Dawn as she put down the plunger. 'Help yourself, there are mugs in the cupboard up there.'

'Sure thing,' she said, choosing a mug with a pleasing

butterfly design. She poured herself a coffee and asked, 'What can I do to help?'

She sat opposite Dawn at the kitchen table.

'Not much really. This is a Fergus thing with a group of his mates and their families. He does the cooking – if you can call barbecuing actual cooking – and I just help with some salads. And really, these days I can buy ready-made salads at the supermarket. So, it's no big deal; so just relax, I expect they will start arriving in about half an hour.

'I predict that Ted and Veronica will arrive first with their two-year-old, Eddy. She's a real cutey. They both play touch footy with Fergus. Veronica manages the local supermarket and Ted is a sales rep for Moccona coffee.

'Hank, I think you met this morning, and Ross, his fiancée, are coming. Ross owns a bicycle shop in Brisbane and competes in triathlons. Hank, as you know works with Fergus. He's a great mechanic. And I think Matthew Crawley may be coming with his Tuesday, his eleven-year-old daughter. I heard Fergus talking to Matthew on the phone this morning. He is the Australian marketing manager for a new jet ski maker, Krogan. He and Fergus used to compete in jet ski races. Matthew and his wife, Lily, recently divorced and I think it must be his turn to have a weekend with Tuesday, who lives with her mother.

'I've set the table and we can take the salads and nibbles down when we see Ted, Veronica and Eddy arrive. As you can see, Fergus is already attending to his precious Weber. Let's just enjoy the quiet before the party begins.

'Tell me how is your new accommodation? I suppose you

were happy to find a place with just the two of you. That Backpacker Central must have been a noisy place.'

'Yes, it was,' said Rachel, 'Exciting, at least at first, but yes, you're right, it was noisy.

'Amelia, who I share with now, is quiet and spends much of her time in her room watching TV. I don't have a set. I prefer to read. Amelia is very particular about the things in the apartment. It's fully furnished with a refrigerator, stove, microwave and washing machine. Her philosophy is: "There is a place for everything and everything should be in its place". So, I have had to learn to be a lot tidier than I would normally be,' she laughed.

'At first , Amelia and I were working together at the bookshop, but she recently got a better job managing a medical centre in Paddington. We don't see so much of each other now, but that's a good thing.'

'What about men? Have you had many dates? I think you would attract a lot of male attention.'

'I don't know about lots, but I have had a few dates, but nothing serious.'

'How old are you now?' said Dawn.

'I'm twenty-one.'

'Oh, you don't want anything serious yet. You have plenty of time to just have fun,' said Dawn

'I'm hoping to have nothing serious for nearly twenty more years, or never,' she thought, as she gave Dawn a very bright smile. *'I have plans that you could not imagine, but if you could, you may not approve.'*

'Oh, look,' said Dawn, 'just as I said, here are Ted, Veronica and Eddy coming through the back gate. I'll take the salads if you bring the nibblies down and you can meet them.'

Together, they went down and placed the food onto the table. Eddy came running ahead of her parents, arms out wide crashing into Dawn's legs, then wrapping her little arms around Dawn's knees.

'Aunty Dawn, Aunty Dawn,' she squealed as Dawn scooped her up and held her tight.

As she held Eddy close, Dawn said, 'Eddy and I know each other well. I babysit her often when Veronica must be at work and her mother is not available to help her out.'

'Ted and Veronica, this is Rachel.'

Hank and his fiancée, Ross, came next and were introduced. The handshake with Hank was unremarkable this time and she suspected Hank was as relieved as she was when it was done.

Fergus left his precious Weber and greeted his guests. He helped with drinks, but Rachel noticed that each guest had brought their own drinks with them. As Ted took out beers for Veronica and himself, Veronica cautioned him, 'Don't forget you're DD today. Only two beers for you.'

'What does DD mean?' enquired Rachel.

'That means he is to drive Eddy and me home today, so he must limit himself to two beers for this afternoon. Next time we go out and have alcohol, it will be my turn to be DD.'

'I understand the situation you describe, but why DD?'

'Oh, sorry,' said Veronica, 'DD means designated driver.'

Just then another guest, Matthew Crawley, arrived with a young girl.

He apologised seemingly to everyone for being late and was introduced, along with his daughter, Tuesday.

As she shook their hands, Rachel was thinking that this was a man she would like to get to know. *'He is gorgeous,' she thought.*

Just then, Fergus announced that the meat was ready and brought over a large platter of steaks, lamb chops and sausages to put on the table for each guest to choose from.

The conversation ranged from many questions to about her trip to Australia, her job, then local issues about business, jet skis, climate change, politics and the weather.

As the afternoon wore on, Tuesday separated herself from the adults and sat at a table on the other side of the swimming pool. She produced a book from her bag and set about reading it. Eventually, Rachel, joined Tuesday.

'Hi, Red,' Said Rachel.

'Hi, Red, yourself,' laughed Tuesday, as she closed her book and smiled up at Rachel who sat opposite her.

'Tuesday is an unusual name.'

'It's a silly name!' cried Tuesday. 'My parents have trouble agreeing on anything, even my name. They decided on Tuesday because I was born on a Tuesday. At least they could agree on that!'

'If it could have been your choice, what name would you have chosen?'

'I would have chosen Imogen.'

'That is a pretty name. Maybe when you're grown up you can change it.'

She smiled and said, 'You know that you look just as I

did when I was young and felt really shy about having red hair and freckles. Boys especially gave me a hard time. Do you find that?'

'I do. I'm the only person in my class with red hair and I'm picked on a lot,' replied Tuesday.

'Yes, I was too, but do you know what? It passes, and now I find that grown-up boys really like redheads like us. So, cheer up there are better days ahead, Red.'

'That's all very well if I end up looking like you. I think my Dad likes you. He seemed to be looking at you a lot during lunch.'

Rachel let that one go through to the keeper, although she would not have put it in those words.

'I hear that you live with your Mum now. It must be very difficult when parents divorce. Do you spend much time with your Dad?' she asked.

'Every second weekend, but sometimes he doesn't make it. He travels a lot with his job. Even when I was growing up, he was often away, working. I wish he had a job like my friends' fathers do, you know, where they go to work each day and come home every night.'

Tuesday began to tear up a little and Rachel moved over to sit beside her and put an arm around her.

'I hope you realise that it's not your fault that your parents have split up. Children often get the idea that their parents split up because of them but that's not true; getting divorced is strictly an adult thing.'

Just then, Matthew appeared, and Tuesday quickly wiped her tears away.

'Two pretty redheads together; you make a wonderful pair. Are you all right, Tuesday? Have you been crying?' he asked.

'No,' said Tuesday. 'Do you know where the toilet is, Rachel?'

'Yes, just over there. It's the door next to the laundry.'

Matthew took a seat opposite. 'I hope my daughter grows up like you.'

'How do you know what I'm like?' she challenged him.

'You're right, I don't really know, but I'd like to find out.'

'I think that you may like to get to know a lot of women.'

Matthew put up both hands, palms pointed at Rachel. 'Whoa! I'm not trying to hit on you.'

'Oh, I think you are, but that's okay. If you hadn't, I would probably have hit on you,' she said bluntly. Matthew narrowed his eyes as he prepared to respond to this unexpected challenge.

But before he could gather his thoughts, she continued 'I bet your divorce has come about because of you hitting on women who are not your wife, or former wife. You spend a lot of your time away from home, or you did, Tuesday tells me. I think she really misses you when you are away working so much and that, even now, when you can see her every second weekend, you sometimes fail to turn up.'

'Whoa, again,' he said but lowered his hands. 'I'd like to separate two issues here. One is a possible relationship, or at least a date with you, and the other being my daughter and the way I lead my life. You could be part of the first, but you are not welcome to be part of the second.'

'That's fair, so let's discuss the first issue. What are you offering me?' she said.

He reached into a pocket, produced a business card, and handed it over to her. As she took it she looked directly into his eyes as she slipped the card in between her breasts.

He dragged his eyes away from her breasts. 'If you call me, I can suggest a good place to eat in Brisbane or do you know a place that you would like to go?' he said.

Rachel feathered the card still protruding from between her breasts.

'And what did you have in mind for after dinner. Am I to be dessert? If you want to have sex with me it will cost you,' again she looked directly into his eyes. 'There's no need to ask. It will be five hundred dollars.'

Matthew showed little sign of the shock he was feeling.

He said, 'That's a high price for a fuck. Are you a prostitute?'

Just then Tuesday reappeared.

'What's a prostitute, Dad?' she asked.

'Well, it's sort of an adult thing, like divorce. You really don't have to know about it now,' stammered Matthew

'But I already know about divorce. It means that I don't have a mother and father at home. You're just a visitor now and sometimes you don't even come to pick me up when you're supposed to.'

She began to cry again and ran off towards their car.

'I'm sorry about that...' he began, but Rachel cut him off. 'You should be saying sorry to her, not to me.'

'Remember, there are two issues here and you are not part

of the second one, so shut up,' he snapped back. He glared at her then walked over to the rest of the party, said a brief thanks to Fergus and Dawn and goodbye to the others with the comment that Tuesday was not feeling well and that they were heading home. After Matthew had departed in such haste the astonished barbecue group looked to Rachel for an explanation. She walked back slowly towards the group of friends with Tuesday's book *Harry Potter the Philosopher's Stone* under her arm.

'What happened there?' asked Dawn.

'I think that Tuesday is not handling the divorce well. Maybe Matthew is not always picking her up when he is supposed to, and Tuesday is really feeling that as a form of rejection. Look, I don't know the situation so well, so I can't be sure that's the reason, but I could feel the tension between them.'

'But why was Matthew yelling at you?' asked Dawn.

'He thought that it was out of order for me to get involved in their family's business and he was right.'

The honesty of her response impressed Dawn and possibly the others at the table.

'I thought he was going to ask you out '

'Oh, he did. He gave me his business card,' she replied as she drew the card from between her breasts to support, unnecessarily, her point.

'Since he doesn't have my contact details, it's up to me to make the next move, if any move needs to be made,' she added as she took her seat again with the others.

For a short interval, no one spoke; each of the group trying to digest the scene they had witnessed.

Only Fergus was hungry at the evening meal; he satisfied himself with a few leftover sausages and some microwaved leftover garlic bread. Dawn and Rachel both picked at crackers, cheese, fruit and a glass of wine. Each was still reflecting on the incident with Matthew and Tuesday.

'Do you think you will go out with him?' asked Fergus.

'At present, I don't know what will happen. But I can tell you this, I will accept his invitation to dinner if he does ask me. He is a fine-looking man, with good conversation skills and a good sense of humour. That was evident at the BBQ. He did become cross with me and told me to shut up but that may be because I pissed him off. He may have taken offence and want nothing more to do with me. All I know about him is what I learned today. There must be more to him than that.'

'Oh, there is, but it would not be fair to put my view of Matthew to you because I know him in a very different context,' said Fergus. 'He and I have been competitors for years in jet ski competition but it was friendly competition and away from the competition we have been friendly enough. But Matthew has never been a close friend, like the others at the barbecue and we have grown apart as a result of his new job. We simply see less of him than we used to. Today, for instance, I had not invited him to the barbecue. He sort of invited himself when I spoke with him of the phone this morning. I think it was convenient if he had maybe not planned anything with Tuesday for the weekend. But this is all supposition and if you do have a date with him, you may discover the true Matthew.'

'How philosophical you can be after eating burned meat, but I thought you said that you were not going to give an opinion?' laughed Dawn as she lifted her glass to toast her husband.

'It was rather philosophical, bordering on the insightful,' said Fergus, 're-toasting' Dawn with his glass. They all laughed at their collective knowledge of human foibles.

Rachel was thinking back to other observations not made in their collective wisdom so far.

She had noted that Matthew and Tuesday were by far the best dressed people at the BBQ. Both wore fashion-branded clothes and shoes. *Deduction: Matthew had money, some of which may come her way.*

Chapter 31
TUESDAY

Fergus was the only one up early after the barbecue. He was attending to the pool filter when Rachel appeared a little after 9 am. She had her togs on and said, 'I'd like to try out your beautiful pool before I go home.'

'Yes, and next time you come, you'll have to try out a jet ski.'

As she was diving in, Rachel thought, *I'm glad there will be a next time.*

She swam a few laps of the twelve-metre-long pool then swam up to the pool filter where Fergus was working.

'Great pool; it's so big!' declared Rachel 'So what do you think of yesterday's ...' she struggled for an appropriate word.

'Fiasco,' offered Fergus, 'Fiasco?'

'Well, it's not the first time we have had to a drama involving Matthew,' said Fergus. 'I have known Matthew since we first competed together in jet ski racing and his marriage to Lily was shaky even when I first met him. I think they believed that having a child would help but clearly it did not. All three of them, Matthew, Lily and Tuesday are wonderful, but it just did not work out for them as a family.

'The main problem, I think, and this is just my opinion, is Matthew's job. He is the rep for Kogan Jet Ski Company and his territory is basically the east and south coasts of Australia. It is a new company in Australia and is up against some well-established brands. He still lives here in Brisbane, but I think he is rarely home. The machines are shipped to Brisbane from South Korea where they are manufactured. He makes sure that they are shipped to the correct locations around Australia. He also had to set up agents to sell and maintain the machines. They hired him because he is well-known in the jet ski world and because of his participation in jet ski racing He is also well-known for his integrity. He has a good reputation.

'I know he really loves Tuesday, but his schedule sometimes means that he can't be there for her on a particular weekend. Lily is cooperative with his work schedule, but Tuesday does not always understand the arrangements her parents make. As you could see from his car and the clothes they both wear, Matthew is very well paid. Companies such as Krogan pay extremely well, but think they own you.'

It seemed that Fergus could not keep still. After breakfast he cleaned up the barbecue area and his precious Weber and then disappeared into the garage. He paused briefly to join Rachel and Dawn for morning tea where Dawn suggested that he take Rachel down to their shop to see some jet skis. She said that she would not go as she had some work to do on a 'swimming schedule'.

Fergus took Rachel down to the shop in their old Toyota about a ten-minute drive away. On the way, Rachel asked about the swimming schedule.

'Dawn has her own business, although she still helps me out with the jet ski business as well. Her skill is in managing a business and mine is in mechanics. When we were setting up the jet ski business it became clear that we would need money over and above what the bank would lend us. So, she started teaching beginners to swim. She had the qualifications already. Our pool is big and suitable for beginners to learn to swim.

'Soon she was teaching eight hours a day and more people were wanting her time. She teaches one person at a time with her special method. She had so many people wanting to learn, she had to train others to teach in her special way. I call it the Drummond Method, but Dawn calls it common sense. It has been so successful that she has four teachers trained in her method at other pools. She now rarely teaches herself but needs to manage the other pools. That's what she'll be doing while we're at the shop.'

'Why the Drummond Method?' asked Rachel.

'That's her name. She did not take my name when we married. She is Dawn Drummond,' replied Fergus.

As they approached, Rachel could see through the display window some of the jet skis on show.

They looked great, fast even, in their stationary display. Rachel had seen these machines from a distance but never close like this. They were awesome.

Fergus invited her to sit on a floor display model. It felt great to be astride the machine and imagined being on one, on the water with the pulse of the engine directly underneath. That thrilling pulse would be a turn-on and she was looking forward to a ride when next she visited.

Fergus pointed out that some machines had seating for two, so when she came next, she could be a passenger on one of those. The shop was full of various items that were accessories for jet skis. There was everything from wet suits to special sunglasses to helmets and gloves. There were large photos of Fergus on one his special racing machines. It had a very blokey image. That was okay with Rachel, she liked blokes.

The weekend, with its attendant drama over Matthew and Tuesday, was coming to an end and after lunch by the pool, she packed up her things, ready to go to the station with Fergus and make her way back to the city.

She and Dawn embraced to say their goodbyes and then she joined Fergus in the Toyota for the short drive back to the station. On the way, Fergus said, 'The next long weekend is for the Queen's birthday in October, so why don't you plan to come and join us and do some jet skiing? It could be the same arrangement as this weekend but there won't be a Matthew fiasco next time.'

'I thought the Queen's birthday was in June sometime,' said Rachel, shaking her head, perplexed.

'It's all over the place here. Queensland recently moved it from earlier in the year to October because there were too many public holidays in the first half of the year or some other crazy idea. Each state and territory choose when to celebrate it and it is also a day for handing out a lot of honours,' said Fergus.

'Without being too personal, what is your clothes size? We'll need to organise a wetsuit for you to go on the jet ski,' said Fergus.

'I'm not sure. Can I get back to you on that?' said Rachel.

'That's fine,' said Fergus.

A quick peck on the cheek from Fergus and Rachel headed back home on the train. This took about an hour, and she used the time to appraise the weekend and to think about Matthew's business card which she had transferred from between her breasts to her wallet.

'What to do. What to do?' she thought.

She felt that somehow Matthew was going to play an important part in her life; but it was certainly not marriage. She had a similar feeling about Tuesday, but she could not see how to rule any relationship with the youngster either in or out. She felt a real affinity for her fellow 'red', but what would a twenty-one-year-old woman and an eleven-year-old girl, not related, have to do with one another?

She took Matthew's card from her wallet. It was high quality print, with a colour photo of Matthew in the top right-hand corner. Anyone receiving the card would have to be impressed. She certainly was!

By the time she got home she had decided what not to do; she would not call him tonight. Maybe tomorrow, Tuesday (the day, not the girl), or maybe not at all. It was all too hard on a Monday night and there was work tomorrow. She would sleep on it, but of course she did not sleep at all! After the sleepless night, she was off to a fuzzy start to the day.

'You look awful, Rachel. What have you done to yourself over the weekend?' said Amelia as Rachel came out of her room.

Amelia always commented on any mood shifts she observed in Rachel but after months of hearing the judgemental observations, Rachel finally decided to react.

'Amelia, will you please keep your comments to yourself; really, it has become quite irritating.' Undaunted, Amelia replied, 'Well, you do look rather seedy.'

'Piss off and go to work,' shouted Rachel as she slammed her bedroom door.

Amelia thought about being told to piss off and was going to respond. However, the slammed bedroom door made any further conversation unlikely, so she huffed, but left for work.

Yelling at Amelia proved to be somewhat cathartic and raised Rachel's spirits. She dressed quickly and headed off to work. Just as she was leaving she noticed Tuesday's Harry Potter book. For no apparent reason she put it in her bag. It was a slow day at the bookshop, so she was doing some dusting when Matthew entered the shop. He noticed her and approached.

'*Where is this going?*' she thought as he grew nearer.

She smiled as he grew close and said, 'How may I help you today, sir?' 'I am looking for Peter Carey's latest novel but I've forgotten the title.'

'That would be *A Long Way Home*, sir'

'That's it, that's it. Do you have it?'

'We certainly do and would that be paperback or hard cover, sir?'

'Hard cover.'

'Excellent choice, I shall get one immediately.'

He was loving this. A great-looking woman who could play word games with him. She stopped and swung around to face him again.

'We also have a used, but very well preserved, copy of *Harry Potter and The Philosopher's Stone*. I could include that at no extra charge if you purchase the hard cover version of the Carey book.'

He smiled broadly. 'That would be wonderful. My daughter will be so excited.'

'I shall get the books, if you just wait for me at the checkout, sir.'

She fetched the Carey book and Tuesday's Harry Potter book and brought them back to the checkout. She placed both in a bag.

'That will be thirty-five dollars for the Carey book and of course the Harry Potter book is at no charge. Will that be cash or card, sir?' said Rachel, looking Matthew straight in the eye. She had not smiled in recognition throughout the entire conversation.

Matthew waved his card over the proffered EFTPOS device. She asked Matthew if he required a receipt.

He said 'Yes' and she printed one out for him.

'Now will there be anything else, sir?' She smiled broadly and made eye contact.

'As a matter of fact, there is. May I take you to lunch? It must be about time for your break.'

Rachel resumed with her poker face. She reached down to the display of stationery which was between the counter and her customer and picked out a small pocket diary. She opened it at no particular page and ran her finger down as if searching for today's date.

'Ah!' she proclaimed, 'It seems that I am free for lunch.'

Because Rachel's break was brief, they went into *Gnoshi's* next door. 'How do you know where I work?' asked Rachel.

'I phoned Fergus. It seemed that he may have been expecting my call. Are you pleased that I have come to see you?' asked Matthew.

'Could be. It depends on why you came.'

'We have unfinished business. I left the barbecue without asking you out.'

'How is Tuesday now?'

'I don't know. She did not say goodbye when I dropped her off at her mother's.'

'Did you say goodbye to her?'

'Yes, I did, but she did not look back at me; maybe she didn't hear me.'

'Have you arranged a date to see her again?'

'Could we please get back to the reason for me being here. It is not Tuesday, bless her, it's about you and I having dinner together.'

'You're right, I am interfering. I like Tuesday and it's a

shame to see her hurt.'

'Okay, but what about dinner? Where would you like to go? And when?'

'Yes, to dinner, you choose where and when. But if I am to be dessert, you know the price.'

'Are you a prostitute?'

'That's complicated and perhaps we could talk about it after dessert. That is, if you want dessert.'

'I know the price of dessert. I'll pick you up at your place at 7 pm on Friday. What's your address? We can eat at *Alchemy*. Do you know it?'

'I haven't been there, but I've heard good things about it.'

'Are we staying someplace nice for dessert?'

'You bet, so bring a change of clothes for Saturday in case we want to do something for the day. The taxi can take our bags to the hotel after they drop us off at *Alchemy*. Maybe include your swimsuit in case we go sailing. Have you sailed before?'

'No, but it's on my bucket list. Do you have a yacht?'

'No, but a friend has, and I am trusted to use it.'

'It sounds like a plan. Now we should, or, rather, I should go back to work. I'll see you on Friday.'

He leaned in and kissed her on the cheek.

She smiled. He was pleased.

Chapter 32
THE PLAN

The dinner at *Alchemy* was great. They walked to the nearby *Aurora*, only a couple of minutes away, on a warm spring night. He had done well: dinner (she had her favourite, prawns); the short walk (they held hands); the hotel (she had never stayed in such luxury, a suite no less); and the sex was good (but not great). He was very impressed with Burning Bush.

Then they talked.

She took the lead and asked him about himself and Tuesday, and what he envisaged his future to be He went with this for a while, but part way through talk of jet skis, he stopped abruptly and said, 'Enough about me. Let's talk about you. I see what you have to offer. I'd like to help you but I don't know the plan. This skill you have is sensational, but if I am to help you restart your career here in Brisbane, I need to know your plan. I had to spend a lot of money and do all the work, as if it were a date.'

Rachel told him of her goal to become a high-class prostitute, use her body in a safe way and to be in control.

'Okay,' he said, 'but that's not a real plan. That's an aspiration. Do you have any money?'

She told him about Arthur Millar and how her savings had been eaten up in her escape from him. She explained that she would receive money from her mother's estate but that would take time to materialise. And her business plan was devised to be applied in Northern Ireland, not in Australia.

'So to be clear, you have long ago planned to be a prostitute because you like sex, but that you do not intend to grant any man exclusive rights to your body?'

'Yes, my life is not going to be about love, conjugal rights, establishing a home and having a family. This is about doing something I really enjoy with someone I choose. I will not choose to sleep with everyone that wants me. It will be *my* choice.'

By now it was late, and they decided to talk more about it on Saturday.

They woke early and after a light breakfast, he asked 'Would you like to go sailing, it's a great day for it?'

'What about a boat?'

'Remember, my friend, Arnie does, and he lets me use it. I'll call him to see if *Delphi* is available.' He called Arnie. 'We're on. *Delphi* is available. Let's go.'

'I'm up for it.' 'Can you swim?'

'First in the 100m freestyle for my age group.' 'A regular Shane Gould!'

'Shane who?'

'Sorry, you'd have to be an Ozzie to understand that.'

'You had better have on light clothes that cover you. It can be very glaring out on the water and your lovely skin will burn easily. Do you have sunglasses?'

'Yes, but I'll need to pick up a few things at home. Can we go by there and I'll get some sailing clothes?'

It took about forty-five minutes to drive to the Royal Queensland Yacht Squadron in Manly where Matthew's friend, Arnie, moored his yacht. Matthew handed Rachel some sunscreen and suggested she apply some to her face, hands, and the tops of her feet.

He produced a basket containing fruit, sandwiches, cakes and pastries, and a bottle of chardonnay. After parking the car, they walked by the clubhouse between a couple of rigging lawns, then to the office for Matthew to arrange to use Arnie's yacht.

Arnie's berth was G7, so they walked along a board walk for about thirty metres and found the location of the G berths. Matthew helped Rachel aboard *Delphi* and motioned to a shady spot where she could sit. He placed the basket in the cabin below deck.

He excused himself and said he was off for a few minutes to find the crew. 'I thought you were going to sail it yourself.'

'Well, I could but I'd rather sit and talk to you.' 'I'm flattered.'

The yacht was an Adams 31, 9.5 metres long with a fibreglass hull. Rachel was impressed but looking around her, she noticed that there were many bigger yachts than Arnie's berthed nearby.

Ten minutes later, Matthew reappeared with Jane and Felix, a British couple backpacking in Australia. They had a passion for sailing and hung around this club waiting the chance to crew on a yacht. It did not matter to them whether it was for the day or an extended trip – they just liked sailing. The Adams could be sailed single-handed, but Matthew preferred to leave it to Jane and Felix who had extensive experience in sailing on Moreton Bay.

It was 10 am and they set off out of the marina and into the bay initially by diesel power. They had all put on their life jackets. There was a light breeze, so soon Jane and Felix had set sails and their trip began.

It was a day made for sailing; some low cloud meant that it was not so glary, the water was smooth, no big waves and a light north-easterly breeze. The conditions allowed for maximum sail, including at times the colourful spinnaker.

At times the Adams dipped to one side and the crew sat on the upper side to balance. They called to Matthew and Rachel to help.

'Do you want to give it a go?' asked Matthew.

'Do I what!' shouted Rachel as she clambered up and sat beside Felix. Mathew joined her.

It was such a thrill to hang over the side of the boat and feel the spray as the boat sped along in the breeze. She noticed many others enjoying the experience of skimming across Moreton Bay, some with multi-coloured sails. After the excitement of balancing the yacht, they went below. Matthew showed Rachel how to operate the stove to make them coffee and then headed back on deck to take Felix and

Jane bottles of water as neither drank tea or coffee.

When he returned below, he found Rachel examining a map of Moreton Bay. She asked which direction they were headed. He pointed to the north.

He said, 'All being well, we will pass Green Island soon and then further on, we will get to St Helena Island.'

'I thought that Green Island was on the Great Barrier Reef.'

'Well, yes, there is another, rather more famous Green Island up north, but we have our very own here, on Moreton Bay.'

'And St Helena is a remote British island in the South Pacific where Nap-ol-eon was imprisoned and died five years later.'

'Nap-ol-eon?'

'Yes, Nap-ol-eon, that's how it is pronounced by the French.' 'And do you call Paris, Paree?' laughed Matthew.

'Of course,' said Rachel, in a badly faked French accent and laughing too. They had their coffee and some cake before they went back on deck.

Sailing was a revelation for Rachel, and she promised herself that she would do it again. Maybe have her own boat.

She was excited and thanked Matthew for taking her.

After sailing past St Helena, they headed west towards the coast and back down to Manly. As they were sitting below again, Matthew took out pen and paper and began to write.

He said, when he had finished, handing it to Rachel, 'This is a proposal; I thought about our conversation last night and I want to propose a business deal between us. I will lend you $20,000 to get you started on your career. And you will pay it back with ten per cent interest. In two years, you pay me $24,000. This is just a preliminary proposal, and I shall write it up and send it to you for consideration.

'What is your email address?'

'I don't have email.'

'I'll just send it to your phone, then'

'My phone can't do that,' as she produced her simple prepaid mobile from her bag. 'Then you will have to use some of the money to buy a laptop and a smart phone.'

This shook Rachel. She knew that she would require funds to get started but this was an enormous amount. She was stunned and did not know how to reply. This was a situation where her extensive reading was of little use. But she knew that she had Jesse to advise her.

Matthew said, 'This is a business deal that could suit both of us. I hope it does. I cannot get anything like ten per cent interest in the current market and you would get nowhere going to a bank. Prostitution is a risky business, but you are going into it by choice, not by necessity. That's a great start. But you will need advice about marketing and just who your target clients will be. Your service is way ahead of others, but you don't have any connections yet. I can help there. Word of mouth works well here in Australia, as I expect it does elsewhere.'

'Matthew, this is a big surprise. I had no idea that you would or could do such a thing. And I am impressed by your confidence in me,' said Rachel.

'I am confident, but it is a measured confidence. The interest rate I'm charging you is very high. That is an indicator of the risk I am taking. I very much hope you succeed. I am not doing you a favour in this. It is a business deal in which I can make a good profit in a short time, but the risk is high.'

They berthed the boat at Manly and Matthew took Rachel back to her apartment.

He asked if they could meet again the following Saturday to further discuss the deal and added that he would have Tuesday with him. He asked her if that was okay.

'I'd be delighted to see her again.'

When she got inside she checked the time. It was a bit too early to ring Jesse yet, but she was busting to do so. However, it gave her time to think it through herself.

What would she do with this amount of money? How much would a laptop and smart phone cost and how much to run them? What else would she need to run the business?

She tried to remember the details of her Northern Ireland plan.

They had planned to have a website, but she could not recall the costs of doing that. It was a detail that Jesse was going to have to help her with.

The excitement was too much. She rang Jesse.

A very sleepy, but anxious, Jesse answered her phone. 'What's wrong? Why are you ringing ...' she paused, trying to turn on her beside light to read her alarm clock, '... at 4 am?'

Rachel related the story.

'It's very exciting, Rachel, but take a deep breath. We need to know exactly what this guy is offering you. This is what you need to do. He is right, you'll need a laptop and a smart phone. Then you need to get an email address. I'm sure there would have been internet access at that Backpacker Central. Do you have wi-fi at your apartment? If not, go there and get someone to help you do that. Also ask if there is a printer so that you can get a paper copy of your emails. When you've done that ask him – what's his name again? – to email you his proposal. Then you'll have that ask someone at the Submarine to show you how to forward it to me. Do not agree, evenly verbally, to any proposal until we have discussed it. Are you okay with all that?'

Rachel agreed and took down Jesse's email address.

On the following Saturday, Matthew came to Rachel's apartment. 'Where's Tuesday?'

'She stayed in the car. She's pissed off with me.' 'Again?'

'Don't start.'

'Sorry. Not my business.'

When they got to Matthew's car, a very sulky looking Tuesday sat in the back reading a book. She did not look up as they got into the car.

'Hi, Tuesday,' said Rachel.

'Hi,' was the barely audible reply.

'Are you going to have coffee with us?' 'I don't like coffee.'

'What will you have then?'

'Nothing. I'm not thirsty.' 'Tuesday!' said Matthew.

'Rachel is our guest. Please be polite.'

'It's not very polite of you to forget my concert.'

'No, and I have apologised for that.'

'You have a lot to apologise for.'

'Hey, it's a lovely day. We are going to...Where are we going?' asked Rachel.

'To the museum. There's a good coffee shop there and Tuesday can spend time in the museum if she does not want to drink coffee with us,' said Matthew.

'I've already been there tons of times. It's boring.'

'If you two are just going to argue, why not sit here in the car while I go and have coffee and visit the museum by myself?'

Silence.

'Do they have chocolate milkshakes?' 'I'm sure they do,' guessed Matthew. 'So, let's go!' said Rachel.

When they got to the coffee shop, Tuesday noticed that a feature for that day was *Big Voices* which her art teacher had mentioned as good and if any in the class could possibly go, they should. Tuesday asked Matthew if she could go.

He said, 'Sure thing, but we will come in with you, so we know where you are; and you only leave to come back to us here. If you want to go anywhere else, come back here first. Agreed?'

'Agreed!' She was smiling now as Matthew and Rachel walked her into the auditorium.

While Tuesday left them so she could enjoy *Big Voices*, Rachel and Matthew walked back to the cafe and had coffee.

Matthew said, 'Although I will make this a bit more formal for your aunt I can show you the simple arithmetic on the back of a coaster.' And he showed her where he had written down the details of the financial plan he was presenting to her to repay the debt.

Chapter 33
Jesse

After Jesse read Matthew's proposal she was in two minds. This guy was offering a great deal of money at high interest, and she thought that given the risk he was taking, it could be worthwhile considering. *But why was he doing it?*

It was true that it was time that Rachel re-launched her career. *How did he even come into the frame?*

Rachel gave her the background to his intervention, which seemed to Jesse to make some sense. But she still wondered, *Why he had made this offer?*

Jesse had some understanding of British law and expected that Australian law would be similar. But she knew that Australia had been formed from existing sovereign states which had their own legal systems before Federation.

She proposed that she would lend Rachel the equivalent of one thousand Australian dollars for her to buy a laptop and a smart phone. She had looked at online deals in Australia and the price for basic used laptops was about four hundred dollars, and a good second-hand phone could be purchased for between four and five hundred dollars.

With these two items, she and Rachel could communicate by email and even use WhatsApp to speak about this deal and have real-time contact while the business was up and running. The money she lent to Rachel could re-paid immediately from the offered loan by Matthew.

Jesse instructed Rachel to set up a bank account so that they could make funds transfers direct over the internet then she would forward the funds for the laptop and the phone. She suggested that this Matthew character could possibly help with this. She also emphasised that under no circumstances was Rachel to accept credit card access to her account. The basic tenet of their business was cash only. She told Rachel that all business and personal transactions should be cash only. She knew that credit card transactions left a clear money trail.

Rachel informed Jesse that she already had a bank account for her wages and that she had decided to use cash for all her needs.

Jesse had also accessed the Australian Government Immigration website and found that Rachel should apply for a working holiday visa which was available for twelve months for four hundred and eight-five dollars, but that could be renewed for an extended stay of three years.

She put together a series of questions to Matthew by email about the type of interest payment he would accept and how Rachel would make these regular payments.

Jesse was satisfied with the repayment schedule and drew up a formal agreement for both Rachel and Matthew to sign.

Having received Matthew's reply by email and secured Rachel's agreement to the new proposal, she sent them off to him.

Matthew took three days to reply. In addition to the repayment schedule, there was a condition to his final agreement. He proposed that over the two years of the loan that Rachel accompany him each time that he had custody of his daughter, Tuesday, which was once a fortnight.

On reading about this condition Jesse was furious.

She was most unhappy about the issue of Rachel spending fifty-two weekends looking after the guy's daughter without any mention of payment.

Her research on Australian pay rates had also suggested that a rate of four hundred dollars for a weekend's work was not unreasonable. In other words, this Matthew would owe Rachel twenty thousand dollars for that service. She would owe him nothing after two years!

After consulting with Rachel, she fired an email written totally in capital letters that they would not accept this service without payment.

Matthew took a week to reply.

The importance of his daughter's welfare was paramount, and he favoured this new proposal but claimed that since it was *his* twenty thousand dollars, that he should have control over how the money was spent. In fact, he wanted total control.

Again, it took days for him to reply.

He expected that Rachel would need the following:

1. A website to facilitate the business which would require funds to set up and maintain.

2. A scriptwriter to extend and polish her Burning Bush banter.

3. A minder to ensure her personal safety and protect his investment; and

4. A professional photographer for web images, and that he personally had access to people who had these skills.

Rachel and Jesse agreed that on those four issues he was

right. Before agreeing to these conditions, they needed to know just how many of the twenty thousand dollars he would require to take on these tasks.

Jesse claimed that he should provide evidence for these estimates.

It took Matthew more than a week to come back with details of payment of the services which were:

1. The website design would cost between two thousand and five thousand dollars, depending upon the complexity with maintenance fees of perhaps one hundred dollars per month.

2. The scriptwriting fee would be about fifty dollars per minute of product, for, say, a total of five hundred dollars.

3. The costs per hour for unarmed personnel were thirty-five to fifty dollars and up to one hundred and fifty dollars an hour for specially trained armed guards.

4. The photographer costs of one hundred and twenty-five dollars per hour includes set up, supply and presentation. A spend of approximately five hundred dollars would yield forty to fifty photos.

'All of his figures are rubbery. We need to tie him down to a figure we can agree on,' suggested Jesse.

They forwarded this request to Matthew. His reply:

'It was difficult to be precise about this but suggested that a figure of eight thousand dollars would cover items one to three, but that the security figure would depend on what level of security you chose and how often it would be required. He proposed an extra one thousand dollars for his management of these services which could be renegotiated after one year.'

Rachel and Jesse were reasonably happy with the proposal and agreed that Jesse have a business agreement drawn up to present to Matthew.

Jesse pointed out that in terms of the child, that Rachel be allowed a few occasions where she could opt out for health or other personal reasons, with twenty-four hours' notice.

So Matthew would retain nine thousand dollars and deposit eleven thousand dollars into her account. At the end of two years there would be no more deposits and nothing to repay. For the nine thousand dollars controlled by Matthew, Rachel would submit invoices to him and if he approved them he would pay them.

Once the document had been prepared Jesse discussed it with Rachel again before sending it off to Matthew.

'Now,' said Jesse, 'we need to discuss how to use the money to your advantage.'

They spent hours discussing the use of the money and how their Northern Ireland business plan needed to be changed to fit Australian conditions. They found that for legal forms of sex work the act of prostitution itself is not illegal anywhere in Australia, but certain activities associated with prostitution are illegal. Prostitution laws vary from state to state. What is legal in one state might be illegal in another.

There are two legal forms of sex work in Queensland. First, sex work conducted in a licensed brothel from which outcalls are prohibited. Depending on the size of the brothel, there may be up to eight sex workers on premises at any one time. Second, sex work that is the work of a sole operator, where a sex worker works privately from a premises that provides outcalls. It is illegal for a sole operator sex worker to operate in conjunction with any other sex worker.

But now with a big task to be set up, Rachel pointed out that the source of the funds depended largely on Tuesday. What if she did not want to hang out with Rachel on weekends? They had been happy with each other's company twice so far but surely the girl needed to know that Rachel would be with Matthew each time he had custody. And would the goodwill of those two occasions carry over when Tuesday came to believe that Rachel had become her pseudo-mother on the weekends she spent with Matthew. And what would they do if Tuesday pursued the question she asked about what is a prostitute on their first meeting?

Rachel assumed that Tuesday was an intelligent girl and would have already 'Googled' it. What would she say if Tuesday asked her or Matthew if she (Rachel) was a prostitute.

'Of course, the girl's cooperation was important, but it was up to Matthew to bear that risk because it was his idea to choose this option in a belief that this arrangement would stabilise his relationship with his daughter,' suggested Jesse.

'I have a good feeling about the girl,' said Rachel. 'She's a redhead like me and we have already spoken about our special place in society and really, I am young enough to be her older sister.' 'How old is she?'.

'Eleven or twelve, I think.'

'And how about her mother?' asked Jesse. 'Does she

know about this proposed arrangement? She could make it difficult for you if she will not agree to your involvement. And what if the prostitute issue is raised with her by the girl?'

'I have met Tuesday only twice and I admit there could be issues, but really this is *my life*, and as such there are no guarantees.'

Jesse and Rachel considered his proposal and agreed that he should have some, but not total, control

'Okay,' said Jesse. 'You're right. Let's concentrate on the necessary changes to our Irish plan and modify it to suit Queensland. The most obvious and probably the most important issue is that I will not be able to vet the clients. You need a minder, but I see no way that he or she would want to take on the responsibility of vetting clients. Do you think you could manage it yourself?'

'I must admit that I sometimes have nightmares about Millar, but this is my life and my ambition to do what I find personally enjoyable for a living,' Rachel said. 'And although I am aware that the way I look now is seductive for men, it is not going to remain that way for ever. I hope the coming years are uneventful in terms of safety and that I can retire at forty or so and possibly buy Barnaby's Boutique and live the quiet life back in Derry.'

'Okay, if you feel confident, then let's send this off to Matthew and see if he agrees or has further issues to address.'

In reply, Matthew claimed another clause be written into the agreement.

He wanted a bail-out clause at the end of the first year if the situation with Tuesday and/or her mother became irreconcilable. In this case Rachel, would need to repay ten thousand dollars within one month of the end of the first year.

This came as surprise, and Rachel began to lose confidence. Jesse, too, was surprised at this last-minute claim but still thought that the deal, even with these final claims, was still a good one and urged Rachel to agree. She did want the one-month demand be three months. This would give Rachel sufficient time to adjust financially.

Jesse thought that for now Rachel's financial future was satisfactory, given that she would eventually inherit Elaine's stake in her grandmother's house, and perhaps Aemon's as well.

One more issue arose when Rachel made it clear that the time spent with Tuesday did not include sex with Matthew. He had received this one and only service already.

Matthew agreed to this final condition and the deal was finally sealed. The issue of implementation of the plan had now to be considered.

Photos and clothing needed to be addressed first and Rachel needed to decide what she would do about her job at the bookshop.

She decided that she should continue with this work unless it became too taxing to be assembling a suitable wardrobe for her career and for the photos required for the website. She looked for some deals for laptops and smart phones. She chose Telstra as her provider, several people she knew suggested Telstra because it was the biggest, but it did cost more. This cost about fifty dollars per month and included overseas calls.

At nearby Brisbane Traders, she found a reconditioned Dell laptop for four hundred dollars, and a reconditioned iPhone 6 for three hundred dollars.

For now, she continued working at the bookshop and on the weekends when she was not working with Matthew and Tuesday. She also began assembling her wardrobe. Jesse had forwarded the clothes she had in Derry and that was a start, but she needed clothes more suitable to subtropical Brisbane. Matthew obtained the services of Wild West Web Design, and he and Rachel spent some of their weekend with Annie Oakley, webmaster. She was thrilled to take on the challenge and after working out the site architecture with Rachel, began work on artwork and narrative, while Rachel attended a photographic session with Toni Blakely at Flash Bulb Photography for the images for the website.

She needed to arrange for security and began searching the web for businesses nearby. The list that she accessed contained Arnold and Overton Security. This sounded somehow familiar. As she was thinking about it, she remembered Dan Overton's card and her visit his business partner Steve in hospital.

Steve had been very grateful to Rachel when she met him in hospital. but she had no further contact with him. That was months ago. Perhaps she should speak to Steve's company. She realised that he may be able to offer the type of security that she needed.

She rang the company number and asked to Steve or

Dan. The receptionist indicated that Mr Overton was on a business trip in New Zealand and Mr Arnold was not in the office. She did, however, offer his mobile if that could help. Rachel took the number and immediately rang Steve. He was pleasantly surprised to hear from Rachel and asked what he could do to help her. She said that she did not wish to discuss the issue on the phone, and they agreed to meet at *Gnoshi's* on the following Thursday during her lunch break from the bookshop.

Steve was looking so much better than he had when she visited him in hospital. He had looked so frail then; now he looked fit and healthy.

He complimented her on how good she looked, and his mind was racing at the prospect of perhaps asking her out for dinner. She could sense his anxiety. She did not wish to be courted and decided to quickly establish what sort of relationship they might have. It would be a business relationship. Before Steve worked his way into asking her out, she asked him to tell her about his business and how she might use his services in her business. She spelt out immediately the nature of her business.

'Prostitute?' said Steve. He was clearly taken aback by this.

'Yes, Steve. That is my career and now you know, you had better tell me if working for a prostitute would be an appropriate thing for your company to be involved in. If you have doubts about it, then it would be best for you to say so now, and I won't take up more of your time.'

He and his business partner, Dan had never worked with prostitutes, but sensed immediately that there was no real reason for rejecting the work. It was a big disappointment, though, that she was not making herself available for a date.

'What sort of service would you require?'

Rachel related her experience with Arthur Millar and her subsequent flight to Australia. 'So, you would want us to be a bodyguard for you?'

Steve then outlined the nature of his business.

He and Dan had met when students at Ajax Karate. They were both keen on getting to black belt proficiency as soon as possible. They were highly competitive and Rang Duan, their teacher sensed it.

He wisely made the decision to confirm their black belt proficiency on the same day. They happily celebrated their new status together.

Dan had an idea to perhaps use this high status in karate to establish for themselves a school of their own, but Steve's plan was much more ambitious. They would use trained students to become security guards; not big, imposing, or armed, guards, but agile people who could inspire respect and not actually have to use their potent skill. And it would not be just men. Anyone over eighteen who achieved black belt status could be employed as guards.

Rachel listened to Steve's story about the evolution of their security business and was impressed.

She asked Steve to put together a plan for her protection so that she could include the cost of their service in her own business plan.

Steve promised that he could give her a quote for the service she had clearly outlined to him.

She was pleased to see Steve again and she felt that with his protection she could operate her business with confidence.

Steve did not dismiss the notion that he could form an intimate relationship with Rachel.

Chapter 34
RACHEL AND DAWN

Fergus stood by Rachel as the paramedics placed a brace on Steve's neck and very carefully manoeuvred him into the ambulance. He was impressed that she had clearly helped this poor guy who had crashed into the sand leaving his head in a very peculiar position.

'I heard what you said to that guy's friend about neck injuries. How did you come to know about it?' 'As I said, I read a lot.'

'But surely, that is pretty special information. Why would you read about that?'

'Do you remember Christopher Reeve, the actor who played Superman? I once read a novel where one of the characters breaks his neck in a car accident and one of the witnesses to the accident pulled the guy's neck into its usual position which resulted in his death. Then I remembered that Christopher Reeve had had a riding accident which resulted in him breaking his neck. So, I looked it up on the internet and learned a bit about these injuries. Reeve eventually died because of his neck injury but before he did, he and his wife set up a foundation to investigate ways in which serious neck injuries could be rehabilitated.'

'Well, as you have seen, riding a jet ski can be dangerous and anyone selling them has duty to inform the buyers of the risks. You remember me showing you the safety equipment that I supply to new owners? Well, given what I witnessed today, I think that I will be recommending that they have a safety helmet as well. We already sell them, but they're not mandated in Queensland yet. Evidence of this type of accident makes me think that it will soon be a requirement.'

'Did you hear how the ski ran out of control?'

'I heard the rider tell the paramedics that something, perhaps a bird, flew into his face. I saw that his sunglasses had been broken and he did have some small cuts on his face.'

'Well let's hope the other guy survives. He would be very grateful that you may have saved his life.'

'Okay, let's go and see what damage has been done to our craft.'

'Oh dear, Fergus, that looks bad. Can you repair it?'

'Well, it looks worse than it is. There is no structural damage that I can see. It will need some fibreglass filler and a new coat of paint. We don't do that ourselves; there are fibreglass repair places about, so I'll take it to them. It's a pity though, that we won't be able to ride today. But since you're here for two more days we may be able to manage it before you go home. I hope that this has not put you off. I have seen the results of collisions like this one, but they are rare.'

Rachel was shaken by the accident but tried to control the feeling that it could have been fatal for her. She had just managed to jump off before her craft was struck by the out-of-control ski.

She may find the offer of a new ride not so attractive. Despite this, she feigned a weak smile for Fergus.

The damage to the hull did not prevent Fergus and Rachel getting the ski onto its trailer and they soon had it locked up at the shop until it could be taken to be repaired on Tuesday.

Back at the house, Dawn was dismayed when she heard about the near-miss Rachel had experienced and asked her how she felt about it.

'Well, it's a bit unnerving to have had it happen and I still feel quite shaken by it.'

'Unnerving would be an understatement!' said Dawn. 'How close were you, Fergus?'

'Pretty close, but not as close as Rachel.'

'And what happened to the person on the other ski?'

'There were two of them. One had minor facial injuries, but the other has a broken neck, I think.'

'How could it have happened? What was this other rider doing to crash into you?'

'We think that he may have been hit in the face, by a bird perhaps, and lost control.'

'Rachel, love, you look a little pale. Why don't you go and lie down for a bit? I'll bring you a cuppa soon. That was very scary for you!' said Dawn.

'Yes, I think I shall,' said Rachel as she went to her bedroom.

She lay down and reflected on her near miss. The incident played over and over in her mind as a never-ending replay of the incident. It was not often that she thought about her mortality; like most young people she believed that death was something for old people to worry about, but here, right in her face, mortality presented its sinister and daunting self.

She eventually slipped into a light sleep but woke immediately when Dawn knocked and entered with a cup of tea.

Dawn pulled over a chair closer to the bed and took Rachel's hand.

'I am so sorry that this has happened to you, especially when you are our guest. It may be an idea for you to postpone jet ski riding for a bit. I can see that it has shaken you and you'll need time to recover.'

They were silent for a minute or so, then Dawn asked, 'How is the new accommodation working out? I remember you saying that your friend is very particular about orderliness?'

Rachel laughed and they spent the next few minutes laughing about Amelia and the bonking arrangement they had.

'Did you ever have a date with Matthew?'

Rachel kept up to date with current affairs. She had recently purchased a TV and noticed that sex workers were being presented occasionally with an opportunity to talk about their lives in the industry on current affairs programs.

These interviews seemed to help legitimise sex work in the public domain. It seemed to her that slowly there was a move towards public recognition that sex work is, in fact, legal, and as for any other employment, it should not be stigmatised. She realised that religious organisations would always condemn it. They sought to control their followers and deny them their chance to behave more naturally in a sexual encounter. The recent plebiscite on the legalisation of gay marriage suggested to her that the public was becoming a bit more relaxed about sex and sexuality.

If a young woman came onto an open discussion on TV about sex work, then it may be time to present *herself* as a prostitute and not a sex worker which seemed to her to be speaking in code unnecessarily.

She wondered, '*Would this be a good time to confide in Dawn that this is my chosen career? Is confide even the right term here?*'

Would she expect her revelation to be kept a secret?

She decided to first talk about Matthew and if it seemed to be going well, divulge her situation. She and Matthew had a contract which would be complicated to fully explain, but she thought she could handle the conversation without explaining all the details.

But before Rachel could reply to Dawn's question about Matthew, Dawn said, 'You know you have created quite a stir here in Sandgate. Many of the women around here who have seen you are a little afraid of your obvious attraction to the local males. They fear that you may steal their men.'

This came unexpectedly and caught Rachel off-guard. '*What is Dawn getting at?*' she thought '*Was she worried about*

Fergus? And did she know about the incident with Hank?'

For a moment Rachel could not speak.

A multitude of thoughts vied for attention in her brain, and she was briefly speechless. But it was time to take over this situation and quickly.

She held Dawn's gaze and asked, 'Are you worried about Fergus?' The challenge caused Dawn to avert her eyes and her face reddened.

'Let me tell you something about me that you would probably do not know. I use my body to make a living.'

Dawn looked up again, 'Are you a prostitute?'

'I am, Dawn, and I sincerely hope that knowing this about me will in no way change our friendship. What I am doing is business. I like having sex with some men, but they must pay for it. Fergus, I'm sure, has made the decision that most happily married men or men in stable relationships make. They enjoy looking at women, but they choose not to pursue the attraction over their marriage or serious relationship. Fergus and I have been alone together a few times now and I have no feeling of him hitting on me. Matthew did, and he paid for it.'

'This is a big surprise,' said Dawn.

'Let's not assume that men are alone in this. I expect that you and your friends have at some time looked with lust on some handsome man, but like Fergus you have chosen not to pursue the matter.'

'It's difficult for me to imagine what it would be like to do what you do and it's challenging to put aside the social prejudice against prostitution that for most of my life was illegal and sex workers, we called them whores, were considered low-life drug addicts soliciting on the roadside.'

'You are right there. That is usually the way they are referred to in movies, TV and in the media. F o r some women, it is one way to make enough money to support a drug habit. I made up my mind to pursue this life when I was a teenager, and I had the support of my Aunt Jesse when I began the business in Derry when I was eighteen years old. My mother died when I was sixteen, and I left home then to live with my aunt. It's a long and complicated story, but I operated with my aunt's help until one of my clients threatened to disfigure me. I was terrified, so my aunt and the man I had been working with for two years helped me to flee. It is only recently that I have recovered enough to start again here in Brisbane.'

'I wondered about your story about coming here. It didn't quite add up.'

'I'm sorry about the deception but I wasn't ready then to tell you the full story then. Will this change or even negate our friendship?'

'Being deceived is hard to forgive, but knowing what I know now, I believe I can forgive it.'

'This conversation has come as a surprise to me, and I sense that you understand my position. I will never forget that you and Fergus welcomed me into your home and into your lives when I arrived in Brisbane. Even if this was the end of our relationship, I shall never forget your generosity.'

The vigour of their conversation left both women fatigued and what happened next would give a clear indication of the continuation of their relationship.

It was a great relief to Rachel that Dawn moved in and kissed her cheek, squeezed her hand warmly and said 'Why don't you continue to rest? We can talk more later.'

Rachel slept soundly through lunchtime into the early afternoon.

When she emerged from her room she found Fergus and Dawn sitting in the kitchen having coffee. She glanced up at the kitchen clock, 'Look at the time. I've been asleep for hours!'

'Hey,' said Fergus. 'That was a close call you had today. I imagine that your brain has been working overtime to come to terms with it. Don't be surprised that it may take weeks to recover. In racing, I have been in situations where my life was at risk and the memories can be difficult to manage but the important thing to me is that I survived and learned from the experience. I hope it works out that way for you too. Now, how about some coffee?'

The talk they'd had was not, of course, enough to satisfy either Dawn or Rachel. The issue of relationships, marital or intimate, is fundamental in society and is a topic that is frequently discussed by women but unfortunately not so much by men.

Rachel knew that broadening the conversation was essential to her and Dawn, but should they include Fergus?

As they sat together for dinner that night, Fergus had prepared fish and chips, Rachel wondered whether they would speak more and include him in the 'women's room'. Many men knew that women discussed personal issues in the presence of other women, but often changed the subject if a man approached. It was unusual for men to be included in the 'women's room'.

But why?

It seemed to be a situation where both women and men lost out.

Rachel thought the decision should be left to Dawn and so she waited.

How would Fergus cope with an intimate discourse? Was he one of those privileged males to be included in such discussions? She imagined that if he was a regular that he would be included and maybe initiate such a topic.

As usual, the conversation at the beginning, when Fergus had served the meal and taken his seat, was mainly banter. But the banter stopped when Dawn after complimenting Fergus on the fish, 'dropped a bombshell' when she turned to him and asked, 'Does Rachel turn you on, Fergus?' Rachel continued to chew her fish even though she felt an urgent need to reach for water. '*This will be a pivotal moment,*' she thought.

She was pleasantly surprised when he replied, 'Of course I do, and I think most blokes would.' He then filled his mouth with chips and looked in turn at both women.

Dawn then steered the conversation towards the issue of local women expressing concern about having Rachel in their midst.

'Look,' said Fergus, 'I can't and won't attempt to speak for all males, but I think most find it very agreeable to look at attractive women; and some are more attractive than most.

Rachel is a standout in the vicinity right now, but there are always beautiful women around. I may be wrong, but I think they may like to be admired. And let's not forget those attractive young men wearing budgie smugglers on the beach, do they not attract the attention of women?'

'What on earth, is a budgie smuggler?' said Rachel.

'There's this urban myth that some bloke tried to smuggle a pair of budgerigars out of Australia in his underwear but was caught, of course. It is illegal to take native birds out of Australia without the necessary documentation,' said Dawn.

'But the term has been shifted to describe those tight, brief swimming costumes that some blokes wear. If their testicles are large enough, they bulge out like a couple of small, sedated budgerigars. Just as some women like to advertise their sex, so do some men,' said Fergus.

Chapter 35
PUBERTY BLUES

Rachel had just completed the first year of her contract with Matthew. They had passed an important date. He could no longer pull out. He was committed to continue for another twelve months, but there had been no good reason to stop having Rachel with him when he had Tuesday each fortnight. They had enjoyed many happy times around Brisbane and nearby localities. Rachel functioned as a sort of catalyst for father and daughter to enjoy the activities they chose for each weekend they had together.

'I need to talk to Dad about Mum's boyfriend and school, but it seems too hard, and I don't know how he will take it.'

'I find that if the topic is difficult, it may mean that you have to be circumspect about it'

'Circumspect?'

'Yes, it means to look around, or another way of putting it is to consider options; other ways of doing things.'

'Tell me more about this situation with this new man in your mother's life.'

'Well, he's an ESL teacher and he teaches at my school, but he does not teach me. He is sometimes in my class along with another teacher.'

'What does ESL mean and why do you have two teachers for the same lesson?'

'ESL means English as a second language. Some kids in my class speak other languages at home and are still learning English. Mr Mowbray comes into the class to help those kids to understand what the subject teacher is talking about.'

'That sounds like a good idea to me.'

'Yes, it is.'

'So how do you get along with him?'

'I don't. I mean I don't have any reason to either get along with him or not. But Mum is talking about him at home, and I think she is soon going to tell me that they are getting married.'

'Okay, let's be a bit circumspect about this. Has your mother *said* that she is going to marry Mr Mowbray?'

'No, but she has stopped calling him Mr Mowbray and is now calling him Phil.'

'So, you have decided that that means they are going to marry.'

'No, of course not. It means that I am now being asked to accept him as Mum's close friend and as well as a teacher at my school.'

'Do you speak to him at school, or does he speak to you?'

'Neither of us speaks but he does smile at me if our paths

cross. My friends give me a hard time if he smiles at me between lessons.'

'Let's go back to circumspection. He is making you feel uncomfortable when he smiles at you because, when he does, your friends embarrass you.'

'There we are a little circumspection shows us what the problem is and probably how to fix it.'

'How does that help?'

'The problem is your embarrassment. The solution could be to tell your mother about it and ask Mr Mowbray politely not to smile at you because it is causing you unnecessary embarrassment.'

'I suppose that could work, but Mum and I are not on good terms at the moment.'

'Oh, why not?'

'Well, Mr Mowbray has a daughter at my school. She is a year above me, so I don't have any classes together and he has a son in primary school. I suspect that when I am here with you and Dad that Mr Mowbray and his children are at my house with Mum. And his children are using my room. I've noticed that some of my things have been moved around.'

'Did your mother say that his children could use your room?'

'I don't know.'

'The secret to getting on with other people, including your parents, is to discuss issues such as this. But the best way to approach this issue is to politely ask that his children not use your room unless you agree to it. I am emphasising *politely* here.'

'Last Monday a girl in the corridor yelled out at me, "Is Mr Mowbray rooting your mother? I saw his car parked outside your house on the weekend".

'She didn't use the word rooting, but you can probably guess what word she did use.'

'Scaramouch!'

'What does that mean?'

'It means a cowardly, outspoken person.'

'Okay. I see why this issue is may be getting out of hand. Have you told your father or mother about this? This is a much bigger issue than Mr Mowbray smiling at you or things being moved around in your room.'

'No, it's too embarrassing to talk about it with Mum and Dad.'

'It is not my job to guide you through this, but I could offer a way forward. It would involve telling your father this account of the incident and if it would help, I could be with you when you tell him.'

'No!'

'I know it will be embarrassing but the embarrassing part won't last long and you can then get his advice about what to do. It must involve your mother as well and let's be clear, this girl is way out of line and I believe she needs to be sanctioned. It is not a healthy way for a teenage girl to behave. The sanctioning does not necessarily mean punishment, but it must be made clear to her that such behaviour will not be tolerated.

'Matthew should be back soon with the pizzas. Would you like to tell him over dinner?'

'No!'

'Embarrassment does not diminish by putting it off. How about I give a lead in by telling him that we have discussed an issue that is causing you distress and that you would like his advice?'

No pizza was eaten.

Before having eaten even a mouthful, Matthew heard the story.

Rachel had never seen him so angry and part way through his rant, she began to have second thoughts about somehow resolving the issue.

He was angry with the girl, her parents, the school, Mowbray, Lily and Tuesday.

Tuesday went off to her room in tears and Rachel was left with this ...?

It was barely describable.

As he simmered down, Rachel prepared coffee for them then went to Tuesday's room to console her and explain that Matthew did not really blame her but could not focus his anger and so was angry with everyone.

Before discussing the matter in detail, Matthew went to Tuesday and apologised to her.

'What do you think I should do?' he asked Rachel.

'I am sufficiently distant from the issue to suggest some steps to deal with it. Obviously, Lily and Mr Mowbray need to know, and together with you decide what course of action to take. Before you do call her we could devise a plan that suits Tuesday and you that you would be prepared to negotiate. I would suggest that we first obtain the girl's name.

There would be little point in approaching her; her parents need to be involved as well.

'If this girl has a history of this sort of behaviour then the school will have a record of it. Since it happened at school, we would have to assume that it will take over, but we, or you, could provide them with some outcomes that you would like as part of its handling of the situation.'

After some discussion, Matthew was satisfied that the school should take charge and decide the outcome, but that he would like to be kept in the loop of the school's investigation and expected the Principal make it very clear to all parties involved the reasoning behind her decision.

Matthew looked in again on Tuesday but found her asleep, fully clothed still, on her bed. He drew up the blankets and kissed her on her forehead.

'How had she grown up so quickly?'

The next morning Matthew and Rachel were preparing to go out for breakfast.

'Come on, Tuesday, we're going to McDonald's for breakfast.'

'You had better come here and look at this before we go.'

He went to her room. She had her laptop on the bed.

'What is it, sweetheart?'

'Look at this.'

On the screen was a Facebook page with a photograph of a house and a car parked outside.

'What's this about?'

'It's a Facebook comment put up by Phillipa.'

'Who is Phillipa? Wait a minute, that's my house. Whose car is it?'

'Yes, it is our house, and that car belongs to Mr Mowbray. See it is dated last Friday night.'

'Phillipa is the girl who yelled out at me last Monday.'

'The little shit!'

Hearing the raised voice, Rachel came to investigate.

'Will you look at this? That little shit has not only called this out at school, but she has also posted it on Facebook!'

'Time for some more circumspection,' said Rachel.

Matthew spoke to Lily when he took Tuesday back home. Mowbray was not with her, so they agreed to meet during the week at the school when he was able arrange for someone to take his class.

They met in the school library.

After presenting the information he had with Lily and Phil, he left it to them to discuss the issue. They agreed with him that the most appropriate action would be to turn over the information to the Principal, Ms Hargreaves, who was surprised that such an incident should have occurred on her watch but resolved to investigate.

After nearly a week, Ms Hargreaves contacted the parents involved and made an appointment for them to meet in her office. They included Matthew and Lily, Mr Mowbray and Ms Ellie Simpson, Phillipa's mother. She outlined what she had found by questioning the girls, with their parents' present, and gave them copies of the transcript of the interview that the school counsellor had with both girls.

'Okay, you can see what has been done, not just by me but other staff members who felt that they had something significant to contribute. I think you will agree that a substantial amount of effort in doing the investigation. I have taken counsel from those teachers who have contributed to the discussion and our recommendation is that we take no further action beyond the steps we have taken in counselling Phillipa. This appears to us to have been a success and we have heartfelt assurances from her that this will not happen again. I received this assurance personally from Phillipa and I believe her.'

She added that other options had been considered. They included removing the three parties involved, Tuesday, Phillipa and Mr Mowbray, to other schools but the consensus was that the issue would diminish over time and that neither Phillipa nor Tuesday wanted to go to another school.

When asked, none of the parents involved had any questions, so Ms Hargreaves stood and thanked them for their support and indicated that her secretary would see Matthew and Lily out. She asked that Ms Simpson and Mr Mowbray remain. Both looked surprised.

'Ms Simpson, because you are not employed here, it would be difficult for you to understand what we are obliged to do to make sure that our students receive the best education we can give them. Mr Mowbray knows and is part of the extra effort we make to assist those students who are not yet proficient in English. I began as an English teacher, moved on to be in charge of the English Department in another school, then became a Deputy Principal and then Principal here five years ago. I am sorry to labour point here, but teachers are trained to help students learn and some like me take on larger administrative positions. We are not trained to investigate issues such as the one, but we have applied ourselves to over the past week. Both of you have made our task more difficult by failing to assist us by not divulging important information which would have helped us in understanding Phillipa's motive in lashing out at Tuesday.'

Mowbray and Simpson looked at each other, both displaying a lack of comfort about what was about to be revealed.

'I received anonymous information in correspondence, together with this photograph.'

She passed over the photograph of Simpson and Mowbray enjoying themselves together at some social function.

'There was also supplied information that seemed to show that you were a couple formed as a result of meeting on Tinder. There's nothing amiss with your activity and dating, but because you chose not to declare it, we were bewildered by Phillipa's actions and the apparent lack of motive. After a number of sessions with the counsellor, she revealed that you, her mother, had again let her down after the divorce, starting up a new relationship only to have that fail as well. She revealed this to the counsellor after you left at the end of the interview, Ms Simpson.

'We deal with many children here whose parents have divorced I'm sure for good reasons. But some of our students are distressed by it and can act in some very inappropriate ways, as you can see.'

Both Mowbray and Simpson declined to comment or raise any issues with Hargreaves, and they left her office.

Simpson went to her car and Mowbray spoke to Lily as he walked her out to her car.

'What was that about, Phil?'

'Oh, Ms Hargreaves wanted to let Ms Simpson know that she arranged for me to no longer be in the classroom with Phillipa and that another ESL teacher will take my place.'

Matthew and Lily decided to meet again with Tuesday to assure her that this very unpleasant issue was not her fault.

Even though she became the focus, the problem was an example of the imperfect nature of human relationships and not with Tuesday herself.

Some problems could be avoided but lack of planning and compromise often meant that the relationship fractures and children are left in a situation of which they were not the cause. However, it did not necessarily become a disaster and could be managed by compromise.

Phillipa's parents' divorce had been acrimonious and left Phillipa in a situation that she did not understand. Her father had left the area and she had no visits from him. When Mr Mowbray came into her mother's life and left after a couple of months, she was thrown again into mental chaos and focused her anger Mr Mowbray, Phil, decided not to mention the relationship to Lily that he had had with Ellie Simpson. He was afraid that if Lily knew, she may not continue her relationship with him.

Whether this was circumspect or wise, only time would tell.

Chapter 36
SECURITY EVE

Rachel: 'Have you spoken to Tuesday about sex?'
Matthew: 'Well no, they do sex education at school.'
'Tuesday has been asking me questions this morning while you were out. I'm not sure that getting advice from me is such a good idea. Has Lily spoken to her about it?'

'I don't know, you'd have to ask Lily.'

'Matthew, I have not even met Lily. You are her parent, and it is your responsibility to tell Tuesday about sex.'

'Has Tuesday told you about sex education at school? The teachers know all about it and can deliver the message in a dispassionate way,' he said.

'Do you remember what you were told in sex education when you were at school?'

He laughed.

'Well, I remember having a same-sex talk given by our PE teacher. It only took him about 30 minutes and besides I knew most of it already. We thought it was a bit of a joke.

He was about ninety years old!'

'My recollection of sex education at school was chaotic,' she said. 'Our teacher was about twenty-five and I could not imagine anyone wanting to have sex with her. Thank goodness my mother looked after that part of my education.

'Look, I can give Tuesday useful information about sex. It is my life's work but you and Lily are her parents.

'You need to get onto this right away, Matthew. Tuesday has just started menstruating and she is not certain what to do about it. I have given her some sanitary pads for now, but please ask Lily about what, if anything, she wants me to do.'

'Shit. Has she started her periods today? I'll speak to Lily when I take Tuesday home this afternoon.'

The following fortnight when Rachel again joined Matthew; Tuesday was not with him.

'Is Tuesday all right?'

'Well, yes and no. Lily said that she would not be coming today, and she did not want Tuesday taking advice about sex from you. Tuesday is not talking to Lily either. I think she's angry with both of us for the divorce and now this.'

'What does Lily know about me?'

'Not much from me. I am unsure what Tuesday has said. She did not want to talk to me.'

'Does Lily think I am your girlfriend?'

'Look, I have chosen not to give Lily any information about you. Whatever she knows about you would have come from Tuesday. The relationship you have forged with Tuesday is outstanding. She really looks forward to seeing you each time. It's not surprising to me that she chose to seek help about her periods from you rather than Lily or me. It is hard to imagine that your parents have or had sex.'

'That's all very well, but you can't leave her languishing in a sea of ignorance. Teenage girls talk about sex all the time and Tuesday needs to know the truth, not some fantasy of pubescent girls at her school,' Rachel said. 'If Lily is not going to do it and Tuesday asks me questions, then I shall give her the answers. It could be done in your presence, and you could add your own thoughts, or you could do it with me present. It's up to you and Lily to work this out quickly.'

'I'll call Lily now and see if we can do this now. If she and Tuesday are ready, then we should do it right away. Why don't you have this weekend off? I'll call you with an update tonight.'

Lily, Matthew and Tuesday did talk about sex the following weekend and eventually agreed that if Tuesday wanted to ask Rachel about sex, she could, but they did not want her to be told about prostitution until she was older.

'What about homosexuality?' asked Rachel.

'Again, we thought that it could be discussed when she was older or when Tuesday brought up the topic herself,' said Matthew.

Rachel informed him that she had plans to move to Sydney as her two-year contract with him was ending. Although she had felt the contract conditions were unusual at first, working with Matthew and Tuesday had turned out well for all concerned. She was sorry to be leaving Tuesday at a time when the girl was having to endure another family issue.

Lily had begun a relationship with a new man.

The new relationship meant a rejigging of access arrangements which added more pressure to already strained relationships between the various components of the two families.

After two years establishing her business in Brisbane, Rachel took stock. She had purchased her own apartment in the CBD. Dan and Steve had supplied the security she needed, and she was making a lot of money.

Many men had sought her services in Sydney and Melbourne, and she faced the situation where enquiries from Sydney and Melbourne far exceeded those from Brisbane. She discussed the situation with Jesse. It was difficult for them to cope with the sheer size of Australia. Sydney is nearly 1000 km from Brisbane and Melbourne is a further 850 km. After much discussion about the notion of relocation to Sydney, Australia's largest city, they decided that a move to Sydney should be tried. But Rachel should not give up her Brisbane apartment but rent it out while she lived in Sydney.

A Sydney apartment was more costly than one in Brisbane, but Jesse pointed out that Rachel's income was remarkably high, so she advised that she purchase an apartment in Bondi, a suburb in the eastern suburbs. She had worked her way through the real estate websites and suggested a one-bedroom apartment would be the best alternative. It would be an excellent asset to have for her retirement.

It was a difficult decision to make. Yes, she would probably make more money faster, but she would be leaving behind friends such as Fergus and Dawn and Phoebe, their newly born daughter.

Jesse pointed out that Rachel could afford to travel and see her friends as often as she liked. She had the money to do it. It was an important discussion to have. The long-term plan was to make a lot of money, enough to retire at about forty and have an income from investments to live a comfortable life.

One aspect of the business success was security. Rachel discussed her proposal to move with Steve and Dan. They had a Sydney branch already established and had assured her that they could continue with her security in Sydney. It was a particularly important issue for Steve who secretly held onto his hope that Rachel would eventually become his partner.

So, when Rachel was ready to set up in Sydney, Steve offered to go as well to oversee how his staff would look after Rachel's special needs.

Rachel's unique service was well established and she took clients in hotels for which she had established good working relationships. She was well known in the hotel community as a reliable and discrete customer.

Stan Jacobs was a successful car salesman looking for sex and had heard from friends who had used Rachel's service in Brisbane. He was pleased to hear that she was now operating in Sydney.

In her chat with him on WhatsApp, she judged him to be misogynist. He handled her mild irony, however. So she decided to pursue the booking with him.

When reception called to inform Stan that he had two visitors coming to his room he was surprised but remembered that Rachel had mentioned security and guessed that the second visitor was her bodyguard.

When he opened the door, he found a slim woman about one hundred and seventy centimetres tall, dressed in black. Behind her stood a second woman perhaps a bit taller dressed in a trench coat, scarf and dark glasses who said, 'Hello, I'm Rachel and this is Eve.'

'Eve just needs to check out the room before I come in.'

As Eve entered the room Stan grabbed her arm saying, 'What's this about?' He sounded cross.

'Please allow Eve to enter,' said Rachel

'I want to know what she is going to do.' responded Stan, crossly.

Eve took his hand in her left hand and punched the inside of his arm just above his elbow joint with her right hand. Stan yelped in pain as he fell backwards towards the floor. Eve's foot was quickly at his throat and she maintained her grip of his hand.

Rachel remained outside.

'Stan, I have the right to operate my business in a safe environment. You have invited me here to provide you with pleasure, but you must guarantee my safety. Eve is here to help you with that guarantee. Now please sit on the lounge over there while Eve searches the suite. Once the security check is complete, we can discuss whether we proceed any further. Perhaps a drink may calm you down.'

Eve quickly searched the suite.

'What would you like to drink? Eve can get it for you while you relax.'

'Gin and tonic,' he grunted. Neither Rachel nor Eve spoke or moved.

Silence.

He finally understood.

'Please.'

'Okay, when you have finished your drink, I want you to go to the bedroom with Eve. There are two more things to do to finalise the security.'

Stan had recovered somewhat from his undignified introduction to Rachel and Eve and calmly went to the bedroom with Eve.

'Covid check and search completed,' said Eve as she led Stan back to the lounge room. Stan now wore the hotel bathrobe and Rachel sat on the lounge looking beautiful.

'How about we talk about making you feel better than you ever have before?'

Eve pointed to a chair and looked over to Rachel with a quizzical look as she was moving towards the door.

'Yes, I think so,' said Rachel

Eve took the chair and as she left, said 'I'll be just outside.'

'Thank you, Eve.'

Afterwards, on their way out of the hotel, Rachel said 'Do you know that is the first-time security has had to show what they are capable of. I don't know if Steve has filled you in on the need for this level of security, but a few years back a client threatened me with acid. Hence, my caution.

'I was impressed with your speed and agility. That man,'

... she had already forgotten his name ... 'could have been dangerous to be alone with. I had a feeling while I was talking to him on WhatsApp that there may be a violent streak in him. I need to be more discerning in future.'

'Yes, Steve and Dan have made it clear to us that speed, agility and technique are more important than strength, and that where possible we are not to harm your clients but certainly show that we could do a lot of damage to them.'

'And in addition, thank you for the chair. I hadn't thought about it myself but intend to use the idea if I meet – what was his name? – that sort of man again.'

'I can't remember either.'

Rachel missed the contacts and friends in Brisbane, especially Fergus and Dawn. She had flown back to Brisbane for Phoebe's christening and spent a couple of days with them as Phoebe's godmother at her christening.

Chapter 37

2031

The past decade had seen in Australia the biggest shake-up in Federal politics ever. In 2021, a change in National Party leadership ushered in an erosion of solidarity within the conservative Coalition government.

In 2022, the Coalition lost government and the Labor Party secured a small majority in the House of Representatives. It was also a time when several independent candidates were elected and the Greens increased their number of seats.

To get legislation through the parliament, the Labor Party had to depend upon the Greens and at least one Independent in the Senate. During the three years in government, the Labor Party failed to pass their signature legislation mainly because of resistance by the Greens.

Inevitably, the failure of Labor and the Greens to agree on legislation cost them both in the election of 2025 when conservatives were re-elected with a significant majority.

During the time leading up to the 2031 election, the new members of the Greens and Labor finally established a relationship of trust and cooperation.

The change was not immediate but from 2025 to 2031 the relationship became so pernicious within the Coalition that the conservative Liberal and National parties began to stand against each other and contest seats, resulting in a split of the conservative vote. Their main point of difference was the issue of climate change. There remained, however, in the years between 2025 and 2031, a general feeling in the electorate that the Coalition government had handled the pandemic with skill, especially with the management of the economy, enough to keep it being re-elected, albeit with very thin margins. Neither party could govern alone.

Labor and the Greens' promises on global warming were obscured by this more immediate threat and the conservative Coalition continued to win elections.

Remarkably, during the same period the Labor Party and Greens quietly worked at forming a temporary alliance which would persist, at least, until Australia could act as a cooperative member of the global community in pursuit of reducing global warming. They had done this before when a previous Labor minority government joined temporarily to govern with the Greens.

In two elections before 2031, Labor had two separate leaders, one man and one woman. In each election, the conservative Coalition managed to win with the slimmest of margins, meaning that the socialist Labor party had not been in office for nearly six years.

The Labor-Greens coalition formed before the May 2031 election was swept to power. This coalition had made clear plans for the abolition of coal-burning power stations, took up scientific advice on non-petroleum energy generation for vehicles, and gave advice and support to former coal miners and petroleum industry workers about how to take up careers outside these industries and to underwrite removal expenses for transition.

In this election, Indira Nori was elected as an independent member for the seat of Carrington, a semi-rural seat north-west of Brisbane. It came as a surprise to all except the voters of Carrington.

Indira was the daughter of Kashmiri immigrants who fled Kashmir because of the treatment of Muslims by the majority Hindu Pandits. They ruled out fleeing to Pakistan as millions of other Muslims had and sought immigration to Australia in 2004. Their departure was in such haste that their property was left behind with no chance of it being sold. The couple literally arrived in Australia with nothing of value. Her father, a lecturer in chemical engineering, quickly found work in that field. Her mother who had no qualifications beyond Year 8 in high school, worked as a nurse's aide in a local hospital until Indira was born in 2006 and reached school age. Indira's parents' marriage had been arranged by their parents through traditional matchmakers. It was not one based on sexual attraction but considered the structure of the families involved and was concerned with status and wealth. Her father's family paid *mahr* to the bride which is money personally granted to the bride to sustain

her through the change in circumstances when her husband
died.

> And give to the women (whom you marry) their Mahr
> (obligatory bridal money given by the husband to his
> wife at the time of marriage) with a good heart; but if
> they, of their own good pleasure, remit any part of it
> to you, take it and enjoy it without fear of any harm
> (as Allah has made it lawful). *Qur'an Chapter 4 An-Nisa*
> *Verse 4.*

In 2030, Indira won eight-seven million dollars in
Powerball and told no one about it.

She knew that she had been granted this money by Allah
and she understood that it required her to use it in good
works.

How would Allah want her to use it? She did not know
yet but believed that Allah would guide her.

Indira worked as a staffer for Craig Ellis, MP for
Carrington, in his local electoral office. She enjoyed
working for Craig who was approaching retirement age.
However, working for a Liberal Party representative did not
mean that she was committed to Liberal Party ideology. It
was a job and she enjoyed it.

Her passion was for the improvement of women's rights
in the Parliament and in the community, particularly the
Muslim community. So, when the election was called for May
2031, she resigned her job with Craig and set up an organisation
to compete against him for the seat of Carrington.

This was Allah's message.

Craig was surprised by this move but dismissed it as a minor annoyance and set about hiring a new staffer to help with his re-election.

He became alarmed when his electorate was swamped with high quality literature describing Indira's pitch to the voters. She made no apology to Craig or for the fact that she was fighting for this seat for three reasons. One, to make sure that the new coalition of Labor and Greens could rely on her vote on global warming pledges; second, to form the Australian Women's Alliance (AWA) within Parliament; and third, to work as hard as she could to attend to the needs of her constituents in Carrington.

She lobbied all female contestants for both the House of Representatives and Senate with details of her proposal to form the AWA which would be convened when the new Parliament sat, and that the AWA would act only where new legislation had significant relevance for women. Women from all parties and independents were welcome to join.

Craig was further surprised and alarmed when local community radio hosted interviews with Indira as well as carrying advertising for her run for Parliament. This was followed by interviews on large commercial radio stations, on ABC Mornings, and commercial TV current affairs and chat shows.

Indira arranged for several public meetings in the electorate and invited Craig and other contestants to speak.

During the last week of the election Indira delivered her campaign ideas at several open invitation meetings which pitched to women voters in general to join her. She made it clear that her efforts in parliament would be to pursue the needs of Carrington, support reforms required to combat global warming, and ensure that women had equal status to men in Australia. When questioned about issues other than these, she replied that her focus was on these issues; she did not have or need to have policies on education, defence etc unless they were relevant to her own stated issues.

This level of publicity was unheard of for an independent candidate and there were questions put to her by competitors and media. She was pressed to reveal the source of her funding for this media blitz and how she could have a support team, not of volunteers, but paid professionals.

She declined to answer these questions immediately but agreed to reveal the truth in her victory speech on the night of the election.

When Indira completed her secondary education, she enrolled in an Arts undergraduate degree majoring in English literature and Islamic studies. As a result of her studies, Indira began to question the nature of her own beliefs as a Muslim woman and that of her parents.

Indira's education was in the context of Australian culture even though she had been tutored at an Islamic school. There were inevitable conflicts between Indira and her parents as the Islamic way of her parents rubbed up against the Australian culture in which she was immersed.

She excelled at school and in her university studies but found that it counted for little in her pursuit of employment.

There was a significant population of Muslims in

Carrington and when his office secretary resigned to become a mother, Craig Ellis saw it as an opportunity to employ Indira. In addition, she was also young and attractive.

In Craig's office, Indira began to see a way forward in promoting the needs of women.

Craig's electorate included a greater than average number of cases of domestic violence. Indira noticed that Craig was sympathetic to women who were suffering violence in their homes, but she also observed that sympathy was all that he seemed to be able to supply. He was unable to attract government resources that could make a significant difference.

She noted that the most urgent need for these women was shelter and security. This was an expense that was acknowledged but not significantly funded by government.

Indira began to pressure government in the lead-up to the election to match her own proposal to build several women's shelters at her own expense in Carrington. She succeeded by building or buying suitable housing for women who were victims of domestic violence. She topped up from her own funds the level of services provided for the women in the form of security and counselling. Unlike previous attempts to advance the cause for women, Indira decided to pursue the matter by the AWA and separate in the sense that it would not be dependent on government for its administration.

She would use Allah's gift to support the cause. The AWA would not be bogged down by political manoeuvres.

It was a significant task. Men had maintained their power over women for centuries and they would not easily give it up.

The process of setting up had extensive video and audio coverage which was freely available online. The efficient way in which the Alliance was organised was often cited as an example of female productivity.

362

Chapter 38
INDIRA'S SPEECH

ndira rose to her feet.

'Madam Speaker

'It is with awe that I rise to deliver my first speech to Parliament.

'I have achieved the honour of addressing Parliament as the independent member for Carrington. As per the tradition of the House I speak through you, Madam Speaker, on behalf of the constituents of Carrington.

'The word 'parliament' comes from the French *parler* meaning 'to speak'.

'Everyone in this country has the right to speak. Free speech is only limited when it incites hate or is racist.

'We, fellow members, have special rights of speech in this place. What we say here, is privileged, but should not be used as a weapon.

'However, to have constituents vote for us, we must be heard.

'In Western democracies like Australia, it costs a lot of money to be heard, as I can personally attest. I am an Australian, a Muslim and a woman, and I wish to use my place in Parliament to support me in my work as the representative for the people of Carrington.

'I have no party allegiances, but I do believe that I am here now, because of Allah's plan for me to make it a better place for women to do their work as representatives of their constituencies.

'It may seem that at the core of Islam is death, destruction and control, an image portrayed too often in the media.

'There are extremist members in all cultures.

'In my prayers, I have promised Allah that I shall use his gift to me for good works and I promise you, my fellow members, that it is my only plan.

'As a believer in global warming, the truth of which cannot be ignored, I shall lend my support to framing policies to mitigate its effects for future generations. I believe that it is one of the reasons that Allah has granted me the means to help all of us, Muslims, Christians and others, to repair the damage we have allowed to occur in the name of progress and profits.

'I have extended an invitation to women members of the House of Representatives, the Senate and all women who work in this place to join with me to form a group to discuss the issues that women here find an insult to them, doing their jobs.

'Do I believe that committees formed in the past created better conditions in which women do their work?

'No. Not nearly enough.

'Those committees were framed in a political way. My suggestion to women in both Houses and all female ancillary staff to join with me, leave party ideology at the door and together find ways of pursuing our work free of the need to justify ourselves as worthy to work alongside men as equals. In previous attempts to secure equality for women, the framework has been a political one.

'The plan that I shall put to the women who choose to join me will not be constrained by politics, but by willingness of women to right centuries of dominance by men.

'Women and men are not equal. They are complementary which allows for reproduction. But aside from this dimorphism, we are equal in our claim for the opportunity, with men, to pursue happiness. I am not offering men a place in this discussion. It is time for women alone to plan a way forward. I am asking all women who wish to participate in this endeavour to leave ideology at the door when coming inside to discuss a way forward, not to analyse past failures or lay blame.

'I join with you today as a novice in the workings of Parliament and I am sure that I have a lot to learn but please note that I will not be treated in any other way than with respect. All of us here have that right.'

Applause.

*   *   *

'Good Morning to *Backdoor Politics* listeners. I am John

Highfield, and today I am joined by Indira Nori, the newly elected member for Carrington in our Federal Parliament.'

'Welcome, Indira, to *Backdoor Politics*, FM101.'

'Thank you for having me.'

'There has been much discussion about you winning the seat of Carrington, which has been a safe seat for the Liberal Party for over twenty years. Can you tell our listeners how you came to achieve this remarkable win?'

'You may remember that I was on the staff of Mr Ellis, the previous member for Carrington, and prior to the election and in 2030, I won eighty-seven million dollars in Powerball. I believe that the win was a message to me from Allah to use it to do good works. But at the time of winning, Allah had not shown me how I was to use the money.

'Mr Ellis is an honourable man and did a good job for his constituents but was constrained by his party and not able to give his constituents, especially women, the funding for system of crisis housing in Carrington. I am not constrained by party politics, and I have a lot of money which I am prepared to use to address this issue.'

'Tell us how you have begun to do that?'

'I understood at the time the election was called, that Allah's plan became clear. I was a good student at school and university and when I got the job to work for Mr Ellis, all the pieces of Allah's plan came together when the Prime Minister called the election for May 2031. I could see the way ahead to stand for a seat in the national Parliament which provides me a way to be heard by the public, the good people of Carrington, and especially the women of Australia.'

'Now, I have heard that you began your project to provide crisis housing for women in Carrington *before* you were elected. Could you tell our listeners about that?'

'Yes, I had already purchased four houses in Carrington which I judged to be suitable for crisis accommodation, with some modifications, of course, and three blocks of land to purpose-build six more.'

'But, Indira, how did you know that you would win the election?'

'Allah does not mislead true believers, and I knew that this plan was provided to me to use for the benefit of my constituents.'

'You *are* a true believer. Could I now turn to your concern about the treatment of women in Australian society? How do you propose to address the problem of sexual harassment in the workplace which seems to have resisted all attempts so far?'

'John, it is not true that no progress has been made. But I believe the problem is the setting. The approach so far has been limited by the setting, which is an adversarial political setting. Opposition and Government seek to belittle each other. Each needs the other to be the enemy, to show the electorate that it alone can defeat that enemy. The steps forward are slow, shuffling steps. I do not intend to work in that setting.'

'In what setting will you work?'

'Firstly, I cannot do this by myself. I am counting on the women of Parliament, not just the elected ones, to join with me to work out the details but I believe that it may have a structure similar to that of a union. I am counting on women to work with me, and I intend to lead by example. My example will be a model for crisis housing in Carrington which will be seen as the gold standard for protection of women who find themselves in dangerous domestic situations.'

'What? The Australian Women's Union?'

'John, I have already said that I cannot do this alone, but I believe that Allah will continue to guide me through the process. In the past, workers formed unions to combat exploitation by employers and to fight for a reasonable wage and conditions for their work. Many battles were fought over these issues and there came a time when some unions became too powerful and unnecessarily disrupted business. Accordingly, governments stepped in to establish a balance between business and workforce. During the second half of the twentieth century, union power declined. Powerful unions survived though, and we continue to this day to have powerful unions, but they are male bastions. Women need to combine to gain the strength to insist that they have the rights of men and equal pay for equal work.'

'Indira, I wish you well in your endeavours and hope to here again from you soon to update our listeners on progress.'

* * *

'How do you think that went?' said Indira.

'It went very well. You remembered not to over-answer his questions and you stuck to your plan which is not to try to run the country by Sharia Law but to focus on rights for women and give support to climate change science,' said Des Murphy, Indira's personal assistant.

At thirty-five years of age, Des was a veteran political staffer. Like many staffers in Canberra, he was looking to build on his experience to run for Parliament himself.

'We have received several requests from journalists to interview you soon. I propose that we schedule a press conference outside tomorrow, early in the morning, say 8.30 am. Would that suit you?'

'Yes, but let's get together this afternoon to go over our tactics for conducting such events. These people can be very pushy and boisterous. I'll need you and Rhonda with me to make sure I am not overwhelmed.'

'Okay, let's confirm now that Rhonda and I will choose whose question you will answer. Rhonda and I are well acquainted with the press and won't allow them to bully you.'

Indira and several other new MPs had meetings with those people charged with acquainting new members about their duties, responsibilities and protocols which frame the way Parliament operates. New members needed to understand and respect the rules for the satisfactory operation of the House of Representatives.

It was an exciting but daunting process, but Indira knew that her fellow new MPs did not have what she had.

She had Allah's backing and he would guide her.

Rhonda Watkins, Des and Indira met after Indira's induction session. Rhonda was also an experienced staffer and had worked in Parliament for several years for Craig Ellis.

'Let's work out what we think the questions from the

journos will be,' said Rhonda.

They predicted that there would be questions about Indira's faith, her wealth and her feminist credentials.

At the press conference, Des announced to the assembled press that he and Rhonda would choose which journalists could put a question to Indira.

The press, as they had forecast, wanted to concentrate on her religion and feminist opinions. They agreed that only those questions that could be answered briefly would be answered immediately and that questions that required a lengthy response would be published on Indira's website.

To the assembled journalists she announced:

'I have written extensively on these issues in undergraduate papers submitted to my lecturers for assessment, but these are written for an academic audience and would not be in a suitable form as a press release. However, the text of a press statement would need to be expansive and not just a couple of sentences. Therefore, I shall rewrite those papers for general release in which I shall make it clear what my opinions are on feminism and my religion.'

'Are you going to have male staff working for you?'

'As you can see, I have Des working with me. I am not in favour of quotas. I wish to have the best person for the job. The gender of my staff is not an issue. I just want the best people I can get to assist me. If I need more than the number of staff than an independent member is allocated, then I shall hire more and pay for them from my own funds.

'Thank you all for coming. A written statement that I alluded to will be on my website by tomorrow.'

Chapter 39
PAUL AND RACHEL

Two people who did not vote in the 2031 election were Paul Arnold and Rachel Doyle. Rachel was not an Australian citizen and was not eligible to vote. Paul, if he had voted, would have given the Antiabortion Party his first preference. It was the first time this party had run candidates in a Federal election. Paul had been the face of their campaign urging people to support the organisation which was now in the human trial phase and close to achieving successful transplants of human embryos from women, who would otherwise have had the embryos aborted, transferred into the wombs of women who could not conceive and therefore, minimise the level of abortion in Australia and perhaps the world.

Paul, eighty-six years old, died in his sleep on 10 April 2031 from a ruptured abdominal aortic aneurysm. Aneurysms are not associated with clear symptoms and are sometimes detected when a patient has a scan for some other condition.

The Coroner at Paul's inquest noted that he had probably died about 3.00 am but his body was not discovered until his brother Frank reported that Paul had not answered his daily call at 9.00 am and had entered Paul's house with his own key to find the body. Paul's doctor was unable to give a cause of death at the site and hence police were called.

Rachel's life as an expensive prostitute meant that she was making an amount of money limited only by the number of clients she was willing to service. She employed a financial adviser and an accountant to manage her affairs but lived a comfortable life without luxury cars or other trappings of wealth.

She had attracted clients from other Australian cities including Melbourne and Sydney and bought apartments in those cities as well as Brisbane.

She did allow herself one luxury item: a Fareast 19R sailboat. She took sailing lessons and had the yacht moored at the Royal Queensland Yacht Club. At the time of the election, Rachel was in Northern Ireland to visit family and consider purchasing Barnaby's bookshop which now bore the name BiblioCHIK Derry.

This was part of a chain of bookshops operating across the UK and they were extending into the EU. There had been a surge of self-publishing in the 2020s and BiblioCHIK built its business model by catering for these writers, received some and distributed them to their stores. The chain had shops which did well with a particular genre and books of this type went preferentially to those stores. After selling well in BiblioCHIK, some authors were taken up by major publishing houses. She was unimpressed by the business model for BiblioCHIK and declined to make an offer for what was once Barnaby's Boutique Bookshop. She was also intending to visit Aemon in Whitemoor prison where he was serving a fourteen-year sentence for his involvement in the bombing of the Winter Wonderland festivities in December 2024, along with Ailsing Byrne and Jimmy O'Connor, where three children died and twenty-five other people were injured.

After speaking with Jesse and others, she declined Aemon's request for her to visit him. Brexit had resulted in renewed IRA action over the clumsy establishment of a Customs authority between Britain and Ireland.

Rachel's original plan for her business evolved over time as new challenges emerged. It had meant that the various hotels in which she operated were changed when a better product became available. She made subtle but necessary changes to her vetting procedure and kept up with innovations in communications technology.

One such change occurred when, one day, she had a call from Steve's partner, Dan, asking for a meeting.

She agreed and they met at the Coffee Pot the next day.

'I watched a documentary about university examinations last Monday and realised that there is a lot of cheating by students.'

'Well, I hope that the university has some way of stopping it, but what does it have to do with us?'

'What it revealed to me was the possibility of it happening to you.'

'I still don't follow.'

'I know it hasn't happened yet, but what would you do if the person in the hotel suite is not the person you took as a client?'

'Oh, I understand. What are you suggesting?'

'Here is what I think would work. First, include a misrepresentation clause on your website which says something like clients who book for other people will not be serviced and will lose their deposit. And have a photo lifted from the WhatsApp with the client on your phone when you arrive. Our staff will protect you if the client becomes objectionable.'

'Thanks so much, Dan.'

Close to three months later, Rachel arrived at room 227 at the Angel Court Hotel in Melbourne, accompanied by her minder, Kyle. The door opened, revealing a man wearing the hotel dressing gown.

Rachel looked at her phone and asked, 'Is Jack here?'

'I'm Jack.'

'No, you are not. Is Jack inside?'

'Look, Jack could not make it, so I'm taking his place.'

'I don't operate that way,' said Rachel, who turned to go the back to the elevator

As Rachel moved away from the door, Jack attempted to follow her, calling 'I've paid you for a fuck! Come back!'

The plan they had developed for this type of situation was for Rachel to say no more and continue towards the elevator.

As Jack pursued Rachel, Kyle stepped between them, moving backwards in a crouched fighting style.

'Come back!' shouted Jack as he attempted to grab Kyle

by the shoulders. Kyle slid under his outstretched arm and rammed his foot onto Jack's knee, side on. There was a loud crack, followed by an equally loud scream.

Jack fell to the floor clutching his knee.

Kyle noticed that Jack's genitals were now exposed. He gently covered them, quietly whispering, 'I think you may have an ACL injury there. I'll let reception know that you need medical attention.'

Kyle followed Rachel and they met in the foyer. Kyle spoke briefly to the receptionist and joined Rachel.

'Is he all right?'

'Sore knee.'

By any measure Rachel had become wealthy but she did not flaunt it. Her one-bedroom apartments in Bondi, Yarra and Brisbane 1 Tower were well situated and tastefully appointed but not expensive.

She told only Steve and Dan where she lived in each of the cities she serviced. She took no one home to entertain and while she was in residence, she had a daily cleaner.

She had a single bed as she had no plans for bonking at home. If she was to have sex with a man who was not a client, they would do it in his bed or in a hotel. That way she did not encourage men to think they might own her. After sex she could stay or leave whenever she liked.

She kept her much-loved Fareast on Morten Bay and sailed whenever she could. She sometimes sailed alone but enjoyed the experience with friends including Matthew and Tuesday.

She maintained her friendship with Fergus and Dawn and

was honoured to be Phoebe's, their first child, godmother.

Tuesday left Lily and Phil, now married, changed her name to Imogen, and in her university years lived with Matthew, who was single, and avoided the company of Phil's children. She enrolled in a new technology course which meant that she would be well placed to write new code for the first quantum computers which were rumoured to be coming onto the market in 2034.

Rachel was invited to Imogen's graduation, but it was a tense affair, mired with family politics and she left early.

Paul's research into embryo transfer in spiny mice presented some obstacles that he had not foreseen. One was the exceedingly delicate surgery on these tiny creatures. He was fortunate to access AI robotic surgery, which by this time was equal to or superior to that of surgeons.

The big problem was tissue rejection of the implanted embryos by the new mother's immune system.

There were already drugs developed for those women whose immune system rejected her own embryos, but these had not been certified as suitable for transplanted embryos.

His work in this field meant that he was often asked to speak about his research, but Paul had already become quite a celebrity by having his first novel, *God And the Big Bang*, published in 2023. His publisher Barton and Baird then offered him an incentive payment to work on his new novel, *Total Awareness*, about the development of awareness in humans.

He did initially think that it would be a biography but changed his mind and confirmed with the publishing firm that he would be writing a novel.

There was a lot to consider. He had given the publisher a copy of the work that he had shown to Jill and Jason years ago, but this was a brief account of his first twenty years and contained nothing of the immense influence of MacKenzie and Stone on his life for nearly thirty years.

From the beginning of their relationship, he found MacKenzie's personality was vast, and it dominated his life. He likened it to the ocean, immense and moody. She always stood out in a group, not because of her beauty – she was not beautiful – but was surrounded by an aura which affected those around her. She immediately liked or disliked those she met.

As the ocean can be millpond calm or have surfable waves or dangerous wind and rain along with treacherous currents and menacing sharks, so MacKenzie's mood shifted.

After she died, Paul began to get a better understanding of his life with her.

MacKenzie's mental and physical health declined after she recovered from a serious operation in 2016 was performed to clear out plaque from her carotid artery which was more than ninety per cent blocked. The other was near one hundred per cent blocked. As they left the hospital, heavy rain began to fall as they headed home. It soon became a deluge and MacKenzie became anxious, then frightened, and finally frantic pushed Paul to stop.

He had judged this to be dangerous, as other drivers were travelling at high speed, despite the heavy rain. He tried to explain but MacKenzie screamed. It was the loudest sound he had ever heard. He carefully pulled over and they waited for the rain to stop. She was furious with him, and they did not speak for days.

When they next went to Stone's house where they both had appointments, Stone abused Paul about the incident and informed him that she would no longer treat him. Paul was not concerned about this or that he was no longer welcome to go to Stone's house. The new arrangement was for him to drive MacKenzie to a nearby park where Stone would collect her and drive her to her home.

In relationships, disagreement, love, hate, and jealousy have a long history, sometimes subconsciously. For Paul, his unrelenting drive to success in his chosen field meant that he ignored the psychological needs of Louise, Benny and Steve. It was all about him. In his relationship with MacKenzie, it slowly dawned that he could not continue this way if he were to remain her partner. During the thirty years together he had with her, a more balanced Paul emerged.

MacKenzie was aware of his progress, but she did not encourage any relationship with Louise, his sons, or his mother. She wanted him for herself. Her need for him was most pronounced in her last few days. He was with her each day as she endured intubation, loss of bladder and bowel control, and panic attacks. She clung to him. Stone came once near the end and Paul handed her a parcel that MacKenzie had prepared before she went into hospital. Paul did not know what was in the parcel nor did he notice that MacKenzie was wearing none of her jewellery.

He later realised that her jewellery and a copy of her will

were enclosed within the package. Her death had a profound effect on Paul, and he sought grief counselling to help him through. The counselling ended but the grief did not. However, there was the strong feeling of release from his role as her carer which had prompted him to write.

He found it an entirely selfish thing to do, and it temporarily relieved him from the task of being her carer. All that they could do for social activity was limited by MacKenzie's declining physical and cognitive condition.

Apart from his work, most of which he could do from home, there was no escape from MacKenzie's needs and her unpredictable mood shifts.

Perhaps the most intriguing nature of his relationship with MacKenzie was that it included Stone. MacKenzie told Paul of Stone's part in her life early in their relationship and as a result he made an appointment for himself with Stone. He was impressed by Stone's gravitas and over the following several years was treated by Stone for major depression. Stone prescribed a high dose of Prozac and Paul remained on this high dose for years until it became no longer effective. He moved onto an equally high dose of a more recently developed antidepressant. His therapy stalled and Stone informed him that he was resisting the process. Therapy became less efficacious and eventually ceased when they argued about Paul's lack of empathy with MacKenzie on their journey home from the hospital in the rain.

When Paul was approached by the ABC to do a segment on *One Plus One* about his book and work with the Antiabortion League, he agreed, but on the proviso that he was interviewed by the creator and original host, Jane Hutcheon. Paul had watched every episode, but his favourite host was Jane, who had moved on in her career to do other things in 2019. Jane graciously accommodated him, and they taped the episode in 2024. Over the last decade 2020 to 2030, there had been a shift against the support for abortion, which was claimed by women as a basic right for them to control what was happening in their own bodies. The issue reached a tipping point in the United States when the Supreme Court was considering overturning the *Roe v Wade* decision of 1978. Abortion clinics closed as access to abortions was limited to clients whose own lives were endangered by the foetus they carried.

For feminist women this was seen as a massive mistake and threats by extremists were made on the lives of the Supreme Court judges responsible. The antiabortion movement in Australia was buoyed by this change and pressed governments to follow suit, to ban abortion. Paul's commitment to embryo transplant technology was strong but he hesitated, then declined, when asked to support some of the more aggressive tactics employed by the more radical members of the Antiabortion League, such as harassing women entering abortion clinics, for he was a feminist and supported women's rights. His research was to help these women keep control over their bodies without killing the developing embryo.

Proponents and activists began to consider the ramifications of his research. Where would these procedures be attempted? Was this a form of adoption? If so, would current adoptions rules apply? Would the new parents have any knowledge of origin of the embryo? Would health authorities keep records of the origins? What would happen if the baby was born with a serious defect? Would embryos sourced from rape victims or incest be allowed? Paul was comfortable for others to debate these ethical issues given that some lives would be saved by his pioneering work.

The connection between Paul and Rachel, and Paul's son Steve, was never revealed to her.

What purpose would it have served? Paul tried several times to contact his son. None of the messages he had left with Steve's office were ever replied to. He had finally decided on affirmative action and confront Steve as he had been confronted at MOMO years before.

Steve had taken him by surprise and declared that he would not discuss the issue of their relationship further. The problem had been relegated to the too hard basket for now. Paul was busy with his work – nothing new there.

After MacKenzie died, Paul began a long slow review of his life and writing was a critical part of the process. As he assigned actions and words to the characters in his book, his own thoughts and beliefs were revealed on the pages in front of him. The incident with Steve at MOMO was included in the narrative in a disguised form. He thought about his claim for respect which Steve had rejected. Of course, Steve had no respect for his father, just as he had no respect for his father, Harvey. Neither had earned it. When he had spoken about Harvey with Frank, he was surprised that Frank felt that Harvey had been a good father. Respect is not something you can demand; it can only be earned. If Harvey had Frank's respect, why did he not have respect from Steve? The answer was quite clear – he had not earned it.

Paul made a resolution that after the upcoming election he would go to Brisbane and make a stand. He would tell Steve that he apologised for his treatment of his family and ask for forgiveness. As is the case of many resolutions made, they are not kept. Other more important things such as being spokesperson for the Antiabortion League were time-consuming. The long put-off apology to Steve died with Paul just before the election. In some families, wrongful conduct is never forgiven. What makes it so? It may be that some are founded on secrecy. The reasons for hurt feelings are not revealed and members of the family may decline even to discuss this injury and the alleged culprit has no way to apologise or explain.

There are no winners in these situations. Steve's hope that Rachel would eventually become his partner was similarly unexpressed and she never knew that he wanted her. She had a selfish, single life and she intended to keep it that way. The big loser was Steve who had no living relatives apart from the hayseeds.

Sometimes, a courageous attempt to confront the issue can mean that a difficult family problem can be resolved. Sometimes, the rage of being subject to hurtful word or deed cannot be maintained.

In the river of life, even the sharpest stone becomes smooth over time.

www.ingramcontent.com/pod-product-compliance
Lightning Source LLC
Chambersburg PA
CBHW061617210726

48287CB00001B/168